Passage
Soul of the Witch Saga - Book 3
C. Marie Bowen

Pixler Publications

Passage
Soul of the Witch Saga – Book 3
by C. Marie Bowen
Copyright © 2015 C. Marie Bowen

All rights reserved.

This book was previously published as *Soul of the Witch, Book 1*.
ISBN-13: 978-1-945215-070 – Paperback

ISBN-13: 978-1-945215-063 – EPUB

Edited by Liette Bougie

Cover Design by C. Marie Bowen

Published by Pixler Publications

Discover other titles by C. Marie Bowen at www.cmariebowen.com

Content Note

This novel contains scenes of violence, attempted sexual assault, suicide, and racial tension reflective of its historical setting.

Reader discretion is advised.

Contents

Chapter 1

Elsewhere, far from Boston and the Colorado ranch, another thread of the story begins.

— ✧ —

Courtney Veau

—

Present-day – Denver, Colorado

Courtney rested her shoulder against the wall beside the second-floor window and looked down on the street below. The diverse Denver neighborhood had a mix of historic homes and new development. The buildings and trees along the block cast tall shadows across the pavement and foretold the approach of evening. Two helmeted bicyclists coasted past parked cars, then passed from view.

A small sigh escaped her lips, and she raised her gaze to the darkening eastern horizon. She waited for the first star to appear. Her thoughts jumped between her two great unresolved questions—why was she still here; and would he come again tonight?

Dust from the heavy tattered draperies tickled her nose as she peered between their panels. The curtains blocked the light from the passing day and left the small apartment behind her in semi-darkness. Her possessions were few. An inflatable mattress shoved into the corner by the closet. Beside the bed sat a small folding table, which held her laptop and cell phone. A sleeping bag, comforter, and pillow were thrown haphazardly across the mattress, and at the foot of the makeshift bed was a large flashlight. Her suitcase laid open in the closet with her few remaining clean clothes inside; the dirty ones were tossed behind the closet door.

The long shadows faded into twilight. She'd found what she came for—proof this house existed. There was no longer a reason to stay; and yet, just the possibility she might hear his voice again kept her waiting one more day.

Outside her window, the night took final possession of the evening. A few porch lights came on down the block. Headlights swung around the corner as a car turned onto the street and illuminated the pavement. The headlights winked off, and a car door slammed.

Behind her, the room took on a familiar chill. She turned from the window and pressed her back against the drapes as the echo of boots pounded up the back stairs. She gasped when he raced into the room, vaguely luminescent in the darkness. He was dressed in denim trousers and cotton shirt, with a silk scarf tied loosely around his neck.

Where's his hat?

Had he lost it in the race up the stairs? That wide-brimmed cowboy hat was such a part of him he seemed naked without it. His hair had come loose from its binding, and he shoved it out of his eyes with a familiar movement. She stood close enough to read the emotion play across his face, a mixture of fear and bewilderment. His breath was labored, and his anxiety tangible as he stopped and looked right at her. Her mouth fell open, and her heart tightened in her chest.

Does he see me?

He took a hesitant step in her direction. "Nichole?" his voice filled with horror, he whispered her name from another life.

"Yes, Merril! It's me." Courtney stepped toward the specter.

His head turned. His attention called away from her open arms. "Oh, sweet Jesus." Merril fell to his knees and reached for something no longer there. "Nicki, please don't go. Stay with me."

"Merril, I'm here." She ached for him and for herself, but her plea went unheard.

Sobs shook his broad shoulders.

Her heart clenched to witness his despair. She longed to comfort him, to assure him she was there, but could not. In defeat, she sank to her knees beside the grieving apparition.

"Nicki, don't leave me. Look at me—" His hushed voice, choked and broken.

"I'm right here, my love," she whispered, but the room grew warm, and Merril Shilo faded back into the past. Courtney hung her head in the darkness and fought back tears.

One question was answered, at least for now.

***

Two Weeks Earlier—Fort Worth, Texas

Courtney stirred. A medicinal antiseptic smell assaulted her nose while the muted beep and whir of machines slipped into her dream like an old memory.

"Miss Veau? Can you hear me, hon? Wake up, Courtney."

Courtney blinked gummy eyes and tried to focus on the speaker, but brightness obscured her vision. She closed them again as pain lanced across her brow.

"Courtney, open your eyes, please."

Icy fingers slipped beneath hers, and a cold palm rubbed the back of her hand.

"You need to wake up now."

She squinted at the dark-haired nurse and struggled to make sense of her surroundings.

Sudden realization hit, and her adrenaline surged. Beside her bed, the silent monitor sounded an alarm as her heart rate accelerated—she was back. She was Courtney Veau again.

What happened?

She didn't want to be Courtney Veau—not now! Not when everyone she loved knew her as Nichole Harris. *Had* known her, she realized. They wouldn't be alive anymore.

A gasp escaped her lips when the nurse came into focus and ended in a choked cough.

"Take it easy, darlin'. You're going to be just fine," the woman comforted in a slow southern drawl. She silenced the alarm and dimmed the overhead light. "Your throat is sore from the intubation tube. They had you on a venti-lator when you first came in. Would you like a bit of ice to suck on?"

Courtney disagreed vehemently that things were going to be just fine. That she was here—at this place in time, and in this body—told her everything was lost. She tried to raise her hand, but plastic straps held her arm tight to the bed.

"Wha?" Courtney grimaced as her voice broke.

The nurse held the small cup of ice chips to her lips, and a few pieces of frozen moisture fell into her mouth. Delicious coolness trickled down Courtney's raw throat, and she moaned at the icy sensation.

"That should help. My name is Vicki. I'll be your nurse until they move you to a room. You gave us quite a scare this morning."

"What happened? Where... Why am I strap...strapped down?" Courtney croaked through her scratched throat. Tears seeped from the corner of her eyes into her hairline. She took a trembling breath and tried to focus on the here and now.

Vicki held the cup to Courtney's lips and tapped a few more chips into her mouth.

"You were brought to JPS by ambulance early this morning. You were in a car accident. We had a difficult time getting you stabilized—then you fought us each time you woke. That's why you're restrained." Vicki offered a few more ice chips and dabbed Courtney's watering eyes with a tissue. "Who is Merril?"

Courtney choked on the icy fluid in her throat.

"Easy now, darlin'. Here, let's set you up." Vicki raised the head of the bed. "I only ask because you called his name while you were waking. Admissions have been here twice asking for a person to contact about your condition. Is Merril a friend or family member?"

Hearing his name nearly broke Courtney. She longed to wail her grief to the entire ICU, but she had grown up aware of her family's notoriety and had learned to be inconspicuous. Instead, she swallowed back her tears and struggled to control her grief. "Merril's not, I mean he's... You won't be able to contact him." A sob escaped her throat.

Vicki eyed her with concern, then pulled two tissues and wiped the tears from Courtney's face. "Are you all right, darlin'?"

"Yeah," Courtney murmured without conviction.

"I hope so. If you promise to stay calm, I'll remove these restraints." Vicki didn't wait for an answer before she unlatched the straps.

"What else is wrong with me?" Courtney's right hand trembled.

Vicki removed the last restraint from Courtney's leg and set it aside. Then, she rolled the bedside tray within Courtney's reach. "The initial diagnosis is a TBI—traumatic brain injury—but that hasn't been confirmed yet." She set the cup of ice on the tray. "The TBI is the immediate concern, of course. That, along with deep bruises on your left side and leg as well as cuts on your face and scalp."

The arrival of a new patient in the ER drew Vicki away from Courtney's bedside.

Courtney slid the cup from the hinged lid and flipped back the tray-top to reveal a mirror. Her breath caught as she studied her reflection. The room seemed unsteady, and Courtney watched the blood drain from the face in the mirror.

The left side of her face was showered with small cuts. Her left iris swam in a pool of red, and she could see the beginning of a black eye in the dark puffy lid. Two of the cuts on her forehead were taped shut, and the entire left side of her face was swollen, giving her a lopsided, grotesque appearance.

Her mouth fell open as she looked past the injuries and studied the face beneath. The dark brown eyes and fine brown hair were familiar but wrong. The last time she looked in a mirror she'd seen the reflection of Nichole Harris's blonde hair and blue eyes. Courtney searched for a possible explanation but failed when the ache in her heart became too great. Nichole Harris felt more real and alive to her than Courtney Veau ever had.

She let the lid fall shut and clenched her jaw to control the tears, but it was no use. Despair welled inside her, and inconsolable sobs shook her frame.

Vicki glanced in as she passed Courtney's room. "What's the matter, hon? Are you in pain?"

"No, no," Courtney muttered. More sobs erupted as memories overwhelmed her. "I shouldn't be here," she gasped. "I would go back if I could, but I don't know how." Bitter tears closed her throat, and she coughed, trying to catch her breath.

"You need to calm yourself down, sugar, or you're going to make yourself sick." Vicki shoved a few tissues into Courtney's hand.

Courtney gulped down her tears and caught her breath several times, trying to even out her breathing. When the sharp rush of emotion passed, it left a dull, empty ache.

"I am going to have the doctor speak to you." Vicki set the box of tissues in Courtney's lap, then hurried out of the room.

Courtney held a tissue to her face. The love of her life, the very beat of her heart, was either a dream or a man long dead. The pain in her chest crawled up her throat, and her tenuous grip on reality threatened to shatter.

The ICU became busy, and she was left alone with her memories. She looked up from the damp tissues twisted in her hands when Vicki approached with an orderly.

"You've been assigned a room, hon," Vicki informed her. She helped Courtney move to the narrow gurney. "The doctor and an admission clerk will be up to see you. Don't forget these." Vicki set a clear plastic tote filled with Courtney's belongings on the transfer bed.

The orderly pushed her out through a set of double doors and into the elevator. As they passed the nurses' station on the third floor, a nurse picked up her chart from the foot of the rolling bed and followed them into the room. The thin, gray-haired woman reviewed her chart as the orderly assisted Courtney into her new bed. He put her tote in a small closet, and then pushed the gurney from the room.

"Lunch will be up in a few minutes." The nurse wrote her name—Rhonda—on the marker board by the door then slid Courtney's chart into a plastic chart holder. "How do you feel, Courtney? Any pain?"

Courtney shook her head and dabbed at the moisture on her face.

"Then, why the tears?" The short-haired nurse leaned against the sink counter, crossed her arms and looked with disapproval at Courtney.

Through watery eyes, Courtney peered at the nurse. She'd never met this woman before, although she recognized the tone of her voice and attitude. Rhonda knew who her father had been and wasn't pleased to have his daughter as a patient.

Courtney matched the older woman's glare and twisted the crisp white sheets in her hands. She would offer no explanation for her grief. Anxiety wound itself into a tight fist inside her stomach and sat clenched beneath her broken heart.

She hated when people recognized her—hated it with a passion built on years of unrelenting notoriety. Strangers made assumptions about her, and it was always hurtful. Whether they were fans or skeptics of her father, it was never pleasant to be recognized.

Rhonda's smile tightened, and she lifted one shoulder in a partial shrug. "Fine. Don't tell me. I'm sure it would be—" She cleared her throat and stood away from the counter as the doctor pulled the chart from the holder at the door.

"Hello, Miss Veau, I'm Doctor Chambers." The short, balding doctor glanced dismissively at Rhonda, then continued to Courtney's bedside as he paged through her chart. "You were in a car accident this morning and were admitted through the ER. Do you remember the accident?" He paused and looked up from the chart for Courtney's answer.

Courtney watched Rhonda scurry from the room before she looked at Dr. Chambers. "No, I don't."

The doctor nodded and returned his attention to the chart. "You had a CT scan and blood work upon admission. Your brain scan was clear. There's no indication of a TBI, and you have no illegal substances in your blood." Dr. Chambers smiled at his small jest and closed the file. "However, from the description of the accident, I believe you're lucky to be alive." He pulled the penlight from the pocket of his coat. "Let's take a look at how you're doing, shall we?"

The doctor tested her eyes and reflexes and then requested she stand to check her balance. He inspected the deep bruising along her left leg and hip while muttering to himself under his breath. When he was done, he assisted her back into the bed and helped arrange the covers.

"I must say again, you are extremely lucky, young lady. If it were possible, I'd say your father was watching after you." Dr. Chambers listened to her lungs, and then hung the stethoscope around his neck.

Courtney's eyes widened. "You know who my father was?"

He didn't act star-struck or hateful.

"Oh, yes. My wife was a big fan. We used to watch his show on television. I know it has been some years since he passed but allow me to say how sorry I am for your loss."

Courtney bowed her head and blinked away the tears, touched by his sincere sympathy. "Thank you," she whispered then gulped back a sob.

"Is there something else going on, Miss Veau? Something that upsets you? Both the paramedics and the ER nurse noted your...odd behavior. I would like to help if I can." He waited while Courtney mopped her face and blew her nose.

"I'm sorry for crying like this." Courtney added more tissue to the pile on her bed. Dr. Chambers lifted the trash receptacle, and she cleared the used tissues.

"That's quite all right, you've been through a traumatic event. However, considering these notes, I need to ask, is there someone abusive in your life? A boyfriend perhaps?" Dr. Chambers stepped back and rested his hip against the counter.

Courtney shook her head. "No. There's no one. Certainly no one abusive."

"The report says you struggled and fought in the ambulance and the ER before you were fully awake. Anything you tell me will be kept in confidence, but please, allow me to help you."

Courtney turned away. She stammered as she searched for the right explanation. "I...experienced something after the car accident...before I woke up in the emergency room. It was so real." She shook her head and blinked moisture from her eyes.

"Something that frightened you?" Dr. Chambers flipped back a few pages. "The first responders did perform CPR." His gaze rose to meet Courtney's. "You may have had an NDE. I'm no expert, but a classic near-death experience is normally associated with pleasant, even peaceful sensations."

"It wasn't like that. What I experienced was different. It lasted much longer. I was somewhere and someone else for days. I can't explain how—and it doesn't make sense—but I know it happened." Her voice trembled and the emotion she struggled to contain broke free.

"Okay, Miss Veau, it's all right. I'm going to order some medication that will help get you over the emotional hump, so to speak. I'll also refer you to a doctor who works with patients who have encountered something similar." Dr. Chambers patted her shoulder, then offered her the wastebasket again.

Courtney deposited her latest round of tissue casualties. "Thank you."

"We'll keep you a few days under observation, but you should be able to go home by the end of the week." The doctor slid the chart into the door. "Get some rest, Miss Veau."

She closed her eyes, lay back and willed her tears to stop. She would never see Merril again, and the stranglehold of grief that knowledge created would not let go. What's more—Merril was not the only loved one ripped from her life. Amy was gone, Nichole's friend and confidant, as well as Jason, Nichole's cousin. Alive yesterday, and yet dead for more than a hundred years.

The line between then and now blurred. She opened her eyes and saw Rhonda pull a syringe from her IV line.

"Sweet dreams," Rhonda whispered in a sing-song voice and cast a cold glance over her shoulder at Courtney as she flipped the light switch off. Courtney could just make out her muttered "Freak" as she left the room.

Chapter 2

Courtney Veau

—

Three days later, a knock at her door woke Courtney, and she opened her eyes enough to watch an orderly deliver the breakfast tray. Although a warming cover hid the food, she could smell eggs. For the first time since waking in the hospital, she felt hungry, and her stomach growled in anticipation.

The marker board by the door showed Debra was her nurse today. A young woman in gold scrubs came in, took her vitals, and then updated her chart. Debra was friendly and professional, a clear sign she'd never heard of Russell Veau.

After she finished breakfast, an admissions clerk entered her room. The middle-aged woman appeared annoyed at the unfinished paperwork. She presented Courtney with several forms attached to a clipboard and indicated which to complete, initial, or sign. Explanations done, she waved toward the door. "I'll wait outside."

Courtney could hear her chat with the nurses in the hallway as she completed the forms. She paused when she reached the emergency contact and bounced the pencil eraser off the form a couple of times. Finally, she wrote a name—Greta James.

Greta had been the trust attorney who administered her parents' estate after their death in the plane crash. Courtney's grandmother, Mary Curtis, had been awarded custody of their four-year-old daughter, and Greta sent them monthly support payments. The young attorney had been an occasional visitor to their home over the years. After Granny passed, Courtney had Greta apply to designate her as an emancipated minor. She hadn't spoken to Greta since the emancipation hearing, but there was no one else.

Courtney set the clipboard on the bedside tray and relaxed against the pillows, her gaze on the date at the top of the form, April 14. She'd been admitted to the hospital three days ago, but for her, time had become tangled.

Four days ago she'd been someone else. She remembered nothing of Nichole Harris's life before waking in her body, but the time spent in Nichole's world haunted Courtney in glorious detail. She could hear the sounds of the ranch; smell the dust in the air and the hay in the barn.

The first time she set eyes on Merril, a rush of emotion had swelled her heart and overwhelmed her with confusion. She'd awakened with Nichole's feelings but without Nichole's memories, and none of her own.

Courtney took a sip from her juice. Her emotions were less volatile today, and she wondered if Dr. Chambers continued to prescribe anxiety medication.

I hope he did.

She could still feel the jagged edges of her broken heart. She closed her eyes and conjured a vision of Merril as if he were in her room. His green eyes, flecked with gold, would flash with concern to find her in a hospital bed. The thought of his expressive eyes and sideways smile made her stomach flip. A knock at the door jarred her from her daydream, and she opened her eyes to find a tall, thin man standing in the doorway.

"Courtney Veau?" the man asked, with an easy professional smile. "My name's Dr. Phelps. Dr. Chambers asked me to speak with you. May I come in?"

Instead of a hospital-white lab coat, he wore a brown corduroy sports jacket with a computer bag slung over one shoulder. Dr. Phelps looked more like a college professor with thinning brown hair and black-framed glasses.

Courtney hesitated a moment then replied, "Yes, of course."

Dr. Phelps tipped his head and entered the room. "Dr. Chambers told me about your condition." He set his computer bag on the counter then took a seat in the bedside chair. "I understand you required CPR at the accident site. Dr. Chambers suspects you experienced a phenomenon we call NDE or near-death experience, and it continues to upset you. Is this correct?" Dr. Phelps peered at Courtney over the line in his bifocal lenses and waited for her reply.

"I ... um ..." Courtney paused to gather her thoughts. "It wasn't the phenomenon that upset me." She shredded a tissue and turned away from his penetrating gaze. "When I woke up and realized where I was—I knew the people I loved were gone. Forever."

"Ah, yes, I see, I see." Dr. Phelps nodded and reset his glasses with his index finger then regarded Courtney. "Miss Veau, your ordeal is not particularly unusual. Many individuals who experience clinical death see loved ones or have visions of light. Most are not upset by it. In fact, most take comfort in these encounters."

"Do they ever relive past lives?" She looked up from the bits of tissue in her lap to Dr. Phelps.

Dr. Phelps blinked in surprise. "Well...the accounts of this phenomenon are many and varied. Entire books and studies have been written on this subject. Almost certainly, what happened to you would fall into one of the categories recounted by others."

"Do they ever become someone else?" Courtney tilted her head and held Dr. Phelps regard with her own.

"Since what they encounter is thought to be caused by a hallucinogenic state, the result of oxygen deprivation, they could imagine they are."

"Oh, really?" Courtney's eyes narrowed. "So, you're saying I imagined it."

"I am not judging your incident by any means. The science behind this phenomenon is still uncertain and based on multiple theories, even though it has been documented for years in every culture of the world. I am simply giving you one possible explanation."

She studied the doctor in silence. Although she seethed with anger, his comment provoked an idea. She hadn't been in some distant undocumented past; she could find evidence her experience had been real.

Dr. Phelps nodded to himself and reached for his computer bag. "Dr. Chambers said you would be released today since your injuries are healing nicely and can be well managed at home." He opened his laptop and tapped briskly on the keyboard. "I would like to visit with you again at my office and have you recount your ordeal in more detail. Perhaps we can find a way to understand why this has upset you to such a degree."

"I already told you why it upset me," she replied immediately.

Dr. Phelps stopped typing and looked again at Courtney. "And why was that?"

Grief and frustration combined to make her statement sharper than intended. "Because I would rather be back there with him than here with you."

Dr. Phelps lowered his chin and observed Courtney over the top of his glasses. "And how would you return to him, Miss Veau?"

"I'm not a suicide risk if that's what you're implying, doctor." She clenched her jaw in aggravation.

Dr. Phelps held her stare for a moment, then turned back to his computer and tapped the keys a few more times. "I can't stay any longer today, but I can see you at ten o'clock tomorrow morning if that is agreeable. The sooner we discuss your experience, the better you will feel."

After he left, she played with his business card and read over the appointment time while she considered her research options.

Debra returned after lunch and confirmed her release, then took her vitals one last time. Moments later, a med-tech came to remove her IV.

Released from the IV tether, Courtney opened the closet and withdrew the clear tote with her personal items. She emptied the bag on the bed and set her shoes and purse to one side. She dressed while considering where to begin her search. A historical society seemed her best option.

She had just pulled on her jeans when she realized her shirt was missing. "Well, crap."

Debra entered the room with Courtney's discharge paperwork and gave Courtney a curious look. "Is something wrong?"

"I don't have a shirt." She sighed in exasperation and rested her hands on her hips.

"They would have cut it off in the ambulance." Debra set the paperwork on the counter and studied Courtney. "I have an old scrub top in my locker you could have," Debra offered with a generous smile. "I don't wear it anymore. Let me get it."

The nurse was out the door before Courtney could convey her gratitude and relief.

I'm alone now.

That realization hit hard, and she pressed her lips to still their quivering. There was no one she could call for help.

It's the same as before the accident. I'll just have to make do.

Courtney pulled her phone from her purse and turned it on. The happy tone assured her she had battery life. She pressed the contact number for her insurance agent while she waited in her bra for Debra to return. The agent transferred her to the claims department where she received a claim number. Next, she looked up a taxi company on her smartphone and pressed the link to call a cab. Technology made modern life convenient, but she hadn't missed it. Although to be honest, she'd had no memory of technology while she was Nichole...not until the end.

Courtney thanked the cab dispatcher and ended the call as Debra returned. She took the shirt from the nurse. "Thank you," she said and pulled the faded blue top over her head. Courtney listened to Debra read her release instructions while she tied her shoes.

"Your medication should be ready at the pharmacy you have listed. Follow up with Dr. Phelps as soon as possible."

"I have an appointment with him in the morning." Courtney placed her phone and earrings in her purse and slipped the bag over her shoulder.

"That's good." Debra made a note in Courtney's file and then indicated the wheelchair in the doorway. "Let's get you downstairs."

Courtney paced with her slow limp at the hospital entrance while she waited for the taxi. Once the cab arrived, she directed the driver to take her to a rental car company near the hospital. She gave the rental agent her insurance claim number and chose a compact car from the vehicles on the lot. A quick stop at the pharmacy to get her prescriptions, then Courtney drove the familiar road to her apartment.

As soon as she unlocked the door and stepped inside, she couldn't help but view the place with new eyes. It was small, but well-appointed with an updated kitchen and bath. Her two-year-old furniture looked showroom new and unused. There were no pictures of friends or family on the wall. She tossed her prescriptions and purse on the kitchen table and walked through the entire apartment, her gaze noticing every detail.

What a small, safe haven I've created for myself.

Its emptiness left a dull ache in her heart.

In her narrow hallway, she stopped her inspection and searched her heart for something positive. She had no family or loved ones, but she did have financial freedom. The trust fund from her parents' estate initially held a substantial amount and had supported Courtney and her grandmother for fifteen years. What remained in her account would see her through college, with a small sum left over for emergencies. It seemed a paltry thing compared to her empty life.

Her thoughts turned to her father. Russell Veau had been a gifted spiritualist and medium. He argued against the term *psychic*. He could not read minds or see into the future. His gift had been the ability to find lost souls and communicate with those who had passed from life. That had been the basis for his television show. He'd also been a philanthropist and worked pro-bono for individuals who needed his help. He'd worked with both state and local agencies to help find missing persons and had often been asked to locate lost or stolen children. The living soul was a beacon to her father. His gift of finding people bordered on magical; however, he was best remembered for his work with the dead.

Courtney had known very little about her father's philanthropy while growing up. Granny Curtis never spoke of it. It wasn't until she turned eighteen that his files, along with articles and newspaper clippings, came to her from Greta. There were boxes of records stacked in the back closet. She'd read through it all, speechless at what she learned. The most personal items—her father's journal and genealogy work—she kept in a box in her bedroom closet. She gravitated to it now and eased her stiff body to the floor. Courtney pulled the small box of mementos onto her lap with a disheartened sigh.

She closed her eyes and fought back the old emotion, the unfairness, and the self-pity. She couldn't miss her parents because she'd never known them, yet their lives and their loss had shaped her own. She shook her head to dispel those thoughts and opened her eyes.

She raised the lid of the box and shuffled through the photographs. There were some of herself as a baby with her mother, and one of her as a toddler, walking and holding her father's hand. There were several photographs of Granny Curtis and her, but they were not what she searched for, and she set them to the side.

She glanced at her father's notes. He'd traced their ancestry several generations but could never get further than Alexander and Catherine Veau. She read a postcard her father discovered during his search. Handwritten by Catherine, and addressed to Alexander, in the flowery cursive of the post-Civil War era, the ink was faded and barely legible. Catherine inquired when Alexander planned to return home from his visit to the capital and signed the card, *Forever yours, Catherine*. Courtney read the card and then set it aside, as well.

Her hands trembled as she picked up her father's journal. She held the book to her chest and spoke to her father through the tightness in her throat. "Daddy, something has happened. I don't...I'm not sure what to do." She swallowed and struggled to regain her composure. "I want to ask you what you thought...what you think I should do?"

She closed her eyes and collected her thoughts. Her father's journal pressed against her breast, expressing more eloquently within her mind the question she asked of her father.

What do I do now?

She lowered the diary and looked at the worn cover, then opened it randomly and read the first line at the top of the page. "*...an item of great significance was found inside the old home.*"

She sat in stillness, the book, open on her lap, as her finger tapped a slow beat against the faded ink. Day turned to dusk, and the apartment grew dark. Her thoughts were far away, reliving her time as Nichole. She remembered the places she went, and finally recalled the route they had taken to the house in Denver. Amy had driven the wagon westward into the city, turning the right at a diagonal thoroughfare and right again at a livery stable. What was the street name? Piper Street? Patch Street? Excitement fluttered in her stomach.

I'm going to find the house.

It took more than one try to get to her feet after sitting for so long. Her left leg and side were sore and stiff. She pulled herself onto the bed with her right arm and sat for a moment as a wave of dizziness swept over her. When it passed, she stood with one hand secure against the wall.

She crept into the kitchen and switched on the overhead light, and then tore open her prescriptions and swallowed one of each with a sip of water. Her backpack was in its usual spot beside the couch. She set it on the counter and slid her laptop from its pocket.

When the screen came to life, she typed in her password and navigated to her favorite map website. In moments, a satellite view of the Denver area appeared on her screen. She followed the highway west toward the city. Ignoring the northern sweep of I-70, she followed Colfax Avenue straight instead.

They'd ridden toward the mountains until they reached a diagonal cross street. Zooming into the area on the map, she saw City Park first—then she spotted the diagonal.

Park Avenue.

"Holy shit," she muttered as her finger traced Park Avenue northwest and turned right on Pence Street. If memory served, the house would be two blocks down on the left, but she'd only been there once.

She clicked the street view icon on the map program and moved the icon house by house down the street until she found it. A chill raced down her spine so sharp it took her breath away. The trees were overgrown and the neighborhood nothing as she remembered, but she was positive. That was her house.

Courtney Veau had never been to Denver. She and Granny Curtis never traveled outside of Texas, yet she knew the inside of that house. She remembered watching Amy walk to the front door and then stop to look up at the second floor. She knew there were narrow stairs at the back of the house that led from the kitchen to the second floor. It was as if she had been there only yesterday.

She bookmarked the page, sent two pages to the printer, and closed the laptop. Had she sat on the kitchen stool and stared at the photo of her house for over an hour? A moan escaped her lips when she stood and tried to stretch. A sharp pain in her side stopped her. She held still until it resolved to a dull ache. The printer ended its chunka-chunka sound, and she limped down the hall to retrieve her printouts.

She looked at the map and the photo of her house and shook her head in amazement.

Dr. Phelps is going to think I'm nuts.

But she didn't care. What happened to her had been real. He could scoff if he liked or add another chapter to his research.

She froze as a crazy idea took hold. Butterflies fluttered in her stomach, and her pulse raced. With a grin on her face, she opened her laptop and began another search.

Chapter 3

Courtney Veau

—

"Courtney Veau?" the nurse called into the waiting area as she examined the patients. Her search halted at Courtney's battered face.

Courtney stood and pulled her backpack over her shoulder. She smiled at the young nurse who directed her to Dr. Phelps's office instead of an examination room.

"Dr. Phelps will be with you in a moment. There is one patient ahead of you," the nurse informed her as she hurried from the room.

On the wall across from the door, numerous certifications surrounded a large framed medical diploma. To the left, behind a wide mahogany desk, long windows faced a wooded area lush with foliage. Courtney took a seat in one of the leather guest chairs and set her backpack on the other. The place smelled of potpourri and furniture polish; both clean and impersonal. Soothing classical music played through a hidden music system, while doors in the hall open and close. Ticking close at hand caught her attention. The hands on the decorative clock above a low credenza showed 10:45. The doctor was running late.

At 11:20, the doctor opened the door then closed it firmly behind him. He stepped around the guest chairs and took a seat at the desk. "I'm sorry I'm late. It's been a busy morning, and I'm afraid our interview will need to be brief." He pulled the keyboard tray forward, and with a few keystrokes, brought the computer to life. His eyes moved back and forth as the monitor reflected small squares on his glasses. He reached up and flicked off the monitor, then turned his attention to Courtney. "How are you feeling today?"

"Better. My leg's still sore." Courtney gave him a slight smile. "The eye looks worse than it feels."

"You do have quite a shiner. The bruise will fade in a few days. The leg will take longer to heal. However, what I meant was, how do you feel about your near-death experience? You were distraught at the hospital. Have you had time to consider your incident, and view it in a more positive light?" Dr. Phelps folded his hands on his desk and waited for Courtney's response.

"I have. I decided to look for a place I remember from my ... journey. I found the house." Courtney unzipped her backpack and took out two sheets of paper—a printout photo of the house and the street map of Denver. She sat them on his desk.

The doctor's brow creased as he studied her documents. "This is where you believe you were?" He looked at Courtney over the rim of his glasses.

"That *is* where I was. That house. This is the road we took from the ranch. We were in a wagon." Courtney indicated the path on the map, following the road east, ending at the house location notated with a graphic pin.

Dr. Phelps nodded and looked from her fingertip on the map to her face. "What does this mean to you—a photo of an old house and a street map?"

"I was there! It proves what happened to me was real.

"Do you believe the people you encountered are still at this house?"

"Of course not," Courtney scoffed in irritation. She scooped up her papers, returning them to her backpack. "I was inside that house during the summer of 1875."

"Miss Veau... Courtney..." Dr. Phelps hesitated, then pulled off his glasses and polished the lenses with a white cloth from his desk drawer. When he finished, he replaced the glasses and gave Courtney a somber look. "I'd hoped you would put your NDE episode into perspective relative to your current life. Your persistent focus on past events, real or imagined, is not conducive to a healthy frame of mind."

"Dr. Phelps, it's all I have. It proves they existed—that *he* existed. Merril wasn't imaginary. He was real. They were all real. I know I can find more evidence; I just need to do more research."

"To what end?"

"What do you mean?"

"How would proof of their existence help you? How does your quest regarding the past allow you to better value your life today? Most NDE patients find a greater appreciation for their life and loved ones." Dr. Phelps paused, then turned back to his keyboard and brought the monitor to life. "I would like you to make a list of things you value in your life. Your *current* life." His eyes flicked to hers, then returned to the monitor. "Try to see how their significance has been enhanced by your recent ordeal. Bring the list with you when you come to your next appointment."

"I'm not most patients, Dr. Phelps, and my experience was not like theirs." Courtney heaved a sigh as she stood and pulled her backpack over her shoulder.

Dr. Phelps updated his notes, typing furiously on his keyboard. "You can arrange your appointment with Marcia at the front desk. Tell her I want to see you in two weeks. I'm pleased with your progress and your frame of mind, although I would like you to work on your perspective."

Courtney stopped at the door, her hand on the knob, and looked back at Dr. Phelps. "I'm surprised you didn't ask if this had something to do with my father."

Dr. Phelps looked up from the keyboard with a genuine smile on his face. "And I'm surprised you didn't tell me it had something to do with him."

"You knew who he was?"

He never said a thing.

"Of course. However, you never mentioned your father or suggested an encounter with him, even though seeing a loved one is not unusual during a near-death experience. A father like Russell Veau might evoke a strong sense of the occult in a child. Perhaps his absence from your experience is what's noteworthy."

"I don't remember my parents," Courtney chuckled at the irony and shook her head. "I don't remember Nichole's parents either, although she would have known them. Just like now, all I had were other people's memories of them."

"Now, *that* is interesting." Dr. Phelps sat back in his chair and regarded Courtney's battered face. "Let's discuss that aspect of your experience more thoroughly next time we visit."

Courtney allowed Marcia to make a follow-up appointment, although she planned to cancel. She hadn't told Dr. Phelps about the boarding pass in her backpack. She was determined to find her house and stand in the yard, just as Nichole had with Amy. If she accomplished nothing more than to look up at the second floor, she would consider her time well spent. She also planned to search historical records while in Denver. She was certain she'd find her cattle ranch existed east of Denver in 1875.

Her departure time was mid-afternoon, and her large suitcase was already in the trunk. She drove from Dr. Phelps's office to the airport and returned the car to the rental agency. She checked the baggage at the counter but kept her backpack with her as she moved through security and boarded the plane.

At thirty thousand feet, she decided she would take a cab to the house as soon as she landed. She couldn't bear to wait. The snow-capped mountains were beautiful and stretched as far as she could see. Her gaze remained fixed on the scenery during the bumpy landing.

When she disembarked, she followed the signs and rode the crowded underground train toward the terminal and baggage claim. After a short wait, a buzzer sounded, and the carousel began to rotate. Her bag was second on the conveyor belt and down the slide. "Excuse me," she said several times as she edged through the crowd toward her bag. She wrestled her luggage from the carousel, and then stopped for a moment to get her bearings. A sign directed her outside to taxi, shuttle and bus transportation.

She left the terminal and tugged her luggage to the taxi line at the second island. The air was sharp and cool, so different from the soft, humid air in Texas. Even the sky was a darker shade of blue. She took a deep breath, remembering the feel of dry air on Nichole's skin.

A woman in an orange vest caught her attention and directed her to a cab. After a quick glance at Courtney's battered face, the woman offered to take her bag. The cabdriver took the suitcase from the woman and loaded it into the cab's trunk. Courtney slid into the back seat and pulled out her notes on the house.

"Where to?" the cabbie asked in a heavy accent as he pulled his door closed.

"Five Points." Courtney shuffled her paperwork in search of the address, too anxious to depend on her memory.

The driver swung around and stared at her. "I need the street address."

"Let me find it. 2433 Pence Street."

The driver typed the address into the small GPS unit on the dashboard then pulled into traffic. The long drive down the airport road was a step back in time, alongside the sharp reality of today. Built east of Denver's suburbs, the ride from the airport toward the city afforded Courtney a view of the wide-open, undeveloped prairie. Much of the landscape was just as she remembered. The metal framing of new hotel construction at each side road exit served as a pointed reminder of the present day.

Courtney focused on the mountains in the distance. They were beautiful, dappled blue and gray with winter white still adorning their peaks. She had never seen them before yet remembered them clearly. She couldn't take her eyes from the majestic view.

The traffic from the airport was light as they merged onto I-70 West. They picked up speed on the interstate then exited onto I-25 South where traffic slowed to a crawl. The cabbie took the Park Avenue exit and turned onto Pence Street. He drove slowly through the residential neighborhood, and then came to a stop at the curb.

Courtney peered out the cab window at the house, mesmerized. She could feel the dopey grin spread across her face as butterflies bounced around in her stomach.

"Fifty-two eighty." The cab driver met her eyes in the mirror.

"Can you wait for me here for a few minutes? I want to go over to that house." She pointed through the window. "Then I'll need to find a hotel."

The driver nodded and picked up his cell phone. "Okay, but the meter stays running."

Courtney shouldered her backpack and pulled herself out of the cab. She limped across the street to the red brick house with white trim and a white picket fence. Her eyes drank in every detail. The trim was different, and the yard was smaller than she remembered. The covered porch had been rebuilt.

An elderly woman with deep brown skin and iron-gray curls swept the front steps in a faded blue cotton dress and apron. She paused when she noticed Courtney, and the two held each other's gaze across the yard.

"You here to see the room, girlie?" the woman called to Courtney across the yard.

Courtney stifled the urge to look around. It was obvious the woman spoke to her, but Courtney couldn't find an answer to her simple question. Instead, she stared speechless at the woman while the surreal sense of déjà vu played havoc with her mind and froze her tongue.

The thin, gray-haired woman leaned her broom against the porch rail and made her way down the step toward Courtney. "The room's 'round back. It's a one bedroom upstairs. Did you call?" The woman stopped at the fence and looked at the cab. "That yours?"

"Yes." Courtney looked from the woman to the cab and back again.

The woman studied Courtney's damaged face for a moment, then said, "Pay up and get your things. If you don't want the apartment, you can call another. Them cabbies will steal ya blind."

Courtney returned to the cab and paid the driver. He retrieved her luggage from the trunk and set it on the pavement. He drove away as she rolled her suitcase across the street and wrestled it up the curb. The old woman held the gate open, and Courtney maneuvered her case into the yard.

"My name's Dessa. I manage the property for the Hawthorns. And you are?"

"Courtney Veau."

Dessa tipped her head and waved her hand for Courtney to follow her. "It's only a short-term lease, mind ya—month-to-month. The Hawthorns are trying to sell." Dessa pointed to a FOR SALE sign in the yard as they stepped past and turned onto a narrow sidewalk that ran along the side of the house. A flowering vine, fragrant with white blossoms and green leaves, clung to the wall they passed, trailing up to the roof. As she looked up, the vapor trail of a jet cut the sky overhead.

The small back yard had a weed-filled garden and a detached garage. On the back of the house were two doors. Dessa dug in her apron and pulled out a key ring with several keys on it. Finding the one she wanted, she thrust it in the lock and opened the door.

"One bedroom, one bath. There's an attic access up there too, but that stays locked. Leave your travel case here and go on up, have a look-see."

Courtney stepped past Dessa onto the landing at the foot of the stairs. Her gaze followed the risers into the darkness at the top. This access was new, probably added during a renovation of the single-family home into small apartments. The stairs she remembered were in the center of the house, between the kitchen and the front parlor.

Dessa reached in and flipped a switch, but nothing happened. "Darned bulb. There's another door at the top, but it's unlocked. Go on, now, and mind your step."

Courtney's hand trembled as she gripped the railing. Each step stretched the bruises on her left side, and she grimaced with pain. At the midway point, she slipped her backpack off her shoulder and set it down. Then she continued up the stairs.

The upper door hid in darkness across the small landing. The handle turned, but the warped wood refused to budge. Without hesitation, she threw her shoulder against the barrier. The door popped open, and she stumbled inside.

What used to be two bedrooms on the front side of the house was now a tiny apartment. Through the small entry and to the right, a narrow hallway extended past the kitchen. She flipped the switch on the wall, but the corridor remained dark. By the meager light of the dirty the kitchen window, she recognized the attic door at the far end of the hall.

"Unreal," Courtney murmured.

Everything has changed, but this could be the same hallway.

She crossed the hall and walked into the main room, anxious to examine the front window. In her mind's eye, she saw Amy push the curtain aside to study the frame.

To the right, the bathroom caught her attention. She peeked into the tiny area and found the sink, tub and toilet were old and discolored. Back in the hallway, she moved past the kitchen and faced the attic door.

It has to be locked.

She wrapped her fingers around the tarnished handle. The metal stung like ice in her grip. A chill reached through her and ran down her spine.

"Girlie, you all right up there?"

Courtney gasped and released the handle at the sound of Dessa's voice. She took a step back and stared at the attic door.

How long did I stand here, caught in a web of memories?

She ran a cold hand across her forehead and considered the door for another moment before she returned to the landing. She closed the warped door as best she could and took the rail in a firm hold. Going down the stairs hurt much more than it had on her way up. She retrieved her backpack at the halfway point, slung it over her shoulder, and eased her way to the bottom.

"I'll take it."

Dessa smiled. "I thought you might."

Courtney left both bags at the base of the stairs and followed Dessa to the front of the house.

The old woman stopped on the porch and turned to Courtney with a chuckle. "I just remembered, I'm plumb out of rent agreements." She cocked her curly gray head and held up a single shining key for Courtney to see. "Why don't you take this now and we can settle up later?"

"Sure. Whatever works." Sunlight flashed off the key as Courtney held out her hand. It dropped into her open palm, and she closed her fist tight. The metal was cold and hard. A slow grin spread across her face as she looked at the silver key.

Unbelievable.

Dessa turned away and picked up her broom. "We've had some utility problems. Nothin' serious, but you might pick up a couple of jugs of water for the commode. The electric comes and goes. If you have gadgets, you'll want to power 'em up good at the coffee shop. It's just two blocks down, along with some eateries. You can walk there, but don't go after dark." Dessa returned to her sweeping.

"Thank you," Courtney breathed. The surreal sensation of déjà vu still surrounded her. She backed from the porch to the center of the yard and gazed up at the front of the old home with the eerie sense that Amy was beside her. Her last clear memory as Nichole was Amy opening the curtains and looking out the upstairs window. The curtain in her apartment moved slightly, and she stared hard at the glass. After a moment, she scoffed at her overactive imagination. She smiled at Dessa, held up the key, and followed the walkway to the back of the house.

Pulling her suitcase up the steps was torture. Her leg and hip ached along with the rest of her battered body. Once in the apartment, she laid the case on its side, unpacked a few shirts, hanging them on old wire hangers she found in the closet.

Finished with her clothes, she pulled the laptop from her backpack and looked up bus stops and routes. She found shopping nearby, even a megastore that sold everything she needed.

She took a pain pill and swallowed the last of her bottled water. Since none of the light switches worked, she added a flashlight to her list of things to buy.

On a whim, she phoned Dr. Phelps. No answer. She left an excited voicemail about the house and hung up with a happy "Buh-bye." She pulled her empty shoulder purse from her backpack and put her phone, debit card, and shiny new key inside.

Courtney worked her way down the stairs and out into the late afternoon sunlight. She locked the lower door to her new apartment and tested the lock. A car passed in front of the house on Pence Street, and she lifted her head at the sound. Not far to the west, the low, constant hum of the highway reached her. All around her, sights and sounds of the modern world intruded. She had come back, but she was as far from Merril as she'd been in Texas. With that discouraging thought, she tucked the key in her purse and walked as swiftly as she could to the bus stop.

I'll need to hurry to be back by sunset.

She bought a collapsible-wheeled cart at the store, large enough to drag her purchases home. It took some time to get the cart up the dark staircase. She hauled it up a step at a time, moving the flashlight rung by rung as she went. At the top, she looked down into the darkness, weary and weepy.

I can't stop yet. Get up, get moving.

The easy setup for the inflatable bed defied her and left her exhausted. Successful at last, she threw the unzipped sleeping bag over the mattress and wrestled the pillow and comforter from their plastic wrap. She switched off the flashlight, shed her clothes in the dark, and collapsed on the bed.

What a day. I can't believe I'm here!

She lay awake under the starchy new comforter, unable to fall asleep. Her thoughts were a jumble inside her exhausted mind, darting from one thing to another. Just as she drifted off to sleep, she heard his voice.

He was in her dream and her head, calling softly, "Please don't go—stay with me, Nicki ..."

Courtney opened her eyes in the darkness. A deep chill permeated the room. "Holy shit," she whispered and listened for his voice. "Merril?" she called, but there was only silence. She waited in the dark a long time, listening.

Merril slipped into her dream each night after she fell asleep and begged her not to leave him. At first, it was wonderful to hear his voice, even though it was only a dream. However, his refrain never changed and the endless reproach, along with her interrupted rest, played havoc with her emotions.

By the fourth day, she wanted more than fast food. She decided to make a morning trip to the grocery store. She caught the early bus at the corner stop and was back in the apartment in less than an hour. Daylight reflected on dust motes as she emptied her purchases onto the cracked but newly cleaned kitchen counter.

"Nicki, where are you?" Merril's desperate whisper sounded from the hallway.

She froze in shock, turning her head from side to side to try and pinpoint the direction of his voice.

Near the attic? In the bedroom?

Her gaze followed the soft sound his boots made on the wooden floor.

He passed the kitchen opening less than a foot from where she stood, but he wasn't there. The footfalls paused in the bedroom then echoed from where the old stairs would have been, falling silent somewhere beneath her.

The apple she held trembled in her fist. Released from her hand, the fruit rolled away. She held the edge of the counter and lowered her head gasping for air. "I'm here, Merril." Her world tilted. Emotion rippled across her chest, and her head spun. Overwhelmed, she sank to the floor, put her head on her knees, and cried.

She waited several hours for Merril to return, but the house remained silent. Unable to sit still any longer, she went down to Dessa's apartment and knocked, but Dessa didn't answer. She tried to peek through the filthy windows, but shadows hid the interior.

After she returned to her apartment, she wandered through the rooms until she found herself in front of the locked attic door.

"Merril?" Her voice quivered as she reached for the doorknob. "Merril!" Courtney shouted at the door and shook the handle, then whispered, "I can hear you, babe. Talk to me." Silence answered her. She leaned her head against the wooden barrier in defeat. Perhaps Dr. Phelps was right, and she'd fed her obsession until she heard voices.

With sudden clarity, it occurred to her that her father might have tried something else.

She stepped back and released the knob. Her hand had stiffened into a claw and ached to the bone. Massaging her cramped palm and fingers, she stalked into the bedroom, turning off all her electronics. After her tingling fingers drew the curtains closed, she returned to the kitchen for the small scented candle she'd purchased at the store. She snatched it, along with a book of matches from the drawer and went back to her darkened bedroom.

The silent house watched as she set her pillow on the floor and took a seat. She put her back to the inflatable bed and struck the match to the candlewick. The flicker of the fire illuminated the small room, empty except for her bed and a scattering of fast food bags along the wall.

She shook out the match, closed her eyes and exhaled, long and slow. Her deep inhale filled her senses with the scent of the lavender candle. Willing herself to be calm, she opened her senses like her father described in his journal.

She imagined the house she remembered, not the run-down apartments building it was now. Extending her senses beyond her body, she paced through the house with her mind.

He is here.

She could feel him in the shadow ahead of her. The heel-toe rap of his boot echoed behind her. Ever elusive. Unreachable. She pictured him, and her memory was so sharp and clear that she winced, but his presence eluded her.

"Please Merril, come back. Talk to me," she whispered. But as the afternoon became evening, he never answered. Defeated, she blew out the candle and crawled onto her inflatable bed.

She stayed in her apartment for the next two days, waiting for his voice. Each time he called to Nicki she would answer, but he never responded. After each failed attempt, she became more convinced that Merril spoke only in her mind.

She called Dr. Phelps late one night and left a message on his answering machine. She told him about the voice in her head and how it called to her. He hadn't returned her call.

***

Present-day – Denver, Colorado

After the visual encounter with Merril's specter, discouragement overwhelmed her. He'd looked right at her and called her name, but never acknowledged her presence. She re-examined her father's journal and decided she was missing one crucial item—a possession of the deceased. She slammed the journal shut and set it on the floor by the bed, elbows on her knees, her head sunk into her hands.

An item from a man who's been dead for a hundred years? No problem.

In the morning, she opened her eyes, stared at the cracked and peeling plaster on the ceiling, and wondered why she stayed here. Tears seeped from the corner of her eyes, tickling down through her unwashed hair to dampen the pillowcase. She didn't care. She waited without hope for the sound of his voice.

By slow increments, the room grew silent. Sounds from the street became muted and then disappeared altogether. Into the vacuum of silence, came the hushed tone of Merril's voice. He called to her, searched for her. Was he a voice inside her head, or a specter only she could hear? His boot heels echoed down the hallway and paused near her bed. His presence filled the small apartment, and Courtney choked in grief.

"Nicki, don't leave me. Please, come back."

"You're killing me, Merril," Courtney whispered as she listened to his voice with a broken heart. She shook her head and muttered, "No—this has to stop."

"Nicki... Please..."

Frustrated, she crawled off the bed. "I'm not Nicki anymore, Merril, I'm Courtney now. Courtney Veau," she yelled. "I don't know how to reach you. I'm sorry." She stumbled against the wall as she gained her feet. He seemed so close, so insistent. If she shut her eyes, she could see him standing there, green eyes flashing with impatience. But, he'd been left behind, and she, confused and seeking answers, sat alone in an empty house.

She'd come in search of a past that was not her own, and now she was trapped in a place she didn't belong. "This is crazy. What's the use?" Even as the words escaped her lips, the voice in her head moved away and faded down the stairs into the apartments below.

Courtney wiped the tears from her face. She couldn't think with his voice in her head; she could barely eat. She couldn't communicate with him, and it was torture to hear him call.

She snatched her bag and key from the floor and fled the apartment. She slammed the warped landing door behind her and hurried down the stairs, desperate for sunlight and fresh air.

Chapter 4

Courtney Veau

—

Courtney squinted as sunshine and fresh air caressed her face. She fumbled with the key until it slid into the lock. Door secured, she hurried toward the front of the house while tucking the key into her purse and stopped her urgent stride with a startled gasp.

Dessa stood on the walkway, not a foot from Courtney, blocking her path. "Don't go tellin' me you're gonna let some silly ghost scare ya now? That spook never hurt nobody, no sirree. Just raisin' a bit of a fuss today, for sure." Dessa nodded once, then grinned at Courtney.

Hand over her pounding heart, Courtney stared open-mouthed at Dessa. "Holy sh—. Dessa! You scared me to death. What? Wait..." She extended her hand and pointed a trembling finger at her apartment. "You... heard that? You can hear him?"

"'Course I heard him. Think I'm deaf? Probably heard him in heaven itself with all that carryin' on." Dessa shook her gray head then stepped over to a concrete bench in the weed-filled garden. "Girlie, you want to hear 'bout that ghost, or you just gonna stand there?"

Courtney didn't respond. She stood rooted to the walkway as her gaze moved from Dessa to her door, and then rose to the darkened windows above.

"Hey, now, are you all right? Why don't you have a seat before you fall down?" Dessa sat and patted the empty spot beside her.

"What? I'm sorry. It's just I thought the voices were only in my head." Courtney spared a glance at Dessa, but her attention drifted back to the upstairs windows.

Dessa rose with a huff, grasped Courtney's arm with a firm grip and guided her to the bench. "Ain't no voices in your head, 'cept if you've been hearin' more than one. Only one poor old soul walks in there." Dessa waited while Courtney took a seat on the bench and then sat beside her. "That ghost been searchin' this old house for years. Keeps callin' that name, 'Nicki ... Nichole', like his sad old heart was a-breakin'.'"

Courtney felt the blood drain from her face. She cleared her throat then reached out and touched the woman's bone-thin arm. "Dessa, do you know who the ghost is? Do you know his name?"

Dessa shook her head slowly back and forth and pressed her lips together. "No, I can't tell ya his name." Her head stilled as her gaze rose to meet Courtney's. A smile creased her face. "But, I could show you his picture."

"You... have a photograph?" Courtney's head spun, and her stomach flipped. She put her hand on the stone bench to stop the tilting sky.

Dessa chuckled. "Now, don't you go lookin' all green, child. You're just shakin' like a leaf."

Courtney gave the old woman an unsteady smile. "I'm all right. I just ... this is ... unexpected." She paused a moment, took a short breath and then asked, "Would you show me the photo, Dessa?"

"I don't see why not. It'll take some diggin', mind ya. Last time I saw that old thing, it was packed in some rickety trunk upstairs." Dessa rose to her feet and nodded her head. "I think it's time. I'll unlock the door and take ya in, but the diggin' part, that's up to you. You're gonna want to watch your step when we get in there. There's things in that attic been there better than a century. Oh, lordy, it's a mess up there."

Dessa chuckled and patted at her apron as Courtney followed her up the stairs to her apartment. When they entered the main room, Dessa pointed at Courtney's large flashlight. "Best bring that." She continued down the hallway and waited at the attic entrance until Courtney joined her. Dessa withdrew the key ring from her apron and inserted one of the keys into the lock. Her gaze held Courtney's as she turned the handle and pushed. The door swung open with an eerie squeal.

Courtney peered over Dessa's shoulder into the shadows. Dust motes floated in a dim ray of light from a dirty window near the eaves. A musty smell emanated from the room and wafted past Dessa and into the corridor. Courtney wrinkled her nose and fought the urge to sneeze.

The landlady paused before she entered and turned toward Courtney. "This picture was shown to me by the woman who lived here before me. Ada Cranz was her name. Never knew how she came across the picture, or how she knew the story behind it." Dessa turned and mounted the five steps to the storage area. When she reached the top, she stopped and looked around. "Kinda spooky up here, ain't it? Ada thought a witch lived here and used this space for her black magic." Dessa winked at Courtney before she shuffled forward.

Courtney climbed the steps and cast a quick look around. The meager light was little better than darkness. Nothing was recognizable. Discarded items were stacked in rows and covered with tarps. The narrow aisles wove through a dust-covered maze in the small room. She took a step forward and kicked something with her foot. It clunked in the shadows and rolled away.

Dessa spoke as though Courtney stood behind her.

Courtney shuffled closer, one hand outstretched in the semi-darkness, to hear the rest of the tale.

"... so, I asked Ada why she thought that ghost been hauntin' this house for such a spell. Well, Ada tells me it's because his lover left him real unexpected like. Caused this poor fella to go sort of insane. He swore up and down that he'd find her, even if he had to search the rest of time." Dessa stopped and turned to Courtney. "Can't say as I believe Ada's story. She was always sayin' somethin' silly and romantic like that. Now me, I figure that ghost fella got hisself murdered. Maybe by that Nichole gal he keeps lookin' for. Revenge, that's a good hauntin' reason if I ever heard o' one." Dessa paused and smiled up at Courtney in the half-light. "Ada's story got ya all choked up, ain't it? Guess it was kind of touchin', at that."

Courtney no longer saw Dessa. Her sight had turned inward. "He'd search for the wind..." she murmured to herself. Dessa's story brought a flood of new memories. She and Merril had sought shelter in an Indian encampment. So many things were revealed that night, if only she had understood. Courtney gasped at the firm tug on her arm.

"You okay, child? Off woolgathering, I guess. Well, Ada told the story better than I do, I s'pose."

"What? Oh, I'm sorry. He must have loved her very much to search for so long." Courtney blinked, and a tear slid down her face.

"Reckon so. Yep, reckon so. Well, if you're ready you can pick a pile and dig in. We'll see if we can find that picture for ya. Why don't you turn on your fancy light there?" Dessa suggested, then bobbed away around the end of a covered pile and proceeded to the far side of the room.

Courtney raised her hand and brushed the tears from her face with her fingertips. Tears wouldn't change things, and she was weary of tears. She turned on the flashlight and waved it around the attic. Shadows danced back and forth, sending the room into motion. She directed the beam toward the dirty floor, reached down and lifted the edge of the tarp. She worked her way down the aisle but found nothing that looked like a trunk.

Dessa stood at one end of the room and waited while Courtney pawed through cobwebs and skirted an old baby carriage, looking underneath tarps and sneezing. When Courtney stopped beside her, Dessa pointed at the trunks stacked along the wall beneath the eaves.

"Here they are. Hope you're not afraid of gettin' a bit dusty. That picture's in one of these cases—I just can't recall which one. It's no matter. Pick one for yourself and dig in." Dessa made an oval shape with her hands, about eight inches wide and six inches tall. "As I recall, the frame was about yea big." She pointed to a trunk on the other side of the room. "You should start with the one on top, over there in the corner."

"This is a ton of luggage." Courtney aimed the light down the wall. Baggage filled the length of the room, stacked four high in places.

We could search for a month and never find a thing.

She stiffened her resolve and strode to the trunk Dessa had indicated. Adjusting the flashlight beam, she set her light on a nearby box and turned her attention to a small travel trunk on top of the corner pile. Time and moisture had rusted the metal latch tightly, and the catch defied her efforts to open it.

"I need something to pop this open." Courtney cast a quick glance around, but nothing suiting her purpose was within easy reach.

"Havin' trouble there, young'un?" Dessa pulled a handkerchief from her apron, waved it in the dusty air and caused more dust to swirl around their heads. In the half-light, Dessa's face appeared gray as she peered past Courtney's shoulder at the metal-banded trunk.

"The latch is stuck." Courtney hit the metal with the side of her fist. "Do you see anything we could use to pry it open?"

"Whoa, there, child. This here's private property. We don't want to go smashin' up Mr. Hawthorn's fine trunk now, do we?" Dessa chuckled. "We'll just have to take a look-see. Could be that picture is in one of these other boxes. Might be no need to take apart that one you got there. I think we should just let that one be."

Courtney examined the nameplate above the latch. She could almost decipher the engraved initials where her hand had smudged away the dirt and grime.

This is the one.

She rubbed the heel of her hand against the tarnished metal several times. Excitement coursed through her as she looked closer at the nameplate.

"What on earth are you doin' child?"

"There are initials here. I want to see what they are."

"We gonna be here all day if you take a notion to clean this place up. We won't ever find that picture. Here." Contrary to her words, Dessa handed Courtney her handkerchief.

"Thanks." Courtney took the cloth and rubbed at the initial plate above the clasp. Already certain what the letters were, she wanted to see it with her own eyes. She pulled her head back to let the light shine on the metal plate. Time had blackened the metal, but the letters were clear—N. H.

Courtney brushed at the grime on the rest of the trunk, and a chill ran down her spine. She cast a quick glance around the attic, but only Dessa stood behind her, watching her work.

"You think this is the one?" The old woman asked in a hushed voice.

"If the picture is up here, it's in this trunk," Courtney's whisper tightened with the excitement.

Dessa raised one eyebrow. "You're sure? Well, let's see what we can find." She kicked at the pile of discarded items behind her, and a thick spoon slid across the floor. "Here, now, that might do the trick." She handed the utensil to Courtney, then wiped her hands on her apron and stepped out of the light.

Courtney placed the tip of the utensil under the latch and pressed down. On the second try, the clasp popped up with a click. Her arm shook as she slowly opened the heavy lid and let it lean against the wall. Her body blocked the light, and she eased over to allow the beam to illuminate the contents. Resting on what had once been a lavender skirt was a tarnished oval frame.

"There it is," Dessa proclaimed, her grin wide and knowing.

Overall, the photograph had weathered the passing of time well in the trunk. The cream and sepia-tone coloring spoke its age. The picture portrayed three people in stiff, formal poses popular at that time. Two men, dressed in dark suits, stood to either side of a blonde woman seated demurely in an ornately carved chair.

"Holy shit." Courtney's vision blurred and then snapped into focus.

Dessa reached over and lifted the photograph. "Yep, this is it—the picture Ada showed me. See the man to the right of the woman?" Dessa pointed. "That fella's the one Ada claimed is our ghost friend. He's a handsome devil. I bet this young gal in the middle is that murderin' Nichole." Dessa grinned and handed Courtney the tarnished treasure. "Now that we found your picture, I gotta run. I need to finish up some weedin' and see to my other chores. You stay here long as you like. Mind your step when you leave."

Courtney's attention was devoted entirely to the faded picture. She looked up in time to see Dessa lift her shoulders in a small shrug and heard her chuckle as she made her way down the short flight of stairs. "Thank you," Courtney called.

Dessa waved the rag above her head as she walked away from the attic.

Courtney remained in the room for hours. Seated on the dirty floor, she stared at the faces with a dull ache in her heart. Now she had another picture for her memory box. Her finger caressed the glass above Merril's jawline. "I love you," she whispered and wiped at the tears with the back of her hand.

She studied the face of the young woman seated between the men. Her name had been Nichole Harris, and she bore no resemblance to Courtney. She would never convince Dr. Phelps she'd been the young woman in this photo.

I don't care what he believes. Not anymore.

With a sigh, she rubbed her burning eyes. She gasped as the car accident, and all that followed, flooded her memory. The flash of oncoming headlights blinded her. The squealing wheels and the tearing screech of metal on metal, followed by the crunch of breaking glass as she flew forward.

Afterward, there was nothing except emptiness, devoid of light and sound. Time had no more meaning than up or down. By slow degrees, the total darkness faded, and ghostly images emerged. She'd found herself in a shadowed corridor, the only source of illumination was a burst of light that rippled in waves from the farthest end. She'd known she was dead, but there was no regret or emotion associated with that knowledge. She'd felt at peace.

Her muscles tensed as she remembered the ghostly corridor. Anxiety crawled up her spine and she fought a gut response to flee the attic. Clinging to the photo for comfort, she recalled how she moved effortlessly toward the light, down the hall and past empty, darkened doorways. Familiar voices called from the warm glow ahead, although their words were never clear.

An opening to her right glowed and pulsed with the beat of a heart. It distracted her. The rhythmic light grew irresistible, and her direction changed.

Beyond the portal, Nichole Harris's heart had begun to beat again.

The pull was overpowering and swept Courtney's soul down and through the glowing passage.

All light disappeared the instant she'd crossed the threshold, and she spiraled into darkness. Terror had seized her as her mind filled with knowledge and memories from another lifetime. People, places, and emotions, foreign to her, and yet as familiar as Courtney's own life.

Both lives were hers, she'd realized, and with that single spark of recognition, they fused. She'd tried to grasp the enormity of her revelation, but all thought had stopped abruptly, and she'd fallen into an empty and barren unconsciousness.

Chapter 5

Amy Harris

—

June 5, 1875 – Denver, Colorado

Amy carried her gathering basket into the kitchen from the small backyard garden and set it down on the kitchen table. She pulled off one glove while glancing toward the stairs and parlor to make sure she was alone. With one finger, she stroked each of the tightly closed marigold heads, her lips moving in silent prayer to the mother. After each gentle touch, the buds would blossom and spread their tiny orange petals as if filled with jubilation. When the last flower awakened, she smiled with satisfaction.

The smile stayed on her lips as she untied her bonnet and hung it on the peg by the door, then tugged at the fingers of the other glove, one at a time. Footsteps on the stairs brought her head up.

June McKay stepped down into the kitchen. Formally, the housekeeper for the Harris-Highlands Ranch, she acted as Amy's companion during their year-long exile to the Harris house in Denver. "More herbs?" June nodded at the basket on the table.

"Flowers." Amy laid her gloves beside the colorful blossoms then took the arching handle on her forearm. "The last of them, I promise. The marigolds bloomed, and the lavender budded." Amy stepped past June to the stairs. "I want to dry them before we leave."

June slipped an apron over her head. "Is Tom back yet?"

Amy paused as she reached the second-floor landing. "I haven't seen him," she called down to June.

Tom Baker had been in Denver for a week. He'd brought the buckboard from the ranch to use on their return trip. Earlier that morning, he'd walked to the public livery to check on their animals and had yet to return.

Amy's trunk was packed and ready. She glanced at it as she passed her room. Her breath caught.

I'll see Jason soon.

Their separation had been hard, but Jason's cousin could not abide her. Amy and Jason decided it would be best if she made Denver her temporary home. Their separation would only last until Jason could make Nichole understand that his marriage to Amy was no threat to the cousins' close relationship. Unfortunately, Jason's plan hadn't progressed at the pace she anticipated.

Amy and June were scheduled to return to the ranch at the end of the spring roundup, just in time for the annual Highlands' barbecue. Amy intended to stay for a month or longer, depending on Nichole. She hoped Nichole would be too occupied with new dresses and summer distractions to pay attention to her.

Once they returned to the ranch, June McKay would reclaim her former role as housekeeper. Although the woman had become Amy's friend over the last year, she had not become her confidant. There were some things she could never share.

She passed two more bedrooms before unlocking the door at the end of the hallway. She had made the attic space her own when she first arrived at the town house. Now pegs for drying flowers and herbs lined the wall above the workbench. Mortar and pestle graced her table along with a row of apothecary bottles filled with herbs, tinctures and oils.

Once in the attic, she opened the small ventilation window near the peak of the eaves to let in the morning air. She set her basket on the workbench and sorted the flowers.

Jason and Nichole riding in a carriage.

Amy gasped in surprise and gripped the bench. The clarity of the vision was startling.

Merril enraged and grief-stricken.

Jason steps from the buggy while Nichole watches.

Anxiety accompanied the vision now, and a sense of loss. A premonition this strong was rare. She left the basket on the bench and hurried down the hall to her room. Once inside, she closed the door and slid home the seldom used bolt lock.

Philip collapsed at his desk. Kevin in tears as Merril stalks out.

Her hands shook as she pulled a candlestick and holder from her dresser drawer. She struck a match, held it to the wick, then shook the match out. She poured water from the pitcher into the black washbasin beside it, filling it to the brim. The locket around her neck held a curl of Jason's blond hair. She withdrew several of the strands and floated them carefully on the water.

She drew the curtains closed to darken the room and returned to the dresser. The candle flame reflected across the water as though it were a mirror.

She crossed herself and said two prayers; the first, to her father's God. Eyes closed, and head bowed, her lips moved as she spoke her father's favorite, Psalms 23. When she finished the prayer, she whispered, "Amen." The familiar words steadied her.

She turned and raised her arms toward her improvised altar and invoked a blessing from her mother's Gods.

"Lord and Lady, I call to thee,
and to the four elemental spirits of this world –
Air, Fire, Water, and Earth.
Attend me now and grant your blessing.
Gift me with understanding and clarity,
from the vision that you send.
Guard and protect my purpose.
Let my will be guided."

Her mother had taught her to cast a circle and call the corners to seek spiritual guidance or command the elements, but today, a simple blessing would have to suffice. She had neither the time nor the privacy to cast a circle, and urgency drove her.

As she finished, she lowered her arms. A deep sense of calm enfolded her. In her mind's eye, her body took on a warm golden glow. Only then did she consider the basin. The trembling had subsided, and her spirit filled with calm purpose. She looked deeply into the water, her eyes unfocused, concentrating instead on her inner sight.

"Show me," she said softly as the vision unfolded.

***

Tom Baker was eating an apple in the kitchen when Amy came down the stairs. "Was everything all right at the stable?" she inquired.

"Yup," he responded, taking another bite.

"Can we leave for the ranch immediately?"

Tom stopped chewing and looked at Amy. "Now?"

"Well, yes. Before noon."

"I suppose," he shrugged and swallowed. "I don't see why not."

"Good. Go back and get the wagon ready. Oh, and give the stable boy a penny and have him stop our milk delivery."

"What's this?" June asked. She came into the kitchen just as Tom stepped out the back door, taking another bite of his apple.

"We're going to leave today instead of Thursday. Can you be ready in an hour?"

"In an hour!" June's eyes bulged wide.

"Yes. I want to be there by tomorrow."

June pulled the apron over her head and hung it on a peg by the door with a sigh. "I can be ready in an hour if you help me close up the house." June's eyes lit and she grinned at Amy. "Are you that anxious to see Jason?"

Surprised at first, then relieved, Amy chuckled. "Of course, I am."

The older woman nodded and turned toward the staircase. "Well, that's good," June said over her shoulder. "It's about time you got that family started."

"June!" Amy laughed, but the smile faded as June disappeared up the stairs.

Chapter 6

Nichole Harris

—

The Highlands Ranch

Nichole picked up her hairbrush, fumbled with it for a moment, then set it back on her dressing table. Anxiety coiled in her chest, but she ignored it as she pulled on a lightweight pair of day gloves. She checked her coiffed hair in the mirror one last time and adjusted the beautiful wide-brimmed sunbonnet. Perhaps this betrothal was an egregious mistake.

It wasn't Kevin's fault that she had fallen in love with his cheating brother. Lord knows, she had willed that emotion away a thousand times. There were no more tears left for Merril Shilo, and yet just the thought of him made her heart beat fast and brought a blush to her face.

She knew it wasn't fair to Kevin. He was a good-tempered man, like his father, Philip. There was no reason whatsoever she couldn't make a marriage with Kevin work. Except she didn't love him. She never would. She'd lost her soul to a scoundrel; as for the rest, she would just have to make do.

The turn of phrase, *we will just have to make do*, reminded her of her mother. How she wished her mother were here right now. If the thought of Merril no longer brought a tear to her eye, remembering the loss of her mother always did. That unspeakable train ride west four years ago was a nightmare that haunted her sleep to this day.

It had been the spring of 1871 when the letter from her father, Quincy, arrived at her Uncle Spencer's home in Boston. She and her mother had lived with her uncle and his family her entire life, while her father sought to strike it rich out west.

She had just turned sixteen, preparing for her Boston debut, when the letter arrived and ruined her life. In the letter, her father claimed to have made his fortune at last. He had built a family home on his new cattle ranch in the Colorado territory, and he instructed his wife and daughter to join him there as soon as possible.

Nichole sank into the chair beside her dressing table. Her hair and sunbonnet were forgotten; her mind fixed firmly on the past. Memories of her mother filled her thoughts. However, in her hope to find comfort, she found only grief.

They had departed Boston within a week of receiving the letter. Arguing her case swayed no one. Her father decided the time had come to begin their new life together, and that was final. She was thankful now that her mother's young maid, Jeanne, agreed to travel with them. She would not have survived that trip without her.

Her mother became ill on the train. One side of her face grew weak, and she stopped speaking. It was evident Emily Harris was having apoplexy, but there was nothing to be done. By the time they reached Cheyenne, the porter had to carry her mother aboard the short line bound for Denver.

Somewhere between Cheyenne and Denver her mother slipped away. Rage and loss had stunned her beyond tears.

What should have been a warm reunion became a bitter and silent meeting. Her father, at first confused, and then distraught at his wife's death, eventually tried to welcome his daughter, but Nichole would have none of it, or him. She'd been both hostile and withdrawn toward her father and clung to Jeanne while *he* made arrangements for his wife.

Her first months at the ranch were as terrible as she could make them, for everyone. Pensive and aloof, she wanted to run away and return to her uncle's home. She missed her cousin and her friends. Although the people at her father's ranch were kind to her, she spurned their friendship.

Then Merril Shilo returned to his father's ranch, and her entire world changed. Merril had just turned twenty-one and had been on his own for six years. He told stories about places and people she had never imagined. Tall and wild, with little respect for authority, Merril had the most beautiful green eyes she'd ever seen. He explained how he had run away after the death of his own mother. Merril understood her anger and emptiness.

Her passion for Merril sprang from more than just similar tragedies, or so it seemed at the time. He became the center of her world, her reason to live in the dusty emptiness that was the high plains, east of the Rockies.

Then he betrayed her. And now, well, she would just have to make do.

Nichole picked up her reticule from the bed and straightened her short jacket before she stepped into the hallway. The door to her cousin's room across the hall stood open. Jason had already gone downstairs.

She raised her chin, squared her shoulders and descended the stairs. She crossed the entry and opened the front door. A cool morning breeze greeted her, along with the sound of her new carriage approaching the front steps.

"Hey-ho, cousin, you look lovely. There is something extraordinarily beautiful about a woman who doesn't keep a man waiting." Jason pulled back on the reins and brought the two-wheeled, single horse vehicle to a stop.

Nichole dimpled her cheek at his remark and batted her eyelashes.

His hair had grown a bit too long, and disorderly blond curls fell over his collar. He brushed them absently from his eyes and smiled at her. Growing up together in Boston, they were often mistaken for siblings. Both she and Jason shared the Harris family's curly blond hair and light-blue eyes.

Despite her anxiety and second thoughts, her cousin made her smile. She waited as he set the brake then stepped down from the carriage and offered her his hand.

"Shall we, my dear? We don't want to keep your future husband waiting."

Nichole cringed at his remark and placed her gloved hand in his—a frozen smile on her lips.

He escorted her to the other side of the vehicle and helped her onto the seat.

The buggy had been a gift from Jason, one she insisted he purchase for her. He'd warned her that it was sprung for the cobblestone streets of Boston and wouldn't travel well on the rough trails around the ranch. She didn't care. Her mother would have loved it, and so did she.

The tassels on the awning swung as Jason climbed onto the padded seat beside her and took up the straps. With a quick shake of the reins, they moved down the short drive to the rutted trail that served as a road between the two ranches.

"We're going to have to proceed slower than usual," Jason warned as he directed their horse around a hole at the base of the drive.

"That's fine by me." Nichole glanced at her cousin's chiseled profile, then quickly away.

"What's this?" Jason grinned at her. "You aren't having regrets already, are you?"

"Don't tease, Jason. This betrothal is a mistake. What if I refuse to go through with it?"

"The agreement has already been drawn up, Nicki. Philip and Kevin expect us at noon. It is too late to change your mind."

The trail wound down a small incline, and the carriage swayed alarmingly. Jason slowed even more until the rutted road leveled out. They continued in silence. The early summer sky was dark blue and interrupted by only a few puffy clouds. Soon, the road began to climb and turn westerly. In the distance, a lone white peak rose to the south.

"Will Merril be there?" Nichole's voice broke the silence as she picked at the folds of her gown. Jason's chuckle brought her head up.

"Is that what this is about? Your beloved Merril? I think marrying his brother would be the perfect revenge for his past indiscretions."

"How dare you throw that in my face? You know nothing about it. Everything that happened between Merril and me happened before you came here." Heat crawled up her neck. She pulled a fan from her reticule and flipped it open to cool her face.

"I know you caught him with Renata. She told me about it," Jason replied casually, his eyes on the road.

"You speak to her? I don't know what could have possessed Philip to bring that woman home with him, and then allow her to live at his ranch."

"I know *exactly* what possessed him," Jason smirked with a chuckle.

"I'm not sure what upsets me more, Jason," Nichole shot back. "That you would discuss my broken heart with that morally corrupt woman, or that you believe revenge against Merril would serve as fertile ground to build a marriage with his brother."

Jason rolled his eyes and turned to Nichole. "Morally corrupt?"

"Well she is, and you know it. She's a harlot, a... a paid companion to men." Nichole hissed at her cousin, unable to find a description any lower.

"You mean she's a whore ," Jason said dryly. His grin stretched even wider.

"Jason Harris, I will remind you to watch your tongue. What would your wife think?" Nichole scolded and hid her smile at her outrageous cousin behind her fan.

"Ah, yes, Amy. I've meant to speak with you about her, as well. She's coming to the ranch for the barbecue, and I want you to be nice. I am going to ask her to stay at The Highlands rather than return to Denver—"

"She's going to *stay*?" Nichole interrupted, appalled.

"Yes. You'll move to The Shilo to be with your husband, and I want Amy at The Highlands with me."

"So, she *is* going to take my place. I always knew she would."

"First of all, no one could ever take your place. You're my cousin, and I love you. Secondly, you have very little idea what goes on in a marriage bed. I miss my wife."

"Jason, I just don't know what to say. You shock me. I believe that was your intention."

Ahead on the trail, a cloud of dust caught Nichole's attention. "Someone's coming."

Jason reached for the rifle at his feet with one hand, while he pulled back on the reins with the other.

As the carriage slowed to a stop, Nichole recognized the rider. She placed a restraining hand on Jason's arm. "It's Merril."

"He must have found out about the betrothal," Jason warned.

"No." Nichole shook her head, never taking her eyes from Merril's face. "This is something else. Put the rifle down, Jason."

The rider was almost upon them. Nichole nudged Jason, who put the rifle on the floorboard. She caught his silent look of aggravation, and then Merril had her full attention.

Merril reined his mount to an abrupt halt beside the carriage and greeted the travelers with a grim expression on his tanned face. "Good afternoon, Nichole. Jason. I hate to be the bearer of ill tidings—especially on such an auspicious occasion." Merril's anger accented his sarcasm. "I do hope you will forgive me."

His distress involved more than just her and Kevin.

I've never seen him like this.

Nichole sat forward on the seat. "Merril, what's happened?" Her gaze met his and her heart pounded in her ears.

The long muscle in Merril's jawline worked for a moment before he answered. "My father is dead," Merril growled between clenched teeth. "He collapsed as Kevin told us his plan to marry our lovely neighbor." Merril's cold stare moved from Nichole to Jason. "His death comes at a rather convenient time for you, doesn't it?"

The stunned silence held for only a moment as Merril's words sank in.

"Philip is *dead*?" Nichole exclaimed in horror. "Dear Lord—Merril, I'm so sorry." Her fan dropped unheeded to her lap as she gasped into her gloved hand.

Jason's head drew back, as though Merril's comment hit the mark. "What the hell does that mean?" Jason stood and looked across at the tall man seated on the coal-black mount. "I am more than tired of your slights to my character. If there's something you want to say to me, then say it, or be damned, for all I care."

"Jason, what are you doing?" Nichole gripped her cousin's jacket. "Stop it this instant."

Jason shrugged Nichole's hand off his arm and stepped down from the carriage as Merril dismounted.

The men circled each other alongside the road.

"Both of you stop this, right now. What's the matter with you?" Nichole slid across the bench, her gaze torn between Merril and her cousin. She couldn't bear to watch, and she couldn't turn away.

Jason raised his fists.

Merril's lips ticked up in a half-grin. "You want to fight me, city boy?" His voice dripped with sarcastic disbelief. "You're sure about this?"

The big black mount edged away from the men, then bolted away as a rattlesnake shot from the grass.

Disturbed by the commotion, the big diamondback slithered across the road and disappeared beneath the carriage.

Nichole exhaled a small sigh of relief she hadn't followed Jason from the buggy. Her gaze rose to meet his just as her head jolted back. The carriage horse bolted in terror away from the snake, across the uneven prairie. Tossed in the air, Nichole screamed as her gloved hand slipped from the front rail. The entire vehicle bounced high and with a loud crack, her world tipped sideways, then went black.

Chapter 7

Merril Shilo

—

A loud crash resounded through the Shilo ranch house as Merril kicked open the front door and stepped inside. In his arms, he cradled Nichole's bloody and unconscious body tight to his chest. Regret and remorse were bitter in his mouth. "Kevin?" he yelled as he stalked across the entry. "Henny? I need some help!"

Kevin staggered to the library door dressed in his best charcoal suit. He held an empty glass in one hand and a liquor decanter in the other. "What?" he bellowed at his brother then fell silent staring at Nichole's long, bloody curls.

Merril stalked past him. "Get Doc Johnson back here," Merril commanded and took the stairs two at a time.

"What happened?" Kevin's footsteps followed him up the stairs. "Damn it, answer me!"

Merril cursed his brother under his breath as he shouldered open the door to his room and laid Nicki on his bed. A horrifying gash gaped along her hairline. Blood ran through her hair and darkened the bedding beneath her head. The bitter scent left a taste of copper in the back of his throat. He bunched the coverlet together and held it to the cut on her forehead to staunch the flow.

"For God's sake Kev, get Doc. I think she's dying."

"What the hell did you do?"

"Doc's on his way back." Jason pushed past Kevin in the doorway and rushed to the bedside opposite Merril. "How is she?" He knelt and took Nichole's limp hand in his.

The men exchanged glances. "I don't know." Merril looked away from Jason's worried blue eyes, so like Nichole's, and swallowed. "I couldn't find a pulse." With his other hand, he brushed the long blonde hair from her face.

"Excuse me, Kevin." Doc Johnson edged around Kevin's broad shoulders and into the room, medical bag in hand.

Merril looked up at the sound of Doc's voice and saw the worried faces of Henny and her daughter peek through the doorway.

The doctor set his bag on the nightstand and knelt beside Merril; his gaze never left Nichole's pale and lifeless face. He placed his hand over Merril's grip on the bedding and looked into Merril's eyes. "I've got it, son. You can let go."

With a shudder, Merril forced his hand to release the material, stood and stepped back from the bed.

A tear slid down Jason's face as he held his cousin's hand, his fingers on her wrist. "There's no pulse, Doc." Jason moved his fingers, felt again, and shook his head.

With one hand pressed to Nichole's head, Doc Johnson rested the fingers of his other hand along her neck. After a few seconds, he repositioned his fingers and closed his eyes.

The weight of silence in the room and the horror in his heart held Merril paralyzed.

This is the fault of my jealous rage fueled by loss. It should be me lying there instead of you, sweetheart.

His vision glued to Doc Johnson's face, knowing the Doc's next words would destroy his world. The wait stretched, heavy as the silence of the men around the pale still woman.

After an eternity, Doc opened his eyes and nodded at Jason. "She has a pulse."

Jason released Nichole's hand and sat on the floor. He covered his face with his bloodstained hands and murmured, "Thank you, Jesus."

Merril rounded the bed and touched Jason on the shoulder. "Here," he said, and held out his hand.

Jason looked up, gripped Merril's bloodstained hand with his own, and came to his feet. The handclasp lasted just a moment longer as Merril reassessed Nichole's cousin. He could see Jason doing the same as their eyes met and held.

Jason pulled away first. He ran a hand through his hair and shoved the curls from his eyes. "I could use a drink," he murmured. His eyes slid back to his cousin.

"Let's go downstairs," Merril suggested, then realized Kevin still stood rooted in the doorway, arms crossed, his face a dull red.

Kevin's clenched jaw sent a rhythmic tic up the side of his face. "I think you'd best explain to me just what the hell happened," he snarled at Merril.

"Take your discussion out of this room, gentlemen," Doc Johnson's firm tone brooked no argument, then it softened, "Henny, would you fetch me some warm water and soft linens."

Henny's dark face bobbed once. "Yes, sir." She wrapped her arm around her daughter's shoulders and disappeared from the hallway.

Merril stretched his hand toward the door, his gaze pinned to his brother's face. "Shall we?" His whole body tense and prepared for whatever Kevin might do.

Kevin spun on his heel and stalked away.

Merril glanced back at Jason, then over at Nichole and Doc Johnson. "We'll wait in the library, Doc. Keep us informed."

Jason watched his cousin a moment longer, and then followed Merril.

Merril pulled the door closed behind them. "I'm going to wash up out back and see if Henny needs a hand." Movement at the far end of the hall made him pause.

Renata lingered in the shadow. Her measured pace took her back and forth across the narrow hall. She appeared hesitant to approach the men. Even in the dim light, he could see her black hair hung to her hips and shone like satin. A high Spanish comb held the fine hair from her face, and a light shawl draped from her elbows.

Merril's lip curled with disgust.

Jason turned at Merril's expression, and his gaze lingered on Renata. "You go on. I'll be down in a moment."

Merril waited until Jason looked back at him. He tipped his head toward the woman in the shadow. "Let me give you a piece of friendly advice. Stay away from her."

Jason's jaw clenched, and he glared at Merril. "What do you care?"

"I don't." Merril nodded toward Renata. "She's trouble, pure and simple. That cat will eat you alive, city boy. If I had to wager, I'd bet she has a claw or two in you already."

"I'll thank you to mind your own business."

Merril's smile ticked up in amusement at Jason's defensive agitation, and he glanced at Renata. "Do yourself a favor," Merril met Renata's lifted brow with a shake of his head. "Watch your back around her." He went downstairs, ignoring their murmured voices behind him. At the base of the steps, he ignored the clink of glass in the library and headed toward the back of the house.

I can't speak to Kevin right now—not with Nichole's blood on my hands.

He crossed the great room and passed the long dining room table with its heavy wooden chairs. The center room had been built large enough to hold half the wranglers during roundup, and often had. The tall northwest windows were bright with afternoon light. The mountains appeared as distant blue hills trailing away to the north. The entire west wall of the room was made from stone encasing the large fireplace, cleaned and empty for summer. Through an arched opening to his right, he went by three small bedrooms his father had built for Henny and her family, then out the back door.

Henny had been a part of his family for as long as Merril could remember. A house slave on his grandfather's plantation in Georgia, Henny was given her freedom when Philip inherited and sold the estate. Henny and her husband, Tobias, were the only freed slaves who didn't take their papers and go north. Instead, they accepted Philip's offer to work for him and moved with the Shilo family to Texas. After the war, Tobias trusted his small family to Philip's care and returned to the Deep South to look for his sister. He never came back.

Merril stepped into the open yard between the house and several outbuildings. He stopped near the well, worked the hand pump into the trough, and washed the blood from his hands. He ran his wet hands over his face and through his hair. "Damn."

My hat's still on the road near the carriage.

The cookhouse door opened, and Henny elbowed out, holding a kettle of warmed water. Katy came right behind her, arms filled with linen towels. "Let Mr. Merril take a towel, Katy. He's like to drip all over my clean floor when he goes inside." Henny sidestepped Merril's attempt to take the kettle. "I got this Mr. Merril, but thank ya."

Merril took a towel from the top of Katy's pile and wiped his face, then tossed it over his shoulder. With two strides, he was ahead of the women and opened the door for Henny.

"You should let me carry that upstairs," he offered.

Henny shook her head. "It helps to keep busy. You need to see to your brother. He's takin' Mister Philip's death hard, and now this."

Merril followed the women through the great room, hesitating at the foot of the stairs.

Henny and Katy made their way up to the second floor. There were tears on Katy's face, and she kept her gaze cast down at the linens.

Merril turned from the staircase and stood silently at the library door.

On the far side of the room, Kevin downed another glass of whiskey. He rested his hands along the mantelpiece, shook his head and mumbled to himself.

Merril watched for a moment longer then walked in. "I could use one of those." To his left, his father's large desk faced the room. Tall windows behind it showed the front porch and the ranch beyond. Two leather guest chairs stood angled toward the workspace. On his right, a small couch and table sat on a carpet before a wall of books. His father had brought the books with him from Georgia, then to here from Texas. The family library was undoubtedly the most valuable room in the house and smelled of liquor and leather.

Kevin faced Merril. The mantel on the stone fireplace behind him held a decanter of scotch and another one half-full of whiskey. There were several clean glasses stacked neatly on a plate beside the decanters.

"Help yourself." Kevin filled his glass and moved to the desk, surveying the yard as he drank.

Merril poured himself a shot of whiskey, then leaned against the fireplace.

"Merril," Kevin snapped without turning around. "You gonna tell me what happened?"

Merril drank half his shot, allowing several moments to pass before he replied. "We met on the road just past the second gully, the one that washed out last spring."

"I know the place."

"They were in that two-wheeled contraption of hers. I told them about Pa." Merril hesitated and took a sip of his whiskey. "Jason got down on the road. Nicki—she was sitting in the carriage alone when a rattler spooked the horse.

It panicked and took the buggy across the prairie. When the axle split, Nicki was thrown. She hit her head on a rock."

Kevin turned and set his empty glass down hard on the desk. He leaned forward and glared at his brother. "Do you expect me to believe you had nothing to do with this?"

"It was an accident." Jason stood in the doorway drying his hands with a towel.

Renata, positioned behind him, peered inside over his shoulder.

Jason entered and took a seat in one of the guest chairs, tossing the hand towel onto the desk. "I didn't set the brake, and I didn't secure the reins before I stepped down. If anyone's to blame, it's me."

Merril poured Jason two fingers of whiskey. "Nicki would never blame you."

Renata smiled at him while she seated herself on the small couch, as though she were a member of the family.

"Like you said, it was an accident." Merril handed Jason the drink. He ignored the wave of Renata's hand and took a seat in the other chair.

"So, we just wait? Is that what we do? Wait?" Kevin grabbed his empty drink and returned to the mantel. Glass clinked against the decanter as Kevin refilled his drink. "You want one?" he snapped at Renata.

"Yes, please," Renata said in her low sultry voice.

Merril caught Jason's questioning glance and shook his head in exasperation. Kevin was an ugly drunk and more than halfway there already.

"What happens if she doesn't wake up?" Renata asked when everyone had been silent for several moments.

"She'll wake up," Kevin growled from his place by the window.

"Yes. Of course, she will," Renata soothed.

Merril took another sip and studied Nichole's cousin.

Jason sat lifeless, his elbows on his knees, staring into his drink. He showed no sign of having heard Renata's comment.

"I knew a man in Santa Fe who was hit in the head. When he woke, he was like a drooling child. He was never the same."

"Shut up, Renata," Kevin and Merril spoke in unison, and then looked at each other.

"Why is she here?" Merril snapped, his knuckles white around his glass.

Kevin downed the rest of his drink. "Because I say she can be here." He glared at Merril with bloodshot eyes, as though he dared him to say otherwise.

"I'm a forward thinker," Renata explained. "Someone must look ahead."

Merril's eyes remained locked with Kevin's. From the edge of his vision, he saw Jason lift his head and look between the two brothers.

"What if she is not all right?" Renata queried. "What will happen then?"

Chapter 8

Nichole Harris

—

The agony in her head woke her. She winced, and then groaned as pain sliced across her skull.

"Easy gal, easy does it," a man's voice whispered. A large, warm hand slipped into hers. "You've a nasty cut on your head, young lady. Take your time. Let me draw the shade."

The warm hand disappeared, and footsteps shuffled across the room. The light against her eyelids softened. She blinked several times and pressed her hand to the pain beneath her brow. The man's slight frame made a blurry silhouette against the filtered light from the window.

"Does that help?" He took her hand again and seated himself on a chair.

"Some," she murmured. Her vision collapsed from all sides to a pinpoint and then blinked out.

When she opened her eyes again the soft-spoken man was still there, asleep in the chair. His elbows rested on his knees; her hand was clasped between his. White hair edged around his bald scalp and matched the beard trimmed tight to his jawline. His wire-rimmed glasses had slid down his nose as his head bowed toward his chest. She squeezed his hand.

Calm hazel eyes opened and stared into her own. "Just restin' my eyes. Do you feel a bit better now?" His smile was easy and comforting.

"A little," she replied. "What happened? Where am I?"

"You're at The Shilo. You had the misfortune to be thrown from a runaway carriage, but you'll be fine now."

"You're a doctor?"

His smile faltered. "Yes. I'm Doc Johnson. This is Merril's room."

"Merril?" She squinted her eyes as pain lanced across her head.

"You don't remember Merril?"

"Should I?" She pressed her hand against her forehead.

He nodded, still searching her eyes. "What do you remember?"

Her eyes fluttered closed. She searched her memory, but the answers slipped away. Her chest tightened with anxiety and her heart rate accelerated. There was nothing—not a name or a face—not one small thread of memory to build on. She opened her eyes and tears swelled. "Why can't I remember?"

"Easy now, Miss Nichole," he hushed her concern. "You took a hard knock to your head. Sometimes, memories take their time comin' back."

"But I don't remember anything." A slice of pain assaulted her each time she reached for a memory.

"You will in a few days, or maybe a few hours. I know it's easy for me to say not to worry, but you shouldn't. Your memories aren't lost. They'll return."

"You said my name—Nichole?" She raised her gaze to the doctor's face, her eyes brimmed with tears.

The doctor patted her hand again and nodded. "Yes. You are Nichole Harris."

She closed her eyes and rolled her head away. "I can't even remember that."

"Not now, but you will. You were with your cousin on your way here when the accident happened."

"I remember none of this. Could I talk to them? It might help to see someone I know."

"It might." Doc Johnson released her hand and stood. "Then again, it might not. Don't get upset if you don't remember right off. Your memory will come back in its own good time." He returned a few items to his black bag, then took hold of the door handle and looked back at her. "I'll send them in, one at a time, for a short visit."

"Would you tell me who's coming? I might not recognize them and I..."

The doctor chuckled. "Of course. I'll send Jason up first; he's your cousin. The Shilo brothers are Kevin and Merril. I'll be right outside to make sure they don't stay too long. Rest now, while you can." He slipped his hat on and carried his bag out the door.

Nichole let her gaze wander around the room. The wall to her left was made of stone and contained a fireplace at its center. The furnishings were minimal, a desk beneath the window and a chest of drawers across from the bed. There were very few personal items in the room, yet the doctor said it belonged to Merril Shilo. Nichole tried to put a face to the name, but the effort was too great. Frustrated, she closed her eyes and let her useless speculations slip away.

***

Merril Shilo

—

The library was silent except for the clink of Kevin's glass against the decanter. He set the empty container on the fireplace shelf, took a large swig of his drink, and then returned to stare out the windows.

Merril sipped his whiskey and eyed his brother with concern.

If I tell him to ease up on the liquor, it will only make him worse.

"We should have heard something by now," Jason commented. "Don't you think?" He looked over at Merril and rolled his glass between his palms.

A knock at the library door captured everyone's attention. Merril and Jason rose from their chairs.

Doc Johnson set his bag on the floor, then rubbed his hands together as he entered the library. He glanced at each person, but his gaze came to rest on Jason. "Your cousin will be fine. I expect her to make a full recovery—in time."

"Thank God." Jason set his glass on the desk and heaved a sigh of relief.

"How bad is she, Doc?" Merril had played enough poker to know the doctor held something back.

Doc's brow furrowed as he looked at Merril. "Physically, she's fine. She has a bruise here and there and a bump on her head. The cut stopped bleeding and should heal well." He paused and shook his head. "She has another injury, however; one I can't mend."

"For Christ's sake, spit it out." Kevin rounded the desk and approached Doc Johnson. "Is she blind? Paralyzed? What's wrong with her?"

"She has a loss of memory—a malady we call dementia." Doc turned and looked at Kevin. "She didn't recognize me. She didn't know her own name until I told her."

Jason ran a hand over his face. "But she'll be all right?"

"I believe so," Doc reassured him. "Memory loss is often a temporary condition."

"When can I see her?" Jason stepped around the chair toward the door.

"Right now. I told her I'd send you three up, one at a time. I don't want you to say anything that might upset her. Make your conversation as brief as possible. She needs to rest."

"I have a question." Kevin took another step toward the doctor. "Nichole and Jason were coming here to sign a marriage agreement and—"

"Merril," Doc Johnson interrupted Kevin with surprise, "congratulations, son. When did you two decide to tie the knot?"

"It's not *his* marriage, it's *mine*," Kevin growled.

Doc Johnson's eyes widened. He looked from Merril to Kevin. "What's this? I thought Merril wanted to marry the girl."

"I did," Merril snapped.

"She hasn't spoken to you in two years." Kevin's tone increased from a growl and ended with a shout, his face a patchwork of red and white.

Merril remained unmoved. "That was before this—dementia." He grinned at Kevin and made a toast of the statement with his glass, took a sip, then set the glass on the desk.

"What? Why, you little shit—"

"Damn you, boys!" Doc exclaimed. "You sound like jealous children instead of brothers. That poor young woman upstairs won't know either of you from Adam. She knows nothing about a wedding agreement—to either of you. She'll meet you today as if for the first time." Doc paused and looked between the brothers. "I don't want any mention of this marriage, or your father's death, for that matter. It would serve no purpose. When her memory comes back, she can sign your agreement. Hell, I'll even dance at the wedding, but not before. Do I make myself clear?"

Merril nodded and tightened the rein on his emotions. Fear for Nichole, the loss of his father, and his brother's drunken remarks pushed him closer to the edge. He couldn't afford to lose his temper with Kevin—not at a time like this.

"Let me stress this one more time. I absolutely *forbid* any of you to apply pressure she won't understand." Doc paused and met each of their faces. "That includes *you*, young woman."

Renata's smile disappeared, and she looked around, her brow furrowed in concern. "Me? How could I upset the poor girl?"

Doc ignored her. "I'll take Jason up first. You boys have a seat. He'll be back down shortly."

Chapter 9

Nichole Harris

—

Nichole lay still in the silence. Once or twice, angry voices reached her from downstairs, but now, the house was quiet. Her emotions were like a tidal wave. They washed over her with fear, then ebbed to frustrated anxiety. She eased to a sitting position and rearranged the pillows to support her back, then pressed her fingers between her eyes, a counterpoint to the pain.

A man cleared his throat. "Are you awake?" Doc Johnson's voice was hushed.

"Yes." She lowered her hand to her lap and opened her eyes. "Is my cousin with you?"

"He's right here. Go on in, son." Doc pushed open the door, and a stranger stepped into the room. He stood silent until the door closed with a click behind him, and then he smiled at her.

Nichole's mind went blank, her eyes wide as she looked at her cousin. Beyond handsome, Jason was beautiful.

His skin, tanned by the sun to a golden perfection, highlighted his light-blue eyes, which shone in the dim light of the room. Blond curls, damp from the heat, clung to his forehead and fell over his collar.

She was speechless.

"So, it's true." Jason looked away as he took a seat in the bedside chair. "I didn't realize what it would mean—how it would feel—for you not to know me."

"Is it...is it that obvious? I'm sorry—"

"Don't apologize Nicki. It's not your fault. I just wasn't prepared for your reaction." Jason chuckled. "We get that look from strangers sometimes, you and me. It used to amuse us, but to see that same look in your eyes, well...it took me by surprise." He raised his gaze to hers.

"Are you saying I look like that—like you?" She shook her head in disbelief. "No way."

Jason's smile grew amused at her denial. "Except for my chiseled jaw and roguishly dimpled chin, why yes, we look quite alike." He winked at her as he stood and stepped to the chest of drawers. Beside the basin and ewer were a razor and a mirror. He handed her the shaving mirror with a grin.

She kept her gaze on his face, cautious of his delight. An emotion stirred inside her chest, tied to his mischievous smile.

He's always been dear to me.

With trepidation, she lowered her gaze to the mirror. At first, she saw only blood matted in her hair and the bandage wrapped around her head. Then, she met her own eyes in the reflection, and they opened wide. "Holy shit," she whispered.

Jason laughed with amusement. "I told you."

Large blue eyes reflected back at her, filled with doubt. Fringed with dark lashes, they were open wide beneath delicate, arched brows. Her hand shook as it rose to her face and touched the smooth texture of her porcelain cheek. On one side, her hair was free of dried blood and hung in golden curls to her shoulder. Her chin was softer than Jason's, rounder with no dimple, and where his nose was straight, her nose turned up at the tip.

"We take after our grandfather. You were named for him."

"I was?" She returned the mirror to her cousin.

Jason nodded. "Nicholas Harris. He had two sons, my father, Spencer, and yours, Quincy."

"And we all look like this?"

"More or less," Jason chuckled. "You and I look the most alike."

"Wow." Nichole picked up one of her curls and studied it. "Do they live close—our parents?"

His smile faded. "Both your parents have passed. Your mother, Aunt Emily, died four years ago. Uncle Quincy was killed in an accident last fall. You were their only child."

"Oh."

What do I feel? Nothing.

She cleared her throat. "What about your parents?"

"Both alive. They live in Boston. You and I are the only ones that came west, except for my wife, Amy."

"You're married?" Nichole asked, startled at each new revelation.

Jason smiled at her reaction. "Yes, I am. She's coming to the ranch for the barbecue. You'll meet her in a few days."

"Coming here? We're at a ranch?" Her face grew warm. She hated how little she knew; how ignorant she sounded.

"Yes, this is The Shilo Ranch, and no, she won't be coming here. We hold the cookout and dance at our ranch, The Highlands, each spring. Amy lives in Denver for now, but I hope she'll decide to stay with us."

"Of course."

Why wouldn't she stay?

There was too much information to process already, and the situation between Jason and his wife was none of her business.

A knock sounded, and Doc Johnson looked in. "Time's up, Jason."

Her cousin stood and took Nichole's hand. "I'll send Amy a note to let her know what's happened. She should receive it before she leaves town."

"Be sure she knows you'll be back at The Highlands. You should return home tomorrow, depending on how Miss Nichole feels, of course," Doc Johnson suggested.

Jason glanced toward the doctor. "I agree. Nicki would be more comfortable in her own bed. Also, Jeanne is there to help." He released her hand and spoke over his shoulder while he walked to the door. "Jeanne is your personal maid. For tonight, Renata or Katy can help you with whatever you need."

"Who are they? Who's Renata?" With each new name, a flutter edged into her chest, and her throat tightened.

Jason cast a worried glance at the doctor, who nodded his permission. "Renata is a guest at the ranch. She is—*was* a friend of Philip Shilo—Kevin and Merril's father."

Nichole looked between the two faces.

What an odd exchange.

The men's behavior and hesitation piqued her curiosity. "You say she was a friend?"

What aren't they telling me?

"Um, yes." Doc paused and pressed his lips for a moment. "Regretfully, Philip passed away only a short time ago. Renata will remain at The Shilo until she can make other arrangements."

"Oh." She looked away and shook her head. "I'm sorry."

"That's perfectly all right, young lady. Now, come along Jason. Two other gentlemen are waiting to see Miss Nichole."

"I'll see you in the morning, Nicki." Jason gave her a smile of encouragement. "Have a good night's rest."

Their footsteps faded, and in moments, heavier footfalls approached. Another man stepped into the room.

He was roughly the same height as Jason, judging by the door frame, but height was the only similarity. Where Jason had a slender build, this man was wide across the shoulders and broad in his chest. Even through the gray suit coat he wore, she could tell his arms were well muscled. He was pleasant looking, with short cropped brown hair that had just a touch of gray. His eyes were hazel and deep-set. He stood awkwardly beside the door and looked from Nichole to the doctor.

Doc Johnson indicated the broad-shouldered man. "Miss Nichole, this is Kevin Shilo." To Kevin, he added, "Keep it short, son." Then, he disappeared into the hall.

Kevin stepped closer, his regard fixed firmly on her face, and stopped at the bedside. "What Doc said about your memory—it's true? You don't remember me?"

Nichole indicated the chair. "Please sit. It hurts to look up." When he sat, she could smell alcohol on his breath.

He remained motionless in the chair, intent on her response. His expression was serious, somewhere between disbelief and anger.

"It's true, Kevin. I'm sorry. I don't remember anything." She touched the bandage, over her injury. "However, Doc Johnson assured me my memories would return."

"Yeah, Doc says a lot of things." Kevin sat forward, elbows on his knees and bowed his head. His hands trembled.

Sympathy at his obvious distress compelled her to reach out to him. "He told me your father passed away recently. I'm sorry for your loss."

Kevin's head came up. His face was taut with anger. "Doc told you that?"

"Um...yeah, he did. He wasn't supposed to?"

"No, he wasn't." Kevin stood and walked to the window. He shoved the curtain aside. The muscle in his jaw worked as he stared into the late afternoon light.

His swift anger alarmed her, and she remained silent.

Is he drunk?

After several moments, he let the curtain fall closed. He turned to her and captured her gaze with his own. "Doc said there were two things we weren't to mention to you."

"Two?"

Kevin's nod was slow; his words harsh and filled with pain. "My father's death...and our plans to wed." His face crumbled as he paced across the room to the door, his hand over his mouth.

"What?" Nichole gasped. "Our plans?" Her voice grew louder. "You mean *our* plans?"

Kevin spun around at the alarm in her voice. "There's no reason to be upset," he said as he approached the bed.

Nichole leaned away from him. "I'm sorry. I don't remember you. I don't remember this place, and I don't remember—"

"Doc was right."

"—being engaged to you. I don't *know* you. I can't marry you. It's not a good time."

"I shouldn't have said anything. Damn."

Nichole stopped and gasped for breath, panicked by the enormity of all she couldn't remember. Tears filled her eyes, and a sharp pain sliced across her head. "Ah..." she cried out.

Kevin captured her hand and stroked it. "Hush now, sweetheart. I'm the one that needs to apologize. This isn't your fault."

Nichole held her other hand to her head and moaned. After a moment, the pain subsided, and she opened her eyes. Kevin was on one knee beside the bed, her hand imprisoned in his, she tugged until he released it.

"I'm sorry I said anything," he repeated.

Nichole looked away. The emotion left her nauseous with a dull ache behind her eyes.

"I should see your brother now." She wiped her face with her hand.

Kevin rose and crossed to the chest of drawers. He withdrew a large white handkerchief and handed it to Nichole.

"I'll send Merril in," he said and left the room.

***

Jason Harris

—

Renata rose from the couch and motioned to Jason the moment he returned to the library.

Jason knew she wished to continue their conversation in private and turned from Merril's curious glance toward the front door.

She followed him onto the porch, then indicated the outbuildings toward the back of the house. They walked past the well pump and the chicken coop, and then paused on the far side of the corral across from the barn.

Jason leaned on the wooden rail and watched the horses while he waited for Renata to speak.

"How is she?" Renata stood with her back to the pen and looked toward the sunset.

"Except for her memory, she seems fine. We'll postpone the engagement, of course."

"Encourage her to proceed with the marriage. It would be best for everyone."

Jason raised an eyebrow at Renata. "What's your rush? After Philip's funeral and her memory returns, she'll marry Kevin. The ranches will merge. I'm not concerned." He looked across the paddock toward the barn. After a moment of silence, he continued. "I'll send a letter to Amy this evening and let her know what's happened. If you have another missive for your friend in Denver, you can send it with mine."

"Such a kind offer. Perhaps I will write a short note." Renata turned and met Jason's gaze with her own. "Do you tell your wife everything?"

"Most things." He turned back to the horses. "She'll be here for the barbecue. I intend to ask her to stay."

"And you would have me forget our dalliance? Have I met your beloved Amy before? I think not. I shall have to introduce myself at your party."

Jason chuckled and looked at Renata. "I can't imagine a circumstance where a woman of Amy's standing would be introduced to you. Besides, if she discovers I bedded you, I believe she would understand. Our *dalliance* is not an affair of the heart, after all—more of a business transaction."

Her dark gaze flashed with anger. "Philip found out about us, you know. Henny must have told him. He was angry and threatened to send me away."

Jason faced Renata. "I hadn't heard."

"No one heard, and now, no one will."

Jason stared, appalled at Renata's triumphant smile. "What are you implying?"

"Let me ask another question. Does your Amy know you invested much of the Harris fortune in other endeavors?"

"No, but Quincy and Nichole were aware of it. What's your point?"

"There is no one now who knows you had approval, is that correct? This is very sad for you. Taking money that doesn't belong to you is theft."

Jason felt his face flush in anger. "Don't threaten me, Renata. They were aware of my plans."

Renata laughed. "How will you prove that? You told me it was easier to change investments if you didn't need Quincy's signature. You hold the new investments in your name alone." She laughed again and walked away.

"You can't blackmail me, Renata. What could you want from me?" Jason followed, noting her self-satisfied smile when she glanced back.

"I want only one thing from you, Jason Harris. Convince your cousin to marry Kevin Shilo. I want it announced at the barbecue. If you don't, I will take matters into my own hands."

Jason stopped walking. "Why would you care about that?" he called at her back.

Renata waved her hand in the air, and chuckled, but never looked back.

***

Merril Shilo

—

Merril circled the empty library. He picked up items then set them down while he waited his turn to visit Nichole.

He'd watched Renata and Jason slip away as soon as Jason came downstairs. Those two were an odd pair. He didn't know Jason well, but after today, he'd gained respect for the man. Renata, on the other hand, was a manipulative little whore. Whatever was going on between them didn't bode well for Jason.

The rush of footsteps down the stairs alerted him and he looked up from the book in his hand. Kevin marched into the library, followed by Doc Johnson.

"You told her about the engagement?" Doc threw his arms in the air as he followed Kevin across the room. "Why? Why in the world would you do that to her? She doesn't know who you are."

Kevin reached the mantel and picked up the empty whiskey decanter then slammed it back down. He grabbed the scotch and poured himself a drink. "She said you told her about Pa." He took a drink, then glared at the doctor. "It was the right thing to do. Once she gets her head around it, everything will be back the way it was."

"You may have set her recovery back weeks with a shock like that," Doc persisted.

"Enough, old man. You're not my father." Kevin took another swallow and turned his back on the doctor. He leaned his arm across the mantel and stared down into the empty fireplace.

Doc Johnson's face shone red beneath his white beard. He faced Merril. "Go up and talk with her, son. Make sure she's all right. I'm going to have a few words with your brother, whether he wants to hear them or not."

Merril slid the book back onto the shelf. "You sure you don't want me to stay while you talk to Kevin? He's had a lot to drink."

Kevin turned his head and glared at his brother. "What's that supposed to mean?"

Doc shook his head. "I need you to check on your young lady. I can handle your brother."

"She's not *his* young lady," Kevin yelled.

Merril grinned at Kevin then walked out the door. Behind him, Doc instructed Kevin to put the glass down and have a seat.

Merril hesitated outside the room until their voices softened. He wasn't about to let Kevin take his anger and grief out on Doc Johnson. He couldn't hear what they said, but they weren't shouting. Satisfied, he climbed the stairs to check on Nichole.

He paused at the door and peeked in the room.

Nichole sat forward, her knees to her chest and her face hidden behind one of his large white handkerchiefs.

She'd broken off their romance almost two years ago, yet the sight of her distress made him want to beat the hell out of his brother. He eased into the room and left the door ajar. If voices rose downstairs, he would be able to hear them.

Chapter 10

Nichole Harris

—

Nichole buried her face in the big square cloth Kevin had handed her. As their footsteps faded down the stairs, she drew a trembling breath, glad to be alone. It gave her a chance to think.

The loss of her memories, her life, set her adrift. With no perspective to reason through what she'd learned since waking, she struggled beneath a layer of confusion.

One last person to meet and then I can rest.

The pain in her head left her exhausted, and she longed to escape into sleep.

At the sound of footsteps in the room, she lowered the handkerchief.

A cowboy stood just inside the door. His head cocked as he listened to something down the hall.

This man must be the younger brother, Merril.

He was taller than Kevin but had the same muscular build and broad shoulders. His legs were long, and he was lean through his hips and waist. He wore a gun belt slung low around his hips; the holster strapped tight to his leg. With his denim trousers and cowboy boots, he lacked only a western hat to complete his costume. His faded blue shirt gaped open at the neck, exposing a portion of his tanned chest, and dried blood stained his neck scarf and shoulder.

I bet that's my blood.

Her puzzled gaze moved to his face.

Deep-set green eyes caught and held her own. A warm half-grin creased a dimple down to his jawline. "Hey, Nic. Doc said I should check on you."

The sound of his soft voice sent a trail of gooseflesh down her spine as her heart skipped a beat. The sudden rush of emotion was more than she could bear. She pressed her arm tight against the pain between her breasts, and her eyes filled with tears. She couldn't tear her gaze from his, and she couldn't speak, her breath had been knocked from her lungs.

"Nicki, are you ill?" His grin disappeared, and he took a step toward her. "Should I call Doc?"

She shook her head as sparks crisscrossed her vision and she struggled to breathe through hiccuped sobs. "How do I... know you?" she managed to ask; her voice hoarse with accusation. "Why does it feel like... my heart is breaking?" She lowered her forehead to her knees and fought to contain her inexplicable grief.

His weight lowered the bed beside her, and he lifted her onto his lap. "I'm sorry, Nicki," he whispered into her hair.

She curled against his chest and gulped air through the tightness in her throat. "Why do I feel these things? What's happening to me?"

"I don't know, Nic." He brushed the curls from the side of her face. "You never told me this before. I never knew you felt this way."

Her lungs filled in short gasps, then her breath rushed out, along with her tears. She hurt all over from the fall. Her broken mind terrified her. Unwanted shame and embarrassment poured out as she leaned against the solid comfort of his chest.

His arms held her close, but she wasn't imprisoned. If she moved, he might release her, so she kept perfectly still. "I can't marry your brother," she sniffed.

He rubbed her back and rested his chin on the top of her head. "I know."

The warmth of his hand felt good. When he kissed the top of her head, she let her eyes fall closed. "I'm scared."

"Don't be, Nic. Everything's all right. You're safe."

He caressed the back of her head and neck, and she relaxed into his arms. His voice was low and even, as he murmured reassurances. She lost track of what he said, and instead, listened to the soft rumble in his chest.

***

Merril Shilo

—

Merril eased Nichole's head onto the pillow and moved her hips from his lap to the mattress. He took up the coverlet from a stack of fresh bedding on the dresser and tucked it around her while she slept.

Downstairs, the front door slammed.

Doc must be heading home. He would want to reach Kiowa Crossing before dark.

Merril sat in the bedside chair and watched Nichole sleep.

Nicki had shocked him with her declaration of heartbreak. When she'd found Renata in his arms two years ago, she acted as though he handed her the perfect excuse to break off their relationship. She'd never let him explain, refused his attempts, and insisted she didn't care.

He'd made the mistake of believing her indifference—hadn't realized her heart held anything more than relief to be away from him.

"Is she asleep?" Doc asked softly.

Surprised to find Doc at the door, Merril nodded and rose from the chair. He crept into the hallway and pulled the door closed behind him.

"How is she, son?"

Merril ran his hand through his hair. "She's upset, frightened her memories won't return."

"Did Kevin upset her?"

"He confused her."

Doc shook his head and walked toward the stairs. "Once Kevin stopped drinking, he left for The Crossing—said he needed to speak with Cecil Cobb right away."

Merril followed Doc downstairs. "Pa's attorney?"

"Yep." Doc picked up his bag and retrieved his hat from the coat rack. "He seemed anxious about your pa's will. I told him he had other things to attend to just now, but he wouldn't listen to me."

"What about Reverend Michael and the burial service?"

Doc Johnson shrugged. "He didn't want to hear that, either."

"Well, damn. Wait for me, and I'll ride with you and speak to the reverend myself."

"I'm in no hurry." Doc covered his bald head with his bowler. "I'll wait outside."

***

Nichole Harris

—

Disturbed by the light, Nichole stirred in her sleep and blinked her eyes. An oil lamp on the dresser cast a steady glow across the room.

What the hell?

Movement near the window caught her attention, and she rose on her elbow, unsure of where she was and who was in the room.

A woman stood beside the open window. Her long dress and hair billowed back in the evening breeze falling still as she lowered the sash. The color outside cast an odd reddish glow onto the woman's face as she drew the draperies closed.

She straightened her long, elaborate skirt, and faced Nichole. "Did I wake you?" Her voice held the hint of a Spanish accent. A tall comb pulled her hair from her forehead. The hairstyle drew her features into sharp focus and accented high cheekbones and a thin, straight nose. She tossed her hair over one shoulder and smiled. Fine lines creased at the corner of her eyes and mouth.

Nichole sat up and ran a hand over her face to give herself time to think.

Where am I?

Then she remembered.

There was an accident. This is Merril's room.

The woman crossed to the doorway and retrieved the lit candle from the top of the chest of drawers. "I did not mean to disturb you. I thought only to light your lamp and close the window. I am Renata."

"Renata—yes, Jason mentioned you. You didn't disturb me. The oil lamp surprised me, though. Everything here is very authentic." Nichole rubbed at the dull pain above her brow and studied her visitor's clothing.

A fold of dark satin draped from her narrow waist over an ankle-length black skirt. A ruffle rounded the skirt at the knees and darted material belled from ruffle to the floor. She wore a white V-neck blouse beneath a matching black satin jacket with tight sleeves. A silver cross between her breasts reflected the light from the candle in her hand. Her clothes were as beautiful as they were inexplicable.

Renata chuckled. "The lamp surprises you? You think we are so backward at The Shilo that we use only candles?" She set the candle holder on the dresser and approached the bed. "The doctor told us you had forgotten everything. That is very hard to believe."

"I know, right? I should know these things...." Unable to articulate her confusion, she lowered her eyes. "Doc Johnson said my memory would return. I wish it would hurry."

"Hmm," the woman made a dismissive sound. "Doctor Johnson is an adequate physician I suppose, for horses. He practices his medicine on livestock as well, did you know?"

"He's a veterinarian?"

"It is true," Renata affirmed. "Perhaps a *real* physician, one who knows this type of injury, would be of more help to you than our Doc Johnson."

"If my memory doesn't come back, I'll ask Jason about a specialist."

"Yes. You should ask. However, I will contact a doctor friend of mine, just in case. How could it hurt?" Renata shrugged and took another step closer to the bedside. "You have always impressed me, you know. A woman so young, with such wealth and responsibility. Owning a ranch in this man's world must be difficult. I suspect it is why you sought marriage. It would be a relief to hand that responsibility over to your husband, would it not?"

"What? You're saying...it's *my* ranch?" Disbelief and panic pinched her voice.

"Why, of course. It belonged to your father, and now it is yours—the ranch, the land, the cattle—even the house in Denver. All yours." Renata uttered a short laugh and gestured with her hands as she spoke. "Jason helped your father with accounting, but he has been here only one year. You must insist he explain about your investments. A woman should know what is hers, don't you agree?"

Nichole rubbed at the constant ache above her brow. "You're right. Jason will help me." Her stomach rumbled, and her bladder pinged its urgency reminding her she had more immediate concerns than investments. "Is the bathroom down the hall?"

Renata hesitated as though she wished to say more, and then tipped her head. "You can ask Katy to draw up a bath." She retraced her steps to the door and retrieved the taper just as footsteps sounded in the hallway. "Here is Katy with your dinner. I'll remind Henny you need a nightdress and some clothes for tomorrow." She wrinkled her nose at Nichole's bloodstained blouse and swished her skirts out of the doorway and around the girl in the hall.

The girl stood frozen until Renata passed, then her eyes lifted to Nichole's. "Good evenin', Miss Nichole. Mama said I should bring you some food. Are you hungry?"

"You are... Katy?" Nichole guessed and smiled at the teenager.

"Yes, ma'am." A sad smile lit her coffee-colored face. "I'm sorry 'bout your accident." Katy walked in and set the linen-covered tray on the corner of the dresser. "Would you like me to pull the chair over, so you can eat your dinner here?"

Nichole estimated Katy to be around fourteen, an awkward age of long legs and knobby knees. Despite her brave smile, she could tell the girl had been crying. "Thank you, Katy. I'm starving. First, though, I need to use the bathroom."

Dark eyes turned to her in confusion. "Miss Nichole, we don't have a bathing room here like you do at The Highlands. Mama said we would set up a bath after you eat. She wants to look at your head before we wash the blood from your hair."

"I don't mean a bath, I uh ... need to use the toilet."

"A toilet, ma'am? For your hair?" Katy's brows rose in concern. "I can fix your hair after we wash it out."

"No." Nichole shook her head. Frustration and urgency compelled her into motion, and she shoved the cover from her legs. She stopped and stared blankly at her clothes. White stockings disappeared beneath white Capri-length pants trimmed with lace. A loose slip bunched around her thighs. Over the slip she wore a blouse, misbuttoned and bloody down the front and right sleeve. "What the hell am I wearing?"

Katy hurried around the bed, arms outstretched, to help Nichole stand. "I'm sorry, Miss Nichole, but your jacket and skirt are ruined. Mama said there was too much blood to soak out. She has your corset and boots downstairs."

"Katy, I need to pee." Nichole edged her stocking feet around until she could place them on the floor. Despite questions about her wardrobe, her need was urgent.

"Oh!" Katy's eyes widened. She shut the door then reached under the bed and pulled out a large ceramic pot. She removed the lid and set it aside.

Nichole looked down at the deep white bowl. "You've got to be kidding me." She pulled up the slip and fumbled with the waistband of the pants. "How do these come down?"

"They don't come down, Miss Nichole, they are split. Just sit, I have you." Katy gathered Nichole's slip under one arm and secured her balance with the other.

Nichole confirmed the opening in her drawers as she lowered herself onto the narrow porcelain seat, and then moaned with relief as her bladder released. When she finished, Katy helped her stand and step away then she put the cover on the pot.

"Why is there no crotch in these pants?" Nichole leaned against the bed.

Katy looked at Nichole. Concern clouded her dark eyes. "So you can relieve yourself."

"Yours are open like this?"

"No, ma'am. Only ladies wear drawers, for modesty. I've never worn a pair."

Nichole rubbed her forehead.

Am I losing my mind?

It was more than merely unfamiliar, it was straight out bizarre, but she couldn't pin down the reason.

"You should eat your dinner before it gets cold." Katy positioned the chair near the dresser, and then returned to steady Nichole as she walked around the bed.

Beneath the linen napkin was a bowl of beef stew with carrots and onions. On top, a wedge of freshly baked bread caused a loud rumble in her stomach. Everything looked fresh and smelled delicious. Famished, Nichole began to eat.

Katy scurried from the room returning with toiletries for Nichole's bath and hair. She built up a small fire in the hearth, then glanced at Nichole. With a quick smile, she disappeared out the door again.

Nichole wiped a bit of gravy from the bowl with the last of her bread, savoring every drop. As she chewed the last bite of her meal, a tall and ample woman entered the room.

She wore a full-length gray dress with long sleeves and a pocketed apron tied around her waist. It was easy to assume this woman was Katy's mother. Both had the same almond-shaped, dark eyes. The woman's hair was gray and black, pinned in a bun on the back of her head. She crossed the room and came directly to Nichole.

"My name is Henny, Miss Nichole. You know me, though you don't remember just now. I've ordered a bath prepared by your fire. Katy will wash your hair and help you clean up. First, I want to look at your injury. Is that all right with you?" There was no joy in Henny's eyes or a smile on her face, only grief.

Nichole nodded her consent and sat still while Henny unwound the linen strips from her head.

The cloth bandage had dried to the injury and Henny had to use a damp cloth to ease it away from the wound. When it came free, Henny studied the stitches. "Doc would make a fine seamstress. Do you want to see?"

"Yes, please." Her head felt light without the wrapping. She took the mirror from Henny and looked at her forehead. The gash ran along her hairline and was held closed with tiny, evenly spaced stitches. The swollen, angry line would leave a scar. Exposed to the air, it burned.

Henny withdrew a jar from her apron and set it on the tall dresser with the other toiletries. "This is Miss Amy's special ointment. Katy will put some on the stitches after she washes your hair. We'll leave the bandages off." Henny took Nichole's hand in her strong long-boned hand and bent to look her in the eye. "We're going to take real fine care of you, Miss Nichole, don't you worry. Katy will bring you night clothes, and Miss Renata will let you choose something of hers to wear tomorrow."

Two men carried a tub into the room and placed it near the fireplace.

Henny paused to survey their work. "Bill, the water in the kitchen is hot. Could you bring it up in the large buckets?"

Bill nodded and kept his eyes averted from Nichole as he left the room.

Henny took the coverlet from the bed and draped it around Nichole's shoulders. She tucked the cover over her slip then followed Bill from the room.

Sooner than Nichole would have imagined, the bath was ready, and Katy closed the bedroom door. She stood, with only a tiny bit of dizziness, and removed her blouse as she walked to the tub. The deep-sided metal tub was half-filled with warm water. Katy helped her remove her long slip and unbutton the back of her drawers, then held her steady as she stepped into the tub and sat down.

Katy moved the chair close and took up a long-handled ladle. "If you lean your head back, I'll wash out your hair. Hold this over your forehead to keep it dry." She handed her a soft cloth.

Nichole tipped her head back and closed her eyes. Liquid warmth flowed through her hair and down her back sending a shiver of delight along her spine.

Katy worked from the tips of her hair toward the scalp, removing the dried blood. She pulled the hardened ends apart, soaped, and then rinsed, working slowly around Nichole's locks.

The ladle dipped, and water flowed over Nichole's scalp. "Katy, Doc Johnson told me this is Merril's room. Is that true?"

"Yes, it is, Miss Nichole." Katy's busy hands continued their gentle work, lathering another section.

"He doesn't keep any personal things in his room." Eyes closed, Nichole let the warm room and water relax her.

"I guess not. I didn't notice before."

Nichole heard Katy lather another portion of her hair, felt her working her way up the long strands as she separated the dried blood from the hair. Rinse, and then repeat.

When Katy was done, she wrapped the hair in a towel, twisted it gently and tucked the end of the towel near Nichole's neck, then took the soft cloth from Nichole's hands. "I'm done with your hair. Did you want me to help you wash?" She handed Nichole a rounded bar of soap.

Nichole smiled at her. "Thanks, but I can do it."

When she was done, Katy helped her stand and step over the edge of the tub.

The girl dried Nichole as she held the chest of drawers for balance, then helped her into a soft cotton nightgown. She helped Nichole to the chair near the fire and then took the salve from the dresser, dabbing it on the stitches. "Miss Amy's salve will make you sleepy, but the cut will feel better tomorrow."

After Katy toweled Nichole's hair dry, she combed through the waist-length curls. "I'm going to put your hair in two braids, so it's not wet down your back if that's fine with you."

"Hmm." Nichole's voice sounded far away in her own ears.

When Katy finished the braids, she held Nichole's arm to steady her and tucked her into bed.

The salve took the pain from the injury, and the dull ache behind her eyes eased. She snuggled against the pillow and imagined it was Merril's chest.

Chapter 11

Merril Shilo

—

Merril rode north along a familiar deer trail toward home. He'd arranged with Reverend Michael to perform his father's services the day after tomorrow. The reverend's first available time. The only thing left to do for his father was to open a plot in the small family cemetery.

Twilight had long since passed, and the sky held only the amber outline of its fading memory over the mountaintops. In the east, constellations glistened.

The path wound down a slight incline. His horse, Midnight, picked his way through the sage and underbrush and crossed a small creek kept alive from the daily spring rains. The heady scent of lilac hung heavy in the night air, and Merril filled his lungs with their sweet fragrance.

He looked to the sky and in his mind's eye saw his father. He ran an exhausted hand over his face. He wouldn't go back to the ranch tonight. He needed a private place to mourn his father, and time alone to reflect on the day's events.

He was younger than Kevin by ten years. They'd never been close. By the time Merril reached the age to do more than milk cows and run errands, Kevin was a man with his own responsibilities. Merril's father was the one who taught him how to rope and ride. He showed him how to hunt deer and pheasant with a rifle.

Each day their father spent with him triggered unreasonable jealousy in Kevin. Their distant relationship became antagonistic. The tension between them grew so intolerable that after his mother's death in '64, he left the ranch without destination or explanation. At fourteen, it was easy to justify his reasons—easier still to think nothing of the worry and pain he caused his father.

He was twenty when he rode onto his father's Colorado ranch, unsure of his reception. Both his father and Henny cried when they saw him. The lost son returned home.

Kevin wasn't as pleased. The years apart had not endeared Merril to his brother. Their father's joy at Merril's return reignited old jealousy.

Merril guided Midnight with the pressure of his knee. They weren't far from the small hunting cabin he and his father built to mark his return home. *I'll stop there.*

The ground rose, and as he reached the summit of the rise, a brilliant full moon broke above the horizon. He would have paused to appreciate the beauty of the moonlit landscape, but Midnight sensed their destination and picked up the pace. The cabin stood at the bottom of an incline, not far from the bend in the creek. A few squat bushes grew around three sides of the structure, and a thin line of brush and trees followed the seasonal stream toward the road home.

He dismounted and looked over the squat building. The little lodge had been built along a rutted trail, distant from the main road between the ranch and Kiowa Crossing. Although it appeared empty, he'd learned to be cautious.

Gun in hand, he stood silent and listened to the night, then became part of it. He moved into the shadows along the wall and approached the wooden door, nudging it open with the toe of his boot. The rough mattress and stone fireplace shone in the milky moonlight. He replaced his revolver and returned to Midnight, then led him to the lean-to shelter surrounded by brush on the side of the lodge.

Once Merril saw to Midnight's comfort, he went inside to find his own. He pulled the lantern from the shelf and struck a match to the wick. Soon he had a small fire in the stone hearth, and a meal of the dried beef, cheese, and a hard biscuit he carried in his bag.

Kevin was going to be a problem. His obsession with Nichole and their ruined betrothal, his grief, and heavy drinking all pointed in one direction. His brother would send him packing as soon as their father's will was read.

Not that he couldn't make his way on his own. He'd be happy to leave—except for Nicki.

The memory of Nicki's pale and bloody face brought back the burden of guilt that clawed through his chest as he had carried her lifeless body up the stairs. His own grief and anger caused the carriage accident, no matter what Jason said. He should never have allowed his rage to take hold of him.

Sam Kline, a mercenary gunfighter he came to know during those six years, warned him never to shoot in anger, with either his gun or his mouth. His Cheyenne brother, Gray Wolf, recognized his internal rage as well and warned him to guard against it.

I thought I'd learned to control my fury.

He vowed to do better.

Merril rubbed a calloused hand over his face and listened to the solitary bark of a coyote. He cast his memory back to when he first met Nicki. She told him how bitter she was about her mother's death, and how alone she felt. He'd never seen a more beautiful woman or known one so fragile in spirit. He groaned as he recalled her in his arms and the trust she placed in his hands.

He never mentioned marriage to Nichole. He assumed she understood how he felt about her. When they consummated their love in this very cabin, he believed her feelings were as strong as his.

Both fathers would have welcomed their union.

Then Renata had come between them. She had rushed into the barn and thrown herself into his arms that day, knowing Nichole was just outside. She had kissed him. A ruse by his father's whore to hurt Nichole.

But to what end?

Renata's motives remained a mystery, and she never approached him again.

When Nichole refused to speak with him about what she had seen, he took his injured pride and walked away. It took a tragedy for him to understand how devastated she had been.

How could I have been so blind?

He rested the back of his hand across his brow and closed his eyes. Outside, the crickets struck up their evening chorus. One question continued to plague him. How was it possible Nichole continued to feel those emotions even though she didn't remember who he was? His feelings for her hadn't changed.

Holding her in his arms tonight brought back every tender sentiment he'd ever felt for Nichole.

How much time did he have before Kevin sent him away?

***

Nichole Harris

—

The window in her room slid open and woke Nichole. Eyes wide in the darkness, she saw the moonlight play across the wall when the curtains moved. She sat up and stared as a man pulled himself onto the desk beneath the window. He rolled onto his back and pulled his long legs through one at a time then sat up. In a day filled with inexplicable events, a man sneaking into her bedroom did not faze her. Somehow, she knew who it was.

"Hey, Nic." His voice was soft and low. He spun around and dangled his legs from the desk.

"What are you doing?" she whispered. "What time is it?" She glanced at the nightstand, but whatever she sought fled her mind. She looked back at Merril, his face shadowed, his back bathed in moonlight.

"Early morning, maybe three hours 'till sunrise." When she didn't reply, he continued, "I had to see you. The more I thought about everything, the more urgent it became. Before I knew it, I had the ladder at the window." He paused as though to measure the silence between them. "I have something I need to tell you."

Her entire body tingled at the sound of his voice, and her heart pounded in her ears. Every comment in her mind sounded asinine, so she remained quiet.

"I'll go if you want. I should go." He faced the window and grabbed the sill.

"No, wait." Nichole pushed the covers away and slid her bare feet to the floor. She stood and took two steps toward Merril before the wave of dizziness struck her. She staggered to the desk and reached for the corner just as strong hands gripped her arms.

"What are you doing?" He echoed her earlier words and pulled her between his legs to keep her upright.

Her head spun. "I stood up too fast," she murmured. Her hands fell on his thighs and her lowered head bumped against his chest.

"You shouldn't be out of bed. Where's your bandage?"

She raised her face and moonlight filled her eyes. "Henny took it off so Katy could wash the blood out of my hair."

The shadow across his face hid his eyes. "You've got pigtails," he chuckled softly. He held her steady with his legs and tugged one of her braids. "Did Katy do this?"

She nodded, unable to find her voice. The ache in her chest had returned, but more immediate was the tingling where his legs touched her.

His knuckle brushed her breast as he tugged her other braid. "I've never seen you wear pigtails."

Her breath caught, and her nipple tightened sending a pulse of sensation between her thighs.

"You're not dressed." He brushed her nipple again, slow and deliberate, with his fingertips.

"I was asleep." She moaned at his touch. Her hands ran up his thighs to his hips, and she pulled herself closer, snuggling against his tightening groin.

Merril groaned and cupped her breast with his hand and lowered his mouth to hers. He kissed her with a gentle softness—lips barely touching hers—his thumb continued to stroke her nipple.

Her hands moved up his arms to his shoulders. Pressing closer, she deepened their kiss and twined her fingers into his hair.

He pulled back after a moment, breaking the kiss, his breath heavy. "Nic, we can't. I didn't come here for this."

She dropped her forehead to his chest. The broken ache inside her heart returned. "Don't say you're sorry you kissed me. I couldn't take that."

"Hell no, I'm not sorry. But we'll get caught if I stay." Merril's voice dropped to a murmur. "Dear Lord, I want to stay." He gathered her close and hugged her to his chest.

They were silent for a moment.

When he spoke, all levity had gone from his voice. "Kevin went to speak with the attorney yesterday. I expect Cecil Cobb will be at the house today to read Pa's will. I think—no, I know—Kevin will send me away as soon as the ranch passes to him."

Nichole leaned back to see his eyes, but they remained in shadow. "But why? Why would your father leave the ranch to Kevin? Why would Kevin make you leave your home?" She paused for a moment and reached up to touch his face. "When did your father die?"

Merril covered her hand with his own and turned his face to kiss the palm. "Yesterday morning, just before your accident."

"Oh, Merril. I'm sorry." She pushed the hair back from his face with her other hand. "Now I understand why Katy and Henny are so sad."

"His death was unexpected, and a shock to everyone." Merril sighed and captured both her hands in his, holding them between their bodies. "Kevin has several reasons to want me gone. When you hear I've left the ranch, trust you will see me again."

"Come to The Highlands. If Kevin makes you leave, come to me."

"Ah, sweetheart, it doesn't work that way. Jason would never allow it."

"What does Jason have to do with us?"

He brushed his lips across her forehead and her mouth in quick succession, then held her tight to his chest. "I've got to go. I'll see you later today before you head home." He kissed her one more time, then slipped from her arms and out of the room. "Close the window or the room will get chilled."

She leaned over the desk to watch him leave, but he was already gone.

Chapter 12

Nichole Harris

—

"Wake up, Miss Nichole. I have clothes for you to look at, and breakfast is ready." Katy struggled through the door with three dresses in her arms and piled them at the foot of the bed.

Nichole stared at the mound of taffeta and satin. "Those are huge Katy, is there anything less?"

"Less what, Miss Nichole? Mama mended your petticoat. You won't need to borrow one. Your camisole, drawers, corset, and shoes were only dirty and cleaned right up. I'll run and fetch those. Oh, and I'll check for gloves and a parasol. You just choose the dress." Katy whirled out the door.

Nichole edged out of bed, careful not to spill the dresses onto the floor and looked in horror at her choices. The first one was a deep rose satin with a high collar around the neck that plunged at the bodice. The long sleeves were tight down the arms and buttoned at the wrist. The skirt was layered satin and lace, with a large bun of satin scrunched at the rear.

What the hell?

A large red bow was attached beneath the protruding bump at the rear. The scent of strong perfume and body odor wafted up as she set it aside.

Phew.

The second dress was two shades of lavender silk with gathered material down the front of the over-skirt and at the wrists. The bottom of the skirt fell in pleats under a drape of satin. Both the red and the purple outfits were more suited to Renata's dark complexion.

The last dress was cream and brown. It had a square neckline, trimmed with brown satin and short, bunched sleeves that could be worn off the shoulder. The drape was brown satin, with a cream ruffled skirt and a jacket that matched. Below the waist in the back was a small brown satin rump with a large bow under the fake ass. It would have been amusing if she wasn't so horrified. The brown and cream dress didn't smell of body odor. Either the dress was new, or Renata disliked it.

Katy scurried in with undergarments, shoes, a parasol, and gloves. She laid them on the bed next to the clothes. Katy's simple skirt was shorter than Renata's gowns, a hand's width above her ankle-high buttoned-up boots. She wore a plain blue blouse over a black cotton skirt, with an apron similar to the one her mother wore yesterday. Her curly hair was tied back from her face with a cream-colored ribbon. "Did you decide, Miss Nichole?"

"These are lovely, but I would like something less ... formal. Is there a skirt and blouse in Renata's closet, like what you and your mother wear? Does she have any jeans?"

Katy's eyes grew wide. "But you're a lady, Miss Nichole. Even Renata wouldn't wear servants' clothes—"

Nichole held up her hand. "Never mind, Katy. I'll wear the brown one, but I want to remove the back part. Can you make that happen?" Nichole pointed to the brown and cream outfit.

"Oh, Miss Nichole, you were teasin' me," Katy chuckled and relaxed. She picked up the drawers from the pile of undergarments and handed them to Nichole.

Nichole held up the split drawers and shook her head. They were ridiculous, but she sat in the chair and gave herself over to Katy's direction. In less than an hour, Katy dressed her and prepared to start on her hair. Even if she'd been familiar with the clothes, these dresses were a two-person operation. Once she was home and had her own clothes, she was sure it would be much simpler—or there would be changes.

Katy unbraided and brushed her hair, then pulled her tresses up the side of her head to the crown and pinned it, creating a cascade of waves that fell across her back. After that, she pulled a few tendrils of her hair around Nichole's face and arranged it over her forehead to cover her injury.

"You're all done, Miss Nichole." Katy stepped back and smiled at her work.

Nichole sat straight in the chair; with a corset, there would be no slouching. She looked into the small shaving mirror. Her hair looked like a rippled Mohawk with side bangs.

So be it.

Katy helped her rise and picked up her gloves and parasol.

"Lead the way, Katy. I'm not sure where we're going." She waited until Katy was in the hall to look back at Merril's room. She glanced at the window and felt a blush rise on her face. Then she followed Katy out the door.

Nichole gripped the rail and made a careful descent behind Katy. As she descended the stairs, the front entrance and the wall pegs near the door came into view.

Katy set the parasol and gloves on the table and smiled at Nichole. "I'll leave these here."

Nichole walked with Katy past a library and into a large open room. Out the window, the day was bright, and the mountains—distant mounds of blue—trailed away in the distance. There was only one occupant seated at the head of the table.

Jason placed his teacup on the saucer and stood as Nichole and Katy entered.

Katy waved as she skipped through an open doorway.

"Good morning." Jason pulled out a chair beside his. "You appear much improved from yesterday."

"Thanks. I feel better." Nichole's movements were awkward in the unfamiliar clothing. She arranged the skirt in front of the chair then perched on the edge, aware of the corset.

"Did you sleep well?" Jason poured her a cup of tea from the tea service, then reseated himself. "Have any memories returned?"

"I did sleep well. Henny put salve on the stitches, and it put me right out. And no, except for flashes of things that have no context, my memory has not returned. It's a start, though." She found the ceramic honeypot and allowed the dabber to drizzle the sticky sweetness into her tea. "Are we the first ones up this morning?"

Jason watched her add honey to the tea. "No. Kevin rode in a while ago and went upstairs to change clothes. I'm surprised he didn't wake you. He said Cecil Cobb was on his way. Since when do you put honey in your tea?"

Nichole paused, prepared to taste her tea. "I don't use honey?"

"No. Just a dash of cream. How does it taste?"

Nichole sipped and sat the cup down. "Delicious. Have you seen Merril?" Her face became hot when she said his name. Her emotions about him were strong and confused, complicated by the touch of his hand and his lips on hers.

Jason gazed at her for a few seconds before he responded. "He's been in and out, no pun intended. He'll be back before Cecil gets here. Quite the scandal in my opinion. Reading a man's will before he's properly buried." Jason shrugged. "Perhaps they do things different in Colorado. I don't know."

Nichole ignored Jason's joke and helped herself to a biscuit, then added a dab of honey. She nibbled on it and sipped her tea. "What?" His continued stare was irksome.

"You seem—different." Jason took another sip of his tea.

"How so?"

Jason shook his head. "I'm not sure. Perhaps I've never watched you eat a biscuit with your face as red as a tomato."

Nichole dropped the biscuit on her plate in annoyance then licked the stickiness from her fingertips.

"You lick your fingers now, too?" Jason chided, and handed her a cloth napkin.

She glared at her cousin and took the napkin.

"Now, there's a look I'm familiar with." Jason smiled and took a sip of his tea.

"She's up." Kevin strode into the room, rounded the table, and took the seat across from Nichole. "Cecil's coming up the south ridge and will be here in no time." His hands shook as he pulled off his leather gloves. "Isn't there any coffee?" He ignored the slam of the front door as he looked Nichole over with a grin. "Have you remembered anything? You look bright as a rainbow."

The chair beside Nichole scraped back, and Merril sat down. "Good morning, Nicki."

"Good morning, Merril." She kept her gaze on Kevin by sheer force of will. "No, I haven't. Every so often, I'll get a flash of something—a fragment of memory—but they're not making much sense, yet."

"It will come back," Jason commented.

"Maybe you should—I don't know—try harder." Kevin's anxious gaze darted between Merril and Nichole.

Merril leaned forward, elbows on the table, his broad shoulders almost touching Nichole's. "You want her to try harder?" His voice grew louder by slow degrees. "How about she doesn't try at all? Doc said it could come back a piece at a time. Oh, that's right, you don't listen to a thing Doc Johnson says."

Nichole felt Merril's breath on her hair as he whispered, loud enough for everyone to hear. "Don't listen to Kevin, Nicki. He had a rough night."

She turned at the sound of his voice and found herself nose to nose with Merril. His startled expression echoed hers for a moment, then he smiled as he looked over her face and into her eyes. His delight was evident and set her heart racing. There were chips of gold in his green eyes, and his grin was irresistible. His lips—

Kevin slapped his hand down on the table with such force the cups and saucers rattled, and he came to his feet. "That's enough, Merril."

Startled, Nichole looked from Kevin's dark, furious face to Jason.

Jason shook his head at her and took another sip of tea.

"Ease up, big brother," Merril snapped. "There's no need for that."

"I won't have you show that kind of disrespect in my home," Kevin provoked.

Merril rose from his seat, glaring at his brother. Anger etched in every line of his body. "It's not yours yet, Kevin. You should show some respect for our guests."

Jason sat his cup back onto the saucer and smiled at Nichole.

"Excuse me," Merril said to Jason and Nichole. "I have a few things I have to tend to before Cecil arrives." Merril stalked from the room.

Kevin resumed his seat as Merril's boots sounded on the stairs and a door slammed upstairs. "I know I should apologize, but damn him. He has a way of getting under my skin."

"That's perfectly all right," Jason replied. "I understand how you feel."

"Merril didn't do anything wrong." Nichole bristled. "I think he's nice."

"You never used to, that's for damned sure," Kevin shot back, then appeared to bite down on his words.

"What does that mean?" Nichole scowled at Kevin.

"He's right, you know," Jason added. "You haven't spoken to Merril in quite some time."

"All right. I've had enough of this. Please, excuse me." She stood and glared at both men. "I need some fresh air." When she turned away from the table, a chair scraped across the floor. She continued down the hall and opened the front door, aware she was being followed.

The bright sunlight blinded her. She shaded her eyes and blinked as she looked across the yard. Hard-packed ground extended to a corral about thirty feet from the porch, a part of the dirt road that ran between the house and a long outbuilding to her left. To the right of the corral stood a long, low-roofed structure where several men had gathered.

"I didn't mean to upset you." Kevin stopped beside her.

She pointed at the cowboys across from the split rail pen. "Who are those men?" Some of them ate from tin plates, while others watched her and Kevin on the porch.

"They're our wranglers. Their cookhouse is on the other side of the bunk." He pointed toward the horizon. "Beyond the ridge is our branding site. It's not far, but you can't see it from here."

She followed the porch around the house where she discovered another group of structures centered around a small yard with a hand pump and trough. Further on was another corral adjacent to a large barn. "This is a big place."

"Mid-sized," Kevin replied right behind her. "Both our fathers hoped to combine the ranches by marriage one day."

"Kevin, I'm sure they had great intentions..." Nichole turned to face him and was shocked when he gripped both her shoulders hard in his big hands.

"You loved me before the accident. I know you did. You could love me again, just give me a chance. Say you'll marry me, and I'll prove it to you."

His fingers bruised her shoulders through her jacket, and his intensity alarmed her. She pushed against his chest with her hands. "Kevin, let me go."

He ignored her demand and pulled her closer. She turned her head away to avoid his kiss. Several cowboys became animated, rose to their feet and nudged each other.

"Cecil's here." Merril's voice was calm as his hand clamped down on his brother's shoulder.

Kevin released Nichole and spun around. He grabbed Merril by the front of his shirt and hissed into his face, "Don't ever come up on me like that again, do you hear?"

Nichole stumbled against the house, numb with shock as the brothers stood nose to nose. The cowboys shouted encouragement, urging them to fight. She couldn't see Kevin's face, but Merril's eyes glittered with rage. A stillness about him radiated both patience and deadly intent.

They stared at each other for several seconds, then Kevin dropped Merril's shirt and looked away. "Damn it, Merril, you know better than to grab a man from behind like that. What's inside that head of yours anyway? Straw?" He shoved past Merril and stomped around the front of the porch.

Merril cast a cold glance toward the men at the bunkhouse. Their jeers and excitement evaporated, and they disappeared like magic to return to work. Merril turned his attention to Nichole. "Are you all right?"

Nichole remained pressed against the side of the house. She nodded and stretched out her hand to him. He took it and steadied her as she came off her heels. "Holy shit, Merril," she whispered and saw his grin tick up.

He wrapped her hand around his forearm and escorted her around the house. "Kevin's not himself. I've never seen him act like that. Keep your distance from him after I've gone."

A buckboard waited in the yard with a boy tending to the horse.

"Don't go." She stopped at the door and looked up at him. "You don't have to leave. You have choices."

He patted her hand and forced a smile. "Cecil's here. They're waiting for us." He opened the door and rested his hand on the small of her back as she stepped inside.

* * *

Jason Harris

Jason watched Kevin follow Nichole out the front door and shook his head. Stubbornness was not the way to win his cousin's heart. It was more apt to piss her off. He learned that firsthand. From the corner of his eye, he saw Renata slip into Kevin's vacant chair.

"What do you think?" She took a biscuit and broke it in half.

"Memory or not, her attraction to Merril runs true. It's quite obvious. Your boy, Kevin, doesn't stand a chance."

"I need you to see that he does. In fact, it is imperative for you that she and Kevin wed."

Jason turned to look at Renata. "I care that Nicki gets well. I don't care who she marries. Your blackmail didn't work, Renata."

"Then let me motivate you a bit more, my love." She tilted her head and grinned at him. "You have been in contact with a senior partner in an investment firm, a Mr. Otis Pierce. Mr. Pierce loaned you several thousand dollars which you have failed to repay, yes?"

"How do you know this?" Jason's face flushed, and the teacup rattled as he set it on its plate.

Renata shrugged. "I know you send him information. I know this information is about the Harris and Shilo ranches and is taken as partial payment on interest for the debt you owe him. Tell me if I am wrong." She tore a small piece from her biscuit and dabbed it with honey. "First, you are an embezzler and an adulterer." She waved the dabber at Jason. "Now, you are a spy. Who knew?" She smiled and popped the honey coated biscuit into her mouth.

"Renata, I offered financial advice on ranching. The information I sent does not harm anyone. These ranches are privately owned, there is no investment loss or gain."

"I agree. It is of no consequence. However, it does prove that I have access to all you send; letters, requests, orders, and that you are something of a shit. Did I say that right?"

"Make your point." His patience was gone.

"You sent a packet of letters to Denver not long ago. Do you recall? A letter for sweet Amy and a report to Mr. Pierce. I gave you a letter to send to my friend. Do you remember it?" She licked her finger.

"I remember. You sent another letter yesterday."

"The first letter to my friend was signed by you. In it, you ordered a quantity of arsenic, enough for your needs. The letter was quite specific."

"What arsenic?" Jason's voice dropped to a whisper. "What are you saying?"

"I'm saying that if a competent doctor were to examine Philip Shilo, his death might not be considered a natural one, and it might not go so well for you."

"You poisoned Philip?" Jason's voice was hushed in disbelief. "Why would you... why would you kill him?"

She laughed and ran her tongue over her teeth. "You should see your face. This is priceless." She paused again, then leaned closer. "Nichole's engagement needs to be announced at your barbecue. It would go better for your cousin if she is agreeable. That is your part. Talk to her, convince her it would be for the best."

"I didn't poison Philip. I wasn't here, and I have no motive to want him dead. An investigation would show this for what it is, an attempted blackmail by a murderous bitch."

"You think so? I think your motive is quite clear." Renata popped another piece of biscuit in her mouth. "Once the ranches combine, Kevin will need help from his cousin by marriage. We already know what you do with other people's money. So, you seduced me with that pretty face of yours and had me poison my lover." She waved her hand in the air. "Besides, I would be gone. I have friends elsewhere, but you—a scandal like this would ruin your life and your family."

Jason said nothing as he stared into her black eyes.

"Make this happen, Jason, for your cousin's sake and your own. Convince her."

The front door slammed. Jason started and looked toward the entry.

Kevin patted Cecil Cobb on the back and showed him into the office. He waved at Jason to join them. "Renata, you come too. Cecil needs everyone mentioned in Pa's will to be present."

Chapter 13

Nichole Harris

—

Nichole preceded Merril into the library.

Seated behind the desk was a heavyset man whose bald head reflected the light from the window. He had only enough hair to fringe his neckline and rise over his ears. White whiskers continued down both sides of his cheeks and over his lip to meet beneath his nose. He rubbed a hand over his clean-shaven chins. He wore a brown suit with a string tie bound at the neck by what looked like a gold nugget.

Merril escorted her to the desk as the large man rose to his feet. "Nichole, this is Cecil Cobb, our attorney. Cecil, you remember our neighbor, Miss Harris."

Cecil wiped his hand down his suit and smiled before he held out his beefy fingers. "Of course, I remember Miss Harris. So nice to see you again."

Nichole took his hand and smiled politely. "Hello, Mr. Cobb."

When she turned to the room, she noticed Jason and Renata sat at opposite ends of the settee.

Jason's elbow rested on the arm of the couch, his hand covering the lower half of his face. His vacant stare was aimed at the fireplace, and he appeared unaware Nichole had entered the room.

Renata toyed with a handkerchief in her lap, a slight smile on her face.

Kevin leaned against the mantel, drink in hand. He gave her a cold stare, then shook his head once and sipped his drink.

Nichole turned back to Cecil and lowered herself onto the leather chair. From the corner of her eye, she saw that Merril remained standing beside her chair.

Cecil resumed his seat and arranged the papers on the desk. "First off, I want to extend my condolences to the Shilo family—Kevin and Merril. Your father was more than a client. He was a good man and a friend. News of his passing came as quite a shock." He paused, nodding to both Kevin and Merril.

"There are a couple of ways we can proceed. I think I would like to read the most recent codicil first and work backward by date. Once the codicil pertaining to you is read, and Phil's wishes are expressed, you may ask questions, or leave the room if you wish. If there are no objections, I will begin." Cecil looked to each person, then reached into his coat pocket and withdrew a pair of wire spectacles. He placed them over his bulbous nose and wrapped the ends around each ear.

"This addendum is dated January thirty-first, eighteen seventy-two.

To my dearest, Renata, I do bequeath the sum of two hundred and fifty dollars. In addition, any and all clothing and jewelry that I have gifted to you shall be yours to keep and shall not be considered part of my estate. It is my request that you be allowed to remain at The Shilo Ranch for a mourning period after my passing."

Cecil looked up from his papers and addressed Renata. "The time given here is arbitrary and at the discretion of the heirs. It can be extended or shortened as they see fit."

Nichole looked to Merril and then at Kevin, but both watched Renata. Nichole peered around the chair just as Renata dabbed her eye with a lace-trimmed handkerchief.

"My Philip was a generous man," she said softly.

"Miss Renata, if you have no questions, I will proceed." Cecil shuffled the papers and gazed at Renata over his spectacles.

"I have no questions," she murmured and sniffed into her hanky.

Cecil nodded and looked down through his glasses at the document in his hand. "This addendum is dated October tenth, eighteen seventy.

To my good friend Quincy Harris, his family and heirs, I do bequeath all use of water and waterways as they originate on my property, The Shilo, and flow northeast onto his property, The Harris-Highlands Ranch. The waterways shall be free from claim or forfeit for as long as The Harris-Highlands Ranch is owned or operated by the Harris family—whether in partnership with my heirs or as an individual interest." Cecil looked to Jason. "Any questions Mr. Harris?"

It was a small thing, but it irked Nichole. The attorney should have asked if she had any questions. She looked to Jason, but he appeared deep in thought and didn't act as though he'd heard the attorney's question. "We have no questions at this time, Mr. Cobb. Thank you." She smiled at Cecil and then looked back at Jason in concern.

Jason's head came up when Nichole spoke. "I'm sorry. No questions at this time, Cecil." Jason rested his elbow on his knee and ran a hand over his face as though he just woke up. He glanced around the room then looked at Nichole.

"Are you okay?" she mouthed to Jason.

He nodded and sat back against the couch.

Nichole's attention returned to Cecil when he began to speak.

"The stipulations and conditions stated herein were witnessed by my hand on the fifth day of May, eighteen sixty-seven." Cecil paused and looked to Merril and Kevin. "I usually read the assets and liabilities at this point, but what is attached here is old. I've had an updated portfolio drawn up for you. I see no need to read this aloud." Cecil handed a sheet of paper to Merril and one to Kevin. He paused a moment while they looked over the document.

Merril folded his and slid it into his back pocket. Kevin slapped his face down on the mantel.

"Is there a problem?" Cecil addressed his question to Kevin.

Kevin downed the rest of his drink and poured another before answering. "Just get on with it, Cecil. Quit drawing it out."

Cecil glanced from Kevin to Merril then cleared his throat and looked back to his papers. "To my beloved sons, Kevin and Merril, I do bequeath each exactly one-half of each of the above-stated interests, to be used and owned in accordance with the stipulations and conditions set forth herein and made a part hereof."

"That is pure bullshit." Kevin interrupted and took a step forward. He pointed at the document in Cecil's hand. "That is not what Pa wanted—I can tell you that."

"Young man, I assure you, these are your father's wishes. He and I reviewed the entire document when the codicil regarding Miss Renata was added three

years ago. There is more, if I may continue." Cecil had paled at Kevin's out-
burst, and although his voice remained firm, his chins quivered.

Nichole glanced over her shoulder at Jason and Renata.

Both sat forward on the couch. Jason nodded at her glance while Renata
chewed her lip.

Nichole looked up at Merril.

He was tense and had his sight pinned on his brother. He crossed behind
her chair and repositioned himself between her and Kevin, only a step from
Kevin's path to Cecil.

Kevin downed the rest of his drink. "Ah, hell, read the goddamned thing,
then."

Cecil gathered the papers into one stack and tapped them on the desk. He
licked his lips and cast a worried glance at Kevin.

"It's all right, Cecil. Go ahead," Merril said.

Cecil took a breath and looked down at the document. "Where was I, then?
Oh, yes, here we are. The following stipulations were added to your father's
will at the same time the codicil for Miss Renata was added.

"Number one: Any commitments requiring legal or binding agreements
must be signed by both owners. Neither party shall carry the option of individual contractual agreements as they pertain to the above-mentioned interests."

"Number two: Any liquidation of assets must be agreed upon in writing by
both owners. Neither shall carry the option of selling his share of the assets.
This includes a sale to the other owner." Cecil looked up from the paperwork
and addressed Merril. "This means you can't sell or give any part of the stated
assets to Kevin, or Kevin to you, of course." Cecil paused for a moment, but
the room was silent except the clink of glass on glass as Kevin poured another
drink. Cecil looked back to his papers.

"Number three: Should either owner abandon their interest, their half of
the above-stated assets would immediately transfer to the owner that remains living at The Shilo."

"I think we know who Pa was thinkin' of there, don't we?" Kevin sneered
at Merril, then looked at Cecil. "How are we supposed to make this work?"

"Your father intended you to work together. This is set up as a partnership
agreement, similar to what he and Quincy considered at one time. There are
only a few loopholes that I see, if you'd care to consider them."

"What are they?" Merril asked.

Kevin stepped up to the desk beside Merril. He glared at his brother, then stared coldly at Nichole, and finally gave his attention to Cecil.

"Agree to sell the entire estate. Liquidate everything and walk away with enough cash for each of you to start again somewhere else."

Kevin swore and walked back to the mantel.

Cecil watched Kevin and swallowed. "If that doesn't suit you, and I see it doesn't, you could sell to a third-party escrow. They would sell the ranch, and other assets, back to you in a predetermined manner. For example, Kevin would purchase back the ranch and Merril would purchase the stock and mining interests. Any difference in value could be settled in cash. Those are the only loopholes I can find in your father's will."

"This is bullshit," Kevin yelled at the fireplace.

Everyone came to their feet at once.

Merril stepped between his brother and Cecil, holding his open hand to the attorney. "Cecil, thank you for coming. We value your advice. I'm sure you understand that this is an emotional time for everyone."

Cecil took Merril's hand and nodded. "Of course, of course. These are your documents to keep. I should really be on my way." Sweat beaded on Cecil's head.

Nichole found Jason by her side, his hand on her elbow. "We need to go, as well," he said. They followed Cecil and Merril out of the library.

Nichole looked back and saw Renata place her hand on Kevin's shoulder as she whispered in his ear.

Cecil and Merril took their hats from the pegs and stepped outside.

Jason picked up the parasol and gloves from the table and handed them to Nichole. "Are these yours?"

"Yes and no. They're Renata's. I didn't thank her for the loan of the dress." Nichole began to turn back, but Jason stopped her.

"Now would be a bad time. Send a note of thanks when it's returned." He plucked his flat crown hat from a peg and set it on his head, and then steered Nichole out the door.

Behind them, glass shattered in the library.

She looked back at the windows as they crossed the porch, but the reflection blocked her view. The heat of the midday sun touched her face, and she opened the parasol.

Cecil climbed onto his buggy and the boy who tended his horse clambered up on the seat beside him. "Send a note if you need anything, Merril. I wish you boys the best of luck."

Merril ran his hand through his hair and set his old hat back on his head. "I'll take that luck, Cecil. I have no doubt we'll need it. Take care on your way home."

Cecil turned the wagon around in the yard and shook the reins. At the end of the drive, he turned to the right. A cloud of dust hung in the still air after the wagon disappeared.

Merril walked to another buckboard that stood hitched and waiting between the long building and the corral. He checked the harness and bridle then patted the horse on the neck before he led the vehicle into the yard. A horse trailed behind the wagon tied with a lead rope and harness.

Jason shook his head as Merril approached. "What the hell are you going to do? I'm not sure you can reason with him. I've never seen Kevin act like this."

Merril reached out and shook Jason's hand. "I know. It's the liquor. Then again, I never thought him a pleasant person to begin with. The reverend will be here in the morning for Pa's service. After that, I plan to hunt mavericks and finish the work at the branding site."

Jason looked toward the house, then back to Merril. "Nicki and I won't be able to attend Philip's service. We'll come by and pay our respects to your father at a more settled time. I hope you understand."

"I do, and I'll see you at the end of the week."

"Yes, at the barbecue." Jason glanced between Merril and Nichole, then climbed onto the wagon and took a seat.

Merril placed his hand under Nichole's elbow to steady her as they walked to the other side of the wagon. "When you spoke of my choices, I don't suppose you imagined this."

She looked up at Merril's face when they stopped. "No. You were so sure you'd be sent away. Are you happy? Relieved? I can't tell."

Merril glanced at the house. "I'm concerned." He looked back to her and captured her gaze with his, then smiled. "I bet you're glad to be going home."

Nichole fought the rush of emotion at his closeness. She could look into his eyes forever, and yet his nearness still caused a worried ache in her heart. "I don't remember home," she admitted. "This is the only place I know—so far."

"You both realize Kevin is watching from the library," Jason commented as he took up the reins, then adjusted his hat. "Make your goodbyes short, or he'll be out here."

"Allow me." Merril took her parasol, closed it, and handed it to Jason. "Put your foot here." He indicated the front axle near the wheel.

"I'm afraid I'll fall." Nichole gathered her dress with one hand and placed her boot beside the wheel.

"You won't," Merril said in her ear.

She took Jason's hand and felt Merril hold her waist from behind as she climbed to the footboard.

"Are you steady?" Jason asked before he released her hand and elbow.

She nodded, arranged her dress, and took a seat beside her cousin. She opened the parasol and then looked down at Merril. "Thank you."

Merril tipped his hat to her and grinned. "You're welcome, ma'am. I'll see you both Friday. Oh, and if you find my good hat, hold onto it for me."

Jason shook the reins, and Merril stepped back.

Nichole kept her gaze on him as long as she could.

When Jason turned left at the main road and they started up a small incline, Merril was lost from sight.

"What is today?" Nichole asked as she turned back to the rutted road ahead.

Jason smiled at her as though he read her mind. "Today is Monday."

Chapter 14

Nichole Harris

—

A cool breeze gusted across the prairie and folded the grass in waves. Nichole lifted her face to the chilled air and was comfortable, despite her heavy clothing. She was glad Katy thought to provide a parasol and gloves to keep her pale skin from blistering. They traveled in companionable silence for some time. Jason appeared lost in thought, and she marveled at the endless sea of grass and tall white thunderheads in the distance. The mountains, which seemed so close this morning, now looked distant and small in the afternoon light.

"See that?" Jason pointed ahead.

She followed his direction and spotted the overturned carriage ahead off the side of the road. "Is this where it happened?"

"Yes, it is. I hope my rifle's still there." He pulled the reins, and the buckboard came to a slow stop. He secured the straps and set the brake, then winked at Nichole. "Not likely to forget to do that again." Pausing beside their wagon, he studied the area before he walked through the grass. While making his way toward the carriage, he bent every so often to look at things on the ground. Finally, he rounded the capsized buggy, bent down, and disappeared from sight.

When her cousin reappeared, he strode back with several items in his hands. "Found it," he called as he reached the dirt road. He slid the rifle onto the floorboard and handed her a woman's hat, a small purse, and a brown felt cowboy hat with a leather band. "No one's been here." He climbed onto the seat and unwound the reins, released the brake, and they moved forward again.

Nichole set both hats on the seat between them and opened the purse. "Someone must have been here. It's empty."

"What did you have in it?" Jason glanced at her, then back to the road.

"I don't know," she paused as several possible items flashed through her mind, but before she could articulate what they were, she knew they could not have been in this bag.

Not yet.

That realization startled her, and her pulse quickened. The knowledge was there, but fleeting—a feeling she couldn't define, and then, it slipped from her mind.

She studied Jason's profile and wished she could ask for an explanation.

"What?" He caught her stare and smiled. "Are you worried you may have lost something?"

"No...I don't think so." She turned away from his curious gaze. "How much farther until we're home?"

"It's roughly two hours from The Shilo to The Highlands, so a little more than an hour left. You seem anxious. Is everything all right?"

She shrugged and twirled the parasol. "Can I ask some questions?"

"Of course."

"How old am I?"

Jason grinned. "You turned twenty on March tenth."

"Oh." She looked away across the prairie.

What is that? A tree?

"I thought I was younger. How old are you?"

"Me? I was twenty-five at the end of April. It's June now, by the way."

"I was going to ask." The object in the distance gained height as they drew closer. After a few moments of silence, she continued. "When did you get married? How old is your wife?" She looked at Jason.

He kept his eyes on the road as a grin split his face. "Amy and I married in August of '73, so we've been married almost two years. Amy is the same age as I am, well, a few months older. She'll be twenty-six in October."

"Is that a tree up ahead?"

"That is a tree." He chuckled at her. "A cottonwood. There's a creek that winds back and forth toward The Highlands from the top of that ridge. It dries up in the summer." His voice trailed off, and he slowed the wagon.

As they drew closer, she could see two men on horseback in the shade. "Who are they?"

"I'm not sure." He reached down and slid the rifle within easy reach.

"Are they waiting for us?"

"We'll know soon enough."

Nichole remained quiet and watched the two men. They had seen the wagon and turned their mounts to face the road.

Jason leaned close to Nichole and whispered, "The older man with the scarf around his hat is Blackwood Jones. Jimmy Leigh hired him this spring to help with the roundup. Jim is the foreman at The Highlands."

"And the young man?"

"I don't know. Wranglers move from job to job. We have several men that are regulars, but most of the crew is new each season." The carriage reached the shade of the tree and Jason drew rein.

Both men wore dusty blue trousers and light-colored shirts, and both wore felt hats. That was where their similarities ended.

Blackwood Jones looked tough and wiry; his skin weathered by years in the sun. One side of his face bulged as he chewed a large wad of tobacco. His eyes shifted from Jason to Nichole with a perpetual squint.

The other rider was little more than a boy, with light red hair and freckles. He appeared upset, almost to the point of tears, and kept his head down.

"Afternoon, Miss Harris. Mr. Harris." Jones rested one arm on the saddle horn. "Jim was wonderin' if you'd be back today. Your wife's been up at the big house for a couple of days now."

"Amy's here?" Jason asked in surprise.

"Yes, sir. She and Tom arrived just after you left the other day. I thought you knew."

"No, but I always welcome good news." He paused, studying the two men. "Is there a problem I could help you with, gentlemen?"

Jones spat a long string of tobacco, and grinned with brown stained teeth at Jason, "Hell no, ain't no problem, 'cept this greenhorn is askin' for time off. Says his wife and babe need his help." Jones snickered.

Jason looked at the young man. "What's your name, son?"

"Timothy Caine, sir," he replied and touched his hat.

Jason nodded and leaned forward, elbows on his knees, the reins held loosely in his left hand. His attention turned to Jones.

"What did you tell Timothy?" Jason's voice was pleasant, but Nichole could sense his uneasiness.

"I told him what I'd tell anyone with a half-cocked story like that. No time off 'cept for a damned good reason—'specially now, with the roundup goin' on."

Timothy straightened, and Jason's cool gaze swung back to the boy. He seemed to be considering something as he regarded the young man. "Is your family at the bunkhouse, Timothy?"

The young man's face flushed pink. "No, sir."

"No? We have a family bunkhouse. It's small but separate from the men's bunk."

Timothy seemed reluctant to answer, which left Blackwood the opportunity to speak instead. The taunt in his voice was unmistakable. "Timmy-boy has hisself a little nigger bride, and a little mulatto babe. I don't imagine they'd feel comfortable around decent folk." Jones spat again and giggled.

Timothy turned his head away. His face flushed red.

Speechless, Nichole looked to Jason to remedy the situation.

He sat silent and bit his lip while considering the two horsemen.

Unable to hold back her shock and outrage any longer, she lifted her chin and found her voice. "Mr. Jones, you will apologize to Mr. Caine this instant for your rude and disgusting remarks."

"Apologize? For what? Everythin' I said was God's own truth. Why, this no-count rebel married a—"

"Enough!" Her sharp shout cut him off, then her voice dropped. "Shut your filthy mouth." She seethed while Jones chuckled at her. "Apologize. Now. Then report to me this evening. You need to understand a few things if you are to remain employed."

Thin, colorless lips drew back as a sneer spread across Jones's face. "I sure am sorry you feel that way, Miss Harris, but I take my orders from Jimmy Leigh."

Nichole drew in a shaky breath. "This ranch is called The *Harris*-Highlands for a reason. You should give *that* some consideration, Mr. Jones. I'll inform Mr. Leigh about our meeting and ensure he attends."

Jones stared at her, chewed a moment, then spat.

Nichole spoke slow, enunciating each word, "Do you understand me, Mr. Jones?"

"Yeah," Jones said and chuckled.

"Yes, *what*, Mr. Jones?"

"Why, yes, ma'am." His eyes narrowed, and his gaze shifted from her to Jason and back.

"I'll expect you at the house this evening." She looked at Jason. "What would be a good time?"

Jason stared at her, concern evident in his eyes. "Come by the house at seven, Jones."

Nichole turned to Timothy. "You can move your wife and child to the bunkhouse, Mr. Caine."

"We tried that, ma'am," Timothy explained, his face still red. "But Lawna was afraid to stay there alone during the day." He flicked a wary eye toward Jones.

"I see." Nichole saw the glance and watched Jones's grin widen. "Where are your wife and child now?"

"Lawna and the babe are in a lean-to just across the rise, over there." Timothy motioned east with a wave of his arm.

What can I do?

A sick babe and his mother alone on the prairie motivated her. "Mr. Caine, go find Jimmy Leigh. Tell him you are to have the use of a wagon and as much time as you need to move your family to the ranch house. If he has any questions, tell him to see me. Also, tell Mr. Leigh that I would like to see him when I speak with Mr. Jones this evening at seven."

"Yes, ma'am," Timothy said, relief evident in his voice. He tipped his hat and turned his horse.

"One more thing," Nichole called, and he paused to look back at her. "When you get to the ranch house with your family, please ask for me. I would like to meet them."

"Yes, ma'am. Thank you, ma'am." He turned and hurried down the road, a dust trail hanging in his wake.

Nichole watched Timothy ride away, then looked back at Jones.

He spat a long stream of brown juice and watched it hit the road in front of the wagon, then looked back at her and grinned.

Nichole lifted one delicate eyebrow and held his gaze. "Was there something more you wished to say, Mr. Jones?"

"It'll wait." He glared at her from his hunched position in the saddle.

"Good. Then I'll see you this evening."

Jason shook the reins, and the buggy moved down the other side of the ridge through the dust left by Timothy. They rode for almost a quarter mile in silence.

When Jason spoke, his voice was tight and strained. "Nicki, I know you're not yourself right now, but I never want to hear you discipline a man like that again. It's not your place. What were you thinking?"

"What was *I* thinking? What were *you* thinking? Why didn't you say something?"

"How could I? You never shut up."

"And what do you mean by it's not *my* place? If that Jones asshole is my employee, I have every right and every intention—"

"Would you be quiet for one minute—"

"I will not be quiet. You sat there and did nothing. How could you let him humiliate that boy like that? It was horrible."

"That's fair," Jason conceded. "I understand your reasons. Nevertheless, it was Timothy's choice to marry the girl. He's from the South, Nicki, no wonder he came west. To top it off, you invite them to move in with us. When they get to the house, you'll have to make other arrangements. They can't move into the ranch house. It would upset the staff. I won't have it."

Nichole turned in the seat and glared at Jason. "It would upset the *staff*, and *you* won't have it? Is that what I just heard you say?" She turned her head and glared over the empty grassland. "Jason, I'm not leaving a baby in the middle of the fucking prairie. They stay with us until we find them a safe place to live."

Jason stared at her open-mouthed for a moment, then shook his head. "I can't believe I heard you say *fucking*. Since when does a lady speak like that?" His voice softened, "Nicki, you've made a big mistake. I see it's useless to argue with you, but I warn you, there will be trouble."

"Trouble," she scoffed. "It can't be that bad." She turned back to the road, unsettled by his sudden change of tone. His warning nagged at the back of her mind.

A part of her realized she'd stepped out of line and acted out of character, even though she still raged inside at Jones. Her thoughts wound around in circles. She replayed their argument, desperate for words to make Jason understand, or help her untangle her own mixed emotions.

She should have encouraged Jason to act—he wasn't a monster. She could tell he didn't like Jones any more than she did. Then why? Why had she spoken her mind as though she had the right?

Because she had every right, another part of her whispered. Her head began to ache, and she looked over at Jason to find him studying her.

He shook his head and eyed her as though she were a stranger. "You sure have changed Nicki. I can hardly believe it's you."

Chapter 15

Nichole Harris

—

Not far ahead of their wagon, a trail of smoke twisted into the summer sky. It rose from behind the white house and drifted east with the breeze. The homestead vanished as the road dipped toward a dry stream bed.

It's too warm for a fire. I wonder what's burning?

Nichole cast an uneasy look at Jason but refused to break their strained silence. Instead, she straightened her shoulders and gritted her teeth against the nervous flutter in her stomach caused by the conflicting rationale that raged inside her mind.

The bumpy road inclined again and turned west as they reached the ranch. Jason directed the team off the main thoroughfare and up the short dirt drive into the side yard. He slowed the wagon to a stop beside the house.

Stone chimneys rose on both sides of the clapboard building but held no trace of the smoke she'd seen. A large, railed porch wrapped the home, and dormer windows near the roof told of a third story or attic.

The ranch road ran between the side yard and a large split rail corral. It continued around the empty pen to a large barn that stood angled toward the road. The barn's double doors had been pinned open, in both front and back, giving her a glimpse of the prairie beyond. To the left of the open structure was a familiar low-roofed building. A bunkhouse.

"What are you going to say to Jones?" Jason asked as he secured the reins, set the brake, and relaxed against the backrest.

"Standard stuff, I suppose." She shrugged. "That I expect people who work for me to be decent human beings. That bullying, and name-calling won't be tolerated."

"I should be the one to talk to Jones and Jimmy Leigh."

"No. I need to do it." Her gaze lifted to meet Jason's. "My feelings about this are clear, and I still know right from wrong. Besides, I want to appear as normal as possible."

"Nicki, there's nothing about you that's normal right now." Jason reset his hat to capture several errant curls. "You've never behaved like this before."

"That means nothing to me. I don't understand how you expect me to act." Her voice rose with emotion. "No." She raised her finger to still his reply. "Don't answer, because it doesn't matter." She snapped her parasol shut and turned to climb down from the buckboard.

"Well, Christ!" Jason hopped to the ground and sidestepped the horses to reach and steady Nichole's descent from the high seat.

"I don't need your help." She swiped at his outstretched hands with the parasol.

"Stop that." He dodged the umbrella and reached toward her again. "I don't want you to fall."

She glared into his face as she settled her anger, then placed the parasol on the bench with precise deliberation. Finally, she took his hand.

"Not like that. Put your hands on my shoulders, and I'll lift you down."

"Fine. Whatever." Nichole braced both hands on Jason's shoulders, and he lifted her by the waist, standing her on the ground.

A shout from the yard caught their attention.

Jason leaned down to whisper in her ear, "The men on the left are Lloyd Baker, and his son Tom. They care for the livestock. Everything that isn't cattle that is. The tall man is our foreman, Jimmy Leigh."

Jason stepped on the hub by the wheel and reached for the items on the seat, while Nichole studied the men coming from the barn. Both Lloyd and Tom had light-brown hair and were easy to identify as father and son. They were of medium height and walked with the same gait to their step.

Jimmy Leigh was a giant compared to the men beside him. The foreman had dark hair and eyes beneath a black cowboy hat. His shoulders were muscular and broad. He frowned as he reached them, his gaze focused on her.

Jason handed Nichole her empty purse, the parasol, and Merril's hat before he greeted the men. "The buckboard belongs to The Shilo, along with the rigged geldings. Our animal is on the lead in back. Check him again for injury. He took quite a tumble when the carriage flipped."

Lloyd and Tom tipped their hats to Nichole, then took charge of the wagon and animals. Tom climbed onto the buckboard and waited as his father untied the lead from the back of the buckboard. Lloyd slapped the back of the wagon, and Tom shook the reins, directing the team toward the barn. Lloyd nodded again to Nichole and led the haltered horse across the yard.

"Lloyd, as soon as you take care of the horses, you and Tom come back to the house. I have some news for everyone," Jason called to Lloyd who gestured he understood with a wave.

Jimmy Leigh tugged the leather gloves from his fingers one at a time. His gaze remained on Nichole even though he addressed Jason, "Amy received the letter you sent last night. We sent the post from Phil's woman on into town." He flashed an annoyed glance at Jason. "Remind her we don't run a mail service." When he addressed Nichole, his voice was low and soft, almost a rumble, although he didn't whisper, "The note said you were injured. If you are, I don't see it."

"I hit my head," she replied, and would have shown him the stitches, but her hands were full.

Jimmy Leigh narrowed his eyes at her. "I was approached by one of the new wranglers not an hour ago. He said I was to rig up a wagon so he could bring his family to the ranch house. He was very clear that it was on your authority."

Nichole squared her shoulders and raised her chin to meet the foreman's fixed stare. "It was. There was an incident on our way here with Timothy Caine and Blackwood Jones. I would like to meet with you and Jones this evening. I hope that doesn't upset you."

A slight smile twitched the foreman's lips, then vanished. "Not much upsets or surprises me anymore. I just want to be clear on the details, is all."

"Come inside, Jim." Jason took hold of Nichole's elbow and directed her up the porch step and to the door.

The entrance opened directly into the living area, bright and inviting. To her right, there was an old-fashioned seating area. The sofa and chairs gathered around a center table where red roses floated in a shallow white bowl. Three paces in front of her was a staircase. The wooden steps and rails, polished to a glossy finish, flared as they reached the floor. The rail curled outward in each direction, welcoming a hand from either side of the room.

Left of the stairway stood a long dining table covered with a white tablecloth and a live floral centerpiece. The scent of roses and lilacs filled the air with fragrance. The table was centered before a stone fireplace and mantel that held several photographs and small paintings. There was a closed door on the wall beyond the table and an open doorway opposite the fireplace

Jason laid his rifle on the table beside the door and took the parasol and hats from Nichole's arms. He hung them on the wall pegs, then turned to speak with Jim and froze—his attention focused on the stairs.

Nichole saw his hesitation and followed the direction of his gaze.

A woman descended the stairs. Her black boots peeked out from beneath a russet-colored gown and cream-colored petticoats with each step. The satin gown gathered at the long waist and contoured close to the body at the bodice. Long sleeves covered her arms to the wrist, showing only her delicate hands, which floated along the rail on each side. One more step, and her face came into view. Her hair was pinned to her head in a loose bun and was just a shade richer than her gown. She had expressive dark eyes with long lashes. Her soft smile was for Jason alone.

Jason stepped forward and held out his hand, and the woman's face broke into a brilliant smile, her eyes glistened with tears. She rested her hand in his as she descended from the last stair. Jason touched his lips to her hand and then drew her close to kiss her forehead. He bent to whisper a welcome in her ear.

Nichole caught her breath as she seethed with jealousy. The strength of the sentiment made no sense to her. She glanced up at Jimmy Leigh and was surprised to see desire flare in the foreman's eyes.

Jimmy Leigh's gaze flicked to her, and his stoic demeanor returned. He removed his black wide-brimmed hat, hung it on a peg, and then tucked his hands into his back pockets as he walked to the table.

Nichole followed him to give Jason and his wife a moment of privacy and to understand her jealous-laden reaction to Amy. Once the force of her initial impression subsided, she recognized it as a child's emotion—she was afraid to lose Jason. She ran a hand over her brow and pressed against the sharp pain.

"You didn't recognize me." The soft-spoken words were a statement, not a question.

She looked into Jimmy Leigh's perceptive eyes. "No. I suffer a few side effects from the head injury."

"Yet, you recognized Amy." His gaze flashed to the couple whispering by the stairs then back to Nichole.

"Not really. I don't remember her, only the emotion I felt toward her. Apparently, I can recall strong emotion."

"Well, she is a lady who provokes strong emotion."

A heavyset woman, her gray and black hair pulled back in a tight bun, entered through the cased opening beside the stairs. She wore a brown dress and white bib apron.

Behind her followed another woman, closer to Nichole's age, with light-brown hair, also pinned in a bun. The younger woman had on a dark blue skirt and white blouse. They moved into the dining room with a smile and a nod to Nichole and Jimmy Leigh.

Moments later, Lloyd and Tom arrived through the same opening.

Jason held Amy's hand as they walked toward the table.

An older woman followed them, dressed in dove gray with a bib apron.

Jason stopped at the end of the table and rested his hands on the back of the chair. "Please be seated, ladies. I have a couple of things I need to say."

Jimmy Leigh pulled a chair out for Nichole.

The two women took seats across from her. Lloyd and Tom shuffled along the wall and stood at the end of the table. Amy remained standing beside Jason, and the woman in gray stayed near the stairs.

The foreman paced away to the front window. He returned and leaned a shoulder against the stone fireplace.

Jason cleared his throat and made sure he had everyone's attention. "On the ride to The Shilo yesterday, we encountered Merril on the road. As I stepped down to speak with him, a rattlesnake spooked the horses. Our rigged horse bolted, and Nichole was thrown to the ground when the carriage overturned."

A gasp of concern moved around the table, and Nichole's face warmed as everyone looked at her.

"Her injuries aren't serious, thank goodness, the worst being a blow to her head. Doc Johnson treated her at The Shilo and stitched her forehead." Jason paused and cast his gaze around the room. "However, because of this injury, she has a temporary condition Doc called dementia."

The room was quiet for a moment. The large woman across from Nichole spoke into the silence. "Dementia? What does that mean, Jason?"

"It means Nichole has trouble remembering things. Doc assured us her condition is temporary and will resolve itself in a few days."

"How much do you remember, Nicki?" The young woman across the table asked.

Nichole met the woman's gaze. "Not much. I get flashes of memory or feelings, but they don't make sense to me yet."

"I never heard of such a thing." The large woman leaned over the table and looked Nichole in the face. "Are you sayin' you don't remember me?"

Nichole shook her head. "I don't. I'm sorry. I don't remember any of you or this place."

Amy crossed behind Jason and approached Nichole. She crouched down beside Nichole's chair and took her hand. "My name is Amy," she said. Her voice was as gentle and soft as her eyes. She smiled and threw a glance at the tall figure leaning against the wall. "I believe you've met Jimmy Leigh. He's our foreman, in charge of the ranch. He helped your father build The Highlands."

Amy indicated the young woman across the table. "This is Jeanne Miller. She traveled with you and your mother from Boston. Jeanne takes care of your clothing and helps with your hair. Beside her is Cookie. She's in charge of the kitchen. She cooks our meals and helps with the garden."

Cookie pressed her lips in sympathy. "I can't believe it. I knew something was wrong. But you're a strong young woman. I know you'll be just fine."

Amy pointed past Jason to the woman who stood beside the stairs. "Back there is June McKay. She's the housekeeper and laundress for the ranch.

"Over here are Lloyd and Tom Baker. They take care of the farm animals and maintain the tack and equipment."

Nichole heaved a worried sigh and looked at all the faces. "I'm going to have trouble with so many names. Let me apologize upfront for not remembering them all."

"Oh, now, don't be silly," Jeanne said.

"That's perfectly all right, dear," Cookie reassured her.

"No need to feel sorry, just get to feelin' better." Lloyd chimed in from behind.

When the well-wishes died down, Jason cleared his throat again to gain everyone's attention. "There's more." He looked down at the table, his tone grave. "I must impart this news with a heavy heart. Philip Shilo has passed away."

"What the hell happened? Phil and Kevin were here not two weeks ago," Jimmy Leigh pushed off the wall and shook his head in disbelief.

"I know," Jason replied over his shoulder. "Doc Johnson called it apoplexy. It was sudden and unexpected. He'll be laid to rest in the morning."

"Kevin and Merril?" Jimmy Leigh took a step toward the table. "How are they taking Phil's death?"

"As you'd expect. Their constant arguing serves as a proper distraction for them." Jason turned back to those gathered around the table. "That's why Nichole and I left The Shilo when we did—to let them figure out the issues of their father's estate."

He paused, but the room remained silent. "I know this is a shock for everyone. I think it best we keep to our regular schedule. There's a lot to accomplish before Friday. If no one has any questions, you can return to your work. Cookie, what time is dinner?"

"Oh, my goodness!" Cookie pushed herself from her chair. "It almost slipped my mind." She turned and disappeared through the open archway. Lloyd, Tom, and Jeanne followed her out.

Nichole watched Jimmy Leigh let himself out the front door as June crept up the stairs.

Amy remained crouched beside her chair.

Nichole gave Amy a grateful smile. "Thank you. I was...overwhelmed."

Amy rose to her feet and patted Nichole's hand. "You are welcome."

"Amy should take you on a tour of the house before dinner. You'll be too busy afterward." Jason walked past the table to the closed door. "I don't know what Jim is going to think about your new sensibilities, but as you said, that's on you." He paused, hand on the doorknob and looked at Nichole. "I want you to tell Timothy Caine you've reconsidered your offer to let them stay."

Nichole released Amy's hand and rose from her chair to face Jason.

He'd opened the door behind the table and stood in the doorway of an office.

"I'm not worried about Jimmy Leigh, and it's too late to change my mind about the Caine family."

"Why can't I make you understand? It's not our place to care for those people."

Nichole rested her hands on her hips. "Oh, but I do care. I also care that people who work on this ranch were allowed to bully him with impunity. I care what happens to his wife and his baby. It bothers me that you *don't* care about those things." Pain lanced across her brow, but she ignored the discomfort.

"You don't realize the consequence of your actions, Nicki." Jason's lips were tight and his face red.

"You're right. I don't. But I know what the consequence of my inaction would be. I can't live with that." Nichole turned and stalked past Amy and around the stairs. She stopped at the closed door in the parlor and pressed her hand against her brow. Understanding Jason's argument wasn't the problem. The discord within herself confused her. The ache in her forehead now pounded. She rubbed her brow as she turned the knob and opened the door.

Chapter 16

Nichole Harris

—

Nichole gaped at the room, her limp hand remaining on the doorknob. A potted ivy hung from the ceiling near the window, and a variety of live plants were arranged around the space. The east-facing glass was open and allowed both the cool breeze and the late afternoon light inside. Tall clouds rose in the distance, their high tops puffy and white against the dark blue sky. The shadow of the house was long on the grassy side yard. The room smelled of freshly watered plants and wild roses. Beyond the settee stood a baby grand piano.

"How beautiful," she whispered as she stepped inside.

Amy entered behind her and crossed to the window. She looked out at the thunderheads. "The storms will stay east of us tonight. Can you smell the rain?"

"I smell roses," Nichole replied. Her hand trailed along the stitching on the settee cushion. "Someone spent a lot of time on these."

Amy turned from the window. "Quincy ordered the settee and chairs for your mother. Jason says she would have loved them. This was to be her special space. She played the piano beautifully, as do you."

Amy moved to the mantel and struck a long match, and then lit two lamps that sat on the shelf. "Let me light the room so you can see it properly." She crossed the room, her hand shielding the flame, and lit the glass lamp set on top of the piano. The lamps were works of art, with delicately etched flowers on red glass.

She blew out the match and then turned to Nichole. "I want to be honest. I didn't know what to think when I received the note from Jason yesterday. He said you asked about me. I was astonished. We were never close, you and I."

"Honesty, then." Nichole rested her hand on the back of the couch and studied Amy. "This memory thing I have going, it's weird. I don't remember people, per se, but if someone evoked a strong emotion in me before the accident, I still feel that emotion."

Amy's brow furrowed at Nichole. "What do you mean?"

"I must have been very jealous of you and your relationship with Jason. I struggled with that sentiment when I first saw you on the stairs. It's a child's reaction, fearful of loss and change." She paused and searched for the words to express herself. "I don't want to believe I was the type of person who would act on such petty feelings, but if I was, then I likely owe you an apology."

Amy opened her mouth to speak, then shut it again, her dark eyes wide as she stared at Nichole. "I'm quite speechless," she whispered. "I didn't anticipate this." Her fingers twined together in front of her skirt as she turned away. When she looked back, her eyes were filled with sincerity. "I always imagined you felt this was your place, your home, that Jason was your dearest friend, and I was—unexpected."

"You're very kind, Amy. It was selfish of me, but I appreciate your empathy." Nichole turned and examined the photos on the mantel. "Besides, unexpected things may be a blessing in disguise. Is this my family?"

"Yes, from when you lived in Boston." Amy crossed the room to stand beside Nichole.

"Should I know these people?"

"Most of them."

Nichole searched the faces but recognized no one. With a sigh of annoyance, she turned to Amy. "What's upstairs?"

"Come. I'll show you."

Nichole followed Amy from the music room, through the parlor, and around to the stairs. The dining room was empty, and the door to the office closed. Upstairs, the afternoon light from the rooms on the west side reflected across the wood floor. They paused at the top railing. At the other end of the hallway, a steep flight of stairs led to an opening in the ceiling.

Amy indicated the first door to the right of the stairs, and Nichole peeked in.

Closed curtains on the west-facing window deflected the afternoon heat, but the room remained bright. A quilt-covered bed stood before her; the headboard centered on the wall to her right. Left of the door was a white chest of drawers, with a matching wardrobe in the corner. Two chairs were positioned near the stone fireplace. Nichole turned back to Amy, still in the hallway.

"That is the room I share with Jason—when I'm at the ranch." Amy blushed and directed Nichole's attention to the two doors at the far end of the hall. "Those are small guest rooms. The stairs go up to the attic, where Jeanne, June, and Cookie sleep. This is your room." Amy stepped into the room across from hers, and Nichole followed her in.

The furniture layout was similar to Amy's room. To her left was a single brass bed with a number of colorful quilts layered over the mattress. A stone fireplace on the far side of the room held more photographs on its mantel. A lamp burned brightly atop a low dressing table beside a chest of drawers. A matching pair of wardrobes stood beside the door.

Amy rounded the bed and indicated a door on the other side of the bed. "You might like this." She opened the door to a balcony and allowed the breeze to gust into the room.

Nichole walked around the bed to the balcony and looked out. The eastern horizon had darkened beneath with storm clouds. Lightning flashed near the ground, and thunderheads billowed in the sky overhead. On her left, close to the back of the house, grew a large cottonwood tree. She took a deep breath and smiled.

Amy's right. I smell the rain.

She closed the door on the distant storm and turned to her room.

Amy sat on the end of the bed. "The opening beneath the stairs in the dining room leads to the kitchen, bathing room, and back door. Across the back yard is the larger cookhouse. I can show you those tomorrow." She paused and met Nichole's eyes. "What do you think?"

Nichole sat in the chair by the unlit fireplace. "It's big and more open than The Shilo. It's more finished and formal."

"You're right," Amy agreed. "Your father designed this house with a wife and daughter in mind. He wanted you to be happy here after living in Boston." Amy paused until Nichole looked back at her. "There was another reason as well. Phil Shilo and your father decided they would use this house to entertain their guests. The Shilo has the more practical ranch house. They had hoped one day the two ranches would merge, along with the families."

"Is that why I was to marry Kevin?" The words were bitter on her tongue.

Amy shook her head. "I don't know how it came to that point with Kevin. I knew your father hoped for a union between you and Merril until you broke that off."

Nichole's heart clenched. Merril elicited such opposing emotions in her. He held her heart, but had he betrayed her? Her feelings for Merril were too personal to share with Amy. "I broke it off?" She rose to look at photos on the mantel and hid her discomfiture. Portraits of the man and woman from downstairs, her parents she assumed, stared back at her.

"You and I never discussed it, of course. I only know what Jason heard, probably from your father."

Nichole nodded and looked at the next photo. It was a recent picture of Kevin, Merril, and herself. She lifted the oval frame from its stand and studied the photograph. She was seated between the brothers who stood to either side of her chair. Both men wore suits, and she wondered if Kevin wore the same outfit he had yesterday. Merril looked so different wearing a suit, that it made her smile, despite her confused emotions. She replaced the picture above the fireplace and turned to Amy.

"Would you like to freshen up?" Amy gestured to the dressing table. Water was already in the bowl and towels set to one side. Nichole wet her hands and splashed water on her face, then used a sweet-smelling bar of soap to wash her hands. She dried them on the towel.

"Shall we go?" Amy prompted when Nichole continued to stand beside the dressing table.

Nichole hesitated. Amy's innocent question sent a surge of nervous flutters loose inside her stomach. After their meal, she would meet with Jimmy Leigh and Jones. Her regret at this confrontation was made bearable only by her fierce determination to set things right. She turned and looked at Amy in consideration. "You heard me speak with Jason about meeting with Jimmy Leigh and Blackwood Jones?"

"Yes, I did." Amy waited beside the door. Conflict etched her face. "I know I shouldn't say anything, but since we are being honest tonight, I must warn you, Nicki—stay away from Jones. He's a dangerous man."

"If he's dangerous, why is he still working on the ranch?"

"I can't say," Amy whispered her eyes downcast. Her gaze rose to Nichole. "The boy and his family, was that the crux of the matter?"

"Yes. It started with Jones's callous racial remarks, but the story came out. The family is homeless and has an ill baby. What else could I do?"

"I'm not questioning your decision. Although, I'm not the one you'll need to convince."

"What would you have done?" Nichole stepped closer to Amy.

"I'm ashamed to say I would have done nothing, which isn't good or noble." Amy looked away again, and when she turned back, her eyes filled with worry. "You realize some people will become...outraged with you over this decision."

"I've discovered that already."

"Still, if it's what you believe—"

"There was nothing else I could have done."

"Then you must act how you feel is right." Amy paused at the sound of footsteps on the stairs.

The sandy-haired girl looked in the open doorway. "There's a couple downstairs to see you, Nicki. The man said you asked them to come here?" Confusion etched her freckled face.

"Yes, I did. Thank you...Jeanne." Nichole remembered her name at the last second.

Jeanne studied Nichole then added, "Cookie says dinner is ready."

Nichole tipped her head in understanding, and Jeanne disappeared, her quick footsteps sounding again on the stairs.

"What are you going to do with your new house guests?" Amy asked.

"I didn't give this much thought, did I? I'm open to suggestions."

Amy tapped her lips with her finger as her dark eyes turned to the ceiling. "Hmm. I'd use discretion to achieve your goals. Perhaps you could suggest they have dinner in the yard tonight. There is a table there, and the weather is mild. Cookie and Jeanne will become acquainted with Timothy's wife and baby." Amy paused in consideration. "Do not let them be thought of as guests. They must have jobs."

"Doing what?"

Amy's gaze returned to Nichole. "Have the young man help prepare the ranch for winter. Jim and Lloyd have no time. Assign him to work for Tom. He can help mend the kitchen roof, restore the shingles, fill the bins with wood. The list is long."

"And his wife?" Nichole followed Amy into the hall.

"Her position in the household will resolve itself in time." Amy paused and looked into Nichole's wide blue eyes. "Be sure everyone understands this is a temporary living arrangement. It will serve only until more suitable housing for Timothy's family can be found."

Amy's suggestions lifted Nichole's spirits and eased her anxiety. "Thanks for your help. I'm glad you came back early."

Amy turned at the top of the stairs and captured Nichole's attention. "You confound me, Nichole Harris. I'm glad you're here, too." Amy turned and descended the stairs before Nichole could respond.

She followed Amy past the long table and through the cased opening. To her left, a short hall led to a larger room where the trailing edge of Amy's skirt disappeared. Nichole followed to the end of the hall and paused.

The kitchen ran the length of the house to her left, where a long cabinet held tonight's prepared dishes, along with many closed containers. The shelves above were stacked with pots, pans, and other assorted items. Across from the shelves on the far wall, a chair propped the back door open and helped cool the warm kitchen.

Cookie stood across from Nichole, in front of a large stove. Sweat beaded the back of her neck as she stirred a big pot. The wall directly to her right had a closed door.

Amy waited outside. She gestured for Nichole to follow, then stepped down into the yard.

Nichole smiled and nodded to Cookie as she passed through her kitchen. There seemed to be a hint of concern in the big woman's eyes. Nichole stepped outside and down a wooden step to the yard.

Timothy stood beside a table in the yard, his hat in his hands. Seated on the bench beside him was a young black woman. Her head rested in her arms as she leaned on the table.

At the other end of the short table, Jeanne held the baby. The bright-eyed infant laughed as Jeanne made kiss noises. She grinned and pulled her head back as the baby tried to capture her hair with a chubby hand.

The sound of thunder rolled across the yard, and everyone looked east to the storm clouds. The breeze carried the scent of rain, cool and refreshing. To the west, the sun edged toward the mountains.

"Miss Harris," Timothy said with relief when the thunder passed. "We came, like you said."

"Yes, you did. I'm glad you made it. Did you bring your belongings?"

"Yes, ma'am. They're in the buckboard over yonder. We don't have much." Timothy shuffled his feet and cast a worried glance at his wife.

"Is your wife feeling ill?" Amy asked. She stepped closer to the young woman who barely raised her head to acknowledge their presence.

"She's just real tired, ma'am. Real tired. She hasn't been able to sleep—"

"She's starving," Jeanne interrupted, speaking over the baby's laughter. "She's nursing, and she isn't getting enough to eat. Look at her arms."

"Dear Lord." Amy slid between Timothy and his wife and put her hand on the young woman's brow. "Jeanne, ask Cookie for two bowls of tonight's stew. Also, have her bring bread with honey and some of the mead from the cellar." She held out her arms to Jeanne.

Jeanne handed the baby to Amy and disappeared into the kitchen.

"What's your wife's name?" Nichole asked and took a seat on the bench across from the woman.

"Her name is Lawna, ma'am. Lawna Caine. Our baby is Hope-Anne."

"Lawna, can you hear me? Are you all right?" Nichole asked, and touched the woman's arm. Her skin was the color of dark honey, and dry from exposure to the sun.

Lawna raised her head and looked at Nichole. Her eyes were the same color as her skin, with dark circles beneath them. She was painfully thin, but Nichole thought she looked more worried and exhausted.

"Yes, ma'am. I hear you," she said in a soft southern drawl. She sat up and tried to smile at Nichole. "I'm sorry I'm so tired. I wanted to thank y'all for what you're doing for us. Then I just fall asleep as soon as I sit down."

"Don't worry about it. You've had a rough few days or few months. How old is Hope-Anne?" Nichole glanced at Amy who was bouncing the happy baby girl who squealed in delight.

Lawna smiled and looked at her daughter in Amy's arms. "Our girl is six months old. She's wantin' to crawl already."

Cookie and Jeanne descended on them with bowls of stew, a platter of bread and mugs of mead. Nichole stood and gestured for Timothy to sit and eat.

"Oh no, ma'am. I can't sit and eat while you serve us. It ain't proper."

"Sit. Eat. When you're done, I need you to take your things up to the smaller room upstairs. You'll stay there until we settle on a better arrangement. Jeanne can show you where it is." Nichole glanced at Jeanne for confirmation. Jeanne nodded and ran back into the kitchen with a smile on her face. "After that, you'll need to return the buckboard. Do you know who Tom is?" she asked.

Timothy nodded.

"Good. You'll be working for him starting tomorrow. He can put together a list of chores he needs help with, but if he has any questions, ask him to speak with Mrs. Harris or me."

Timothy seated himself before the aromatic beef stew and swallowed. He licked his lips as he put his face over the bowl. "Yes, ma'am."

Jeanne came back to the table with a bowl of stew for herself and a large quilt. She spread the quilt on the ground near Lawna and then took Hope-Anne from Amy. "Cookie said to tell you your dinner is ready, and your husband is waiting for you." She sat Hope-Anne on the blanket and handed her a spoon. The baby's eyes grew wide as she tried to grasp the silver utensil. Lawna and Jeanne both laughed, and Amy drew Nichole away.

"Cookie will be out here before long. Lawna will have all the help she needs, I think," Amy whispered as they stepped closer to the back door.

Nichole glanced back at the table. Both Timothy and Lawna were eating, while Jeanne played with Hope-Anne and talked to the young couple. She left them to their dinner and followed Amy through the kitchen and into the dining room.

Jason looked up as Amy and Nichole entered the room. "Finally!" he exclaimed in exasperation and pulled out a chair for his wife. Nichole rounded the table and seated herself to Jason's right.

There was already a large server of beef stew on the table, and Cookie added a plate of biscuits and a jar of honey as Jason took his seat. Each table setting had a glass of water.

Cookie disappeared into the kitchen and didn't return. Nichole suspected she had taken her dinner outside to be with Jeanne and the young family.

Dinner was family-style, serve-yourself, with Jason especially attentive to Amy. The conversation was sparse as they ate. Nichole discovered she had no appetite for the delicious-smelling stew. Her anxiety about the upcoming meeting with Jones and Jimmy Leigh had her stomach in turmoil. She picked at a biscuit as Amy told Jason about Timothy's wife and baby.

"I don't believe the baby is sick. His wife is the one who's suffering."

"Well, that changes everything, right?" Jason looked from Amy to Nichole. Both women shook their heads.

"It changes nothing," Nichole stated.

Amy smiled and patted Jason's hand. "They need our help."

Outnumbered, Jason turned his attention to his meal. As soon as Amy set down her spoon, Jason suggested, "Let's take a walk before the rain sets in, shall we?"

Nichole understood the invitation did not include her.

"Cookie will clean the table once she's finished with her dinner." Amy stood, and although she spoke to Nichole, her eyes were on Jason.

"No worries," Nichole told them, but they had already crossed the room to the front door.

Jason took a cloak from one of the pegs by the door and wrapped it around Amy's shoulders, then ushered her outside. Almost as an afterthought, Jason looked back at Nichole. "Use my office for your meeting, if you like." Then, he closed the door and left Nichole alone at the table with her unfinished meal, and her nervous stomach.

Chapter 17

Nichole Harris

—

Nichole paced Jason's office, impatient for her appointment with Jones and Jimmy Leigh. In an act of cousinly defiance, she lowered herself into Jason's leather chair and rearranged all the papers on his desk. A tall grandfather clock stood beside the doorway. The intricate hands told her the time. Ten minutes after seven. From the open office door, she could see past the dining room table, across the house to the front door. The butterflies in her stomach kept time with the pendulum on the clock.

Cookie and June had cleared the table, and she had watched the Caines move their few belongings upstairs. Jason and Amy remained outside. The house was quiet—fertile ground for an active imagination.

What if Jason was right?

Two guest chairs were pushed tight to the front of the desk. She peered around her own high-backed chair and looked at the papers on the low credenza. With an impatient sigh, she turned back to the desk, opened each of the drawers, and scrambled their contents.

Outside the window, a cloud of dust rose to mar the perfect blue sky. She could see the trails of dust twist in the sunlight, but not what caused them. She half rose to peek out when the front door opened, and she dropped back into the chair.

Jimmy Leigh was alone. He closed the door and hung his hat on a peg. He looked toward the office, caught her eye, and crossed the dining room with long strides. He ducked the doorway lintel as he entered the office. A concerned frown creased his forehead. "Hello, Nicki."

"Hello, Mr. Leigh, thank you for coming."

His lips twitched. "Plain old Leigh or Jim works best, Nicki. We've been on a first-name basis for a while now. I'd like to keep it that way."

"Yes. That's good." She cleared her throat. "Please have a seat, Jim."

He pulled back the guest chair nearest the door and folded his long frame into the seat. "Jones will be a while yet. I asked him to take care of some things. I wanted to talk to you first. Alone."

She couldn't read his face. "All right." Her fingers laced themselves in her lap.

Jim leaned the chair back and pushed the door closed with a click, then eased the chair legs to the floor. He rested his elbows on his knees and looked her in the eye.

"What's this I hear about Jones steppin' out of line?"

"It's true." She paused to choose her words. *Breathe.* "We came upon Jones and Timothy on our way back from The Shilo. Jones said some terrible things to the young man about his family. When I told him to stop and apologize, he spat at the wagon. Jones said he only answered to you."

"This started over Caine?" Jim ran a big hand over his face. "Well, hell."

"You disapprove of Timothy's family?" She clenched her jaw, and her hands tightened.

"Nicki, I hired Timothy Caine." He paused, leaned back, and crossed one long leg over the other at the ankle. "Caine doesn't need my approval to live his life as he sees fit. Although all choices—especially the hard ones—come at a price. He chose a hard road." He brushed at his trouser leg and shrugged. "That's my opinion. It ain't worth a pile of... beans."

"Why not? You're the foreman."

"Well, that's true. But being an opinionated foreman doesn't change the way other men think." He chuckled without mirth. "Caine told me about his wife when I hired him. I knew there might be trouble, but the man needed a break.

"The truth of the matter is Caine is shunned by most of the men. He knew he would be." Jim caught her gaze with his own and held it. "The men who work cattle are a mixed lot. Less than half are white. We have Mexican vaqueros, over a dozen freedmen, and a handful of Red Indians this year. They all get along—for the most part. This isn't about Caine's wife or what Jones said to him. Hell, Caine's heard worse. That's not what bothers me."

"It's not?" Her soft voice trembled, and heat suffused her face. She'd jumped into the deep end.

I didn't know.

Her twisted fingers ached, but she ignored them.

"I'm more concerned about how he spoke to you." Jim paused, lowered his leg, and sat forward. His voice dropped a notch. "A couple of the men came to me not an hour ago. Jones is sayin' things—about you." He paused, then growled, "I won't tolerate that."

Amy's warning about Jones ran through her mind. "He's dangerous."

"He could be." His eyes were calm and serious. "Do you want me to let him go?"

He's asking me?

"I'm not sure. Do you need him? I've already taken Timothy from you." She looked down at her hands. Her fingers knotted together, the knuckles white. She unlaced them and flexed the stiff joints. She exhaled into the silence.

You always trusted him.

"I don't know what would be appropriate. What do you think we should do?"

The big foreman shifted in his chair and rubbed the stubble on his chin. "Well, there might be some mavericks out past Willow Ridge that need rounded and branded. It's a long, ugly ride. Whoever goes will miss the barbecue, but I've got to send someone. Might as well be Jones. Once the drive starts, he won't be here to bother you. I'll release him when we finish at the railhead."

Nichole nodded. "That sounds good." She rubbed her forehead. "Will he know this is about me?"

"He'll know, and so will the rest of the men. It will serve as a reminder. You deserve their respect, and anything less won't be tolerated." Jim almost smiled. "These are good men, for the most part, hardworking and honest. Since your pa died, there's been some confusion about who runs The Highlands."

"I thought you did. Who else?"

"I do, and I don't. My name's not Harris." His gaze softened. "Your pa built this ranch. I was the foreman, but I followed his orders. He often spoke of you, and I know he would want you to take the reins." Jim paused and squinted one eye. "Still, it might not be something you feel up to...."

His challenge straightened her back, and her chin came up. "This is my responsibility, isn't it?" She looked at him and saw approval in his eyes. She gave Jim a tremulous smile and blew out her breath. "I don't know how to run a cattle ranch. If I ever did, it's gone now."

"You'll learn, and you'll have help. It won't be as hard as you think. No one expects you to ride herd or brand." His smile ticked up again, as he looked at Nichole. "I do wonder what Jason will say, though."

Nichole frowned and studied the foreman's tanned face. "This ranch belonged to my father, not his. Jason's an accountant and a lawyer. I love him dearly, but The Highlands is my ranch."

Jim leaned forward and placed his hands on the desk. "That's true, but remember, your pa sent for Jason to help him." He paused for a moment, then continued, "To be honest, you never cared a lick about the ranch. You're not wrong to want to step up, but you need Jason's help and support. It might be best to use discretion...."

"...to achieve my goals," she finished his sentence with Amy's earlier words.

Jim narrowed an eye at Nichole. "You a mind reader now?"

A laugh burst from Nichole. "No. It's something Amy said earlier."

His eyes opened wide, and his face flushed. He looked down at his hands. "Well, Mrs. Harris is a woman wise beyond her years. It's best to listen to what she tells you."

"What's up with you and—"

Nichole was interrupted by a quick knock on the door. It was thrust open, and Jones stepped into the room.

"Mr. Jones." Nichole waved to the empty chair. "We've been expecting you."

Blackwood Jones pawed his dirty brown hat from his head. The polite gesture didn't match the hostile look in his eyes. He stared daggers at Jimmy Leigh.

"I don't know why you agreed to this meetin', Leigh. There ain't nothin' to discuss."

"I came for the same reason you did. I work for Miss Harris." The foreman's tone brooked no argument.

Jones ignored him. His sneer shifted from Jimmy Leigh to Nichole. "Why, yes ma'am." Anger and hate filled his eyes. "Anything you say, Miss Harris."

Jim shot to his feet. "Watch your mouth, Jones. That, and your filthy attitude toward Miss Harris, is why you're here right now."

Jones cocked his head back in a defiant gesture. Their size difference would have been comical were the situation less volatile.

"I ain't workin' for a skirt, Leigh," Jones sneered. "You know that. If you were half the man you claim to be, you wouldn't, either."

"You've said enough, Jones."

"There you're wrong, *Mister Foreman*, it ain't near enough." Jones slammed his fist on the desk. "Besides handin' out orders all of a sudden like she's all high-and-mighty, she took the side of that stinkin' nigger-lovin' kid."

Nichole's attention went back and forth between the men. She'd planned to hold her peace when the trouble began, but this was too much. "Mr. Jones," Nichole shouted, "if you can't work at The Highlands without name-calling and bullying—"

Jones swung around and leaned across the desk. "I sure as *hell* ain't workin' for you, bitch!"

Spittle sprayed her cheeks, and she turned her head as the rank odor of his breath assaulted her. From the corner of her eye, she saw Jim reach over the desk and pull Jones back by his collar. Quick as a snake, Jones spun and swung low.

Jim doubled over as his breath slammed out of him. He stepped back and gasped.

Nichole came to her feet. "Get the hell out of my house, Jones."

Jones ignored her and hammered two more hard blows to Leigh's midsection.

Jim stumbled back and crashed into the door, slamming it shut. Nichole could hear running and shouts throughout the house.

"Jason!" she screamed, as her fingers tightened around a large stone paperweight on the desk.

Jim regained his balance, brought his huge fist up and connected with Jones's jaw.

Blackwood's greasy head snapped back. He stumbled away from Jim knocking over the chair. He came to rest against the desk. An animal growl filled the room as Jones's lips pulled back in a snarl. "You're gonna die for that, Leigh." Jones drew his gun.

Nichole brought the paperweight down on his head with both hands. He crumpled to his knees, then to all fours as the door burst open.

"What the hell is going on in here?" Jason rushed in; Amy close behind him. He stopped short and stared at Jones. "Who started this?" Jason demanded. He looked hard at Nichole. Then his gaze slid to Jim.

Jim pulled Blackwood Jones from the floor. With one hand under Jones's arm, the other hand snatched the gun from the floor.

Nichole lowered the paperweight onto the desk.

"Jones walked in lookin' for a fight." Jim shook Jones for emphasis. "There's no use keepin' him around. He'll just cause trouble."

Jones ran his free hand over the back of his head. His fingers came away bloody.

Jason walked over and stood before Jones. "What's the problem, Jones? This isn't an issue that should have come to blows."

"I won't take orders from a woman," Jones gritted out, his hand still massaging the back of his head.

"Seems you won't have to," Jason said. "Jim, escort him off The Highlands property, and Jones, I don't want to see you around here again. Do you understand me?"

"Yeah," Jones sneered. "I'm beginning to understand a lot of things." He shook his arm free of Leigh's hold and turned to glare at Nichole. "I'll leave, for now, fancy lady, but we might just meet again."

"You better hope you don't, Jones," Jim warned as he pushed the man past Amy and through the door.

After the front door closed, Jason turned to Nichole. "Are you all right?" he snapped.

"Of course I am." Nichole walked around from behind the desk. "Why wouldn't I be?"

"What the hell did you say to him?"

Nichole's jaw dropped "What? I told him to have a seat. I didn't start this."

"Like hell, you didn't! I could hear you yelling from outside."

"Well... yeah." Nichole settled her hands on her hips.

"Jason," Amy warned, "there's no need—"

"Amy, please." Jason held his hand out to Amy, and then turned back to Nichole, "I want to know what went on in here."

Nichole narrowed her eyes and ground her teeth. Jim's advice about discretion flitted through her mind.

Nice thought. Not happening.

"Jason, I'm sorry, but I don't owe you an explanation."

Her smile was honey-sweet as she crossed in front of Jason. At the door, she turned and leveled an icy stare at her cousin. "I'm tired, and I'm going to bed. Why don't you discuss your problem with Jim? If you still have questions, we'll talk in the morning."

She heard Jason slam his fist on the desk as she walked away and started up the stairs. Movement caught her eye when she reached the second floor, and she paused to wait for Amy.

Amy was pale. Her hands trembled when she reached the top of the stairs. She leaned against the stair railing, her eyes pleading with Nichole.

"Amy, are you all right? Jason wouldn't—"

Amy shook her head. "No. This isn't about Jason. It's about Jones."

Nichole motioned Amy into her room.

Jeanne had been there already. A full-length white nightgown lay at the foot of Nichole's turned-down bed.

When the door closed, Nichole faced Amy. "What about Jones?"

Amy rubbed her arms and paced away, then spun and looked at Nichole with thoughtful consideration. She began to speak, then stopped, pressing her lips.

"What's wrong?" Nichole asked.

"Jones isn't going to let this drop," Amy whispered. "You need to be careful."

"Jones is gone. Jim won't let him come back. We're safe." Nichole saw her words only increased Amy's anxiety.

Amy nodded, tried to smile, and stepped past Nichole to the door. "I know. You're right, of course. Just, please...please, be careful."

Amy closed the door behind her. Nichole stared at it for several minutes. What had Amy been trying to tell her?

Chapter 18

Nichole Harris

—

The house was quiet when Nichole woke. Sunlight filled her room, and dust motes danced in the rays from the east window. She stretched and felt the pull of healing muscles, then relaxed and closed her eyes. She lay still and recalled the last two days, the only two days of her life. Try as she might, her thoughts returned to Merril and the kiss they shared in his room. The touch of his hand set her on fire, and yet, along with her desire, her emotions were tangled and confused.

What happened between us?

She had no answers. Yet.

Unsure about the household routine, she finally crawled from bed and made use of the chamber pot. She replaced the porcelain lid then stood and raised her arms over her head. Her back popped and the muscles along her spine pulled, but it felt good. She rolled her shoulders, stepped to the wardrobe, and peeked inside.

Five beautiful dresses hung beside several colored blouses. All the dresses had either bunched folds behind the waist or short trains in the back. The drapes across the front of the skirts were rife with intricate needlework or pleats, both along the skirt and down the bodice. They were gorgeous and sported as many embellishments as Renata's had. The second wardrobe held undergarments. Long slips were sewn taut over narrow hooped cages, often with a pillow attached at the waist in the back.

Crinoline and bustle.

She knew what these were. In one sense, they were important to her, in another, she was appalled. She needed to find something both beautiful and practical to wear.

Discouraged, she sighed and turned to the chest of drawers. She picked out a soft, cream-colored chemise and matching stockings. The third drawer held knee-length underdrawers, all without crotch material.

How bizarre.

She took a pair of those as well.

Out of curiosity, she opened the cedar chest at the end of the bed. There, folded neatly, were some simple skirts with matching jackets.

This is more like it.

There were six or seven different outfits with varied styles and colors, but with clean and simple lines.

She went back to the wardrobe and found a lightweight blouse to match the first skirt in the chest. Once dressed in the dark green skirt outfit, she went through the dressing table and found a matching green ribbon. She brushed her long curls to one side, tied them tight with a bow, and then stared at herself for several moments in the mirror. The face had become more familiar, yet she couldn't help but see a stranger in the reflection.

She set the brush aside and stood to view her ensemble. It was nice not to worry about crushing the back of the skirt. Being able to breathe without a corset was a bonus.

Why aren't there any jeans in my room?

Because ladies never wear slacks.

But I've worn them before. Haven't I?

She made a mental note to ask Amy or Jeanne about riding pants, at least. She lived on a ranch, for Christ's sake.

She eased from her room with a pair of tall boots in hand and padded down the stairs to the dining room. Sunlight filled the open room, and a delicious smell emanated from the kitchen. There was no one in the room or Jason's office. Following the aroma of baking bread, she continued through the open archway and down the short hall to the kitchen.

Cookie was busy at the table beside the oven, her back to Nichole as she kneaded the dough with her knuckles, and then turned it over repeating the process.

"Good morning, Cookie."

"Oh!" Cookie jumped, and faced Nichole, one hand on the dough, one on her chest. "Miss Nichole, it's you. My lands, you gave me a start. I didn't hear you come in."

Nichole raised her boots as if in explanation, and took a seat on the wooden chair beside the door. "I didn't mean to scare you." She smiled an apology as she pulled on her boots. "Where is everyone?"

Cookie wiped her hands on her apron and smiled in delight. "Muffin had her pups this mornin' out in the barn. Eight of 'em. They're the cutest little things. Run out and take a look. I'll put your tea on."

Nichole chuckled at Cookie's excitement and stepped out the back door. Morning dew coated the empty picnic table and hand pump. There was a chill in the morning air, but the sun on her back warmed her. She looked toward the barn and corral, and her vision was captured by the mountains. Yesterday, they had been distant blue hills, but the morning light made them appear much closer.

Horses tossed their heads and played in the corral near at hand. She smiled at their antics and crossed the hard-packed dirt toward the barn. She could hear voices filled with exclamations and laughter ahead of her. A group of people stood just inside the open doors. Fresh hay and the musty scent of animals greeted her as she stepped inside. She stopped to let her eyes readjust to the dim interior.

"Nicki, come and look at the pups." Delight filled Amy's voice as she took Nichole's arm and guided her around the first stall. "Aren't they adorable?"

Nichole nodded a smile to everyone before she turned her attention to the dogs. The puppies were fat, wiggly, and had a fine coat of fur with marks like their mother. Even though their eyes were closed, they had enough strength to push each other aside for their mother's milk. Muffin lay on her side, tongue hanging from her mouth with what looked like a doggie smile. With her tall ears and bright eyes, she appeared to take great interest in the people gathered around her babies.

"They're so tiny," Nichole said in awe. "Can I touch them?" She looked to Tom and Lloyd, who both had an expression of pride on their faces.

"Let Muff smell your hand first. She'll let you know if she wants you to stay away. She won't bite," Tom instructed.

Nichole nodded at Tom and knelt near the mound of hay Muffin had chosen to birth her litter. She held out her hand to the foxlike face of the little mama. Muffin sniffed her knuckles then gave her a lick of approval.

She ran her fingertips across the little bodies lying side by side, noses pressed to Muffin's belly. "Wow. They're so soft."

When the memory came, it was sharp and clear. Around her, the happy chatter and exclamations faded. Their words became unclear, and a tingling sensation tickled her scalp. For a moment, she no longer saw the barn.

It was Christmas. Red and green lights blinked merrily on a tinsel-covered tree. The smell of pine and cinnamon rolls filled the room. Presents were scattered around the floor. Colorful paper and ribbons were discarded everywhere. She was young—maybe seven or eight years old. A dark-haired man with a beard placed a large, unopened present on the floor in front of her and a younger child. The whole package moved, and excitement spread through her chest.

"Go ahead," the man urged. "Open it. I've saved the best for last."

She stared at the box, wide-eyed, before tearing into the paper. When the last of the wrapping was gone, and the lid was open, she heard the boy beside her shriek with delight.

"It's a puppy, Courty! A puppy! Oh, wow, look Courty, for us!"

The tiny ball of fur, happy to be released from its confinement, licked and wiggled, soaking the giggling children with puppy kisses.

As suddenly as it had appeared, the recollection vanished.

Amy's hands were tight on her shoulders. "Nicki, are you all right?"

She let her held breath escape her lungs. White lights darted across her vision, then disappeared. She looked up at Amy's concerned face. "My memories are coming back."

"You fell back against my legs, and I thought you'd fainted." Amy touched Nichole's face and neck and then smiled. "Let me help you up."

"I've got her." Jim pulled her to her feet. "You sure you're well? I don't want you to fall."

Nichole smiled and laughed. "I feel great. Doc Johnson was right. They're coming back." She turned from Jim and sought Jason. "It was the Christmas we got a puppy. I remember it, clear as a bell. You were there, and a man with a dark beard gave us a puppy. Muffin's beautiful pups helped me remember."

Jason nodded, a half-smile frozen on his face.

"That's wonderful." Amy stepped forward and took both her hands. "You'll remember more and more every day."

"I know, right?" Nichole happy gaze took in everyone. "It wasn't much, but anything is better than what I've had. I was worried I'd never get any memories back."

"Ah, now," Jim scolded. "We knew better than that, didn't we, Jason?"

Jason didn't say a word. He looked conflicted as he gave a wary smile to Nichole.

"Let's go inside," Amy suggested, turning her back to Jason with a look of exasperation. "We can celebrate your memory's return over breakfast."

"I don't think I could eat. I know I couldn't sit still." Nichole laughed again and gave Jim a quick hug.

"Let's go for a ride, then," Jim suggested. "It'll work up your appetite and give me a chance to show you the ranch. What do you say?"

"That would be perfect." Nichole looked up at Jim's face and thought she saw him smile.

"Jason?" Jim looked from Nichole to Jason. "Do you have any concerns with me showin' our young lady around her ranch?"

"Hmm? Oh, no. No concerns. Don't go too far or be out too long. Nicki is still recovering."

Jim tipped his head at Jason, then turned to Nichole. "Well, come on then, gal. We've got two geldings just waitin' for us." He indicated the large corral across the yard, occupied by several horses.

***

Amy Harris

—

Amy watched them cross the open space to the pen and waited for Tom to wander back to his pups before she turned to Jason.

"What's the matter?" She stepped closer and took his arm as they left the barn. "Aren't you happy for Nichole?"

Jason's smile was strained. "Her memory hasn't returned. At least, not yet."

"What? Are you sure? I know it was a small memory, just Christmas, and puppies. It could be a sign the rest will return, and soon."

Jason shook his head and kicked his toe in the dirt. He stopped outside the back door to watch Jim and Nichole move through the horses in the corral "We never had puppies at home. My mother didn't care for them. She claimed they made her sneeze and wouldn't have them in the house. And that man with the beard she spoke of? I don't know who that could be."

Amy stared at Jason in surprise. She turned to watch Nichole and Jim. They followed Lloyd as he led two horses toward the barn. She glanced at Jason as he leaned against the backyard table and bit one side of his lip. "I'll be inside. Come in and have some breakfast." She touched his arm, and he nodded, still watching his cousin.

Amy crossed the yard to the door. Her thoughts troubled. She smiled at Cookie as she made her way through the kitchen. In the dining room, June was setting the table for breakfast.

"Good morning, Amy," June said as she aligned the chairs and straightened the silver.

"Good morning, June. The table is lovely."

"Thank you. Oh, before I forget, Jeanne mentioned that she and Tom plan to head to Kiowa Crossing before lunch. Cookie and Lloyd have a few items they need for the barbecue. If you need supplies from town, be sure to let Jeanne know."

"Thank you," Amy replied. "I will."

June hesitated beside the table, a sour look on her face.

Amy paused. "Is there something else on your mind, June?"

"It's that Lawna Caine." June walked around the table to Amy. "Poor Cookie has her hands full trying to keep her out of mischief."

"Mischief? What kind of mischief could she possibly find?"

"Well, not so much mischief as underfoot and out of her place. That woman and her baby came downstairs this morning, looking for things to get into."

"She wants to be helpful, June," Amy chided. "It will be nice to have another pair of hands around the place. What with the barbecue this week and fall canning in mind, there's no such thing as too many hands."

"Not *that* pair of hands," June muttered in agitation. She stepped forward and confronted Amy squarely. "It's not fair. Nichole has allowed that woman and her family to live in this house like guests." Her voice lowered perceptibly, "Amy, you must understand how we all feel about this."

"I know the situation is unusual," Amy stated, "but I met Timothy and Lawna last night. They seem to be very determined and quite in love. Their baby, Hope-Anne, is a beautiful child."

"It isn't proper, and you know it. Those rooms aren't meant for their type. Cookie, Jeanne, and I live in the attic. But these ... strangers get a guest room."

Amy narrowed her eyes. "Let me understand you with clarity. You're unhappy with your current living quarters?"

"I'm not unhappy with mine," June hissed, "but with theirs."

"I see," Amy said, her voice both soft-spoken and hard-edged, as only she could manage. "It appears that I'm in the unfortunate position of reminding you who decides the accommodations in this household. Miss Harris employs Mr. and Mrs. Caine, and their living arrangements are only temporary. If you wish to make your complaint formal, you should bring it up with Miss Harris."

"But Amy," the older woman protested, "Nichole isn't in her right mind. Heavens, just last night she didn't know our names. Two days ago, she didn't know her own."

"I think that's quite enough," Amy's tone was harsher than she intended. "Miss Harris is capable of making decisions without your approval. Any further discussion about her well-being or her choices will be considered idle gossip."

Amy left June in the dining room and stalked into the kitchen, past Cookie. She didn't necessarily agree with Nichole's decision, but she was family, and June—regardless of their friendship —was hired help. She would not allow June to criticize Nichole. Besides, Lawna was a sweet girl. Timothy was earnest and eager to please.

Her anger carried her through the kitchen and out the back step in a fury. She almost knocked over the dark-skinned girl laden with the laundry.

"Oh! Lawna, I'm sorry." Amy held her shoulders to steady her.

"I was in the way, Mrs. Harris." Lawna bent to retrieve a dropped piece of linen from the ground and smiled at Amy.

"I needed to do some laundry, what with the baby and all—living rough. Miss Cookie showed me where the washtub and the well are and let me use some of her soap. I asked her if she had any laundry she needed scrubbed."

An excited grin split the young girl's face. "Miss Cookie has all types of things that need laundered and mended."

"That's wonderful, Lawna, but where is Hope-Anne?"

"She's asleep in that basket under the tree, near the laundry tub. I think she is feeling better already."

"I think her Mama feels better, and she knows it."

Again, Lawna's infectious grin animated her face. "I know, Mrs. Harris. Timothy has looked at the roof and gave Tom a list of supplies to pick up in town."

"I'm glad for you, Lawna."

Lawna waved and carried Cookie's laundry to the tub near Hope-Anne.

Amy scanned the yard, but Jason had disappeared. She walked to the corral and leaned on the split rails. Only a few horses remained in the pen. She watched the clouds move east overhead. Her thoughts circled and returned to Jones. Anxiety tightened in her chest, and she released a deep breath.

Let it go.

There was still trouble ahead with Jones—if only she knew when and how. She released a prayer into the wind to watch over Nichole.

Chapter 19

Nichole Harris

—

Nichole followed Jim, Lloyd, and the horses into the barn. She stood to the side as Jim saddled the brown horse while Lloyd took care of the bay. A rich, brown coat with black legs, mane, and tail, the bay had a single white spot on his forehead she longed to touch.

What a beautiful animal.

Her fingers itched to rub him from his nose up to the white spot and give him treats. Then, she noticed the saddles. "Why is my saddle different?"

Lloyd looked at her sideways as he tightened the strap around the girth. "Whatcha mean different? It's yours." Lloyd looked back at the belt and adjusted the stirrup.

Jimmy's saddle had a single horn and a stirrup on each side. Hers had curved leather horns with a stirrup only on the left side. She cast a quick glance at Jim. He rested his back against his horse and watched her with a bemused look on his face.

Lloyd placed a wooden step beneath her stirrup and turned to her.

She hesitated. Her mind raced as she looked at the two saddles. She knew why they were different but couldn't bring the knowledge forward. The thought teased her but remained just out of reach. The bay swung his head around and looked at her as well. She could almost feel the horse's impatience. It made her smile. "Sorry. I'm still a bit confused."

It's a sidesaddle.

The image came to her, how to sit, how to mount.

I've never been on a horse.

"It's a woman's saddle," Jim called over his shoulder as he mounted.

"I know that," she replied without conviction. She stepped on the small platform with her right foot, draped her skirt and petticoat over her left arm. Lloyd braced her as she stepped into the stirrup with her left foot, rose, and hooked her right leg around the top pommel. She adjusted her left leg beneath the lower horn and draped her skirt over her legs.

Mounted like a boss.

"Yes." She made a fist and pumped it in victory.

Lloyd picked up the wooden step and walked into the tack area.

Her breath hitched when she realized how far she was from the ground. "Holy shit," she muttered as her gaze measured the distance.

Jim reined in beside her. "You all right?"

She looked from the ground to Jim. "You heard me?"

His half-grin was gone, and a smile creased his face in amusement. "Did you say something?" He laughed aloud and guided his horse out of the barn into the sunshine.

"Ya might want this thing, here." Lloyd held up a closed parasol.

"Thank you." She lifted the dark green parasol, opened it, and laid it over her shoulder. "Lloyd, why are there parasols in the tack room?"

Lloyd shrugged. "It's where you said you wanted 'em. You want 'em moved again?"

"No. They're fine." She patted the bay's neck "What's his name?" Her mount followed the brown horse out of the barn.

Lloyd walked beside her. "Ya call him Sugar 'cause he's so sweet." He grinned and stopped walking.

Nichole chuckled and urged Sugar to step up beside Jim.

Their path took them northwest across the plain. Sweet-grass and wild-flowers cast their fragrance into the air with each gust of the breeze. Tall, yellow flowering weeds and thistle bushes rose above the knee-high grass. They followed a beaten trail, less than a road, but flattened with recent use and wide enough to ride side by side.

"Where are we going?" Nichole asked. Although the prairie appeared flat, the subtle rise and fall of the ground hid their destination beyond a low hill.

"Thought we'd mosey over to the brandin' site. It's just yonder."

Nichole stared at Jim for a moment. "Last night, you spoke with no accent. Today, you twang like Lloyd. What's up with that?"

He looked at her in surprise and tugged the reins to a stop. Nichole's bay stopped beside him. "All right, then. Maybe you can tell me what's happened to your Boston accent? I only hear it half the time."

Nichole blinked at him. "My... you mean how Jason and Amy talk? I'm supposed to sound like them?"

He nodded. "And you did, until yesterday. Now, I hear the west in your voice, Texas maybe, but that could be the Shilos' influence. My point is, your speech is different, and not just the accent, but also the content and expressions."

"Well... I'm not doing it on purpose. I have an injured brain. Why are *you* doing it?"

He ran his hand through his hair and reset his hat, never taking his gaze from Nichole. "I musta picked it up from bein' around Lloyd and Tom this mornin'. Can't say fer sure."

Nichole narrowed her eyes at him. He grinned and urged his horse forward. Nichole's mount stepped up to keep pace.

"I brought you here for a reason. I want you to see the ranch and understand what we do. The spring roundup is finished, for the most part. We're about done with branding and notching the calves. We'll keep the cattle close for a few weeks, then drive 'em to the railhead."

"Why wait?"

"Normally, we don't. But this spring has been unusually wet. We decided to sit tight for a spell, let the ground dry out some. The railheads aren't that far from the ranch. It's not like we're driving 'em from Texas."

"Who decides? You and Jason?"

"Phil, Kevin, and I. That's why they were here a couple of weeks ago. Jason doesn't know anything about cattle. He keeps track of the men and wages, and makes sure we have supplies for the drive."

"Merril wasn't with them?" Nichole shot Jim a quick glance and saw him grin at her question. Heat suffused her face.

"Merril works the cattle, like these men. He's learning."

Nichole nodded, as though everything made perfect sense.

The path they followed inched up a slow incline, away from the squat bushes and cottonwood trees that grew in clusters along the streambed. Jim paused for a moment at the top of a rise, and then descended the other side.

Sugar chose that moment to change direction. He turned to follow the ridge, but Nichole pulled the reins and directed him back to the path. Sugar snorted and sidestepped, but gave in and started up the rise after the brown.

At the crest, Nichole caught her breath. Below her was a shallow but wide basin, covered in prairie grass. Cattle grazed across the valley and filled it from the ridge to the stream that swung wide to the north. Nearby, several men worked with branding irons and calves.

Jim turned to her with a smile. "Here we are. Winter pasture. This shallow depression shelters the stock from the wind." He pointed across the valley. "The tree line on the north side helps keep the snowdrifts down. It's close to the ranch and easy to reach in the winter. It is also convenient for the roundup. Your pa wanted the sight and smell of the branding away from his ladies."

Nichole guided Sugar alongside Jim's mare. "They're almost done?"

"Yep. A couple more days and they'll be finished until we drive. Time for these boys to celebrate."

"Celebrate at the barbecue?" Nichole chewed her lip, her brow furrowed.

"You don't seem very excited," Jim observed.

"I am, then I'm not. These men know me. They'll expect me to know them. My memory is difficult to explain and impossible to hide."

"You'll be fine. Just smile and flash those pretty blue eyes. They won't know what hit 'em."

Nichole's laugh was tinged with uneasiness. "You're sweet, Jim, despite your diabolical air of mystery." She smiled and looked across the valley. "I've changed, though. You've seen the difference. I know Jason sees it. How do I act normal when I can't remember what normal used to be?"

Jim wrapped his reins around his saddle horn and leaned closer to Nichole. "Nicki," he said, his tone sincere, "you are better company now than you were before. You're more interested in the ranch and easier to talk to. I don't know anyone, 'cept maybe Jones, who would say any different. Don't worry about what they think." He gestured toward the valley. "Just enjoy the party."

"Hey, Leigh!" A man near the branding irons called out. He wrestled a half-grown calf that kept stepping away. "How about a hand with this one? Seems this little girl don't want to lay down for me."

Jim swept the hair out of his eyes and under his hat in one motion. "John needs a hand. This should only take a few minutes."

"You go ahead. I'll head back. I've had a wonderful ride."

"You remember the way home?"

Nichole nodded. "The path leads straight to the house. I can't miss it."

"That's true. I could have Kelly see ya home, to be safe."

"No, please. I know the way. I won't get lost," she promised.

Jim narrowed his eyes in warning. "You fall off your horse, that cousin of yours will have my hide."

Laughter burst from Nichole. "I'll be fine, Jim. We haven't gone that far."

"Hey, Jim, you want to speed it up?" John had lost his hat, and his nose bled. "This little gal ain't gonna wait forever, ya know."

"I'm comin', John, keep your pants on. She ain't that big."

"Like hell, she ain't!" John struggled to hold the calf. "Year and a half in the brush, wild as you please. You come hold her down and tell me she ain't that big."

Nichole laughed and tugged Sugar's reins. "See you at home, Jim," she called as she topped the rise. Sugar picked his way down the other side with delicate precision. To the east, the path through the grass was clear. She started that way then paused to consider her options. Doc Johnson would kill her if he knew, not to mention Jason and Jim, but the sun warmed her legs, and she simply couldn't give up the day and return to the house. Not yet. With a lift of her head, she pulled the reins and headed south, into the wind.

I'll follow the ravine for a while.

She couldn't get lost if she kept the rise on her right. Retracing her path would be simple.

Sugar picked up the pace when their path merged with a worn track.

"Is this a trail you know?" she asked Sugar, then felt foolish, but Sugar bobbed his head as if he understood. Nichole giggled. "All right then, boyfriend, you take the lead. Where does this go?" Nichole gave Sugar a nudge, and the bay stepped up the pace. They followed the ravine until the trail turned east. The scenery took her breath away, a virgin wilderness of prairie and sky. Peaceful and empty—just the tranquil atmosphere her mind needed.

Sugar slowed and then came to a stop near a thicket of bushes. He pawed at the ground and nibbled the leafy vegetation. "I take it we've arrived." Nichole closed the parasol and pulled her skirt back. She unhooked her left knee, stood in the stirrup, and then lifted her right leg out and over the saddle. Sugar turned his head to watch when she hesitated. She sighed at Sugar's impatience and lowered her right foot to the ground. "There, see?" She drew the reins around Sugar's head and rubbed his nose with a gentle hand. "Thanks for putting up with me, fella."

Sugar bumped her hand, then pushed at the bushes.

"Is this it, Sugar? Is this what you like?"

The bay stomped and nosed the bushes.

"In there? Sure. Why not?"

Nichole shoved at the brush, and it moved. The limbs were long and thin, but not anchored to the ground. She pushed them up into an arch as Sugar passed beneath them, then she slid under them behind the bay, letting them fall back into place.

When she turned back to Sugar, she gasped at the hidden thicket. Her gaze traveled around a wild, unkempt garden, surrounded by tall brush on three sides. Near the rocky outcrop, a small clear pond glistened in the sunlight. A delicate waterfall fell from the rocks above. Even on the ridge above her, brush grew thick and lush. She stood in a private sanctuary of her very own.

"Oh, wow, Sugar." She patted the horse as he grazed on the thick green grass. "Look what you've found. It's perfect. I see why you like it here."

Nichole placed her parasol near a large flat rock. The water beckoned, so cool and refreshing, like a mirage in her wildest dreams. The brush and rocks blocked the cool breeze, and the sunlight warmed the small grove. She unbuttoned and folded her jacket, and then laid it beside the parasol.

This is perfect.

The blouse came next, then the boots and skirt. After a suspicious glance at the bushes, she relaxed—even the birds had begun to sing again. With quick movements, the thigh-length chemise and drawers came off, and she was free of her clothes. She hurried toward the small pond.

She tested the water with her toes—ice cold and clear. She flashed Sugar a mischievous smile. "I'll bet we've done this before. Fess up."

Sugar huffed and shook his dark mane.

"Don't lie to me, horse," she scolded. "You were just a little too eager to back out now. We're in this together, so don't give me that look."

Sugar flicked his tail and turned away.

"Fine, be that way." Nichole took a few hesitant steps into the pond. The bottom was rocky but smooth, and the cold water sent chills up her spine.

Get on with it.

She jumped forward into the center of the pond and popped back up with a gasp. The pool was shallow. When she stood, the water lapped at her waist. Nichole took one more careful inspection of her private garden. The birds sang in the bushes and Sugar grazed on the lush grass. Surrounded by tall bushes and rock, the clear blue sky and warm sun were the only witnesses to her wild escapade.

Just a quick swim.

She dove into the water and surfaced with a splash and a laugh, her worries about privacy forgotten.

Chapter 20

Merril Shilo

—

Merril reined Midnight in the morning stillness. The vast, empty prairie acted as a soothing balm to his shattered soul after his father's funeral. Kevin had attended, but the brothers hadn't spoken. As soon as the reverend left The Shilo to return to town, Merril had ridden out. He'd come more than two miles along the Shilo-Highlands boundary in search of strays. He pushed his hat to the back of his head and relaxed. It looked good. Unless the other wranglers found any calves, they were ready to call the branding and notching done.

He recognized Shadow Creek ahead. He'd ride home along the streambed on the Highlands side. If any missing cattle were here, they'd be near the water. He urged Midnight into a trot parallel to the waterway. Ahead, the foliage thickened where the creek dropped over the plateau ridge. He could never see this place and not think of Nichole.

Merril made his way down the ravine along the brush and stopped near the secret opening he and Nichole had made years ago. He dismounted and wrapped Midnight's reins around a low-hanging limb.

"I'll be back," he whispered as he lifted his rope from the saddle. Then he stopped. Random splashing from within the brush enclosure confirmed his suspicions.

I'll be damned if I wasn't right. And I'd hoped to get home early today.

There were too many loose ends to resolve. The most urgent being a conversation with a sober Kevin about their future. Like it or not.

He parted the greenery with slow movements, careful not to startle a skittish calf.

"Michael, have mercy!" he gasped, as Nicki's little gelding, Sugar, nuzzled at the leaves near his head.

"What are you doing here?" He rubbed the bay's nose and accepted his greeting. "Just like old times, huh, Sugar? Is Nicki with you, or are you just playing tricks on old Lloyd?"

Sugar huffed and sauntered on to better grazing. A loud splash brought Merril's attention to the pond. A smile spread across his face as Nichole surfaced on the far side of the pool.

She stood in the shallows, her back to Merril, as water lapped at her waist. Then she turned. Clear rivulets of icy water ran over her high, firm breasts and arms.

Merril's groin tightened as she called for Sugar to watch, then splashed her way back to his side of the pond. Before he had time to change his mind, he crouched beneath the foliage and walked into the sunlight. He stopped beside her folded clothes.

Nichole hadn't noticed him as she swam across the pool and stood again in the sunlight. When she turned and saw him, she uttered a squeak, and sank into the deepest part of the small pond. The clear water bumped against her chin but hid little.

"What are you doing here?" she hissed. "You scared me to death. Give me my clothes." Heat rose in her cheeks as she sputtered her demand.

"What do you mean, 'what am _I_ doing here'?" He sat beside her parasol and loosened the handkerchief around his neck. "It sure is nice here. Good view."

She glared at him in silence, her nose just above the waterline.

"How did you find this place, Nicki? Is your memory back?"

She raised her chin from the water. "I wish. Give me my clothes, you Peeping Tom."

"Can't do that." Merril lounged on one elbow and crossed his boots at the ankle.

***

Nichole Harris

—

Nichole gave him the most threatening glare she could muster.

Well, crap.

He was having a great time at her expense. Then again, she could see the humor of the situation if it hadn't been to her disadvantage. "You're a shit, Merril Shilo. What are you going to do? Sit there all d-day?"

"If I have to," Merril replied. He peeked from under the brim of his hat. "Such language. Does Jason talk like that around you?"

"I guess I'll f-freeze to death," she stuttered.

"You could." He kicked off his boots, one after another. "But I wouldn't advise it. Truth is, it's a little early in the year for swimming. Especially dressed the way you are. Miss Harris, I am shocked."

"C-creep," Nichole managed, through chattering teeth.

"Come, get your clothes Nicki, before you *do* freeze to death. I won't look," he said with his lopsided grin that told differently. "I promise."

"Yeah, right," she muttered. She studied the handsome cowboy a moment longer as he tipped the brim of his hat a bit lower.

Oh, he's going to watch all right.

She suppressed a nervous giggle and inched her way forward. She moved as close to the edge of the pond as possible and still keep the partial cover of the water.

In a burst of motion, she sprang forward, throwing water at him as she dove for her clothes. Her garments weren't far, but he'd positioned himself for precisely this purpose. Her clothes were but an arm's-length from his side.

***

Merril Shilo

—

Merril smiled as she splashed water at him, then raced up the slight bank. *What a beauty she is.*

He'd almost forgotten—or at least he'd tried. Nichole's golden hair, dark with moisture, hung heavy around her shoulders and back and tangled strands clung to her swaying breasts. Her nipples were as he remembered, rosy and hard-tipped from the icy water.

At the exact moment she bent to reach for her chemise, he sprang. He wrapped both arms around her shoulders and rolled her away from her clothes—taking his weight on his arms—and came up as planned, on top.

Nichole's laughter filled the small enclosure. "You're such a Neanderthal." Her brows raised as her mirth faded. "Let me up."

"A what?" He'd lost his hat and hair fell over his face. "I have to be quick to take down a little orphan calf and not hurt them. This is a tried-and-true maneuver." He gave his head a shake, tossing his hair from his eyes, and grinned down at her. "You know, we used to meet here a couple o' years ago, before—well—before we stopped meeting at all." His grin widened. "I guess you remembered this place?"

"Sugar brought me here." Her gaze dropped to his lips. "But it's good to know I had finally come to my senses about such a cow herding caveman."

"I like the way you talk now," Merril said. "With such charm. Same Nicki, but without all the fluff and nonsense." He bent his head to kiss the droplets of water from her throat.

***

Nichole Harris

—

His lips scorched a trail from her neck to her breast, and she gasped when his warm tongue made contact with her icy nipple. Slowly, he kneaded the tip, pulling at it with his lips. A sensation of pleasure flowed from her breast to her stomach, coming to rest between her legs with a delightful pulse. She pushed halfheartedly against his shoulders. "Merril," she breathed a warning, as he changed sides and nibbled gently. "This is a bad idea. Anyone could find us. You should stop."

"Are you sure?" The warmth of his mouth retreated. "I'll stop if that's what you want."

His soft deep voice only added to the yearning inside. With a groan, she closed her eyes and arched her neck. "No—don't stop."

He chuckled, and his tongue returned to her throat. Tender kisses trailed up her neck making her catch her breath. His lips, soft and patient, urged her to respond. Despite her better judgment, Nichole's resistance dissolved, replaced instead by an awakened desire to love this man. His familiar touch inflamed her and stirred a craving for more.

And I do want him. I always have. Now and forever.

"You're beautiful." His calloused hand ran up her waist and cupped her breast. "Let me make things right between us. Let me love you."

Nichole's lashes fluttered open, and she stared into Merril's gold-flecked green eyes. "I don't remember what we were like." Her hand curled into his unruly hair.

"Then let me show you," he breathed as their lips met once more, this time with passion.

Nichole quivered to the depths of her soul. She fumbled with the buttons on his shirt, needing to feel the warmth of his skin against hers.

Merril brushed her fingers away and removed his shirt and vest himself.

The heat from his naked chest pressed against hers, and their passion slowed. There was time now, and a lifetime remained to learn and explore each other. His hand slid down the curve along Nichole's side and caressed her hip, while her cool fingers stroked the corded muscle of his arm. Content for the moment to stroke and kiss each other—his skin, warm as the sun, and hers, icy-cool and damp from the pond.

She slid her hand down his hard, flat stomach, past his belt.

A low growl rumbled from his throat. In moments, he'd tossed his belt and trousers to the ground, and his entire body pressed tight to hers, his skin so hot she shivered. The warmth of his hands caressed her, and his lips drank in each of the droplets on her skin.

She moaned when his hand found the heat at her center. Her breath hitched as the coil of pleasure tightened low in her belly. "Oh, Merril," she breathed.

"Yes?" His voice, soft in her ear.

"Oh, yeah," she replied and shifted beneath him as spasms of pleasure shook her.

He took his weight on his arms and paused, centered between her legs. "Ready?"

Nichole nodded and pressed toward the touch of his hardness along her heat.

His eyes held hers as he slowly entered her, filling her emptiness. "Better?"

"Such a Neanderthal," she whispered in response to his cocky grin and thrust her hips up in time with his movements.

His grin disappeared, and he groaned, gathering her to his chest. He buried his face in her neck and lifted her hips with one long arm. He held her steady, thrusting harder and deeper as his passion peaked. "Ah, God, Nicki."

His softly spoken words tickled her neck. She wrapped her legs around his hips as another wave of pleasure rocked her. "Holy shit," she whispered and opened her eyes to the azure sky.

Sedated in the afterglow of satisfaction, Merril cradled her to his side, while the puffy clouds high above them floated by in a mirage of characters over their hidden garden.

"The summer begins," Merril whispered as Nichole snuggled closer to his lean muscular body. "And maybe a new start for us." He kissed the top of her head and lay back.

"Mmm," Nichole agreed, still tipsy with emotion.

He turned his head and opened his magnificent eyes.

"You said we'd done this before."

"We have."

She looked away, her face heated, embarrassed to ask, but curious nonetheless. "I feel cheated." She pulled a blade of grass and ran her fingers down the edge. "I'm envious of your memories. I... I don't know what it was like... you know... when we did this before." She turned her sleepy eyes towards Merril.

He studied her with a serious expression on his face. "Go on," he urged.

"Well, was this time... was it like the others?"

"I'm not sure what you mean." Merril chuckled.

Nichole rose on her elbow and glared down at him.

"Truthfully, no. This wasn't like the other time." He nuzzled her hair with his nose. "We've only made love once before, and this was much different."

Nichole eased down beside him, and Merril planted a small kiss on her forehead.

"In some ways, it's the same, I suppose," he continued, "if you mean the mechanics of it. But in the way that matters, much different."

"Explain." Nichole nestled her head in the crook of his arm.

His brow furrowed. "It's hard to describe what makes one woman different from another."

Nichole looked at him from the corner of her eye. "You're not comparing two women, Merril. You're comparing one. I'd think that should make things a bit easier."

"You could be two different women." His eyes searched hers. "The Nichole I know today and the one I was with two years ago." He paused again and looked away. "You enjoyed making love with me this time. I could tell."

"And I didn't enjoy this before?"

"I'm not sure, to be honest." The lopsided grin Nichole had come to love so well flashed across Merril's handsome face. "Does it matter?" He drew her close to his side.

She melted into his arms. Her joy permeated her to the tips of her toes. Everything would work out, and all was right with her world. In just a few days, she went from a sick, frightened girl to a woman who stood her ground, managed a ranch, and made love to the most handsome man she'd ever seen.

"I love you, Nicki. I always have." Merril cupped her face in his hands. "If it weren't for Renata, we'd be married by now with a yard full of kids and another on the way."

"Renata?" Nichole drew back in confusion.

"I shouldn't have said anything—"

"Too late now. You have to tell me." A cloud passed in front of the sun and darkened the thicket. "You can't expect me to let a comment like that go."

Merril clenched his jaw, lay back and looked up at the sky. He cleared his throat and cast a quick glance at her. "You and I had been together for a couple years. We had our problems, like everyone, I suppose, but the consensus was that at some future date we would tie the knot and settle down."

She waited, but he continued to look at the sky. "And?"

"This isn't easy." Merril turned away and picked up a small stone. "I always believed it was the reason you agreed to marry Kevin."

"It must have been pretty bad," Nichole said, her tone more serious than she intended.

"It was." Merril nodded. "We had learned to trust each other. You meant everything to me." He lowered his head and concentrated on the rock. "I was stacking hay in the barn and I don't remember exactly when Renata came in. She said she needed my help with something. One minute, we were talking, and the next, she threw herself into my arms and kissed me."

He raised his gaze from the rock in his hand and met Nichole's eyes. "When I looked up, you were there, standing in the open doorway. You stared at us with a blank look I couldn't read, then you whirled and ran.

"I tried to stop you, but you were gone before I could get Renata from around my neck. You refused to speak to me after that until the carriage accident took your memory." His attention returned to the stone he rolled between his fingers.

"The accident stole the good memories too, like the trust you say we shared." Nichole shrugged and tried to cover her grin but began to laugh. "I can't believe I stopped talking to you and agreed to marry your brother, all because I saw you kiss Renata."

"You were jealous."

"Probably. But I would handle the situation much differently if Renata kissed you today."

"You would?" He looked from the stone in his hand to her face.

"Well... yeah." She chortled. "How could I be so jealous of you and Renata that I would agree to marry Kevin?" A giggle erupted, then a laugh. "A revenge marriage?"

"Forget it. I should never have said a word." Merril rolled away, came to his feet and grabbed his shirt. "Get dressed."

Nichole continued to laugh. Merril's irritation with her mirth made it even funnier. She wiped the tears from her eyes and held her sides.

"I said, get dressed," his voice tinged in anger.

"Are you mad?" She giggled. She couldn't help it. His icy glare made the situation comical, and she bit her lip to stop her laughter. "Whew, I'm okay." She sat up and took a deep breath. His glare made her smile again. "I'm sorry I upset you. I just can't imagine—"

"You can't imagine being jealous of me. You've made your point." Merril frowned at her. He picked up his trousers and pulled them on. "Now, go on and get dressed."

"Look, Merril, I said I was sorry. And I am." Her mouth twitched, but she held back her grin.

Merril reached for her chemise and tossed it in her face.

She pulled the cotton shift over her head. "Okay, fine," she conceded. "I'll get dressed. It's what I wanted to do all along if I remember right."

"You remember well enough when it suits you," he replied sharply.

Nichole rose to her feet and gauged the distance between Merril and the pond.

"Oh, I remember a number of things," she said.

Merril looked down to buckle his holster strap around his leg.

With a quick shove, she pushed him backward into the icy pond. He disappeared beneath the surface with a big splash.

"You were acting childish." Nichole stuck out her tongue, her hands on her hips. "So I thought I'd be childish right back."

Merril struggled to his feet and shook the water from his face.

Nichole took a step back, uncertain if she'd gone too far.

He walked toward her through the water and growled, "You little spitfire! I'm going to give you what your daddy never did." The sparkle in his eyes gave his amusement away.

Nichole's uncertainty dissolved in laughter and she ran behind Sugar, peeking over his rump at Merril.

***

Kevin Shilo

—

On the ridge above the couple, the bushes rustled closed. Kevin turned back to his large sorrel gelding. He'd seen enough. "Damn those two conniving backstabbers," he swore as he mounted and headed home. "They planned this all along. There was no dementia. Hell, how do I know there was ever an accident, for that matter? They're all in on it—making me out to be the fool. I'll show them."

He kicked his horse into a gallop as his mind raced ahead. There had to be some way to get even. He wanted Nichole—now more than ever if that was possible. Only now, he wanted her as a trophy—something he could hold over Merril. He didn't care about her happiness. After what he just witnessed, he was done trying to win her affection.

Renata waits at the ranch.

There was a woman who didn't pretend to be something she wasn't. She knew how to please a man, and he needed a woman in the worst way.

She'll help me decide what to do.

Renata always had good ideas. He spurred his horse faster. "I'll show them, and when I'm through, they'll know they've messed with the wrong man."

Chapter 21

Merril Shilo

—

Merril staggered from the pond, more amused than angry.

"You started this game." Nichole's nervous laughter erupted as she backed behind Sugar.

His grin ticked up just a notch on one side. "You've been playin' *your* game a lot longer." Merril lunged at her with a growl—and missed.

She ducked through the brush, and she escaped to the other side of the thicket.

"Damn you, woman!" he hollered with a laugh as he slid through the bushes after her.

The sound of her amusement floated back to him as she ran. Her bare legs flashed beneath her chemise. She looked back at him, her hair a riot of curls. Just as he caught her, she tripped and pulled them both into the tall grass.

Three gunshots barked as bullets whistled overhead.

Nichole froze. "Was that... gunfire?" She tried to sit up.

"Shit." Merril pushed her head down. "Stay low." He peeked over the grass toward the shooter. "What the hell's the matter with you?" he yelled at their assailant. He ducked as another bullet flew over their meager cover.

"I got no quarrel with you, Shilo," an unfamiliar voice called. "It's that bitch you got with ya. She and I have some business to take care of. Send her out, and you can be on your way."

He looked at Nichole. "Do you know him?"

The color had drained from her face, and her eyes were wide with fright. "His name is Blackwood Jones."

"Why does he want to shoot you?"

She opened her mouth, then closed it again and shook her head. "It's a long story."

"How long can it be?" Merril shook his head. "In one day, you've managed to make a mortal enemy—one that packs a six-shooter."

"Well... you've got a gun, too."

"I do." He gave her an annoyed look. "But it's soaked. It won't fire."

"Oh, yeah." Tears welled in her eyes. "He was supposed to be gone. Jimmy Leigh made him leave last night."

"Seems he came back."

"Hey, Shilo," Jones hollered. "I'm givin' ya ten seconds to send 'er out, or you're both dead. Matters little to me."

"Listen, and do exactly what I say," Merril whispered in her ear. "To your left, about ten feet away, are some low bushes. Crawl on your belly until you get there. Follow them back toward the pond. Midnight is on the other side of the thicket. Mount him and stay there until I come for you." He searched her eyes. He could feel her tremble with fear. "Can you do that?"

She nodded and rolled onto her stomach.

"Good, then go." He pushed her rear down. "Use your elbows. Keep your ass down." He saw her look back as she crawled away. He motioned for her to keep going.

"Time's 'bout up, Shilo. What's it gonna be?"

"I want to talk, Jones." Merril raised his hands above the grass in a show of good faith, and as a distraction from Nichole's movements.

Another shot whizzed past, and Merril dropped back to the ground.

"Next one ain't gonna miss, cowboy," Jones called. "Send out the bitch."

Merril lay on his back and checked his revolver. The powder was soaked. He holstered his gun and looked toward Nichole. She'd disappeared behind the bushes.

I'll have to chance it.

He rolled over and rose to peer through the grass and get his bearings.

Jones stood roughly eighty feet away. The man's horse danced skittishly behind him. The damned fool had dismounted and walked toward him.

He was still far enough away that Jones's aim would be hampered by distance. If Jones had a good aim, he wouldn't miss in another twenty feet.

I need to draw his fire now.

Merril dove from one place to another. Jones fired one shot, and then another.

A sharp pain in his shoulder knocked him back. "Christ!" Merril raised his head and peered at Jones.

Jones stood, waiting. He raised the pistol and took careful aim. His thin lips pulled back from his yellow teeth into a grin. He squeezed the trigger. The hammer slammed into a spent cylinder with a click.

"Goddammit!" Jones yelled and holstered the pistol. "I ain't done with you, Shilo." He reached for the rifle on his saddle but found his horse had shied away from the gunfire.

Merril rose and sprinted into the shelter of the bushes.

Shortly after, Jones's rifle sounded. "I'll find you, Shilo," Jones called. "You won't get far—not with a woman."

Merril emerged on the far side of the thicket and found Nichole seated on Midnight. "Stay low." He pulled himself up behind her with a grimace. "We're gettin' the hell out of here."

"You're hurt." Nichole tried to look, but he stopped her.

"There's no time." He wrapped his arms around her and urged Midnight forward. They fled east across the prairie.

The Highlands branding site lay behind them. The ranches were at equal distance north and south. Jones would catch them before they could turn and reach the safety of either home. He'd have to outdistance Jones and find shelter somewhere ahead.

The bullet wound in his shoulder sent sharp pains down his arm. With each jolt of Midnight's hooves, sparks of light flashed in his vision. He was losing too much blood.

The gunfire behind them ceased, but they would be followed. By how many men—Merril had no idea. Whatever they were going to do, it had to be soon. Loss of blood made him dizzy and nauseous. He saw a line of low brush and trees ahead.

That must be Box Creek.

They'd crossed the eastern edge of the Shilo-Highlands boundary. There was nothing ahead but renegades and rattlesnakes.

If we reach the trees, we'll have to make a stand.

***

Nichole Harris

—

The treeline grew closer as they raced across the open stretch of ground. Nichole cast a cautious glance around Merril's side. There was no one behind them, yet she knew Jones was still back there. On the rise, three riders appeared. They stopped for a moment, and then raced down the other side toward them. She looked over the sweat-soaked mane of Merril's horse. The trees were close—they would be in them within minutes.

Merril's grip on her waist weakened, and he sagged, slipping to one side.

"Merril!" She twisted to gain a hold on him, but instead, her motion caused both of them to fall just short of the trees.

Branches snapped as Midnight continued into the brush.

"Merril, you need to get up!" She cried as she tried to pull him to his feet. "Oh, shit." The right side of his body soaked in blood. His arm stretched out at a strange angle from his shoulder. He'd taken the full impact of the fall on his injured arm.

"Come on, Merril. Come on, come on." She pleaded as his eyes rolled and focused on her frightened face.

"Go, Nic." He pushed her away. "Find Midnight. Get the rifle. It's your best chance."

"What do you mean *my* best chance? You've got to come."

"No, just... go." Merril shook his head, and his breath caught at the movement. "There's not enough time."

"There's plenty of time." She pulled at his belt and glanced up in fear as the riders drew closer. "Please. Try."

"Do what I said. Bring the rifle back here as fast as you can." He pushed himself up with his good arm.

His face bled of color, and she feared he would pass out. She waited, ready to catch him, but he opened his eyes and nodded. "Go. I'll try to make it to cover, at least."

Nichole spun on her bare heel and raced into the trees.

Where was his horse?

She found Midnight not far from where he'd entered the bushes.

"Easy, now," she soothed as she approached. She retrieved the rifle then raced back to Merril.

"Over here."

She heard his call just before she broke the cover and sidestepped to him. "You made it." She held out the rifle to him.

"My arm—I can't hold it."

The hoofbeats of the approaching riders pounded in her ears. They called to one another, but she couldn't make out the words. She looked down at the rifle in her trembling hands. "I can't shoot this." Her chest tightened, and her breath came in short gasps.

"It's easy." Merril smiled at her, his eyes dull and his face pale. "It has a lever action. Pull the lever down, then back—there, that's right. Just like that. Now, place the butt tight against your shoulder. Good."

Nichole looked over at him. Her arms and legs were shaking. "I can't do this, Merril."

"Sure, you can." He gave her a weary smile. "We're out of choices."

"Damn." Nichole held the rifle and exhaled slowly. The entire barrel trembled.

The riders crossed the low field. Nichole watched in horror as all three men pulled rifles from their saddles. "Shit, oh shit."

"Brace yourself between those trees. Stay down. Now, look down the barrel. You have one shot, Nicki, make it count."

"One?" Nichole looked back at him, "What good is one fucking shot?"

"You take one with us." He laughed, then groaned. "Or they scatter. You might have time to pump the lever again. But try to hit one of them."

She peered along the barrel at the one she believed was Jones.

"Wait," he whispered.

As their faces became clear, Nichole pinned the tip of the sight on the closest man, then eased the trigger back. The recoil slammed her against the tree trunk. She had missed. Worse yet, Jones and his companions didn't scatter. Instead, they turned toward them and charged.

"Run." Merril urged, trying to push her away.

"To where?" Nichole searched Merril's eyes for an answer. Jones and his men were almost upon them. There was no place to run. A gunshot rang out, and Nichole buried her face in Merril's uninjured shoulder.

"Nic, look." Merril poked Nichole's arm. "They got him."

"Who?" Nichole raised her head and looked through the bushes. "Who got who?

"Someone shot at Jones and his pals. Whoever they are, they got one of his friends."

Jones turned his horse, yelled at the fallen rider, and gestured toward the line of trees.

Another shot rang out.

Jones dug his spurs into his horse and galloped away with one man, leaving the other on the ground.

"The coward," Merril murmured and closed his eyes.

"Who fired the shots?" She lowered the rifle to the ground and curled beside Merril.

"We'll find out soon enough." He leaned his head against the spindly tree behind him.

They waited in silence. Nichole had nothing to stanch Merril's wound except her hands, and they were filthy. Her chemise was no cleaner. The injury looked bad. His shoulder—either dislodged or broken—was swelling.

"What should I do?" she whispered.

Merril opened his eyes and stared straight ahead. "Don't move."

The urgency in his voice held her and made her stomach drop. Despite his command, she turned her head, inch by inch, in the direction of Merril's gaze and drew in a short gasp.

A tall, dangerous-looking man gazed down at them from his great height. Muscular brown arms folded across his massive chest, and his dark straight hair hung past broad shoulders. Colorful paint decorated his face and chest.

He grunted a command, and Merril nodded. "He wants us to come with him," Merril told her.

"You speak his language?"

"Yes. He's Cheyenne."

"Tell him we're the good guys."

"He probably knows that already." Merril laughed, then grimaced. "Why else would he have shot Jones and not us?"

The Cheyenne grew impatient. He reached down, grabbed Nichole by the arm and hauled her to his side.

She yelped and struggled against his tight grip.

Merril spoke to the brave who grunted a reply and released Nichole's arm.

"What did you tell him?" She rubbed her arm and stepped away from the big man.

"I said you were my wife and I was blood brother to the Cheyenne people."

"He believed you?"

Merril's chuckle turned into a cough. "He's taking a wait and see attitude."

The brave spoke again, and two more dark-haired men appeared. They talked for a moment, and then the two men linked arms beneath Merril's legs and back. They lifted him from the ground.

"It's all right, Nicki," Merril said through clenched teeth. "They're taking us to their chief."

"Their chief's here too?" The big one gripped her arm and led her through the trees.

"Somewhere close. These are renegades, hiding from our army."

There was so much bitterness in his voice when he spoke of the army, Nichole looked back at him in confusion.

"Don't make them mad," Merril warned.

"Don't worry," she called over her shoulder. "I don't want them to go all Blackwood Jones on us."

They followed a path through the brush. The small thicket became darker as the sun dipped lower in the sky. When they drew close to the encampment, Nichole could smell the smoke from a campfire and hear the movement of their animals, but she saw no sign of life, aside from the three who accompanied them. No one spoke. The big Indian had made that clear from the start.

Nichole studied him as they walked. He made no sound as he moved through the trees, only her footsteps were audible in the silence. Her unshod feet became bruised and tender.

The tall warrior wore no shirt but had trousers of light brown animal skin. The other two wore dark blue army pants. Each carried a quiver of arrows and a bow strapped to their backs. Her massive captor held a rifle in his hand, decorated with feathers and leather strips.

Nichole glanced back at Merril. He sat motionless as the Indians carried him, seated upon their locked arms.

The foliage parted, and their group stepped into a clearing. There were three small cook fires. A dozen Indians sat around the fires and spoke to each other in soft voices.

When the big one led them to the center of the camp, the quiet conversations ceased. Her captor made a short speech, motioned for Nichole to stay put, and then entered a conical shelter covered with different types of animal skins.

The men put Merril down near a tree. He gasped in pain at the slight movement.

The braves, who had grown silent at their arrival, muttered to each other as the wait stretched. A few of them rose and approached Nichole. She backed up and bumped into the man who stood guard over Merril. The Indian said something short and forceful to the approaching braves and drew his knife from its sheath.

His point made, the other Indians turned away. The guard looked hard at Nichole as he sheathed his blade, and then turned his cold, dark eyes away from her in disgust. Her attitude changed from one of gratitude to one of fear.

He doesn't want my thanks. He'd just as soon let those men have me.

She shivered as much in apprehension as with chill. The temperature dropped as soon as the sun set and her chemise offered little protection from the cold. She moved to where Merril lay, sat down beside him and wrapped her arms around her legs.

There was something altogether wrong about being here with Indians. She rubbed at the gooseflesh on her arms and looked down at her bare feet.

What was it?

More than once, she'd experienced a sense of displacement. As her memory came back, she'd been beset by conflicting ideas—this is right, no—this is wrong. But not this time. She did not belong in her undergarments in the middle of a bunch of Indians. She tried to shake off the dull ache that began at the front of her head.

Indians.

What did she know about American Indians that evaded her?

Nichole swallowed the lump in her throat and blinked at the annoying tears in her eyes. She was confused, afraid, and thoroughly sick of not having answers. The flap on the conical shelter opened. Nichole came to her feet.

Tall and Ominous was back. He stepped out of the structure and stood to his full height, arms folded across his broad chest.

She held her breath and waited.

Another man followed through the opening and stared solemnly at Nichole. He was a hard, lean man with multiple scars on his dark, hairless chest. He approached and stopped in front of her, studying her in silence.

She returned his stare, afraid to show the fear that overwhelmed her, but too frightened to look away.

The warrior, or chief, she presumed, glanced briefly at Merril then back at her. "Who are you?" he asked, startling her with his excellent English.

"Nichole Harris." She gestured to Merril. "This man is Merril Shilo—"

"I know his name," the chief interrupted. His expression didn't change, and he never looked away from her eyes. "What are you doing here?"

"We were chased—"

"I know you were pursued," he interrupted again.

"If you knew, then why—"

"Be silent." His tone was angry.

Nichole's words died, and her mouth snapped shut.

He motioned to another man who stood in the group of observers.

"This man will see to my brother." The harshness left his voice when he spoke of Merril. It came back when he regarded Nichole. "You will come with me."

The chief turned and disappeared into the shelter.

Nichole hesitated before following him between the flaps.

So, Merril is related to the Cheyenne.

If the chief hadn't been so irritable and grim, she would have questioned him about their relationship. It was doubtful he'd welcome her curiosity.

A small fire burned in the center of the shelter. It warmed her chilled flesh when she entered. Soon, however, the heat became uncomfortable.

Another man, older and smaller, sat cross-legged on the other side of the tent. He only glanced up as she entered, and then returned to his trance-like meditation on the fire.

"Sit." The chief motioned to a place near the door. Nichole sat as he moved around the fire and took a seat beside the old man.

"Why have you come?" Both men stared at her across the flames.

"I'm not sure I understand your question." *Stay calm.* "Three men chased us to the creek. Your men saved us. They brought us here."

The chief shook his head and turned to the white-haired Indian. They spoke in their language for a few moments. When the conversation ended, the chief turned to Nichole again.

"My grandfather asks again." His tone turned formal. "The spirits told him you would come. They say you are searching. What do you seek?"

She had no idea what the spirits meant.

What do I say?

How could White Eagle know they would end up here? What was she searching for? Her past? Her memories? How could he know about that? Nichole shivered despite the heat, and gooseflesh rose on her arms. The silence stretched, and they continued to stare at her, waiting for her answer.

"Your grandfather's spirits are wise." She bowed her head to White Eagle. "I do search, but I don't think I'll find what I am looking for here."

The white-haired man addressed his grandson.

The chief nodded. "White Eagle says you have lost yourself. You are between places. Tell me, how can this be?"

"Um." She swallowed. "It's hard to explain."

Both men watched her and waited.

Her face heated, and she shrugged. "I had an accident. I hit my head." She raised her curls and showed them her scar and stitches. "I injured the part of my brain that keeps my memories. Now I can't remember people or things that happened before the accident."

The chief spoke to White Eagle. Nichole assumed he translated what she had just said. White Eagle shook his head.

"My grandfather does not accept your answer."

"That's the only answer I have." Nichole's breath hitched, and panic fluttered in her chest.

"Silence," he commanded. He raised his hand and pointed two fingers at her. "You believe your words. But they are not true."

White Eagle again spoke to his grandson. The chief's face was puzzled as he turned to Nichole. "You do not belong to this place and yet you stand in it," he translated. He looked from Nichole to his grandfather, and then back at her.

She wanted to laugh, or cry, or even scream, but she fought it down.

White Eagle began to rock back and forth where he sat. A strange, low chant filled the tiny enclosure with its haunting melody.

"We must go." The chief rose to his feet. "My grandfather desires to learn more. Come."

Chapter 22

Nichole Harris

—

The chief left the tent and Nichole followed close behind. She had no desire to stay and watch White Eagle converse with his spirits.

Outside, a breeze rustled the leaves on the bushes and trees. It chilled the sweat on her skin, and she gulped at the cool air. The chief stalked away and left her to wonder where she should go. She turned, and the big guy stood beside her. He motioned for her to follow and strode away.

She struggled to keep up. The campfires were shielded, and she didn't want to lose him in the dark. None of the men looked up as she passed, their attention diverted with eating or mending equipment.

Tall and Ominous stopped beside a small army pup tent and pointed at a blanket on the ground. She looked from the woven covering to her guide, but he'd walked away. Her stomach growled. When had she last eaten? Breakfast? No—it had been dinner, last night.

I wonder where they've taken Merril.

She lowered herself to the blanket and rubbed her feet. The refreshing coolness had worn out its welcome, and the chill of evening descended. Hungry, cold, and no way to ask about Merril.

Marvelous.

Easy to identify, Tall and Ominous returned from across the camp carrying two carved bowls in his oversized hands. He stopped beside her, then handed her a bowl of thin brown gravy.

"Thank you." She smiled up at the huge man and cradled the warmth close to her chest.

His stern face softened, and he smiled. "Toma."

"Thank you, Toma." She inclined her head.

He lowered himself beside her on the blanket. "Toma," he repeated and then pointed at her.

"Nicki." She touched her chest. "I'm Nicki."

"Nic-ki." Toma gave a satisfied nod of his head and began to eat.

She observed him for a moment, then followed his example and scooped the thin gravy with the pieces of beef. When the last drop was gone, she licked her fingers and set her bowl aside. Her gaze touched on the men she could see from where she sat.

Where is Merril?

A few men stood, stretched, and wandered away from the fire. They disappeared into the darkness around the camp. Most stayed seated and spoke in low voices. Their leader was nowhere in sight.

A low moan caught her attention, and she turned to the tent behind her. She looked at Toma for permission, and he motioned for her to go inside.

It was warm and dark inside the structure. Nichole crawled through the opening on her hands and knees, then paused to let her eyes adjust. A subtle movement to her left told her where he lay, and she scooted closer to the sound.

Behind her, Toma folded the entrance flap back allowing the dim light of the campfires to brighten the inside of the shelter.

Merril lay on a woven blanket along one side of the tent. His shoulder wound had been cleaned and bandaged. His arm was bound tight to his body with torn strips of material.

He opened his eyes and lifted his head as she crawled to his side. "Is that you, or am I dreamin' again?" His voice was hoarse.

"It's me." She took his hand and rubbed it against her cheek. "How do you feel?"

"I've been worse, I guess." His eyes closed, and he eased his head back onto the blanket. "I ache all over, and my shoulder is on fire."

She laid her hand against his face. "You have a fever."

"I'm not surprised."

"Nor am I, my brother." The leader ducked into the tent and sat near the opening.

"Gray Wolf." Merril smiled, his eyes were bright with fever. "I'll be damned. I hoped this was your band of renegades. Last I heard, you were raising hell around Laramie."

"True," Gray Wolf nodded. "We fell back to regroup. We are lying low, as you would say. We steal your cattle to eat." A brief smile flashed across Gray Wolf's face, vanishing so quickly Nichole wondered if she'd seen it. "I did not think you would mind, old friend."

"You know I don't. You could have let me know you were here, though. I would have given you the cattle."

"We are outlaws. I would not endanger you by imposing on our friendship."

"How long will you stay?"

"Not long. We move north. Sitting Bull has called for us to gather. Custer would kill us all if he could. It is rumored he plans to ride against the Sioux."

"General Custer?" Nichole looked from Merril to Gray Wolf, a sharp pain seared across her forehead.

Merril's gaze turned to Nichole. "Lieutenant colonel recently, but yes."

"Custer..." *I know this.* "Does Custer's Last Stand sound familiar to you?"

Merril's glazed eyes stared dully at her. "I know who Custer is. I've never heard of his last stand."

"I learned this in school. I'm positive. Custer and his men were wiped out—" She looked from Merril to Gray Wolf, and her voice dropped to a whisper. "—by the Sioux and Cheyenne."

Gray Wolf leaned away from Nichole. His face reflected both wonder and fear. "Where did Custer die?"

"I... um... let me think. I know this." She held one hand to the ache in her temple, the other she held up at Gray Wolf. "One of the northern states. Montana...I think." She opened her eyes and smiled. "He died at the Battle of the Little Bighorn, in Montana."

Merril closed his eyes and lay back on the blanket. "You're wrong."

"She speaks the truth." Gray Wolf's eyes were wide.

"George Custer isn't dead." Merril didn't open his eyes.

Gray Wolf stared at Nichole. He spoke just above a whisper. "It is as he said."

"Who said?" Merril's voice was sharp with annoyance.

"My grandfather."

Merril's eyes snapped open. "White Eagle's with you?"

"Yes. He knew you would come." Gray Wolf rose and left the tent.

Merril raised his head to look at Nichole. "What's this all about?"

She pulled the loose strap of her chemise back on her shoulder. "I don't know," she muttered, hesitating to elaborate.

"Where did you hear of Custer's Last Stand?"

Nichole shrugged in frustration and blinked at the sudden sting of tears. "I don't know Merril. I thought I learned it in school. I shouldn't have said anything, but it was right here, in my head." She pressed her fingers against her forehead.

Merril laid his head back and closed his eyes. He winced whenever he moved, and his face was drawn and pale. "I need to rest." His soft, hoarse voice broke her heart.

"I know. I'm sorry I mentioned Custer. It's like... I knew it happened."

"*Will* happen, Nicki," he corrected sleepily. "Now, let me rest."

She crawled outside. Her mind and heart in turmoil.

The banked fires burned low. Several men sat and talked, but most lay upon the ground.

She walked from the camp into the brush, stopping a few yards away. Silent tears slid down her face. Merril needed a doctor, and she had lost her mind. She wiped her eyes and her nose and turned back toward the tent.

Toma loomed up out of the darkness in front of her.

"Holy shit, Toma." She gripped his arm with one hand and held her chest with the other. "You scared the crap out of me." She chuckled at her fright and looked up at the tall brave. "You need a bell around your neck."

Toma grunted and reached down to touch a teardrop that trembled from her chin. He looked from his fingertip to her eyes and shook his head, a question in his gaze.

"I'm just tired, Toma. Sleep?" She placed her palms together and laid her head on top of them.

Toma nodded and vanished into the thicket in the direction of their camp.

She followed, trying to imitate his silent movements but without success. Her bare feet had taken a beating today and were more than tender.

Outside Merril's tent, Toma waited with an old coat draped over his arm.

"Nic-ki sleep." He pointed to the blanket on the ground in front of the shelter. "I watch."

She raised an eyebrow at him and smiled, and then sank to her knees on the mat. She took the coat and wrapped it around her shoulders. "You're not so bad." She curled into a ball on the blanket and shivered

A few feet away, Toma sank gracefully to the ground by his bedroll.

"You're just a big softy at heart." Her eyes closed.

***

Jason Harris

—

Jason gritted his teeth in a fury and watched Jim pace around the dining room table.

What the hell had he been thinking?

"I swear, Jason. She said she was coming right back here." His deep voice boomed across the room. "The last I saw her was around noon or better at the branding site. She told me she could make it home from there." He turned and glared back at Jason "Hell, I know she could have."

"We thought she was with you." Amy sat her teacup in its saucer and glanced from Jason to Jim.

"She should have been with you, Jim, the whole time." Jason tapped a pencil on the polished wood table. "I thought you knew better than to let her go off on her own. It's your fault she's lost."

"Do you think I don't know that? I could kick myself for lettin' that little girl ride away by herself. I told her to come straight back here." He pointed to the floor and glared at Jason, and then turned and paced away to look out the front window. "For all I know, she could be lying out there, hurt." His voice dropped to a whisper. "Or worse."

"She's not dead." Amy's calm voice caught both men's attention.

"What?" Jason snapped. His glare turned from Jimmy to his wife.

"I said, she's not dead." Amy enunciated clearly to Jason. Her serene eyes held his.

"I hope you're right," Jim muttered, his face gray with worry.

"She's all right, Jim. I know she is." Amy rose from the table and rested a comforting hand on Jim's arm. "You couldn't have changed what happened. Nichole would have found another way to go off by herself. Believe me. Please."

"Thank you." Jim smiled for the first time since he walked in the house. "Jason doesn't appreciate you enough."

"He will." She smiled at Jim's compliment and winked at Jason as she crossed the dining room and began to ascend the stairs. "But for now, I'm going to bed. Tomorrow promises to be quite a day."

Jason's curious gaze slid from Amy's disappearing skirts to the pencil he fumbled with his hands. "There's no use going back out tonight," he commented morosely. "We'd never find her in the dark."

"We have to do something." Jim crossed the room and stood before Jason. "We could put the men on horseback with torches. Ride from here to the branding site. Make sure I didn't miss anything."

"No. You didn't miss anything this afternoon." Jason rubbed his face and eyed the tall foreman. "She's not between here and the branding site. Nichole's gone off somewhere else."

"Damned if I don't know that, Jase." Jim turned back to the window and stared into the night. "I just wish I knew where she was."

"Tomorrow we'll ride to The Shilo. For all we know, she's been there the whole time. If not, then we'll search from there. Either way, you'd better get some rest."

"Yeah." Jim slipped his hat onto his head. Anxiety made him look far older than his thirty-five years. "That shit ain't likely to happen. Good night, Jason."

"Good night." Jason watched Jimmy Leigh head out the door and disappear into the darkness. Both anger and sympathy surged in his chest at Jim.

Where could she have gone?

Jim was right. The branding site wasn't far, or hard to find, especially in the light of day.

Then where could she be?

He shook his head and ran a weary hand through his golden hair.

Where in blazes are you, Nicki?

Abruptly, the pencil stopped its rat-tat-tat. A cold sweat broke out on Jason's forehead.

Jones.

That one name—one thought—sent a chill of terror rippling along his spine. Blackwood Jones. If that son-of-a-bitch touched one hair on Nicki's head, he'd kill him.

Chapter 23

Nichole Harris

—

Nichole shivered in the darkness, and her eyelids fluttered open.

What was that?

The banked fires cast no light across the camp, and clouds covered the night sky. She huddled beneath the oversized coat and stared into the black silence—senses alert.

Soft footsteps drew her attention, and she lifted her head. The raised perspective showed the muted glow of the small fires. In front of her, Toma stood, outlined by the red coals.

Has he been there all night?

A voice spoke in hushed tones to Toma. Then the coals disappeared as a shadow passed to the front of Merril's tent and slipped inside. Unintelligible voices and the sound of movement came from inside the small shelter. First one, and then another shadow emerged from the tent. The soft stir of their footsteps disappeared into the camp.

Where would they take Merril in the middle of the night?

She gripped the coat around her shoulders, sat up and leaned toward the big man. "Toma," she hissed as quietly as she could.

Toma turned toward her makeshift bed and knelt on one knee. "Nic-ki sleep."

"Where has he taken Merril? I want to go with him."

"No." His deep voice was gentle. "You sleep."

So, he does understand English.

"I can't go back to sleep. I want to go with Merril."

Toma rose and stared into the dark camp. After several moments, he spoke in a hushed voice. "Wait." Then he vanished into the dark without a sound.

Nichole waited.

In the bushes along the creek, the faint stir of morning birds and animals intruded on the night's silence. The sky lightened to gray as she chewed her lip and prayed for patience. Then morning broke with a brilliant display. The sky changed from dark gray to orange-gold when a glimmer of sunlight slipped between the horizon and the cloud cover.

She tried to find someone she recognized in the weird red light, but the camp of strangers had lurched into motion. She blinked, and Toma stood beside her.

He's a damned Ninja.

He motioned for her to follow him and moved away.

She tightened the leather jacket around her chilled shoulders. Her calf muscles cramped as she staggered upright. She rubbed them for a moment, never taking her eyes from her tall friend, and then limped after him through the camp on sore feet.

Toma stopped before the shelter she'd been in yesterday. He turned his eyes away, crossed his arms, and watched the men break camp.

"Thank you, Toma." Nichole entered the tipi.

The white-haired man sat in the same place and chanted to the fire. Merril and Gray Wolf were seated on either side of the fire, both silent. They looked up as she entered.

"Sit," Gray Wolf commanded in a quiet voice. He indicated a fourth seat that would make the square complete. "Be silent."

Nichole sank to the ground beside Merril. She studied him in the firelight. Rest appeared to have done him some good. His face had color, and the improvised bandage had stopped his bleeding. He needed some real medical attention though.

He needs a hospital.

Dark circles shadowed his eyes, and he grimaced in pain with every movement. He offered her a smile and returned his attention to White Eagle.

The shaman's low, hypnotic chant grew louder, and he swayed in time with his song. He continued that way for some time.

Both Gray Wolf and Merril gave White Eagle their full attention.

The chant came to an abrupt halt. In the sudden silence, White Eagle raised his arms and spoke in a slow, monotone voice.

She didn't understand the words, but from Gray Wolf's wary glances and the stunned expression on Merril's face, she knew the old man spoke about her.

White Eagle's abrupt speech ended, and he lowered his arms to resume his rhythmic chant.

She sat forward to ask Merril what he had said, but Merril forestalled her with his hand. He looked at Gray Wolf.

The Indian leader gave a short nod then turned back to his grandfather.

Merril bent close to Nichole and whispered. "White Eagle said time is a child's toy to the Great Spirit. Life and eternity are one within His grasp." Merril paused for a moment, then lowered his voice even more. "He said you walk the path laid before you by the wolf spirit—the spirit who warned White Eagle you would come."

"Why is this about me?" Nichole spoke softly in Merril's ear. "What path?"

He held up a finger and looked at his friend's grandfather.

White Eagle's chant had paused once more, and he raised his arms again. His voice, low and old—his words unintelligible, but filled with power.

Merril leaned close and put his lips beside her ear, never taking his eyes from the old man. "Once a door has opened, the wind may pass through. You are that wind. Time holds the key."

Nichole turned her face toward Merril and mouthed, "What does that mean?"

Merril shook his head, his attention fixed on White Eagle.

The old man's trance deepened. Beads of perspiration collected across his brow as he continued to speak.

Merril leaned close again. "A day will come when the wind choose a direction." He paused to listen, then continued. "There will come a time when the door must close."

"I don't understand," she whispered.

"Neither do I." His breath tickled her ear. "He says your past will haunt you, and your future will divide."

Nichole sat back. White Eagle's words didn't make sense, even translated. Why were his cryptic remarks about her? She pushed the coat off her shoulders and sat in the silent heat, wishing for the ritual to end.

White Eagle's supplication to the spirit continued through the morning. Her back ached from sitting motionless on the hard ground. She cast a glance at Gray Wolf and Merril. How did they sit like this for so long?

Gray Wolf added more wood to the fire and the heat inside the tent became unbearable.

The sun was well into the sky when White Eagle ceased to chant and became as still as a stone.

"We will leave now." Gray Wolf stood in one fluid motion. "Grandfather must rest."

Nichole struggled to her feet and wobbled. She pushed her tangled hair out of her face and brushed at her chemise, but it didn't help. By the light of the fire, she could see the bottom trim had torn loose and trailed behind her, as filthy as the rest of her. Her calves were scratched and bruised, and her unshod feet were cut and tender. Her sorry state didn't distract her from what she had witnessed.

"What else did he say?" she asked as Merril followed her out of the tent.

"A lot," Merril replied uneasily. "Most you wouldn't understand, 'cause I sure don't."

"Tell me anyway."

"I will," he evaded. "Right now, I need to figure out how to get you home. Your cousin's going to be worried sick about you."

When they reached Merril's tent, he lowered himself onto the blanket with great care, cautious of his shoulder.

"You need a doctor." The color in his face had been from the fire. In the light of day, his skin was pale. She ran her hand across his brow and down the side of his face. He still had a fever.

"That's the other reason we need to get home."

She settled beside him on the blanket. "It was bad, wasn't it? What White Eagle said about me."

Merril shook his head and eased himself into a more comfortable position.

"It wasn't bad, Nic, it just didn't make much sense." He fell silent as Gray Wolf approached.

Gray Wolf carried two canteens. He handed one to Merril and one to her before sinking to his haunches in front of Merril. "We will be gone by sunset." He looked and spoke only to Merril. "I wish I could offer you more time to recover, but we must keep moving."

Merril nodded. "I know. Where will you go?"

"North." Gray Wolf's voice held both determination and sadness. "I think we will not meet again, my friend."

"I fear you may be right," Merril replied softly.

Gray Wolf reached out and grasped Merril's good arm. "I wish you great happiness, my brother."

Toma entered the camp leading Midnight and two other horses. He stopped beside Gray Wolf.

"Toma will ride with you." Gray Wolf rose to his feet. "Then he will ride like the wind to catch us. Be at peace, my friend." Gray Wolf turned and walked away.

Nichole got to her feet. "How do you know him?" she asked, as she helped Merril to stand.

"I traveled with his family to Sand Creek." His eyes were sad as his gaze followed Gray Wolf across the encampment. "Most of his family died there."

"You were there?" Nichole asked in concern.

Merril shook his head, his eyes still on Gray Wolf. "I was at Fort Laramie when the soldiers came. I didn't know about the massacre until it was over. He and I—we were little more than children."

"Gray Wolf is a bitter man who's bound to meet a bitter end someday. Not that I blame him, or any of them, for that matter." Merril sighed and took Midnight's reins from Toma. "Gray Wolf's hunting party was not at the Sand Creek camp when Chivington butchered his people. He blames himself."

Nichole stared wide-eyed at Merril—speechless—finally taking the reins from Toma.

Toma looked over her head and refused to meet her eyes. Then he held out a pair of moccasins to her.

"Are these for me?" She looked from the leather footwear to Toma.

Toma ignored her and kept his gaze on Merril who struggle to mount his horse.

Once in the saddle, Merril turned to Toma and spoke to him in his native tongue. Toma replied, and Merril smiled.

"He says they are a gift from his people to Lost Wind, wife of Dark Moon."

Around the camp, the men were preparing to depart. Several of them glanced their way.

"You are Dark Moon, I take it?" She looked up at Merril.

"I am," he replied with his half-grin. "And you, my love, are my beautiful wife, Lost Wind. Welcome to the family."

"Tell them I am sincerely grateful." She bowed her head to Toma, and then looked back at Merril.

Merril faced Toma but spoke loud enough for the men in the camp to hear.

Nichole slipped the soft leather shoes onto her torn feet. They were old moccasins, well-worn and just a little large, but they were perfect, in her eyes. She saw several of the men nod while Merril spoke.

"Thank you," she whispered to Toma.

He held the stirrup as she mounted the gelding they captured from Jones's fallen friend. Toma nodded but never met her gaze. He turned and pulled himself onto the back of his spotted horse.

"Let's go home." Merril's smile was tired as he winked at Nichole. "Your cousin will see me in irons, I know."

They rode away from the encampment, but Merril's injury kept their pace slow. As they rode, Nichole's thoughts returned to White Eagle.

I must know what he said.

She urged her horse to catch up and keep pace with Merril's. "Can I ask you something?"

His attention came to her slowly. Both fatigue and pain apparent on his face. "What's that, sweetheart?"

Her question about White Eagle died in her throat. "How are you still in the saddle? We should stop."

He shook his head. "No. We'll be there soon." His gaze focused on her. "Talk to me. I feel better when I hear your voice."

She stared at him—uncertain—then spoke her question. "Does White Eagle actually talk to spirits?"

"I don't know. Gray Wolf believes he does." He stared at her for a moment. "Did you notice he wouldn't look at you when we left?"

"Not really. Your friend didn't like me to begin with." She searched his face. "Are you saying there's more to his behavior than simple... dislike?"

Merril nodded. "White Eagle said to look at you was to see one who had walked through the halls of the dead. But that's a rough translation." He tried to laugh, but it turned into a cough, and he winced.

Nichole's stomach lurched. "That has to be about the carriage accident. You said you were afraid you'd lost me. That must be what he meant."

Merril remained silent for a while. When he spoke, his head lowered so that she had to strain to hear him. "White Eagle believes you crossed from life into death."

"Well, that's ridiculous." She stared at Merril's gray face. Their talk had tired him. He wouldn't be able to stay in the saddle much longer. She pulled on her reins and fell behind.

Did he believe White Eagle?

She glanced back at Toma.

He looked over her head and past her as if she wasn't there.

Chapter 24

Nichole Harris

—

The line of brush along Box Elder Creek had long since disappeared when Merril held up his hand. "Let's stop for a spell."

Nichole slipped gratefully to the ground and winced when her sunburned shoulder brushed against her mount.

"You're a bit red." Merril walked around Midnight and opened one of his saddlebags. He pulled out a wrinkled blue shirt. "I should have thought of this earlier. Here." He shook the shirt out and handed it to her. "It'll keep the sun off your shoulders."

"What about you?" she asked, and then glanced away in embarrassment. His muscular chest and back were tanned almost as dark as Toma's.

"I'll be fine." The lopsided grin brought out the long dimple on the side of his face. "I'm more concerned about what Jason will say when he sees you. Your sunburn's the least of it."

Nichole shrugged. She couldn't think on that. She knew how bad she looked. "How's your shoulder?"

"Tight and sore as hell." He turned around and surveyed the barren landscape of grass and sky. "We're on Shilo land now. We'll be home soon."

"It went quicker going the other way." Nichole eased the blue shirt over her tender shoulders.

"We were movin' a bit faster." He winked at her and smiled.

She leaned against her mount and stretched her back as she took stock of his condition. Her chest tightened with concern. He tried to be playful to ease her fears, but he wasn't doing well. His face was sallow, and beneath his dull eyes were dark circles.

His fever's back.

Their brief stop ended and Merril helped her mount, and then pulled himself onto Midnight's saddle. "Another hour and we'll have you home."

Nichole nodded and fell into line behind him. Fatigue and exposure made her nauseous. She could only imagine how much worse Merril felt. They rode in silence for another quarter-mile.

Ahead to the west, the sky grew dark and threatening. The horizon disappeared, and a low wall of clouds rolled across the grassland toward them.

"All hell's about to break loose," Merril commented over his shoulder as a clap of thunder swept past the riders.

"We're not going to make it before the rain, are we?" The wind picked up and tossed Nichole's snarled curls about her head.

His response was lost in another clap of thunder.

Toma called out, and Merril's head came up. "On the ridge," Merril said. He slid his rifle from the saddle scabbard.

A quarter-mile south, on a low rise across the flat expanse of grass, several riders watched their progress.

"Do you think it's Jason?" Nichole whispered to Merril as she pulled beside him.

"Or Jones," Merril replied and nodded to Toma.

Toma pulled his rifle from behind him and held it ready.

The three moved forward, wary of the other group as they approached the ridge.

"It's Jason." Merril's voice was flat. He laid his rifle across his lap. "And Kevin." He glanced at Nichole and raised one eyebrow.

Nichole looked down at her attire: a filthy torn chemise under Merril's wrinkled shirt, bare scratched legs ending in a pair of old moccasins. Her calves and arms were sunburned, and by the sting at the tip of her nose, her face as well. Her gaze lifted to Merril. "What do we tell them?"

"The truth, I guess. Well, most of it." His smile widened. "This will be interesting."

Six mounted men waited for them. Three were men she'd met at The Highlands. Jim, Jason, and Kevin rounded out the number.

The riders moved to meet them.

Nichole could just make out the expressions on the faces she knew. Jim appeared relieved, while Jason looked angry, his jaw clenched and his face red beneath his blond hair and black, flat crown hat. Her appraisal of their rescuers stopped at Kevin.

Kevin's eyes bulged from his flushed face as his horse raced ahead of the others. "That savage bastard!" Kevin bellowed and pulled his rifle from his saddle scabbard.

"Kevin, stop!" Jason yelled.

Instead, Kevin cocked the lever action on the rifle, raised himself from the saddle, and took aim.

Merril cocked his rifle, and with a grimace of pain, brought the weapon to his shoulder and aimed at his brother.

"What's he doing?" Nichole stared in horror as Kevin approached them. "He's lost his mind."

Jason and Jim had kicked their horses into motion to catch Kevin.

From the corner of her eye, Nichole saw Toma stop beside her and raise his rifle at Kevin.

"Well, shit." She shook the reins and kicked her horse forward, darting between the two groups, and then pulled back hard on the reins. Her mount reared in protest, and she hugged the saddle with her knees to keep from falling. "What's wrong with you, Kevin?" Her voice broke as she fought to stay seated. Her horse spun and reared again. "Are you going to shoot us?"

"Damn it, Nicki," Merril said as Midnight shot past her and raced toward Kevin.

Kevin didn't appear to notice either his brother or Nichole. His sight was pinned on the big Indian as he squeezed the trigger.

The butt-end of Merril's rifle caught Kevin beneath the chin. The impact lifted Kevin from the saddle with a wretched crack. Kevin hit the ground on his back. He tried to rise but fell back to his hands and knees. His head hung down, and he wheezed in short gasps. Blood ran from his open mouth.

Merril slid from Midnight and staggered to his brother. "What the hell are you thinking?" His voice was harsh as he glared at Kevin. Merril reached down and gripped his brother by the collar.

Kevin's head lolled back, the color in his face returning as he gulped air, his mouth full of blood.

"Why are you so bull-headed ignorant?" Merril shook him again. "Christ, I can smell the whiskey from here. What's wrong with you, Kevin?"

"That's enough, Merril." Jason slid from his mount, his voice cold and hard. "I said, that's enough."

Jason grabbed Merril's shoulder, but Merril pulled away from his grip and stumbled back. "Keep your hands off me." Blood ran from his bandaged shoulder down his tanned torso. The bandage was brown and soaked with blood.

Toma laid his rifle across his legs and watched the reunion in silence.

Nichole climbed down from her horse.

How can Toma know these are friends?

Satisfied he wouldn't shoot her cousin, she ran to Merril's side.

"I want to know what's happened," Jason yelled at Merril and then turned to her. "And I want to know right now."

A crack of thunder followed his words. He gestured at Kevin, who staggered to his feet with the help of one of The Highlands' ranch hands. "He couldn't have any worse thoughts than I have. For Christ's sake, you've been gone for two days."

"Nicki's fine." Merril's face was as white as Kevin's. Tight lines of pain creased his brow and around his mouth. "She's been with me."

"Fine, you say?" Jason bellowed, his chiseled features contorted in rage. "With you she's fine? Where are her clothes, Merril?" Jason turned his wrath on Nichole. "Where the hell are your goddamned clothes?"

"If you would just shut up for one minute—"

Jason's hand cracked across her cheek.

Caught off guard, she spun and fell to her knees. She shook her head in disbelief and glared at her cousin.

"Why you—" Merril started at Jason, then stopped.

Jason had pulled a small revolver from his vest. "I'll say this just once, Merril Shilo, and I mean it most sincerely. I may not be able to stop dealing with your half of The Shilo, but by God, you'll leave my cousin alone." He jerked his head at Toma. "Who the hell is that?"

"His name is Toma." Merril wiped his hand across his face. He reached out a hand to help Nichole stand, but Jason raised the small pistol again. Merril stopped and faced Jason.

"He's Cheyenne," Merril stated in a calm even voice. "If it hadn't been for Toma's aim with that rifle, Nic and I would be dead now."

"Jones?" Jason queried, and Merril nodded. Crystal blue and green-gold eyes met and held in both a challenge and complete understanding.

Nichole lurched to her feet. A husky sob escaped her throat and rose in a frustrated scream as she turned to face the men. Her chin jutted toward her cousin. The side of her face where Jason slapped her flamed beneath her sunburn. She pushed the tangled hair from her face and pointed at her cousin. "You're crazy." Hysteria took hold, and she threw her arms in the air and screamed. "You're all fucking crazy."

"Nicki..." Jason warned. His pistol still leveled at Merril's bandaged arm and chest.

She fled backward, out of his reach. "Do you care what happened to us?" She stumbled on the uneven ground, and then regained her balance, still backing away. "Are you blind? Merril's been shot and needs medical attention, and this asshole tries to shoot us." She pointed at Kevin who watched her through bloodshot eyes. "Then you hit me and pull a gun on Merril. What the hell is wrong with this picture, Jason?" She turned and ran.

"Nicki!" Jason yelled at her retreating back.

She wobbled past Toma and screamed in rage at the sky.

"Hell." Jason threw the pistol to the ground at Merril's feet and chased her. "Nicki." His voice softened as he came up behind her.

She spun and glared at him with tear-filled eyes. "Don't you touch me."

"Nicki, I—"

"Get away," she shouted as sobs erupted.

Jason grabbed her arm just as she turned to run again.

"No! Let me go." She punched Jason in the chest and arms. Her fist slid past his face.

He pulled her close and wrapped his arms around her. He held her against his chest as her efforts to escape him lessened. In the end, she clung to him as all the terror and anger rushed out in a storm of bitter tears.

"I'm sorry, Nicki." He smoothed her hair and plucked a leaf from it. "I was terrified for you. I thought you'd been hurt or killed. Then to see you like this—I was wrong. Please, say you'll forgive me."

She nodded, unable to speak. Jason rocked her gently in his arms. After a moment, she swallowed her tears and disengaged herself from Jason, wiping her eyes. "I'm sorry, too."

She moved away from her cousin and captured her horse's reins, and then hoisted herself up and looked down at Jason with red-rimmed eyes.

"Hear me, Jason Harris," she hissed. "You have nothing to say about who I choose to see. I don't intend to fight with you about this now, or ever. I will do as I see fit." Their blue eyes met and clashed, held by love and doubt. "Don't expect me to seek your approval and don't *ever* hit me again." She pulled the reins away and turned her attention to Toma.

"Goodbye, Toma," she said softly to her friend, knowing he would understand. "Thank you."

Toma nodded his head once, but never looked at her.

She turned her mount toward Merril and the rest of the search party.

Jason retrieved his revolver from the ground and mounted his mare.

"Let's go home," Jimmy Leigh called to the others as they turned to head south across the valley.

Merril raised his good arm and waved to Toma.

The tall Indian lifted his rifle high above his head in reply and then rode swiftly back the way they came.

Nichole gazed after Toma, sorry to see the gentle giant leave. A cold, heavy rain began to fall just as a movement to her left caught her eye.

"No!" Her scream echoed across the grassy plain, but she was too late.

The sharp crack of a rifle stung her ears. A spot of red appeared in the center of Toma's broad back. He slipped slowly from the saddle and fell to the ground.

"That ought to teach those damned red bastards not to steal Shilo cattle," Kevin shouted as he slid his Winchester back into its scabbard. His eyes were glazed with hate and satisfaction. Kevin cocked his head and smiled sardonically at Merril.

Jim edged his mount between the two brothers. "Don't do it, Merril," he cautioned, as Merril reached for his Colt. "That won't change anything, and you'd be putting your own neck on the line."

"This murdering bastard deserves to die, Jim." Merril's voice was ragged, filled with loathing and disgust at Kevin.

"The judge won't see it that way. It ain't fair or right, but no one's gonna take any special circumstances into account."

"He was our friend," Merril yelled at his brother's smirk.

Jason and Nichole turned their mounts and raced toward the fallen warrior and slid from their saddles.

Nichole fell to her knees beside her friend. She placed her hand on his back, then turned her head to watch Merril.

Merril yanked Midnight's reins, turning away from Kevin, and followed Jason and Nichole to where Toma lay. He dismounted beside their friend as lightning flashed. A deafening crash of thunder followed immediately and rolled away across the plain. Merril knelt in the wet grass beside Nichole.

She leaned against Merril and glanced up at Jason. "He's dead. Why would Kevin shoot him in the back? He—" She covered her face with her hands, unable to continue.

"I suppose you're goin' to bury that son-of-a-bitch now?" Kevin called at them as he wheeled his mount about in the rain. "Well, I ain't wastin' any more time here. Yah!" His horse shot forward and disappeared beyond the ridge.

Merril rose to follow Kevin, but Nichole grabbed his hand. "Let him go." Her voice was hushed and broke as sobs wracked her shoulders.

Merril squeezed her hand and turned his head away. "God, I hate this." Merril stared back over the trail they'd just ridden.

"He's sick, Merril," Jason said. "He did this to hurt you."

Merril nodded and lifted his face into the rain. "We can't leave Toma here." Rain plastered his hair to his head, and water ran in rivulets down his face.

"Lloyd, grab a blanket. We'll take him to The Highlands," Jason directed.

Lloyd, Tom, and John dismounted. Lloyd untied a blanket from his bedroll and spread it on the wet ground beside Toma. Together, the men rolled the tall Indian onto the blanket and tied it tight around his body. Then, they lifted and draped him across his pony.

"We have to get you out of this weather," Jason said softly to Nichole.

She shivered, and her teeth chattered as the ranch hands rode away. Hatred of Kevin boiled inside her but was small compared to the ache in her heart for Toma. She had been so afraid of him at first, and then came to know his gentle soul.

Lloyd led the pony bearing Toma toward The Highlands.

Jason wrapped his jacket around Nichole, helped her to her feet, and guided her to her mount.

"I'll go with Merril," Jim announced. Another crash of thunder rolled across the plains. Far to the west, a clear line of blue sky appeared. "I'll make sure he gets back to The Shilo safely and know things are—good there. I'll send one of their men for Doc."

"Thank you," Nichole said to Jim and saw Jason nod as well.

"Can you make it?" Jim asked Merril.

Merril pulled himself onto Midnight's saddle. A shiver shook him even as he nodded to Jim and he lifted his gaze to Nichole. "I'll see you soon, Nicki." Then, he grinned at Jason.

"He wants me to shoot him," Jason whispered to Nichole.

Nichole watched her foreman and Merril ride away. "He doesn't look good."

"You don't look much better. Let's get you home and into a hot bath."

"Will Kevin try anything?" Nichole tracked Merril and Jim until they disappeared into the rain.

"He won't. Not with Jim there. Come on now, let's go home."

Nichole shook the reins and rode beside Jason. "Jim can't stay there forever, though," she whispered.

Chapter 25

Jason Harris

—

Jason lifted his face to the last droplets falling from a blue sky. The storm had blown east and left a gorgeous rainbow in its wake. "Look at the rainbow, Nicki."

Nichole nodded but continued to stare at her reins. The skin on her bright red nose and the tangled rat's nest of her hair were bound to give Jeanne fits when she saw them. His cousin looked like a ragamuffin.

I'm more concerned with her frame of mind.

She hadn't said a word since they parted company with Merril and Jim.

Their horses climbed the slight incline into the yard and stopped in front of the house.

Lloyd waited for them on the porch. He took the lead of Nichole's mount in one hand and steadied her with the other as she dismounted. After he gathered Jason's reins, he headed toward the stable.

"The Indian?" Jason called to Lloyd, one foot on the porch.

"He's in the barn." Lloyd paused and stared at Jason. "Not sure what to do with him."

"We'll talk to Merril." Jason rubbed his hand over his eyes. "He might know how to contact the man's people. If not, he'll know their customs."

Lloyd nodded and continued to the stable.

Nichole remained where she was, staring at her dust-covered moccasins.

Jason took her elbow and guided her up the step and into the house.

Once inside, Nichole shrugged out of Jason's jacket and handed it to him. "Here," she said softly. "I'm going to my room."

Concern kept his gaze on his cousin as she mounted the stairs. He stood at the base, jacket folded over his arm, and watched her drag herself up each step. "Everyone will want to know what happened."

"Tell them what you like." Her words floated down to him as she disappeared from view.

He draped the jacket over a high-backed dining room chair and ran a weary hand over his face.

What else could happen?

He'd send men out again this afternoon to look for Jones. If the bastard were smart, he would have hightailed it out of the territory.

As if the whole fiasco with Nichole and Jones weren't enough, Renata had hatched some new scheme. The note she handed him this morning at The Shilo made that plain enough. He pulled the scrap of paper from his vest and read it again.

J ~

I have made new plans and set them in motion.

Others are now involved, but you should not be displeased.

It will not be long now. Trust me.

~ R

Jason folded the note and replaced it in his pocket.

What new plan? What others?

A knot tightened between his shoulders. His eyes moved to the stairs. Whatever Renata planned, she would have to call it off. Nichole had been through too much already.

"You've returned."

Amy's voice startled him. "Only just." He smiled. "Nicki went up to her room."

"Is she all right?" Amy seated herself across the table from where Jason stood.

"I think so. She needs a bath and a good rest. It's been one hell of an afternoon—for everyone."

"What happened?" Amy's eyes filled with concern.

Jason pulled out the chair and tossed his hat on the table as he took a seat. "She wasn't at The Shilo, but Kevin was. When he heard she was missing, he insisted he come with us. Jim found a trail, and we followed it east." He looked up at Amy. "We found them on their way back, from wherever the heck they were. Nichole, without clothes. Merril with no shirt, and shot to hell. The biggest damn Indian I've ever seen rode with them."

"Nichole was naked?" Amy's brows rose, and her eyes grew large.

"No... not exactly. She had on her undergarments and a shirt of Merril's. She's badly sunburned. I know her skin will blister and peel."

"Who's the dead man Lloyd brought in?"

Jason sighed and ran his hand through his hair. "The big Indian, and a friend of Merril's. Kevin shot him in the back as he was leaving."

"He did *what*?" Amy rose from her chair in shock.

Jason nodded. "It seems our neighbors' disagreements are about to come to a head."

Amy sank into her chair, reached across the table and took her husband's hand. "Should you cancel the barbecue?"

"No." Jason shook his head and lifted his gaze from their hands to Amy's face. "We can't do that. The men deserve it. Besides, the invitations have been sent. Other ranchers have made arrangements to come and stay the night." He murmured, "There won't be any trouble between the Shilos. Not here."

Jason placed his other hand on top of Amy's. "I'm glad you're here. We haven't had much time together since you've been back, have we?"

"No," she said softly. "We haven't."

"I've not behaved as a good husband."

"What? Why do you say that? There's no need—"

"Please, Amy." He waved his hand to dispel her arguments. "You should have been here, at the ranch, instead of in Denver." Jason paused to collect his thoughts and studied his wife's face.

She's so beautiful and carries a peaceful spirit within her. She's had to, being married to me.

"Amy." He spoke with hesitation. "There are things you don't know—things I've been involved with that if you knew—"

"Don't," she interrupted. "Not right now. There will be time later for confession and absolution." She leaned forward and ran a hand along Jason's firm jaw. "Besides, even if I knew, it wouldn't make any difference to me. Not between us. We started over when I came home."

Jason pressed her soft hand against his lips, eyes closed and nodded, expelling a sigh of relief. His thoughts moved to another concern. He opened his eyes and gazed across the table. "Something must be done about Jones. I'm afraid he'll come back again."

"He will," Amy stated with conviction. "Hate can drive people mad. Jones is riddled with it, like wormwood."

Jason released her hand, stood, and stretched. "Kevin Shilo is another man eaten with hate. Until today, I wouldn't have traded Kevin for a dozen of his brother. Now, I'm not so sure."

Amy smiled. "To be honest, I've always preferred Merril, even if he is a bit wild at times."

"Well, you would." Jason laughed as he turned to his office. There were several things he needed to see to right away. He looked back at Amy from the doorway. "Don't make any plans for after dinner, Mrs. Harris," he said with a grin. "I intend to make up for lost time."

***

Amy Harris

—

Amy looked up at Jason with a smile, but he'd already turned away and disappeared into his office. Her smile faded, and she released a worried sigh. She rose from the chair and walked down the short hallway to the kitchen door. "Cookie, have you seen Jeanne? Nichole's back, and she'll need help with her bath." Her gaze lifted toward the second floor—where Nichole cried alone.

Amy firmed her resolve, despite the apprehension that tightened in her chest. She'd have to share what she knew, what she guessed, and how she knew it. Despite her fear of discovery, she had to make Nichole understand the danger.

***

Merril Shilo

—

Merril rode with Jimmy Leigh and took shelter in the relative safety of The Shilo bunkhouse. The cowhands were at the branding site, and the place was empty, except for Bill, who had stayed behind to mend his saddle.

Jim helped Merril to his cot and sent Bill to Kiowa Crossing for Doc Johnson.

Merril reclined on his bunk, hand over his eyes, and listened to Jim pace the floor. He knew his fever had worsened. He'd been shot before, but he'd never had a gunshot wound go bad, though he'd seen it.

Not a pretty way to go.

When the door opened, Merril turned his head and blinked his eyes. His vision swam in and out of focus as he tried to see who had entered.

Henny bobbed her head and gave a guarded smile to Jimmy Leigh. She took a hesitant step toward Merril. "I brought bandages and Amy's salve." Her eyes moved from Jim's furrowed stare to Merril. She lifted her chin and carried her basket around The Highlands' foreman to Merril's bunk and set it at the foot of the bed.

"I've already sent for Doc Johnson," Jim informed her. He paced away across the room again.

"I know ya have, and he's a good man, but this needs tendin' right away. Miss Amy's salve is a wonder. If I didn't know better, I'd think the woman was a witch." Her dark gaze rose to meet Jim's glare, and she crossed herself. "A green witch, mind ya. I wouldn't say an unkind thing about Miss Amy—a miracle worker is what she is."

Katy followed her mother in and set a pot of steaming water by Merril's cot. Her eyes grew wide as she stared at the blood on Merril's chest and trousers.

"I'll be all right, Katy." Merril smiled and winked at the young woman. "Your mama's here to take care of me, and Doc Johnson's on the way."

"That's right." Henny placed one of the bandages in the scalding water. "You run back up to the house and keep an eye on dinner. I'll be along shortly. Go on, now." She shooed her hand at Katy, then turned to the strips of colored cloth that bound Merril's chest. "Let's get these rags off and get you cleaned up proper."

Henny unwrapped the bandages with delicate care. Before the last strip of cloth was unbound, Merril could see red streaks of infection worming their way down his chest, and across his shoulder, from the wound. He let his head fall back onto the cot and clenched his teeth as Henny tore the pus-encrusted dressing free.

"Damn," Jimmy muttered and stepped away.

"Don't you listen to him, Mr. Merril. We are goin' to clean this right up. Miss Amy's salve will turn this around, you wait and see."

Merril opened his eyes and saw tears on Henny's dark cheeks, then hissed as she pressed a scalding hot compress against the wound.

"This will draw the poison out." She looked over her shoulder. "Mr. Leigh, if you could help me, please?"

Henny rinsed another compress in the water and folded it.

Jim moved to the head of the cot. "What do you need me to do?"

"I need to see his back to know how much poison is on that side."

"I can roll over," Merril muttered, then grimaced as he leaned to one side.

Jimmy steadied him as Henny studied the injury. "This side is better." She flipped the metal clasp from the jar of ointment and scooped two fingers through the cream-colored paste. "I'm goin' to work this into the wound as far as I can, then bandage your back."

Merril closed his eyes and bit back on the scream that crawled up his throat. His brother might be in the ranch house, and he didn't want Kevin to hear his cry of pain.

When it was over, Jim held his shoulders as he eased down onto his back.

"This side ain't goin' to be any easier. I need to press as much of the poison from the front as I can. Then I'll douse it with alcohol." She wrung out a compress and rinsed it again. The stench of infection fouled the air. "Before I bind up the wound, I'll use more salve. Are you ready, Mr. Merril?"

Merril nodded and held up his hand. "Wait, Henny." His gaze turned to The Highland's foreman. "Jim, if I don't —"

"You'll make it, Merril. It's not that bad."

Merril could see as well as hear the lie in Jim's voice. His one-sided grin ticked up, and he shook his head. "We both know how bad it is. I need something from you. A promise."

Jimmy tipped his head and looked Merril in the eye. "Whatever you need."

"Watch out for Nicki. Don't let Kevin— Pa's death, and everything that happened changed him. After what he did today, I don't know. I couldn't bear it if he hurt her."

Jim gripped Merril's arm and nodded. "You have my word. I'll do what I can to keep her safe." His eyebrows rose as he spoke. "You know as well as I do, she never listens to anyone, except maybe you. Fight this, Merril Shilo. Don't let that bastard win."

Merril nodded and let his head fall back.

Henny handed him a piece of leather, the size of a flat biscuit, from her basket. "Bite down on the leather, Mr. Merril. This... won't be pleasant."

Merril closed his eyes and slipped the leather piece between his teeth. Pain exploded in his chest as Henny's strong hands expelled the matter from the wound. He didn't want to open his eyes and see their faces. He could smell the corruption.

"This will be the worst part, Mr. Merril." Henny's voice was soft and apologetic.

A heartbeat later, a fire tore across his skin and burned deep into his chest. Jim's big hands pressed his shoulders onto the cot. The horrible sound of a man's tortured cry echoed in Merril's ears—and then, he knew nothing.

Chapter 26

Merril Shilo

—

Merril's consciousness returned enough to hear boots pace in the silence. They came toward him, paused, and then moved away. He tried to open his eyes but couldn't. The sound faded, and he slept. Sometime later, he heard voices and felt a firm hand touch his shoulder.

"Doc just pulled up to the house. Can you wake up?" Jim's voice was soft and close.

Merril tried to blink, but his eyes were crusted shut. He wiped them clear and squinted at Jim. "How long have I been out?"

"About three hours. How do you feel?"

How do I feel?

Such an easy question, yet he wasn't sure.

Numb? Alive?

Merril took a breath, then a deeper one. Nausea and fatigue were gone, along with the bone-deep weakness. "I'm better." His eyes opened wider and sought Jim's. "How is that possible?"

Jim's head shook in short, slow motions, never breaking their locked gaze. "I'm not sure. Henny has a healing touch, or Amy's salve has magic in it." Jim smiled and sat back in the chair beside the bed. "Now, you can do me a favor. Don't mention the salve or Amy to Doc. Henny already named her a witch. She doesn't need a rumor like that gettin' started."

Merril pushed himself up and leaned against the wall. He looked down at his chest; the poisonous red streaks were gone. "The Cheyenne have some powerful medicine men." His gaze lifted from his chest to meet Jim's.

"Damned if they don't. Besides, that gunshot wasn't as bad as we first thought." Jim rose to his feet as the door opened. "You were worn clean out."

Doc Johnson walked across the long room with his black medical bag in hand. "I went to the big house first." He stopped and looked from Jim to Merril. "Henny thinks you're dying."

Behind him, Bill's brows had risen into his hairline as he stared at Merril.

"Henny was pretty upset. I passed out when she poured alcohol in the wound," Merril offered.

Jim crossed the bunkhouse with his long strides, took Bill by the arm, and steered him out the door.

Doc Johnson ignored the ranch hand and set his bag on the foot of the bed. "Well, since I'm here, I'm going to have a look." He removed Henny's bandages and looked at Merril's injury. He pressed several places around the wound on his chest, grunted, and then asked Merril to sit forward so he could examine his back. "This looks good. I didn't need to make this trip."

"I'm sorry for that. When Jim brought me in, Bill and Henny thought the worst."

"Hmm." Doc removed new bandages from his bag. "I'll dress this and advise you to take it easy. Not much more you need from me." He placed a compress over the chest wound. "You'll have quite a scar." Then he wrapped a strip of white cloth around Merril's chest to hold the bandage. He did the same for Merril's back. When he finished, he stepped to the chair and took a seat.

"Why aren't you up at the house?" Doc's voice was soft as he repacked his bag.

"Because Kevin's there." Merril murmured, surprised at the venom he tasted in that one name.

Doc heard the anger, and his gaze rose to Merril's face. "Is he the one that shot you, son?"

"No." Merril heaved a short sigh. "He didn't shoot me. He did shoot one of the Cheyenne men that helped us."

Doc shook his head. "I've seen grief change a man." He was silent for a moment, then looked up and met Merril's gaze. "I've known your brother for nigh on ten years, but I can't say I know the man I spoke with at the house just now."

"So, he is home." Merril swung his feet to the floor and reached for his boots. "I'll walk you to your wagon, Doc. Then I need to speak to my brother." He reached for a small bag beneath the bunk, pulled out a shirt and shrugged it on.

Doc stood and watched Merril with a concerned look on his face. "Are you sure you feel up to that? He's more'n half-drunk already. Maybe you should wait till mornin'."

Merril's grin ticked up, and he gave Doc a half-smile. "It won't matter, either way." He buttoned his shirt and pulled his hat from the hook by the bed. He picked up his gun belt and Colt from the floor by the side of the bed.

"Do you need your gun to talk with your brother?" Doc Johnson asked.

Merril shrugged and tied the string around his thigh. "No. At least, I hope not." He straightened and walked with the doctor to the door. "Will you head over to The Highlands?"

"I thought I might since I'm out this way. I want to see how my other patient is gettin' on." Doc Johnson walked to his wagon with Merril. "You rest that shoulder, and take care of yourself, son." Doc frowned and looked uneasily at the house.

"Thanks, Doc, I will. Would you let Nichole know I'm doing better?"

"Of course, son."

Merril stood away from the buckboard and watched the doctor guide the wagon out of the yard and turn onto the road toward The Highlands.

Jim walked up beside Merril, leading his brown gelding. "I'm going to ride with Doc back to The Highlands. You'll be all right?"

"I will. Thank you, Jim. Give Amy my thanks as well."

Jim mounted, tipped his hat, then pulled the reins and trotted his horse to catch the wagon.

Merril turned and looked at the library window. A shadowed figure moved back, and the curtains swayed. Kevin. He needed to talk with that son-of-a-bitch—reach him, somehow. Merril scrubbed his face and shifted his gaze to Midnight pacing in the coral.

Or I could ride away.

Freedom versus responsibility held him paralyzed in the yard.

To walk into that house, which had never felt like home, and reach out to a brother he loathed, would be the hardest thing he had ever done. Kevin had become dangerous, to himself and others. What he did to Toma was unforgivable.

He needs to be stopped. He needs help.

Men had begun to return from the branding site. Merril turned at the sound of their voices and watched their camaraderie with envy. He'd known that freedom. But it wasn't just him involved anymore. Whether he could help his brother or not, there was a singular pair of blue eyes he couldn't bear to disappoint.

"Well, damn." He ran a hand through his hair and reset his hat, and then crossed the yard to the porch. He left the door open behind him as he stepped into the library.

Kevin stood by their father's desk, whiskey glass in hand, and glared at him. "I hoped you'd be dead by now."

"Well, I'm not. Put the liquor down. We need to talk."

Kevin laughed. "Talk? To you? What the hell do we have to talk about?" He took a gulp from his glass, pressed his lips, and looked back at Merril. "You know nothing about this ranch and have no business being part of it." The volume of his voice increased as he spoke. His face turned red with anger. Spittle flew from Kevin's mouth, and he wiped it from his face with the back of his hand. "I'll be damned if I'll talk to you." He crossed to the decanter, refilled his glass, and then returned to the desk.

Merril shook his head in disgust. Any hope he held to help his brother, if only enough to work with the man, disappeared. Merril hooked his thumbs in his pockets and matched his brother's hate-filled glare. "What a disappointment you would be to Pa. You're nothing but a despicable drunkard, Kevin."

Kevin took a long drink and set the glass on the desk. "That's downright funny, coming from someone as worthless as you."

Merril felt the heat rise under his collar. "You shot a good man in the back today, you murdering son-of-a-bitch." He took a step toward Kevin.

"If you love those red-skinned bastards so much, you should have stayed with them." Kevin picked up his glass, found it empty, and slammed it on the desk. "Instead, you come back here and fuck our goddamned whore neighbor." Kevin pointed north, toward The Highlands.

Merril became motionless. His vision shrank to a point between Kevin's eyes.

"Didn't you hear me?" Kevin took another step forward and tilted his head, looking his brother in the eye. "I said Nichole Harris is a rutting slut. That cunt fucks her cousin and that giant foreman of hers." He leaned his face in close to Merril's and grinned. "She'd even fuck a piece of shit like you. She—"

Merril's fist smashed against Kevin's cheekbone with ferocity, knocking him back.

Kevin stumbled against the guest chairs and lost his footing, but never reached the floor.

Merril brought his other fist up into his brother's midsection, driving him up hard against the desk. Rage surged through his chest. He punched Kevin twice more in the stomach as his brother gasped for breath.

Kevin's jaw snapped shut on his tongue as Merril's bloody fist connected with the side of his chin. Kevin fell back across the desk, and Merril wrapped his hands around his throat.

"Merril, stop this!" Renata ran into the room. "What are you doing? Merril, dear God stop!" She flung herself at Merril and clung to his arm, but her efforts didn't loosen his grip on Kevin's throat. The sensation of his gun being drawn from his holster startled him, and he turned to find Renata.

She held his gun with both hands. Its barrel pointed at his head. Her eyes sparkled, and she chuckled with glee. "You are such a fool. Let him go."

With a cry of rage, he flung his brother away with disgust. Kevin fell and lay in a motionless heap beside the desk. Merril turned and yanked the gun from Renata's grasp with one hand, then backhanded her across the face with his other. She fell between the table and the settee, and then pulled herself onto the couch. Her fingers touched the trickle of blood from her nose and lip, and she grinned.

Merril stood over her, panting with fury, and stared at her excitement in bewilderment. The pounding rage in his head and chest eased.

She reached up, grasped her bodice with both hands and rent it down the middle to her waist. Beneath the garment, her camisole was already torn and bloody. Bite marks and bruises covered her breasts.

"Your brother likes to bite." A laugh escaped her, and then her eyes grew serious and filled with tears. "Release me, Merril! Dear God, someone help me. No—stop it!" Renata's terrified cries echoed down the hall and through the open front door.

Merril blinked at her. "What the hell are you doing?" His harsh voice frayed as he stared down at her in confusion.

"No, no ... let me go. Look what you've done. Get out! Don't touch me," her scream trailed off.

There was no fear in her eyes—only spite and triumph. The sound of footsteps on the porch brought a hint of a smile to her lips. "If I were you, love, I would leave now." Her voice bubbled with laughter. "If you wait for the sheriff to arrive, it will only make things harder. He knows how violent you can be. All those men outside, they have witnessed a brutal crime."

Her gaze locked with Merril's and her expression became terrified once more. "You've killed him... you've killed your brother! Someone, help me!" Her voice sounded ragged and terrified, and then, she smiled.

Merril staggered back. He looked from Renata to his brother, who lay still on the floor.

I did just what they wanted.

Without a word, he spun on his heels and stalked out. He slammed through the curious cowboys, knocking two off the porch. No one tried to stop him or speak to him.

Renata continued to cry for help, and several men rushed into the house.

Midnight stood at the water trough in the corral. He raised his head as Merril swung onto his back. With one last glare at The Shilo ranch house and its occupants, he turned and rode away.

Chapter 27

Nichole Harris

—

Jeanne prepared a bath for Nichole in the small, windowless room attached to the kitchen. Constructed near the stove for hot water, it had a built-in drainpipe, which made the tub easy to empty. Jeanne washed Nichole's hair and set a plate of Cookie's fried chicken within reach. She smiled at Nichole as she dried her hands. "Relax. Enjoy your lunch. Call out if you need anything. Cookie will hear you and find me."

Nichole leaned against the slanted back of the tub and plucked a chicken leg from the plate. "Thank you, Jeanne."

Jeanne nodded and closed the door behind her.

The warm bath and the luxurious sensation of Jeanne washing her hair and scalp helped calm Nichole's spirit. Still, each time her eyes closed, she saw Toma lying in the muddy grass, or Merril's pale, gray face as they parted. Her stomach turned, and the chicken leg fell to the plate half-eaten.

After her skin had been scrubbed clean, she draped the warm washcloth over her face and tried again to close her eyes to relax. A sharp rap on the door jolted her from her rest, and she pulled the cloth from her face. "Who is it?"

"It's just me." Amy eased into the room with a smile and closed the door behind her. "I've come to see how you are, and if you need anything. Jason told me you had a terrible experience."

Nichole stood without response and wrapped a cloth around her. Careful of her balance, she stepped from the metal tub onto the wooden floor. She took another towel from the shelf and glanced at Amy. "He told you about finding us, and what Kevin did?" She pressed the water from the ends of her hair and then toweled the rest of her hair.

"Yes, he did." Amy sat on a stool in the corner. "I'm sorry about your Indian friend."

Nichole stopped rubbing her hair and peered out at Amy from beneath the towel.

"Kevin should be arrested for murder." Tears tightened her throat, and her glare dared Amy to disagree.

"Unfortunately, killing an Indian makes him something of a hero around here."

"So I was made to understand." She wrapped the towel around her hair and finished drying herself off with angry motions. "It makes me sick."

Amy nodded. "I'm sure you're tired of hearing this, but it would never have bothered you before."

Nichole pulled a clean chemise over her head and drew the laces tight. She took a comb from the shelf and teased the snarls from her wet hair. "That doesn't say a hell of a lot for me, you know."

Amy shifted in her seat and changed the subject. "Jason also said Blackwood Jones tried to kill you." She took a deep breath before she continued. "I must warn you. He'll try again."

The comb stopped, and Nichole shot a curious look at Amy. "You sound as if you already know he'll show up again."

"I do know." Amy's calm eyes returned Nichole's stare.

"How would you know that?"

Amy pressed her lips and looked away. "Ever since I was young, I've been able to glimpse events that will transpire at some point in the future. Occasionally, I can see distant events as they occur. People don't understand this—gift. It frightens them."

Nichole's scalp tingled. "And what do you see for me?" Her voice was hushed.

Amy shifted on the stool and cleared her throat. "I realize this sounds preposterous. I wasn't going to tell you. I've never told anyone." Her gaze lifted and met Nichole's. "But how else can I warn you about Jones and have you believe me?"

Nichole slipped her robe over her chemise and gathered her comb and brush. "Let's talk upstairs."

Amy nodded, stood, and opened the door. Dry, fragrant air filled the small bathing room as the women stepped into the bright kitchen. Amy smiled and nodded at Cookie, then continued into the dining room and followed Nichole up the stairs. They were silent until they reached the privacy of Nichole's bedchamber and Amy closed the door.

Nichole paced across the room to her dressing table. "You believe Jones hasn't given up trying to harm me."

Amy took a short breath, then opened her eyes and stared at Nichole with calm resolve. "Yes. I'm positive." She leaned her head against the door and spoke in a hushed voice. "I knew he planned something the other night after he fought with Jimmy Leigh." She paused and gazed steadily into Nichole's eyes. "And I know, with certainty, he'll come after you again."

Nichole set the comb down and shivered. Gooseflesh raised the hair on her arms in the warm room. "I wish you had told me earlier." Nichole's flat voice masked her astonishment. *Holy shit*. What Amy confessed was similar to what she had experienced herself.

"I know. But would you have believed me?" Amy expelled a long breath. "Besides, I thought I might be wrong."

Nichole looked up. "Are you often wrong?" Her thoughts skipped back to Custer, and all she'd told Gray Wolf and Merril.

"Only once." Amy shrugged and paced away from the door. "The day before your accident." She paused and regarded Nichole. "I had a premonition in Denver. A strong one. I saw the carriage accident and your injury. However, in my premonition, you—" Amy spun and paced toward the door, gesturing with her hand. "You didn't survive. So, you see, I can be wrong."

Nichole's throat tightened, and she gripped the edge of the dressing table. Her hand rose trembling to her mouth.

When Amy looked back, her eyes widened, and she rushed across the room, putting her arm around Nichole. "Are you faint?" She drew Nichole to the bed, sat beside her, and took her hand. "That was thoughtless of me, to tell you such a horrible thing. Of course, I was mistaken." She patted Nichole's hand.

Nichole glanced at Amy, then looked away and swallowed. "It's not that, or at least, not *just* that. I ... it's something the old Indian said about me when we were with the Cheyenne."

Amy tipped her head. "What is that?"

Nichole looked down at their hands. "White Eagle said that to look at me was to see someone who had been through the hall of the dead." She looked back to her friend.

Amy searched Nichole's eyes. "What does that mean?"

"I'm not sure," Nichole admitted.

"Who was this man?"

"White Eagle is a shaman or medicine man. He's also Gray Wolf's grand-father." She bit her lip. "He talked to his spirits, or they talked to him, about me. He only speaks Cheyenne, so I didn't understand what he said. All I know is what Merril translated for me." She blinked tears from her eyes and sighed. "Amy, what's happening to me?"

Amy opened her mouth, and then shut it. She rose and walked to the dressing table. "I don't know, Nicki." She turned and gazed at her friend. "Has anything else happened? I can't make any sense out of this, and I can't—"

Nichole held up her hand, and Amy fell silent. Nichole chewed at her bottom lip for a moment more, and then her gaze jumped to meet Amy's. "Do you know who General Custer is?"

Amy's brows drew together. "I've heard talk of a Lieutenant Custer, but I don't know him personally."

"Have you ever heard of the Battle of the Little Bighorn?"

"No, I haven't."

"Last night, I told Merril and his friend, Gray Wolf, that General Custer died there... and Amy, I know he did." Nichole lurched to her feet and paced across the room to the balcony door, rubbing her arms. "The battle where General Custer loses his life is called Custer's Last Stand. Or, it will be." Nichole turned to gauge Amy's reaction, but Amy only shook her head.

A knock on the door broke the silence and startled them both.

"Nicki?" Jeanne's voice sounded muffled through the door. "Doc Johnson is here to see you. Shall I send him up?"

Nichole looked from the door to Amy. "He must have been to see Merril." She wound her wet tresses in a loose bun on top of her head, picked up two pins from the dressing table and secured it.

"Yes, Jeanne," she called and tightened her robe belt. "Send him up, please."

"What will you do?" Amy opened the door. From below, they could hear Jeanne's voice call to the Doc, and his laughing reply.

Nichole's shoulders rose with her eyebrows. "I don't know. Wait and see if something else happens—hope more of my memory comes back."

Amy cast a quick glance at the empty stairs, then back to Nichole. "I'd like to discuss this more if you don't mind."

"Not in the least. It's good to have someone to talk to about... weird things."

"Well, well," Doc Johnson's voice boomed out. He stopped in the doorway and gave Nichole an appraising look. "I must say you look better than my last patient."

"Is Merril all right?" Nichole took an involuntary step forward.

"Oh, yes, Merril's fine. I wasn't implying you were any healthier, only that you are better looking." Doc laughed at his own joke. He adjusted his glasses and grew serious once more. "How do you feel, young woman?" He set his bag on the chair near the door and then searched through the contents. "Not resting and not following your doctor's orders, I hear."

"I'm fine," Nichole replied and smiled at the funny old doctor.

The doctor quirked an eyebrow. "Well, we shall see about that. Please, have a seat." Doc indicated the end of the bed and Nichole perched on the mattress. "Have you been able to remember anything yet? No? I wouldn't worry about that. These things take time."

"Yes." Nichole glanced at Amy who stood in the doorway. "They must."

Doc Johnson listened for a moment to Nichole's back with an odd horn device, then probed her head gently. "Still a little tender, I see. Well, that is to be expected. Other than the sore head, how have you been feeling? No dizzy spells? No fainting?" At a shake of her head, he replied, "Good."

He withdrew a small pair of scissors from his case and pushed the hair from her forehead. With quick, sure snips, he cut each tiny stitch and pulled the threads from her injury.

"Doctor," Amy spoke as soon as Doc Johnson finished. "The spring roundup is ending."

"Yes, yes." The doctor acknowledged as he returned his instrument to his case. "There should be no problem with this young lady attending the festivities," he said as he patted Nichole on the cheek with a smile. "It is good to see you doing so well, little girl. Now, I have to run. Amy, tell that husband of yours I said hello." He nodded to Amy as he passed her to step from Nichole's room.

"It seems to be one thing after another with you folks this year. No need to see me out. I can find my way. Good day to you both."

Chapter 28

Nichole Harris

—

Nichole listened to Doc Johnson's footsteps descend the stairs and the front door close. "He's become a regular here and at The Shilo, hasn't he?" Nichole opened the chest to find another plain skirt to wear.

"Skirt and blouse again?" Amy inquired.

"These are more comfortable than the heavy gowns, less frilly and fancy." Nichole indicated Amy's clothes. "Not that there's anything wrong with your frilly—" She touched her heated face.

Amy chuckled. "Let me choose one I think you might like." She opened the wardrobe and pushed several outfits aside, finally pulling out a blue cotton day dress, and presented it to Nichole. "We should also choose one for the barbecue. Jeanne or Lawna will need to press it."

Nichole sighed at the ruffled sleeves and hemline on the gown Amy presented.

At least it doesn't have a bustle.

Amy unhooked the garment from the hanger at Nichole's reluctant nod. "You never cared for this one, although it's like what I wear when I'm here. It's loose enough to pull over your head, then tied snug with the ribbons down the back." Amy chatted as she slipped the material over Nichole's wet hair and helped her find the armholes. "Jason didn't explain how you and Merril ended up without your clothing."

Nichole's face warmed again, but she couldn't keep the smile from her face as she settled the neckline well above her cleavage.

"I see." Amy laughed and spun Nichole around. She straightened the seams and pulled the ties tight in the back. "You always did have a soft spot for that wild one."

"Jones started shooting at us before we could get our clothes," Nichole confessed. A glance in the mirror showed her how red her face had become.

"Ah," Amy said as if that explained everything. Once the dress was fitted to her liking, she picked up the hairbrush. "Have a seat. I'll brush this out."

Amy had just finished tying a blue ribbon on the bottom of the braid when a hard pounding at the front door reverberated through the house. Amy stiffened immediately, then turned and left the room.

Nichole rose and followed her down the stairs.

Amy paused at the bottom and looked hesitantly toward the kitchen, then, she stepped to the door just as the pounding began again.

A young cowboy, no more than fifteen years old, pulled a dusty felt hat from his head. He looked apologetically at Amy. "Excuse me, ma'am, for disturbin' your afternoon, but we wondered if you might have seen Merril Shilo ride by this way?"

Amy glanced at the other young wrangler who held the reins of two horses, then back to the boy at the door. "Has something happened?"

"I ... I don't know what you mean, ma'am," the cowboy stammered, and looked away.

At the mention of Merril's name, Nichole rushed down the remaining steps. Her ice blue eyes caught and held the young cowboy's nervous glance. "Has something happened to Merril?" She stopped in the doorway beside Amy.

"No, ma'am." The youngster gripped the hat in his hands and shifted his glance from one woman to the other.

"What, then?" Amy countered. "Why would you come here to find him?"

The cowpoke looked from Nichole to Amy and swallowed hard. He glanced over his shoulder at his friend in the yard, and then sighed and scuffed his boots on the wooden deck. "We'd jus' got back to the bunkhouse when we heard Miss Renata screamin'. She was yellin' about someone being crazy and somebody dyin'."

He glanced up at the women in the doorway, and then looked back down at his boots. "We all ran up to the house to see what the matter was. Right then, Merril came bustin' out on the porch. He dang near knocked me clean over the railin'—and ma'am—he never even saw me. He walked straight to that big black horse of his and rode away."

"Go on," Amy urged when the boy hesitated.

"Ma'am, I don't know if I should, you bein' ladies and all—"

"Just say it." Nichole's tone was harsh and brooked no argument.

Startled, he gawked at her. "Nobody wanted to go after Merril, not then. We didn't know what was goin' on, and most of us felt it weren't none of our business, anyway. It was about then that Miss Renata ran out on the porch."

The boy blushed and looked back at his boots and shrugged. "Miss Renata's dress was torn real bad across here." He motioned to his chest, but never looked up at the two women. "She was still carryin' on, only not as loud. She said Merril had tried to... touch her, and when she refused him, he got really mad and tore her dress." A noise from Nichole's throat made him look up, but he continued his tale. "She said Kevin tried to stop him, and he just went plumb crazy. He tried to kill his brother, ma'am. We ran into Doc Johnson and sent him back over to The Shilo."

"Oh, my," Amy breathed.

"Amy, you don't believe him, do you?"

"I'm tellin' the truth, ma'am. I swear to God. I was there. Mr. Shilo's in real bad shape like I said, he couldn't even stand up. We had to carry him to his room, and Miss Renata—"

"That's enough." Nichole's short command stopped the young man from speaking.

It's not his fault.

She softened her tone and added, "If we see Merril, we will send a message to The Shilo."

"I appreciate it, ma'am. Sorry to have been the one to tell ya." He put the felt hat on his head with something akin to relief in his boyish features and raced back to his friend.

Nichole closed the door and leaned against it—anger and fear combining to drive the breath from her lungs.

"I must find Jason." Amy turned toward the dining room, so deep within herself and her own thoughts she seemed to have spoken to herself.

"Merril wouldn't do this, Amy," Nichole stated. "He hates Renata. He would no more make a pass at her than the man in the moon."

"That may be, but the fact remains that whatever happened, Merril is running from it. I must find Jason." Amy didn't pause.

Nichole watched as Amy walked away. She passed the dining room table and disappeared into the back of the house.

She must know something.

Anxiety built in her chest, and she knew she couldn't just wait here. She had to find Merril; he was injured, hunted, and wrongly accused. Before she could change her mind, she slipped out the door and hurried to the side of the house and peeked around the corner.

Jimmy Leigh stood next to the old man with the puppies. They spoke for a moment then Jim's head came up sharply, and he looked toward the back porch.

Nichole held her breath, afraid he'd seen her.

Instead of heading her direction, he made his way to the back of the house.

Now was her chance. She grasped the hem of her dress with one hand and ran to the edge of the corral. At the wooden fence, she paused. The horses snorted and pranced, wary of her strange scent. She spoke gently to the shy animals, but they paced away. Movement near the house forced her hand, and she crept behind the barn.

The double doors were open on the back side of the barn. Tied to a post near the corner was Jim's gelding, rested from his return from The Shilo, and awaiting the stableman's attention.

Inside, someone shuffled around the front stalls and spoke softly to the puppies.

Without pause, she untied the reins and led the big horse away from the barn. The gelding was a much larger horse than Sugar, but it didn't matter. There was no other way.

Nichole hiked her skirt above her knees and slipped the toe of her boot into the stirrup. Pulling herself up, she swung her leg over the saddle and wiggled onto the leather seat. Jim's horse acknowledged her weight and pranced uneasily as she tightened the reins. Her feet didn't reach the stirrups, but that couldn't be helped.

"Come on now," Nichole spoke softly. "Work with me, here."

With a shake of the reins and a small amount of pressure from her heels, the gelding shot away from The Highlands ranch house. Her braid came undone, and her long, blonde hair streamed out behind her.

Where would Merril go? Where can I look that Kevin's men haven't?

She retraced the trail past the branding site, to the small thicket surrounding the spring pool. Merril wasn't there. She sat still and tried to imagine where he might have gone. Why couldn't she remember where he would go? She should know that, shouldn't she?

"Nicki!"

The shout brought her around, and she scoured the prairie behind her; panic fluttered in her chest.

Where had the shout come from?

Abruptly aware of her vulnerability, Amy's warning flashed through her mind.

I'm like the dumb blonde in a slasher flick. Shit.

She didn't even have a gun with her. Movement caught her eye as a rider made his way across the field to her.

Jones wouldn't call my name, would he?

Then she recognized the rider. The relief of seeing Jason's angry face made Nichole practically swoon in the saddle.

"Damn it, Nicki! What the hell is wrong with you?" Red-faced and furious, Jason pulled rein beside her.

Relief filled her head and sounded in her voice. "It's you."

"You're damn lucky it's me! I knew—*I knew* the minute I found you gone, along with Jimmy Leigh's horse, where you would go. Thank God you're predictable if nothing else. Did you think Merril would sit by your lovers' pond, and wait for you to save him? After what he's done, he's bound to be out of the area by now."

The gelding danced away from Jason's horse, and Nichole tightened her grip on the reins. "Merril didn't try to rape Renata. She's lying, Jason. She—"

"Do you think I don't know that? Do you think you are the only one who could find Merril and set things right?"

"If you know she's lying, then why don't you—"

"Renata isn't the problem." Jason interrupted. "Those two brothers have been working up to this for years, and nothing I say is going to change that. But you— You have caused me enough grief and worry in the last two days to last a lifetime. It is going to end." Jason's face had grown redder as he spoke. "You are coming home with me right now. You're not to leave that house without my express permission and an armed escort."

Nichole breathed a deep sigh and looked at the barren plain. Now, she could imagine Jones behind every tall blade of grass. "You're right. I'm sorry I frightened you. I just... I want to find Merril. This story—what they say happened—it isn't right."

"I know." The anger drained from Jason's face. He turned away and gazed over the prairie.

Nichole studied his profile, so similar to her own. He clenched his jaw several times, lost in thought. She reached over to him and pulled a blond curl from beneath the collar of his jacket. "What are you thinking?"

When he faced her, his gaze was firm. He met her blue eyes equally with his own, studying her silently for a moment as if he weighed his words. "I was thinking about your father. What he would have said about all this."

"What would he have said?"

"I don't know anymore, Nicki. I just don't know."

He ran his fingers through his hair and replaced his hat on his head, turning his mare away without meeting her eyes. "Let's go home. If Kevin can't find Merril, then he doesn't mean to be found. We have a barbecue to prepare for. And even if the Shilos don't attend, I intend to make sure it's a good one."

They didn't speak on the ride back to the ranch house. When they reached the yard, Jason dismounted and held the bit while Nichole climbed down from the big horse, then he took both animals to the barn.

As Nichole walked to the house, she saw Amy watching from the window. She met her gaze when she stepped inside. "Sorry I took off like that."

"No apology is necessary." Amy waved her hand. "I understand."

"You're not angry?"

"Angry? Whatever for? Worried, yes. However, I was in much the same mind to do what you did; that's why I went to find Jason. I knew he'd talk me out of it. Now, come with me. There are many things to do and decide on before Friday."

Nichole followed Amy through the house to the kitchen. Lack of sleep began to have its effect, and before long, Nichole excused herself to her room.

As she struck a match to the lamp on her dresser, another pain raced through her head. She pressed against the dull ache it left in its wake. All she could think of was closing her eyes. After she turned down the bedcover, she sat and removed her boots.

Nichole struggled with the ties on her dress and considered calling Jeanne to help, but asking to be undressed seemed absurd. Finally, she found her way free of the laced ribbons, and she let the gown fall in a heap on the floor. She was asleep the minute her head hit the pillow.

She slept late the next day, waking only when the sunlight moved across her room to her bed. Her sunburned skin stretched tight and dry across her shoulders and stung her nose, reminding her of yesterday and what happened to Toma. She rolled over and buried her face in the pillow, wishing to escape into slumber once more.

Outside her window, Jason called instructions to one of the hands.

Where is Merril?

She rolled over and gazed dispiritedly at the ceiling.

I wish he were here.

Inch by inch, her legs slipped from beneath the covers, and she rose from the bed. Taking the photo of him from the mantel, she lowered herself to the dressing table chair and stared into his eyes.

Tomorrow night would be the big barbecue. She should decide what she would wear, but sorrow weighed her down. She rubbed her forehead and turned to look woefully at her wardrobe.

How can I even pretend to care about this celebration?

A knock sounded at the front door.

More bad news she supposed, but she didn't care. Merril was gone, and the parts of her memory that were coming back made no sense.

It was frightening.

She couldn't find any part of her that cared what frilly dress she might wear. Toma was dead. Merril was missing. And her mind was coming apart.

She put her head in her hands and listened to the murmur of voices that floated up the stairs.

Chapter 29

Jason Harris

—

Jason held the door handle in a vise-like grip. A muscle twitched along his jaw. This was too much. First, the boy arrived from The Shilo early this morning saying a couple of the hands had seen Jones hanging around. They had tried to follow him but had finally turned back. It probably saved their lives. And now, this. He expelled an exasperated breath and opened the door wide. "Well, Renata, what brings you here this early? I hadn't expected guests today."

"This isn't a social call, I'm afraid." She stepped into the house, drawing with her a tall, bearded man Jason had never met before.

"Jason, this is Dr. Clemens." Renata placed a hand on each man. "Dr. Clemens, this is Jason Harris, the cousin of the woman I spoke to you about."

Jason eyed Dr. Clemens with suspicion as they shook hands.

"Dr. Clemens agreed to visit with Nichole." Renata continued speaking as she removed her gloves. "He has studied cases like hers, haven't you, doctor? I'm sure if anyone could help Nichole, Dr. Clemens could."

Renata bit her bottom lip and gave Jason an innocent smile that didn't deceive him. He studied her a moment with a cold, hard look, then turned to Dr. Clemens.

"Dr. Clemens." Jason acknowledged the stranger coldly. "Your name is familiar. Have we met before?"

Dr. Clemens shook his head. "No. I don't believe so."

Jason released his hand and stepped back. "I'm sorry to say you've come a long way for nothing. My cousin still sleeps, and after yesterday, I don't want to wake her for uninvited guests."

"Nonsense," Renata scoffed. She removed her hat and tossed both gloves and hat on the table near the door. "She'll be down before long. We shall wait."

"Renata, I'm sure Dr. Clemens has better things to do than to—"

"I'll wait." The bearded man cut Jason short. "Cases like this fascinate me."

"So you see, love, the doctor can wait." Renata smiled over her shoulder at Jason.

"I'd like to speak to you privately for a moment, Renata. Doctor, if you would excuse us."

"Certainly, sir. I'll wait over here." Dr. Clemens set his bag near the settee in the parlor and took a seat.

Jason took Renata's arm and escorted her around the stairs, past the dining room, and into his office. After he closed the door, he turned to her, not bothering to conceal his anger. "What is this?" he demanded and paced around the desk.

"Didn't you get my note?" Renata laughed and batted her lashes. "Surely, you understand the need—"

"What need? Nichole does not require medical care. She's doing fine."

"Oh, Jason," Renata purred. "You are so very wrong. Dr. Clemens is convinced that further study of her condition is—how did he put it? Imperative."

"How much did it cost you to have him reach this conclusion?" Jason snapped.

Renata straightened slowly. Gone was the soft teasing smile. Her eyes were cold chips of black ice as she looked Jason up and down.

"Understand me, Jason." Her voice dripped venom. "This is my game now. I will suffer no interference from you. Stay out of my way."

"I won't let that doctor near Nicki."

"Oh, I think you will." Renata trailed a delicate hand along the top of the desk, turning partially away from where Jason stood. "I heard that since Amy came back to The Highlands, you two have been getting along quite well."

"That's none of your business."

"Wouldn't she just be devastated if she found out about our little affair?" Renata giggled, and then covered her mouth with her hand. She looked over her shoulder at Jason with a pout. "It would just put the flame right out of your rekindled romance."

"How thoughtless of me to forget your fee." Jason opened a drawer. He found some coins and threw them on the desk. Renata didn't even flinch at the sound.

"It's not just what happened between us." She paused and studied Jason for a moment. "Consider your part in Philip Shilo's murder."

"That was you. I had no part—"

"You already know I can prove you did. What about your associates in Boston?"

"What does that—"

"Your work for them was hardly legal. Then, you embezzled money from The Highlands. You could be in a lot of trouble, and not just with Amy."

"I have not taken The Highlands' money," Jason enunciated in anger. "On Philip Shilo's recommendation, I diversified The Highlands' holdings."

"In whose name are these new investments held?"

Jason was silent, his jaw clenching.

"You have been a very naughty boy," Renata laughed.

"Those investments are for The Highlands," Jason explained. "I would never steal from Nichole."

"I'm not the one you would need to convince. Nichole seems much more in charge of everything since her accident, don't you agree? I am not sure she would understand your financial strategy. I'm not sure Amy would. I know I have questions." Laughter bubbled from her lips.

Jason did not comment. He looked away, anywhere to take his sight away from her. There could be legal consequences should Nichole make a case against him. Old Nichole wouldn't have cared. New Nichole might, and with Renata's urging, they could take him to court. If they made a strong argument, he could face jail time. Of course, all of that paled in comparison to being complicit in Philip's murder. A murder charge would bring Renata down as well. She would play that card only as a last resort.

Without moving, or looking away from the window, he asked, "What is your plan?" He turned and met her eyes with a steady, icy glare. "And what do you get out of all of this?"

"It is very simple, love. I think you will approve." She swung her full dress around the chair and seated herself across the desk from Jason, motioning him to have a seat.

"Your precious cousin isn't going anywhere," she cooed. "We only want to make that a real possibility to her. That is Dr. Clemens's part."

"So?" Jason replied. His stomach churned as he tried to follow her twisted logic.

"Don't you see? She will be frightened, with no one to turn to. Merril is gone. You are just her cousin, with no authority when it comes to something like this—"

"I do have the authority."

"She won't know that." Renata sat back. "She would have no one to turn to except—" Renata let the words trail off and raised an eyebrow.

"Except?" Jason snapped.

Renata huffed in aggravation and rolled her eyes. "*Kevin*, you idiot! Who do you think? She will have to marry Kevin to stay here and be safe."

Jason's startled laughter filled the room, taking Renata off guard.

"You think Nichole would agree to marry Kevin after what he's done?" Jason laughed again. "She will never do it. Never. She hates him."

"Oh, she will. I shall prove it." Renata smiled.

"You do that," Jason replied. "It appears my hands are tied. But if Nichole refuses to marry Kevin, no matter what the consequences are to me, she will not be taken from The Highlands."

"Think about it, love." Renata purred and leaned over the desk, exposing a good portion of her full breasts to his view. "If she does refuse and is forced to leave, then the ranch and all The Highlands holdings would be yours. Don't tell me that would not please you."

Jason looked from her breasts to her eyes. "If Nicki does agree to marry Kevin, what do you get?"

An evil smile spread across Renata's face, and she threw back her head and laughed. "I get everything."

***

The clock on the parlor mantel chimed the hour of ten when a door opened at the top of the stairs.

Jason stole a quick glance at Renata, who conversed in a quiet voice with Dr. Clemens.

Their conversation stopped, and Renata stood, arranging her skirt. She smiled at Jason. "Showtime, love. Let's see a smile."

Jason's eyes blazed. His fists clenched at his side as he stood. *I never understood the desire to murder until now.* "I should mention that Nichole isn't very happy with you."

Before Renata could reply, Amy and Nichole were descending the stairs. Amy stopped abruptly at the sight of Renata. Nichole, a step behind Amy, looked up in confusion.

"Christ," Nichole stated.

"You must be Renata. What a surprise," Amy managed, as she stepped down and into the room. "And, you have brought a guest. How nice."

"Pleased to meet you, Amy. Good morning, Nichole." Renata's eyes moved from Amy's shuttered face to Nichole's angry one. "May I present Dr. Anthony Clemens, an acquaintance of mine from Santa Fe. I wrote to him about Nichole's injury and was surprised when he replied in person. He was in Denver and was interested in meeting with you. Dr. Clemens specializes in your particular type of injury. Tony, this is Amy, Jason's wife, and Nichole Harris, whom we discussed."

"Ladies," Dr. Clemens greeted both women with a smile. "A pleasure to meet you both."

***

Nichole Harris

—

Nichole eyed the doctor with suspicion. He was an innocent enough looking man, balding, with a short-cropped beard and dark brown eyes hidden behind wire-frame glasses. However, since he stood next to Renata, she didn't trust him.

Amy continued over to the doctor and extended her hand. "So nice to meet you, Dr. Clemens. Would you like some refreshments? There is more room for all of us in the dining room if you would follow me."

Amy continued into the dining area, but no one followed; their eyes were on Nichole still hesitating on the stairs. One step at a time, Nichole descended, her eyes locked with Renata's.

"You have some nerve, coming here."

"I have more than nerve, darling." Renata smiled with glee. "Look, I've brought you a present. Dr. Clemens is a specialist. He's here to help."

"Help whom?"

Renata's smile widened in delight.

The doctor reached out and took Nichole's hand.

"I'm very pleased to meet you, Miss Harris. Renata spoke to me about your injury and memory loss. I'm something of an authority in this field. I've studied many cases such as yours. I would dearly love to speak with you and evaluate your condition."

Nichole looked from Dr. Clemens to Jason, who shrugged and nodded as if to say, *what could it hurt?*

"Let's move into the larger area." Jason took Nichole by the elbow and deftly maneuvered her away from Renata and into the dining area.

"I'm afraid I can't stay for refreshments. I have a train to catch in Denver. I need to be in Kansas City by Monday to meet with a colleague of mine." Dr. Clemens apologized to Amy and then turned to Nichole. "Is there someplace we may speak privately?"

"I'm not sure that's a good idea." Nichole looked from Jason's hand on her arm to her cousin's face.

Jason gestured with his free hand. "You can chat in the office."

"Excellent. After you, young lady."

Eyes narrowed at Jason, Nichole walked past Dr. Clemens and into the office.

Dr. Clemens followed, with Renata close behind. At the door, the doctor turned and smiled. "Excuse us. We will only be a few moments." He closed the door soundly with a click in Renata's face.

Chapter 30

Kevin Shilo

—

Kevin's mount snorted with impatience, tired of standing in the hot sun. Kevin tightened the reins. He had waited for almost an hour on the rise behind The Highlands' main house. Anytime now, Renata would signal, and he would make his appearance.

Just in time to rescue my beautiful and terrified bride-to-be.

He had checked in with Lloyd at the stable and learned Jimmy Leigh was over at the branding site. He told Lloyd he'd come by to discuss the upcoming drive with Jim, but it could wait. Lloyd showed him the puppies, and they spoke about Blackwood Jones, and then Kevin said he would look for Jones's tracks up on the rise behind the house. Now, he waited.

He chuckled to himself and caught his breath at the pain in his side. Merril had cracked his ribs, blackened his eye, and bruised his jaw. Two of his teeth were loose, and he had spat blood for almost two hours from biting his tongue—but what was to come would be worth it.

That lying whore.

His stomach rolled at the memory of her bare limbs wrapped around Merril. He hated her and his brother, but he couldn't get her naked body out of his mind. Merril had ruined everything, including the purity of his future bride.

Now, it's my turn.

He shook his head and exhaled through his mouth to clear his thoughts. The second part of Renata's plan would go as smoothly as the first. He smiled to himself when he saw Renata wave a scarf from the kitchen door and then disappear back inside. He shook the reins and urged his mount forward.

***

Nichole Harris

—

Nichole and Dr. Clemens took seats in the office guest chairs.

"You must allow me to apologize for intruding into your home this way, Miss Harris. I don't make it a habit of arriving unannounced." His smile didn't quite reach his eyes.

Nichole nodded with irritation. "That's fine, Dr. Clemens. Let's get this over with."

"Please, call me Tony. I hate to stand on formality, especially in my profession, where it is important for my patients to feel comfortable."

"I'm quite comfortable with Doc Johnson."

His eyes narrowed at her honesty. "Well then, shall we proceed?" He pulled a writing pad and pencil from his case. "How are you feeling, Miss Harris? Any headaches, dizziness, or vomiting?"

"I have an occasional headache." She couldn't see what he wrote on his pad.

Clemens looked up from his notes. "I've spoken with Kevin Shilo and Renata. Both are perplexed by your behavior since the accident."

Nichole's face heated with ire.

Dr. Clemens's sharp eyes took in her unintended reaction and made another note.

Regardless of Dr. Clemens's diagnosis, she was confident it would not be close to what she had begun to suspect. No one, except herself, Amy and an old Indian shaman could even begin to fathom the truth. She knew he waited for a response, but since he hadn't asked her a question, she only stared at him.

Empty.

Dr. Clemens looked from her face and back to his pad. "Are you aware of your personality changes?"

"No. I don't know what you're talking about." Her tone was dismissive and cold. "My memories are returning, just as my doctor predicted."

"Doctor Johnson is not a specialist in the field of mental illness, and I am. What memories have returned?" He held his pencil ready to notate and his gaze flicked to hers.

"You consider memory loss a mental illness?"

"Of course. Now, which memories have returned?"

"Christmas in Boston with my cousin, and several that include Merril Shilo. Personal things that I find to be none of your business."

"Ah, yes, Kevin's troubled younger brother. Interesting." Dr. Clemens made additional notes.

"We're done here." Nichole began to rise from her seat.

He held out his hand and urged her to remain seated. "Please, if I may. Before you dismiss me, I have some information you should hear about cases like yours." He finished making notes and folded them away in his bag along with his pencil. "From what I have learned about your injury, several things disturb me. I believe further evaluation and care is warranted."

"What are you suggesting?"

The doctor leaned forward, elbows on his knees, and smiled. "What I have in mind for you would be what I call intensive therapy." He smiled again at Nichole's hard stare. "My facility in Kansas City offers sedation therapy. You would have a private room, and we have an excellent nursing staff."

"Sedation? Are you kidding me?"

He leaned back in his chair. "It's an effective treatment for mental illness. Many of my patients go on to lead happy, productive lives."

"My life is already happy and productive. Now, if you'll excuse me."

"Miss Harris ... Nichole. I'm sorry to say this, but this is not your decision. I feel psychiatric treatment will be beneficial for you, imperative in fact, with regards to your serious ailment."

"What ailment is that?" Nichole sneered and struggled to contain her anger.

How dare he?

"Your malady is one of acute nervous reaction, brought on by the concussion to your head last week. From what you and others have told me, it would seem you are bordering on nervous hysteria, dementia, and melancholia. That is to say—"

"Don't bother with explanations." Nichole rose from her seat, hands clenched at her sides. "I see what's happening here. Now, if you will excuse me, I have a happy and productive life to get back to. Goodbye, Dr. Clemens."

The doctor stood. "Don't be too quick to prepare for your festivities, Miss Harris." His smile had changed from friendly and professional to angry and offended. "Based on my diagnosis, you will instead instruct your maid to pack your bags. You will accompany me to Denver, where I intend to catch the train to Kansas City."

Nichole stared at him in shocked silence. When she found her voice, she spoke in a harsh but audible whisper. "No. Fucking. Way."

Dr. Clemens's eyes widened. "I beg your pardon?"

"You can, but it won't do you any good." She leaned in and glared into his eyes. "I said no. I'm not going anywhere with you. I don't need your treatment or your advice. Now, I suggest you leave before I call my cousin and have you thrown out."

"Perhaps it would be a good idea to include Mr. Harris at this point." He gave her a confident smile and resumed his seat. "Not that I need his approval to remand you to my facility, but he should be informed of my decision."

With a huff of frustration, Nichole stalked to the office door. As she flung it open, she was surprised to find Kevin and Renata talking at the far end of the dining room. She stepped to Jason who sat at the table, sipping tea.

He eyed her warily as she approached, and the look in his eyes made her heart drop.

He expected this.

"Can I see you for a minute? Alone?" she hissed at his head.

Jason turned to her with surprise. "Now?"

"Yes. Right now."

"Mr. Harris," Dr. Clemens's voice reached across the dining room. "A word, if you please."

"Jason, we need to talk now." Concern tinged with panic edged up her spine. She'd been set up, that much was clear.

Is Jason involved with this?

"It will only take a moment." The doctor had followed her from the office and was upon them. Nichole turned to face him, but he ignored her and addressed Jason.

"I've just had a very disturbing visit with your young cousin. I'm afraid to say her disorder is much worse than any of you realized. It was a wise decision on Miss Renata's part to have consulted me."

Jason swallowed and looked into his tea. His face was drawn and gray. "Go on, doctor," Jason whispered.

"It appears Miss Harris has developed an acute mania and melancholia, brought on, no doubt, by the injury to her head. The shock of these last few days has been a tremendous setback. I believe she must be treated immediately to forestall permanent dementia."

Dr. Clemens glanced briefly at Nichole, and a shiver of panic ran up her spine. With horror, she heard Jason ask the crucial question in a casual voice.

"What is it you recommend, doctor?"

"He wants me to leave with him for Denver right now, and then travel to his facility in Kansas City." Nichole gripped Jason's shoulder, but he wouldn't look at her. "I told him absolutely not. I'm not leaving with this... this quack of Renata's."

Jason rose and turned to face Nichole. He put a hand on each of her shoulders. His eyes were serious and apologetic. "Nicki, this man is a doctor, a specialist in this type of injury. If he says it would be best for you to go with him and be in his care for a while, I think we should consider it."

"What?" Her stomach dropped, and tears welled in her eyes. "Jason, you can't mean that. I don't need sedation treatments. He can't help me with my problems; no one can." Her voice rose as he closed his eyes to her. "I... dammit, Jason, look at me. Tell him no."

"I'm sorry," Jason shook his head and turned away. "It would be in your best interest to accept treatment."

"My best interest?" Nichole shouted, stunned. "Are you fucking kidding me, Jason? Where's Amy? Where's Jim?" She glanced at Renata and Kevin. They had moved closer and listened avidly. No surprise showed on their faces. Then, Renata grinned at her.

"Don't touch me." Nichole yanked her arm away from the doctor and tried to put Jason between them.

"Miss Harris, please." Clemens reached around Jason and gripped her by the wrist. "As I said before, I must return to Denver without delay."

Nichole jerked her arm but failed to break his hold. Panic tightened her chest.

Jason stepped away and turned his back.

Clemens captured both her wrists and twisted her arm in a practiced gesture, which brought her back tight against his chest. Nichole screamed and bucked her head against the doctor's chin and raked the hard edge of her shoe down his shin bone.

"No!" she shouted again as he yanked her back and wrapped his arm around her neck.

"Calm down or I will sedate you." His voice was low and cold in her ear.

"Let me go!" Nichole continued to struggle. "Put me down, goddammit!" There was no calm inside her. "What is wrong with you, Jason? Help me!" Her voice broke, and she screamed with rage.

Jason covered his face with both hands and walked away.

"Renata, fetch my bag." Dr. Clemens motioned toward the door. "Miss Harris appears to need something to calm her down."

Renata opened the case and withdrew an already damp cloth. "Is this it, Dr. Clemens?"

"Yes. Keep it away from your face. That's right; now hold it over Miss Harris's nose and mouth. Be careful she doesn't bite you."

A sickly-sweet scent came from the cloth Renata held to Nichole's face. She tried to turn her head, but the doctor held her throat tight. Heaviness pressed down on her head, and her eyelids fluttered. She heard a door slam in the distance and Amy's voice. Then, the day went black.

Chapter 31

Nichole Harris

—

Nichole's eyelids fluttered, struggling to stay open. From the blank depth of her drug-induced sleep, she clawed her way to the surface. There was something she had to do. Something urgent. She could hear movement near her—an irregular step on the floor.

She tried to say Merril's name, but the words didn't form. Her face was numb—rubbery. It would be easier to sink back down into the darkness, but she resisted the urge. Her instincts warned her to run, but to do that she must open her eyes. A blurry outline captured her attention through watery vision. Color in motion came toward her, then paced away. Nausea gripped her, and for a few moments she struggled against that, gagging.

"You awake?"

The voice was wrong.

Why am I so sick?

In a flash, she remembered why, and panic seized her. She fought to sit up. The cold porcelain of a bedpan thrust into her side, and she wrapped her arm around it, retching.

"He said you'd need that when you woke up."

Agonized heaves clenched her gut as her head pulsed with pain. She knew Kevin watched her as she tried to gain control of her stomach. She hated him just a little bit more for that. She spat out the last bitterness and wiped the tears streaming down her face.

"Holy shit," Nichole muttered.

"Yeah, you look like shit." Kevin took the bedpan and set it near the door. He handed her a damp towel.

She held it to her face as she sat the rest of the way up. She recognized her bed. "Where's that doctor?" Words were hard. Her mouth wouldn't cooperate. Pain pounded behind her eyes.

"He left."

Nichole lowered the towel and blinked at Kevin's blurry form. "Why?" She reapplied the cool cloth to her face.

"I didn't let him take you, so he left." Kevin chuckled.

"You didn't?" She wiped her face one last time and tossed the towel toward the bedpan. "How did that... what happened? Where is Jason?"

"Jason is downstairs with Amy. She's rather upset. Renata rode back to The Shilo with Dr. Clemens."

"Kevin." Nichole's numb mouth refused to cooperate, and she spoke slowly. Her eyes were gritty and burned. They watered as she squinted to focus her vision. It hurt to blink. The sickly-sweet scent of ether clung to her face. "What did you tell... that doctor?"

"I told him he couldn't take you from me." Kevin walked around the bed and squatted down in front of her. He grunted as though it hurt to move.

"Why did he— How could you—" Kevin's face swam into focus. "Holy crap, Kevin. You look terrible."

Kevin ignored Nichole's comment. "Dr. Clemens told Jason only a close relative could stop him from placing you in his hospital. A father, or a brother, or... your husband."

Nichole blinked at him. "I don't understand."

"As your betrothed, it was left up to me. I saved you."

"You saved me." She whispered his words and tried to make sense of his explanation. "But... we're not getting married."

"Oh, I think we are. Either we marry, or the good doctor comes back and takes you away." Kevin studied her face.

Horror filled her. She opened her mouth to speak but couldn't take a breath.

The grin on Kevin's battered face grew wide and gleeful.

Two short breaths wheezed into her lungs, and she held his gaze as she spoke. "You would force me to marry you? Why would you do that?"

"I have my reasons." He stood, the grin gone, and stepped away from the bed.

He paused at the door, and a strange smile spread across his bruised face. "In case you think your pretty cousin will stop the marriage, you'll need to think again. Jason has his own reasons to keep his mouth shut." He captured her gaze and grinned. "I promise you—he won't interfere."

Nichole turned her head and blinked tears from her still-burning eyes.

"You're a mess," Kevin said from the doorway. "Clean yourself up and come downstairs. We will announce our engagement at the barbecue tomorrow night. You have fifteen minutes, or I'll be back for you—and you won't like that one bit."

The door swung closed with a click.

***

Amy Harris

—

Amy paced the length of Jason's desk, her nails tapping angrily on the corners each time she turned. She had stepped out of the room to speak with Jeanne and Lawna about the barbecue. When she heard Nichole scream her name, she had run through the kitchen in time to see Kevin lift the unconscious Nichole in his arms and carry her up the stairs.

"No, Jason, I don't understand. You say that doctor of Renata's sedated Nichole after she became hysterical, but that doesn't make sense."

Jason rose from his leather chair. He didn't speak until Amy stopped pacing and looked at him. "Dr. Clemens was gracious enough to examine Nichole and provide us with his recommendations." He looked away from Amy's intense gaze and adjusted his cufflinks. "I intend to help my cousin in any way I can. Dr. Clemens studies injuries of the brain. Doc Johnson is a country doctor and a part-time veterinarian."

"That still doesn't tell me what upset her." Amy countered. The whole situation, Doctor Clemens, Renata's involvement, and now Jason's indifferent attitude, gave her a sick feeling in her stomach.

"Dr. Clemens recommended Nichole be committed to a hospital that specializes in treating this type of brain injury—"

"A sanitarium?" Amy said before Jason finished speaking. "How could you even consider that?"

"She's still here, isn't she?" Jason yelled. He paused, took a slow breath, and lowered his tone. "I agree Nichole should remain here with us, and she is. She is upstairs in her room, as we speak." Jason dropped his gaze to his desk. "Now, please. There are some things I must take care of this evening. I don't have time for your hysterics as well."

Amy stood completely still. Anger coursed through her and made her heart beat fast. Her hands, clenched into fists at her side, opened into claws and took on a luminous blue glow. "I see." Her voice was soft—controlled—and the glow slowly faded. "Then, I leave you to your work." Her glare burned unspoken accusations into Jason's equally cold stare as he raised his head and met her eyes. She turned and stalked to the office door when Jason's voice stopped her.

"Perhaps you should consider returning to Denver for a while."

Amy's back straightened. "Yes, of course, Jason," she replied without turning. "I had already thought of that myself."

***

Nichole Harris

—

Nichole stared dumbfounded at the closed door. She had fifteen minutes to—what?

Change my clothes? Slit my wrists? Become presentable?

She closed her eyes and let her head spin.

Well, shit.

The room smelled of ether and vomit, or was that her?

She struggled to her feet and held onto the tall dresser for balance, then wobbled over to the dressing table. One look in the mirror and she laughed out loud. Her laughter dissolved into sobs as she sank onto the chair and covered her face.

A sanitarium or marriage to a madman.

Was everyone in on this heinous plan? They had to be. Why else would Jason let this happen?

The realization that her fifteen minutes were ticking away—and that Kevin would return—sent a shock of fear into her gut and got her moving. She sniffed, wiped her nose, and glared at her pathetic reflection. The tip of her nose had peeled and showed pink through her unbecoming tanned skin. There was vomit on her bodice. Her hair bun had slid down the side of her head. Her eyes were puffy and red.

Fifteen minutes. I hope he doesn't expect too much.

She pulled the pins from the bun, brushed her hair, and repinned it. Cool water and a moist towel couldn't wash the smell off her, but she felt better. She rinsed her mouth and spat into the bowl, then took one last look in the mirror.

She choked back the urge to fall to the ground and weep. Instead, she stiffened her spine.

I'm not dead, or married, or locked away just yet.

Anger at the injustice kept her on her feet. When she reached the bottom of the stairs, she looked at Jason's office. The door was closed. The sound of clinking glass turned her attention to the music room. Despite her anger, her stomach fluttered with nerves and her knees trembled.

Kevin is dangerous. He's already proven that.

Cautiously, she entered the room.

Kevin looked up at the clock and grinned. "Two minutes to spare. I almost hoped you wouldn't show." He downed a full glass of whiskey and set the empty glass on the mantel. He hissed as the alcohol burned his throat, and then turned toward her. "I'm glad you've decided to accept the situation, Nicki," he drawled and pointed to a seat. "It'll make things so much easier for us." His satisfaction was apparent as she seated herself where he had indicated. Then, he stepped to the door and slammed it shut.

"Would you like a drink? A glass of water?" He pulled a decanter from the liquor cabinet and poured a glass half-full of water. "You're mighty quiet, sweetheart. Perhaps you'd like to tell me what's bothering you?"

Nichole's glare shot to Kevin, but her furious words died in her throat. There was madness in Kevin's eyes—the same violent madness she'd seen yesterday when he killed Toma. She tried to swallow, but fear had sucked the moisture from her mouth. Those insane eyes were trained on her. He smiled, reading her reaction and set her water on the mantel. He took a step toward her.

"I saw you and Merril at Shadow Creek the other day. I know what kind of lies you've been telling me." He smiled again and advanced another step. "That wasn't very nice, you know."

Oh shit!

She rose to flee just as his thick-fingered hand closed around her throat and pressed her back against the cushion. His mouth descended over hers and cut off her scream of terror along with her breath. She pushed against his chest and shoulders, but he only increased the pressure of his hand on her throat and stuck his tongue between her lips when she gasped for breath through whiskey fumes.

Darkness closed around her vision, and bright sparks flashed, just as the pressure released. She sucked in a shaky breath, and then Kevin forced his tongue back into her mouth. She gagged and pushed against him. Then, the devouring mouth was gone, fastened instead on her breast he had freed from her torn dress.

A sharp pain shot through her nipple as he bit painfully into her tender flesh. One of his hands clawed frantically at her thigh where he had bunched up her dress. The other clutched greedily at her other breast leaving dark red marks on her white skin.

Nichole panted, and anger exploded in her mind. She wove her fingers deep into his thick hair, then yanked back and down with all the strength she could muster.

His head came up and away from her breast with a smacking sound.

She drew back her arm and launched her fist as hard as she could into his face. As her fist connected with his eye, she rolled toward him. Her movement dumped him off the settee and onto the floor.

A deadly growl grated from his throat, but she had already gained her feet. She raced to the door, her bodice clutched to her breast, and was out of the room before Kevin could get to his feet.

She looked back as she rounded the banister.

Kevin stood in the doorway and their gazes locked.

He's going to kill me.

Terror galvanized her, and she picked up her skirt and raced up the stairs.

His boots pounded into the parlor behind her.

She didn't pause at the top of the stairs to look back. She ran to her room, shut the door and wedged her chair beneath the handle. Trembling, she sank to the bed and waited for the door to burst open and her life to end.

***

Kevin Shilo

—

Incensed, Kevin dashed after her. His eye had already begun to swell where she'd hit him. He stopped for a moment at the base of the stairs and heard her bedroom door slam shut. A thrill of anticipation shot through him as he placed his boot on the first step.

"Kevin." Jimmy Leigh's harsh voice jerked him to a standstill. "What are you doing here? I thought you left with Renata."

Kevin glared at the tall man who stood in front of the closed office door.

"No, I decided to stick around... see if I could help out for tomorrow night."

Jim nodded, stepped around the table, and approached the stairs. "What happened to your eye?"

Kevin winced. "That damned brother of mine. You heard what he did?"

"I heard some nonsense. I find it all a bit hard to believe. Can't imagine what got into Merril, can you?" Jim's voice had a hard edge of anger. He took another step toward Kevin.

Kevin eased his foot off the stair and stepped back. He shoved his hands in his pockets and shook his head. "No, can't say that I can." He backed away as the big foreman continued to approach. "I really ought to head back. What with Merril running off, there's no one at the ranch to keep an eye on things. Wages go out today."

"That's true," Jim agreed stoically. "I think you should run along."

Kevin opened the door and hurried outside. He glanced back just long enough to see Jim turn and look up the stairs. Kevin closed the door and ran to his horse, who stood saddled and waiting in the corral.

Chapter 32

Nichole Harris

—

Nichole sat on her bed and tried to control her ragged breath to hear Kevin when he came up the stairs. The adrenaline eased, and she began to tremble. She waited in apprehension, listening for his boots on the stairs, but the sound never came. She stood and pressed her ear to the door. No sound in the hallway. No noise on the stairs.

She shifted the chair from beneath the knob and cracked the door enough to peek out. Kevin should have broken down her door by now, but the house remained silent. Whatever his reason, he hadn't followed her upstairs. She shoved her hair from her face, closed her door and leaned against it, tense as a coiled spring.

He could be anywhere.

She wedged the chair beneath the knob again, crossed the room and peered out the balcony door. The clopping of hoofbeats caught her attention.

Kevin galloped his horse down the drive toward The Shilo.

He's gone.

She slumped against the doorframe in profound relief and shut the door. She shook her head and covered her mouth with her hands. Sobs erupted, and she sank to her knees beside the bed.

This isn't over. He'll be back.

She needed help, but to whom could she turn? Jason let this happen—why? Merril beat Kevin bloody then ran away—why? Why did they want her to marry Kevin?

A shudder of disgust went through her.

Kevin—ugh.

She rose from her knees and staggered to the dressing table. Her face appeared ashen and blotched, with dark circles underneath her eyes. Her lips were swollen, and her hair hung in tangles around her face. But it was the bruises on her neck and breast she studied. Red tooth marks stung where her skin was scored beside her nipple.

With a cry of rage, she tore the dress to the waist, pushed it over her hips and let it fall in a pool at her feet. Wishing it was Kevin's head, she stepped out of the bunched material and kicked it with fury under the bed. Her torn shift followed the dress. She grabbed the brush and drew it through her tangled hair.

She wasn't going to marry Kevin—that much was certain.

How can I stop him? They'll lock me away.

They can try.

They can, and they will. Kevin was quite clear about that.

But why? It didn't make sense. What was their motive for wanting this marriage? Kevin's motive certainly wasn't love. Then, what? Money? If she married Kevin, what would happen?

That was easy—the two ranches would combine.

Then, it would all be his.

Bullshit. Half would still be mine.

Not true. Here and now, marriage would make both ranches his.

Half of The Shilo Ranch belongs to Merril.

Not if he abandons his share.

Merril was set up too, so Kevin would get both ranches. What did Renata get?

Nichole froze, the hairbrush suspended in mid-stroke. Renata only stood to gain if Nichole was out of the picture—after the marriage.

They intend to lock me away after the marriage—or worse.

What did Jason get? He would lose everything. Besides, she knew Jason. He wouldn't let them do this to her unless there was a reason. She had to find out what that was, and she needed someone she could trust.

A knock at the door startled her, and she dropped the brush. "Yes?" Her voice broke. She cleared her throat and spoke louder. "Yes?"

"Dinner's ready, Nicki," Jeanne called through the closed door. Moments later, her footsteps skipped down the stairs.

Nichole pulled the first skirt and blouse she found out of the trunk, grabbed a new chemise from the drawer, and slipped into them. She moved the chair from beneath the door handle and went downstairs.

Lawna and Jeanne were setting the table when Nichole walked into the dining room. Both women stopped and stared at her with concern.

"Are you all right, Miss Nichole?" Lawna asked.

"You don't look so well," Jeanne said. She and Lawna exchanged worried glances.

Nichole gestured vaguely with her hand. "I'm fine. I must have allergies."

"You mean the hay fever, Miss Nichole?" Lawna supplied.

"That's it." She pointed at Lawna. "I have hay fever."

"Cookie has hay fever too." Jeanne poured cool spring-house water into the glasses. "She swears eating honey helps her."

"Thank you, Jeanne. I'll try that."

Jeanne smiled as she and Lawna turned together and returned to the kitchen.

It was nice to see Jeanne and Lawna getting along so well. Nichole had forgotten about Timothy and Lawna. At least one thing appeared to be on a good track.

The door to Jason's office opened, and Jim stalked out, his face like a thundercloud. He pulled up short when he saw her standing near the table. He looked her over carefully, from the hem of her skirt up. His gaze lingered on her face and grew even darker than before. "Nicki." He gave her a short nod and then continued out the front door, slamming it closed behind him.

Nichole turned to watch as he passed her. She'd never seen Jim other than stoic or slightly amused. His piercing angry gaze unsettled her. What had made him so mad?

"How are you feeling?"

Nichole's head swiveled from the front door to Jason. He looked annoyed as he stepped from his office to the table and pulled out Nichole's chair to seat her.

"What the hell, Jason?" Her voice rose as she prepared to vent her anger at his abandonment. She hadn't intended to jump down his throat, but the sight of him, so calm and slightly put out, pissed her off all over again.

Jason raised his finger and pointed at her nose. "Be silent. There has been enough fighting and screaming and arguing in this house today. I will brook no more."

She rolled her eyes and battled tears. "Why are you doing this to me?" she whispered.

He indicated her chair. "Sit."

She sighed and refused to meet his eyes as she lowered herself onto the chair and stared at the empty china plate, simmering in rage.

Jason took his seat in silence and served himself from the platter of sliced beef. He took another slice and gestured questioningly at Nichole's plate. Nichole nodded. Their pretense of normalcy was absurd. She refused to speak as he filled her plate.

When he finished placing the second slice of beef on her plate, he cleared his throat. "Let's just say I was under some... pressure to act contrary to my feelings earlier today. However, that has been resolved."

"Resolved?"

"Indeed. Yams?"

The front door opened, and Amy came in.

Jason rose and pulled out her chair across from Nichole.

"Thank you, Jason, but I need to wash up first." Amy sailed past them and into the kitchen, but not before Nichole saw her tear-stained face and reddened eyes.

Jason waited by Amy's chair for her to return. Almost immediately, Amy was back, her face clean but her eyes still red and puffy. Jason seated her and returned to his seat.

"Beef?"

"Thank you," Amy replied.

Jason served his wife, setting the plate before her and returning to his meal. The change in the dynamic between husband and wife was obvious.

Nichole picked up her fork just as Cookie stepped into the room with a large pot of honey and a dipper. She set it down by the biscuits and nodded her head at the family.

"The hay fever is takin' this family somethin' awful this year. Y'all be sure to have some honey on your biscuit. It will help." She nodded her head at Nichole and Amy and returned to the kitchen.

They ate dinner in silence. Jason stared morosely into his plate, and Amy only picked at her dinner. Soon after the strawberries and shortcake were served, Amy excused herself to her room. Jason tossed his napkin onto his plate and returned to his office when Amy disappeared up the stairs.

Left to her own devices, Nichole wandered into the music room, careful to avoid the love seat. She moved around the baby grand piano and sat on the cushioned piano bench. She laid her hands on the keys. Only the tips of her fingers caressed the ivories.

At first, the tune was forced and awkward. Discordant notes and difficult tempos made a cacophony of her song. Eventually, the melody gained strength and rang true as she played it repeatedly until it felt right. The words to the song filled her head and she spoke them softly with the music. So many melodies and lyrics competed in her head that she stopped playing and sat with her eyes closed, listening to the playlist inside her head. She knew the words, the tunes, the artists. Her eyes flew open and searched the room.

Why do I know these things? How?

Anxiety crushed her chest, and her head began to pound. She lurched to her feet, blew out the lamp, and then made her way around to the stairs.

Jeanne and Lawna had already cleared the dinner dishes, and Jason was behind closed doors.

Nichole climbed the stairs, a few steps at a time, one hand on the railing and the other pressed to the aching pain in her brow while an oldies station played songs in her head.

She closed her door and slumped heavily against it. Weariness weighed on her, almost as though she'd been drugged again. Her body fought against her and hampered her every movement. She moved in a fog. Pain and music competed for her attention. At last, she found herself undressed and in her bed. She pulled the covers over her head and escaped into sleep.

Nichole woke late the next morning with a dull pounding at the base of her skull. Immediately, she realized the noise came from the bedroom door. She raised her head and looked dumbfounded at the chair braced beneath the handle.

"Nichole? Are you ill?" Amy called. The door shook again. "Open the door, please. It's getting late."

Chapter 33

Nichole Harris

—

Nichole stared at the chair. Why would the—

Oh, yeah. Kevin.

Still half-asleep, she rolled out of bed and paused to let the dizziness pass. She gripped the chair and moved it away from the door.

"Are you all right?" Amy asked. She walked into the room and eyed the chair in Nichole's hands. "What's this?"

Suspicion colored everything and everyone. Nichole shrugged. "My future husband made unwanted advances last night. I thought it best to take precautions."

"What?" Amy exclaimed. Her startled eyes opened wide. "What future husband?"

Nichole stared at Amy. "You don't know?"

"Know what?" Amy's brow furrowed, and she closed the door behind her.

"About the doctor... about Kevin."

Amy shook her head. "Jason became angry when I questioned him about Dr. Clemens, and I know nothing about Kevin."

"So, you don't know what's happened?"

"Apparently not. I know Dr. Clemens sedated you—that his recommendations upset you, and rightfully so. I saw Kevin carry you to your room. Everyone from The Shilo departed, while Jason and I... discussed Dr. Clemens's absurd ideas."

Nichole's anger ignited at the mention of Kevin. She paced away from Amy. "Dr. Clemens intended to take me out of the house by force yesterday. When he grabbed me, I tried to fight him and begged Jason to help me."

Amy sank slowly into the chair as Nichole continued her tirade.

"Jason turned his back. He walked away, Amy. He did nothing to stop them. Nothing!"

"I don't understand." Amy shook her head. "None of this makes any sense."

"When I woke up, Kevin was in my room." She paused and looked at Amy, her fists clenched at her sides. "He told me he had saved me from Clemens and that unless I married him, the doctor would return and take me to his asylum. He said Jason wouldn't stop him."

"This is unbelievable." Amy's eyes were wide with sympathy and horror.

"Believe it." Nichole wiped at angry tears.

"Why would they do this?" Amy's hands twisted in her lap. "Why would Jason allow it to happen?"

"I don't know. And to be honest, at this point, I don't care." Nichole swiped at another tear. "I won't go into that asylum, and I will not marry Kevin Shilo." She spat his name as though it burned her tongue to speak it. She bit the back of her hand to keep from crying.

Merril, where are you?

"No, of course not." Amy sat back and stared at Nichole. "Those are no choices at all."

Nichole cleared her throat and took a breath. "I gave this a lot of thought last night." She paced across the room. "If I stay here, they'll eventually get their way—one way or the other." She stopped and turned to Amy. Her lip quivered, but she fought the emotion back. "But I don't know where else to go." The tears won and tightened her voice. "I own this ranch, but I have no money and no resources." She pressed her lips and gripped her sides with her arms. "I have nothing."

"That's not entirely true." Amy's shoulders sagged, and she looked away. "In fact, I was told I should consider returning to Denver." Her voice was a harsh whisper. She wiped her cheek before she raised her gaze to Nichole. "The house in Denver is yours. We could go together. I know attorneys in Denver and doctors. I have friends there. You wouldn't be at anyone's mercy. And you wouldn't be alone."

Nichole leaned back against the dressing table, her knees weak with relief. She released a sigh and felt her heart begin to pound with determination. "When can we go?" she whispered.

"After the barbecue." Amy sniffed and wiped her face with the heel of her hand. "We should leave in the morning, before dawn. We'll blend in with the other ranchers heading home after the big celebration." She nodded once and smiled at Nichole. "I'll talk with Jim. We'll need his help."

"No one can know." Panic fluttered in Nichole's chest. "What if he tells Jason?"

"He won't. I'll explain the situation. We can trust him, I'm sure of it."

Nichole ran her hand over her face. She pushed her curls away from her eyes and considered Amy. "How long will it take to get there?"

"Between eight and ten hours."

"Ten hours?" Nichole murmured.

Was Denver that far?

"I think that's the best we can manage," Amy explained. "I usually camp halfway and make it a two-day trip. Although, I think that would be unwise in this case. If we're careful with the animals, we can make it in one day."

"How far is Denver?" Nichole asked.

"At least forty miles, though it seems much farther in the winter."

"Wait... what?" Nichole narrowed her eyes and rubbed at the pain behind her eyebrows. "Forty miles in ten hours? That's—"

"Remarkably quick, I know." Amy finished Nichole's sentence. "But we don't want to be stopped. It won't be easy on the team. We'll need to use the buckboard." Amy's finger tapped her chin. Her eyes focused on the floor as she verbalized their escape plan.

Nichole sank into the chair, both hands on her brow.

Maybe I am on the verge of hysterics. Amy's time and distance didn't make sense.

I can fly from Dallas to El Paso in less than two hours. Fly? She squeezed her eyes shut.

I can't fly—I have flown. Pain erupted across her skull.

"Jim will make sure the team is well-cared-for. Let's hope the rains haven't washed out the road. If that's the case, it will take two days."

Amy's voice sounded distant, as though Nichole's ears needed to pop. She peeked at Amy from beneath her hands. Amy stood at the wardrobe.

Nichole's gaze darted around the room and paused at the oil lamp, the bedpan, the bowl and pitcher on her dresser. She searched for a light switch near the door, and her gaze rose to the middle of the empty ceiling. There was no overhead light.

What's happening to me?

"You should wear this tonight." Amy pulled a dress from the wardrobe. "It was always my favorite of yours." She held up a deep burgundy Victorian dress with white lace accenting the sleeves, bodice and skirt inset. A matching double slip and bustle hung together with the dress.

Nichole looked at the dress, and the room began to spin. "Amy, I... " Tears streamed down her face, and her breath hitched. Panic paralyzed her. She struggled to inhale but couldn't, as though she'd been punched in the gut.

Amy looked up from the dress to Nichole's face. "Nicki, what?" She shoved the dress back into the wardrobe and knelt before Nichole. She brushed the hair from Nichole's face, and her gaze dropped to the front of her gaping nightgown. She pushed the neckline open and exposed the bruised and bitten skin. Amy's hand covered her mouth in horror as her gaze lifted to meet Nichole's. "Nicki is... is this... did Kevin do this?"

Nichole pulled the nightgown closed and doubled over. A ragged breath filled her lungs. Amy's warm arms wrapped around her. She rested her head on Amy's shoulder and cried.

Amy straightened Nichole's long curls and rubbed her back. "Oh, my dear, I didn't know. I thought Kevin left with that doctor and Renata. Shh. It will be all right. I promise you. We'll leave here, and you'll be safe. He won't touch you again."

Nichole held on to Amy until the room stopped spinning. There was darkness everywhere her thoughts turned.

There's something wrong with my mind.

Even that knowledge was somehow less painful than Merril's abandonment.

Where are you? I need you.

Jason's betrayal and Kevin's despicable scheme made the third point in her trinity of horror. Her ears popped, and Amy's voice was suddenly clear.

"You need to be strong tonight." Amy pushed Nichole away and held her at arm's-length. They looked into each other's tear-filled eyes. "The most important thing will be to act natural. No one can suspect what we plan. You can't let them know they don't have you cornered. They are counting on that. We want them to believe you have no way out."

Nichole nodded and whispered, "You're right. One thing at a time."

Amy rose to her feet, still holding Nichole's hand. "Pack what you want to bring in your trunk when you're alone. You don't want Jeanne or Lawna to ask awkward questions."

Amy released Nichole's hand and returned to the wardrobe for the burgundy gown and laid it on the bed. "Jeanne will be up to help you dress and fix your hair soon." Amy paused at the door and looked back at Nichole. "Throw on a robe and get a bite to eat in the kitchen. You'll feel better for it. You need to eat something before tonight." She smiled at Nichole, and although her smile was sad, it gave encouragement as well. "We can do this. We only have to get through tonight."

Chapter 34

Jason Harris

—

Jason looked over the guests who socialized across the yard. Ranchers and wranglers had begun to arrive around noon, and now the barbecue was in full swing. Jason lingered near the ranch road, not far from the house, to greet late arrivals.

Cookie and Lloyd's barbecue pit had been uncovered a few hours ago with grand ceremony. Succulent pork and beef trays graced the dining tables, both inside and out. Lloyd had placed the outside table angled from the back corner of the house. The table separated the guest area in the side yard from the food preparation area behind the kitchen. Cookie and Lawna maintained a constant supply of meat, sauces, biscuits, yams, and mint tea to both tables.

The rails from the corral had been taken down the day before and stacked behind the barn. Every other corral post was decorated with ribbons that fluttered merrily in the early evening breeze.

The dance platform Tom and Timothy had built stood in the center of the circle of corral posts. It proved so popular that the wranglers began to display their hoedown skills long before the musicians commenced to play. Even after the music started, the lack of female partners didn't discourage their good time. The men didn't hesitate to partner up and do-si-do with each other.

The rhythmic chant of the square-dance caller sounded like the steady flow of an auctioneer. Between called sets, cowboys would take to the stage and perform solo dance routines that consisted of fast footwork along with boot and knee-slapping.

Jason cheered with the crowd as the latest performer bowed and stepped down to his back-patting buddies. The group of young men headed toward the beer wagon. There were two fiddle players and a banjo player seated near the dance platform. The music in the yard never seemed to stop.

Jason smiled and greeted Mickey Carpenter, a ranch owner who grazed his herd south of Fort Morgan. "I'm glad you made it. No trouble on the way, I hope."

Mickey shook Jason's hand. "No trouble at all. Glad to be here." He tipped his hat to the back of his head. "I've got several men with me. We planned to stay the night. Where do you want us to set up camp?"

Jason pointed west, beyond the barn and bunkhouse. "There's a flat area past the outbuildings. A few folks have already set up camps. Go back to the road and head west. You can't miss it."

Mickey shooed both hands at the men behind him. "Back the wagon up. We need to move over there." He pointed toward the setting sun then grinned at Jason. "Thank ya, son. I'll see the boys set camp, and then we'll be back here lickety-split. I hope to dance with that pretty little cousin of yours."

Jason's smile faltered, but Mickey had already turned away. Jason slapped Mickey on the back as he walked to his wagon. "It's good to see you, Mickey."

Mickey and his men backed down the drive, and Jason found himself alone for a moment. He scanned the crowd in the yard but couldn't find Amy. He had seen her an hour ago on the porch. The icy look she sent him when their gazes met sank his heart.

Nichole had yet to make her appearance.

Near the vittles table, Cookie joked with several cowboys as they made sandwiches with biscuits and meat. On the other side of the barn, the beer wagon stood surrounded by men. Most brought their own tin cups, but there were also house cups with the HH brand painted on the side stacked beside the oak kegs. Jimmy Leigh and Lloyd stood near the barn, close enough to watch both the beer wagon and enjoy the dance platform entertainment.

Jason glanced at the house just as Kevin and Renata crossed the porch to the rail. His eyes narrowed at the pair.

I wish they hadn't come.

Kevin and Renata paused to look over the festivities, chatting softly.

Jason stood close enough to the porch to see Renata avoid a tipsy cowboy with a quick sidestep to her left.

"Drunken fool," Renata hissed at the wrangler. She brushed at her deep red skirt and returned to whispering in Kevin's ear.

Jason saw Kevin nod and step from the porch into the yard, while Renata turned and made her way back inside.

"Jason! Wonderful barbecue this year, just wonderful."

Jason smiled and turned his attention to Gary Bishop, and the two men shook hands.

***

Nichole Harris

—

Jeanne took a hairpin from her mouth and wove it into Nichole's hair.

Nichole winced as the pin scratched across her scalp.

"There," Jeanne proclaimed. "Shake your head." She pulled the remaining hairpins from her mouth and tossed them onto the dressing table, her attention fixed on Nichole's hair.

Nichole shook her head side to side, then up and down.

"Does it feel secure?" Jeanne asked.

"Yes. It's good and tight."

"It needs to be. You'll be dancing."

"Oh, I don't know about that." Nichole struggled to find an emotion other than dread reflected in her eyes.

Jeanne laughed as she tucked the hairpins in the drawer. "There are a hundred or so cowboys outside and maybe twelve women. What do you think?"

Nichole met Jeanne's gaze in the mirror with a look of horror on her face.

"Stand up." Jeanne's smile crinkled her eyes as she chuckled at Nichole. "Let me take one more look at the dress."

"The dress is good. It's huge." Nichole stood, glanced at her reflection and cringed.

Jeanne giggled again and adjusted the lace handkerchief Nichole had asked her to stitch into the plunging neckline of the gown.

"This is a good idea," Jeanne commented. "It's stitched to stay put, and it covers the... bruises." The question in Jeanne's eyes remained unspoken.

Nichole felt her face flush and looked away. "Yes. You did an excellent job. Thank you." She smoothed her skirt and turned, keeping her eyes on her reflection. "You should get dressed, as well. We're late as it is."

Jeanne sighed and waved away Nichole's concern. "It won't take me but two shakes to get dressed and pull back my hair. The party will go on all night. We won't be late at all." Jeanne glanced back as she stepped through the doorway. "I'll see you downstairs."

"Yes. Thank you, Jeanne." When the door closed, Nichole straightened and let out her breath. She admired her costume for a moment in the mirror. It was gorgeous and weighty. She both loved it and was confused by it. Jeanne insisted she put on a corset, three stiff petticoats, and a small bustle at the back to hold the gown away from her legs. It was beautiful and as foreign to her as the chamber pot. And yet, she knew, without doubt, the dress had always been her favorite.

She walked around the room and looked through the dresser drawers.

What do you pack for an escape?

She wouldn't be coming back anytime soon, that was certain. She'd already packed the clothes she liked. She opened the trunk and placed her hairbrush beside chemises, underdrawers and several freshly laundered skirt sets and blouses. She'd also packed an extra set of shoes and boots. The small trunk was full.

She was about to lower the lid when she remembered the photograph. She retrieved it from the mantel and gazed at the faces one last time. Merril, Kevin and herself—so serious and formal—in happier times, perhaps. She wished she could remember when the photo had been taken. She placed it on top of the lavender skirt and closed the lid. The latch clicked shut, and she ran her hand over the nameplate. N.H.

She picked up her shoulder wrap from the bed then turned to face the door.

How can I do this?

There were too many outlandish ideas and bizarre recollections to sort through. It was as though her memory had been double exposed—each thought had a slightly altered ghost image. What she suspected wasn't possible, or there were so many impossible explanations, it made her head spin.

Either way, she needed to walk into this party and pretend to be normal. After all, she was the frickin' hostess.

I can't think of that. It's more important to make Kevin and Renata believe they have me trapped.

She took a deep breath and closed her eyes. Her heart pounded in her chest and echoed in her ears. She would smile at Kevin and Jason. She would dance with a hundred cowboys. Then she would leave this place before dawn.

I have to sell this performance tonight. I'll sort out the rest in Denver.

Nichole opened her eyes and prayed she could keep it together. She straightened her back, squared her shoulders, and then opened the door and went downstairs.

***

Kevin Shilo

—

Kevin moved leisurely through the crowded yard. He stopped now and then to speak with one of the cowboys he recognized or share a toast in his father's memory with one of the neighboring ranchers. Most guests had first learned of his father's death when they'd arrived tonight. To his disgust, the cowboys asked about Merril's absence as many times as he received condolences for Pa's passing. It irked him. He nodded absently at Gary Bishop's eldest daughter. She smiled back with gusto, but Kevin looked away.

Then, on the far side of the yard, near the porch, he saw Merril speaking with Tom Baker. Kevin's thoughts grew grim. He ground his teeth and balled his fists. The crowd obscured his view for a moment, and when the gathering of people parted, both men were gone. He growled deep in his throat and scanned the crowd again.

"Kevin Shilo! Yoo-hoo! You're just the man we hoped to find." Gary Bishop's plump wife, Buela, smiled up at him and indicated her daughter. "Nancy Mae asked if she could come say hello to you and your brother. How are you both doing? We heard about your pa, and we're sure sorry. Was it his heart?"

Kevin nodded to Nancy Mae and her mother. "We believe it was, yes. Excuse me."

"But your brother? Where is he?" Buela clucked her tongue as Kevin stalked away. "Well, I never! Nancy Mae, go find your father and tell him I want to leave."

"But Mama—"

Their voices faded as Kevin stalked through the crowd. He saw Renata glance his way and then step into the house. If Merril dared show his face to him, there would be hell to pay.

***

Nichole Harris

—

Nichole paused a moment on the last rise of the staircase. The step gave her the height to see around the room. She could smell roasted meat on the table, but her nerves made the aroma unappetizing. Several men stood in the dining room and talked as they ate Cookie's dinner offerings. They were all older gentlemen dressed in western-cut suits and vests. They would be the ranchers, she decided. On her left, several ladies chatted together in the parlor. Their evening finery marked them as ranchers' wives.

From the music room, she heard the piano begin to play. Boisterous voices chimed in and sang along. Outside the open windows, fiddles and a banjo played lively dance tunes. Her gaze skipped through the faces, looking for anyone she knew.

A bearded gentleman near the table looked up and caught her attention, then moved toward her with a smile.

"Miss Harris, how lovely you look this evening. This is a wonderful barbecue. I've rarely seen The Highlands so festive." He gave her a short bow, then raised his gaze to hers and smiled.

"Thank you." Nichole returned the man's smile, and her mind went blank.

He cleared his throat in the awkward silence and then gestured toward the table. "Your cook appears to have outdone herself this evening. Would you care to sample her mint tea?"

"Yes, I would like that. Thank you."

By the look on the man's face, she should have recognized him. His brow furrowed, but he had the good manners not to remark on her lapse.

I shouldn't have come down by myself.

These people knew her and expected her to know them. Her stomach dropped, and she stumbled on one of her petticoats.

"Here, let me help you." The gentleman's glance became solicitous. He took her arm, guided her to the table, and filled a small round glass with mint tea. He handed the drink to her with a slight bow and a concerned smile.

Nichole took a sip of tea and nodded her thanks.

Marvelous beginning.

If asked, this guy would be the first to sign her up for the asylum.

"There you are, love. You took your time coming down. Mr. Iliff, how good to see you again." Renata glided to a stop beside Nichole and extended her hand to the gentleman.

"My pleasure, ma'am. I just congratulated Miss Harris on this wonderful barbecue. I'm sure Quincy and Phil would have approved wholeheartedly."

"I'm sure they would." Renata agreed and then turned to Nichole with a grin. "Kevin has asked for you. You know how anxious he is to see you."

Nichole's eyes narrowed at Renata.

What a bitch.

She gave Renata a wide smile and then turned to the man beside her. "Thank you for the tea, Mr. Iliff. I'm pleased you're having a good time."

"I am. I truly am." His head lifted as a new tune resonated from the music room. "I'm sorry ladies, but I believe I hear my wife's concerto beginning. If I don't attend her concert this evening, she'll never forgive me."

"Certainly, Mr. Iliff," Renata replied. "I hope we have the opportunity to speak later."

"Yes, of course." Mr. Iliff smiled politely and walked away.

Nichole's smile faded as she turned to Renata.

Renata raised one perfectly formed eyebrow. "I'm surprised."

"Why's that?" Nichole sipped her tea and allowed her gaze to drift over the room.

Where is Amy?

"I could almost feel some admiration for you, were you not so... defense-less."

Nichole gave Renata an annoyed look. "Shut up, Renata. You're a scheming little whore."

Renata's eyes opened wide in surprise at Nichole's attack. She leaned close and hissed into her ear. "I'll be glad to see you get what you deserve. You're nothing but a spoiled bitch."

"Really?" Nichole's smile grew, and then she chuckled aloud. "Meow, Renata. You can do better than that."

Renata stared at her. "You should use some caution. Perhaps you *are* insane."

Nichole looked up at the door just as Kevin entered the room from the porch. His attention locked on her and he moved directly toward her.

Renata turned at Nichole's anxious expression and smiled to see Kevin approaching. "Did you find—" Renata began.

Kevin silenced Renata by a grip on her shoulder as he moved her aside. His regard never left Nichole. "We'll go outside now, and you're gonna take my arm. I'll ask the musicians to take a break, and then I will announce our engagement." His grin was controlled and angry. "You, my dear, will smile. If you get out of line, even once..." He left his threat implied.

Nichole stared at him in horror.

I can't do this.

Her gaze darted around the room, but there was no one close to them at that moment. Trapped, she looked into Kevin's smug face. "You wouldn't dare touch me in front of all these people."

"Don't tempt me." His red-rimmed eyes and bruised face begged her to defy him.

Renata clutched Kevin's arm and spoke in his ear. "She'll get what she deserves." Her dark eyes smiled at Nichole in elation. "I will enjoy watching her beg."

Kevin chuckled deep in his throat and wrapped Nichole's hand around his arm. He bent her fingers and pain exploded in her hand. "Don't forget what I said. And don't forget to smile."

Nichole resisted until he crushed her fingers again.

Kevin led the two women away from the refreshment table. He smiled and nodded at everyone who glanced their way, stopping several times to speak with people he recognized as he directed their path out the door.

Outside, the evening had cooled with the sunset. A large bonfire blazed in the yard, and elevated torches lit the dance platform, the beer wagon, and the vittles table. On the dance floor, three couples stepped and whirled their partners in time with the music. The yard was crowded with people from the porch to the barn. Beyond that, the unlit prairie was dark.

Nichole pulled back when she saw that Jim watched them from across the yard, but again, Kevin squeezed her fingers, and she continued toward the musicians.

"Keep smiling, little lady, if you know what's good for you. These people are about to receive a very happy announcement."

"She's not smiling, love," Renata remarked as she scanned the crowd.

"Maybe not yet, but she will. She'll smile, or I'll break her hand."

Nichole gasped as he twisted her fingers beneath his calloused palm. She was livid. She tried not to snarl as she looked up at Kevin's profile. "People don't get away with this kind of shit. You know that, right?" Her eyes never left Kevin, but she spoke loud enough for Renata to hear.

"What did she say?" Renata asked. Her gaze darted back to Kevin. She moved behind them to avoid several cowboys who stood near the dance floor.

"Hell, I don't know," Kevin hissed. "Keep your mouth shut. Understand?"

"Do it now, Kevin. Hurry. The song is almost over." Renata crossed her arms and stepped to one side.

Kevin whispered in the fiddle player's ear, and the musician nodded. The music wound down to the last few measures, and the couples on the dance platform completed their promenade.

Nichole's desperate gaze sought a familiar face, but there were none nearby. Finally, her sight landed on Jim.

He remained near the beer wagon, on the far side of the platform. He bent to let Amy speak in his ear, and when he looked up, his gaze landed on Nichole and Kevin. He nodded.

Nichole breathed a sigh of relief.

I just need to live through this.

She held onto that thought as she stepped on the platform beside Kevin. She winced as he twisted her fingers again and then smiled down into her face. His swollen eye promised she would suffer.

When the music stopped, Kevin slid Nichole's hand from his arm to the crushing grip on his left side. He raised the other hand to gain attention. "Friends, neighbors, if I could have your attention for a moment, please. You in the back, come on forward." He waved his hand to encourage the guests to step closer. "I want to make an announcement."

Chapter 35

Jason Harris

—

Jason strolled to the fire with Gary Bishop and Dale Green. Both men were Uncle Quincy's contemporaries and provided a wealth of information about various ventures and investments. He listened respectfully as they discussed the proposed statehood for the territory and what it would mean for the local businessmen. He was surprised to find his attention wandered and he missed valuable information he could send to his associates in Boston.

He turned when the music stopped and watched Nichole and Kevin step hand in hand onto the platform.

"Looks like your cousin settled on one of the Shilo boys." Gary Bishop patted Jason on the shoulder with a hearty chuckle.

"Hmm," Jason replied. He stepped toward the dance floor to hear Kevin's announcement.

"I have to say I'm a bit surprised though." Gary took a sip of his drink. "I always thought she fancied the younger boy, Merril."

"Well." Jason chuckled over his shoulder. "You know how women are."

"That, I do." Gary laughed. "Have two women at home. My little Nancy Mae's had her heart set on the younger brother for some time. Maybe now she'll have a chance."

"Isn't it rather odd to announce their engagement so soon after his father's death?" Dale Green asked. "Some people might take that as a... well, an ill omen, of sorts."

Jason nodded and looked back at Dale and Gary. "The families discussed a union before Phil and Quincy passed. I suppose Kevin felt his father would approve."

"You're probably right." Dale moved forward to stand beside Jason. "Phil flouted convention himself with that gal of his from Santa Fe."

Jason studied the couple on the dance floor. The prospective bridegroom led his fiancée in a waltz. Nicki didn't look happy; in fact, she seemed terrified. Jason turned his back on the couple and wondered if he would ever be able to look himself in the mirror again. He shook his head in disgust at himself and downed his drink.

***

Nichole Harris

—

Nichole thought every bone and knuckle in her hand had broken. The heartfelt congratulations from the sea of strangers around her were almost more than she could bear.

Kevin's eyes smoldered into hers as he waltzed her across the platform. "You don't appear excited at the prospect of becoming my wife. Why is that?"

"You're criminally insane," she replied. Her eyes darted to his, then away.

"My sweet bride," he cooed. "Why do you make such horrible accusations? Have you no love for me? Perhaps you would be a more eager bride if I visited you tonight."

Nichole's stomach clenched, and she swallowed the hot bile that rose in her throat. She tipped her head back and met his smug gaze. Her anger flared. "Try it, and I'll blacken your other eye... oh, wait, Merril already did that."

"You'll pay for that. There's an awful lot I intend to make you pay for." He jerked her waist closer to his hip, and a few of the cowboys up front hooted at the couple.

Nichole hissed as he wrenched her fingers even more. "So you keep saying."

"Maybe a little lesson right now would teach you to respect your future husband. Just a taste to get you ready for our wedding night."

Before Nichole could respond, Kevin whirled her around the dance floor one last time, and then stepped down, drawing her with him. Held in his muscular arms, he spun her into the crowd that parted before them, and toward the darkness behind the barn. She pushed her free hand against his shoulder, and struggled for release—but it was no use. His superior strength held her captive, and his cruel smile terrified her.

Kevin's momentum came to a sudden stop as he backed into a man who stood between the couple and the darkness. He growled and turned his head, then stilled.

"Could I have this dance?" Jimmy Leigh's face was grim. He slid his hand between Kevin's iron grip and Nichole's fingers and forced Kevin to relinquish her hand. Then, he stepped between the couple and put his arm around Nichole's waist.

"This dance is taken," Kevin spat but stepped back from Jim's angry glare.

"Yes, please." Nichole felt her knees begin to buckle with relief, but Jim held her waist in his firm grasp and moved her away from Kevin.

Kevin hesitated for a moment and glowered his frustration as Jim led Nichole back to the dance platform. Finally, he stalked away across the yard and into the house.

"Thank you," Nichole whispered. Tears filled her eyes as blood rushed back to her hand.

Jim's brow furrowed in concern, but he remained silent as she struggled to control her emotions. When she smiled up at him, he spoke softly. "Amy tells me you want to leave with her in the morning. After what I've seen, I'm inclined to agree with you."

"I'm already packed."

Jim made no reply as they danced across the platform. His great height made it impossible for Nichole to study his face. After a few turns, he slowed near the corner of the dance floor closest to the back of the house. The torch beyond the vittles table had gone out, and the kitchen yard was in shadow. They stepped from the platform as the music became lively once again and stopped near the table at the edge of the torchlight.

Nichole shivered in the chilly night air. Her wrap was lost somewhere in the crowd.

Jim touched her shoulder hesitantly. "Are you sure you're all right?"

"I will be... after tomorrow."

He brushed his hair back and reset his cowboy hat with one easy movement. "Amy told me Jason could have stopped this and didn't."

"It's true."

"That doesn't make a lick of sense to me." Jim shook his head. "Jase loves you like a sister. He would never let harm come to you."

"I don't know." Nichole shrugged. "He acted as though he loved me, but when I needed him, he turned away."

Jim let his gaze pass over the crowded yard. "What are you gonna do now? Go back in there?" He gestured to the crowd of people who talked and danced in the yard.

She shook her head. "No. I'm going to sneak up to my room and stay there. I'm freezing, and I don't want to run into Kevin again tonight."

"If we cut across the back, behind the kitchen, we can get you to the front door from the other side. I think it's your best chance to get upstairs unnoticed."

On the porch, Kevin and Renata surveyed the crowd from their height advantage.

Nichole slid further into the shadow. "I think you're right, but please, I need a few moments to myself. Keep an eye on Kevin while I go around back. Thank you, Jim, for everything. I'll see you in the morning."

"Take care, gal. Amy said she wants to be away before dawn."

She nodded, rubbed her arms and made her way around the back of the house.

As soon as she stepped away from the torchlight, darkness took her sight. She put her hand on the side of the house and took a few hesitant steps, then stopped to allow her eyes to adjust. As she listened to the music and voices behind her, she glanced back at the party.

Jim stood watch by the table, his arms crossed, guarding her retreat.

The cloud cover broke, and a gibbous moon spread thin, silver light across the prairie. She rounded the corner of the house just as a shadow detached itself from the darkness under her balcony and stepped into her path.

Nichole halted her step with a silent gasp. She stepped back and felt the hard, unyielding frame of the house. Too startled to run or cry out, her eyes widened as a match flared, and then rose to the tip of a cigarette.

Angry green eyes glared into hers and then vanished as the match extinguished. Sulfur and smoke scented the night air.

"Holy shit, Merril," she croaked, hand on her chest. "Why didn't you say something?"

He stood silently as smoke curled up through the moonlit branches of the cottonwood tree.

She waited for him to speak, but he only watched her. The moon in her eyes left his face in shadow. A cheer went up on the other side of the house.

He stepped from beneath the balcony, crossed in front of her and leaned against the tree trunk. The tip of his cigarette glowed for a moment, then disappeared—crushed beneath his boot. "It seems I should extend my congratulations to you and Kevin." His voice was cold and laced with sarcasm.

"No, of course not." She took a breath to say more, but it caught in her throat. She swallowed and blinked back the sting of fresh tears. Heartfelt or heartache, he overpowered her senses. Her chest fluttered at his closeness.

I've no time for this. I must be away at first light.

Her shoulders sagged, and she stepped away from him—and her heart. Merril could lurk out here all night if that's all he wanted.

Before she took the second step, his hand gripped her arm. "Don't leave so fast, Nic, we need to talk."

His touch warmed her chilled arm as he led her away from the house, along the shadow line of the tree. His hold didn't hurt; it guided her in the dark and held her steady. Part of her wanted to throw herself into his arms and weep. His hateful comment crushed the other part.

He stopped several paces from the house and turned to study her face. "Calm down for Christ's sake. You'll be back with your sweetheart soon enough."

"Kevin's not my sweetheart. He's a cruel psychotic monster."

The side of Merril's mouth ticked up. "What's this? It sounds like you can't decide between us—or maybe you just saddle up with whoever stands next to you."

The sting of his words left her speechless for a moment. Then anger brushed her heartache aside. "Me? I heard you forced yourself on Renata. She's quite a catch, Merril. It seems you've always had a thing for her." The words were out before she could stop them.

He dropped his hand from her arm and stood, fists on his belt, and glared at her. "I never touched that whore." He looked away and down. "I don't know what kind of game you three are playing, and I don't care. What's important is that you, and that lying brother of mine, understand that I'm not out of this yet." He raised his head and glared into her eyes. "Tell Kevin I'll be around."

What?

Nichole stared dumbfounded at his profile in the dappled moonlight. She wanted to caress it and slap it. The cork in her kettle of emotions came loose, and she laughed. It started as a choked chuckle and ended in a sob. She pressed the back of her hand hard against her mouth—so hard she tasted blood. If her emotions slipped now, she would be lost.

She swallowed back the tears and cleared her throat. "Tell him yourself. I won't be here." Her voice quivered. She sniffed and wiped her face. "For the record, I would never have anything to do with them." Her gaze rose, and she frowned at him. "And if you think I would, then you don't know me at all." She raised her hand to her brow and rubbed her forehead. Her voice dropped to a whisper. "Then again, how could you? I don't know myself anymore."

Merril stared at her. A dozen different emotions flitted across his face. He ran his hand over his mouth then stepped closer. "What the hell does that mean, Nicki?" He leaned toward her. "After what I just heard—" He gestured toward the party.

She heard the catch in his voice, and her anger softened. "What Kevin announced was a lie. The same kind of lie Renata told about you." She reached out and touched his arm, then lowered her hand. "I don't intend to be here for a wedding."

Merril looked into her eyes. "Tell me." It was an offer to listen, and a need to understand. "How could you step on that stage with Kevin and let him announce your engagement?"

Nichole sighed and brushed at her skirt. "I wasn't given a choice. Renata brought a doctor to The Highlands yesterday. They knew I would never marry Kevin. Dr. Clemens is their way to make sure I do. Either I marry your brother, or they lock me in the doctor's private insane asylum."

Merril shook his head. "You have an injury. You're not insane."

"I'm not?" Her words both defiant and questioning hung between them for a moment, suspended and unanswered. "I'm afraid there's more to it than simple insanity. I've... changed."

He searched her face. "I don't understand."

"Yes, you do. You've even said it yourself—how I act like a different person." She gripped his shirt in her fist, anxious to speak her mind, to lay it before him. "I don't think like Nichole anymore. I don't act or talk like her."

"What?" Merril pulled her hands from his shirt. Eyes wide, he tilted his head as though considering her anew. "Are you trying to tell me you're not... Nichole?"

Nichole stiffened. Her chin raised, but her attention never left his face.

Merril dropped her hands and turned away. "You make me plumb loco—you know that? You make me think I'm the one who's lost his mind."

"Maybe you're not the one who's lost." Nichole stepped around to face him.

Merril raised his gaze to hers. "What are you saying, Nic?"

"Nothing you didn't just say yourself. I'm not Nichole—or maybe—I'm not *just* Nichole anymore." Her breath caught as she said it, as though saying it aloud made it real.

Merril looked away. "Christ."

She grabbed his arm to make him stay. "Merril. Look at me." When he didn't turn, she stepped into his line of sight. Her eyes captured his. "What else did White Eagle tell you?"

"White Eagle?" Merril's brow furrowed. "I already told you what he said."

"Not all of it," she insisted. "I want to know everything."

Merril ignored her and ran his hands over his face.

"Please, Merril. What did he say?"

He closed his eyes. His voice was low and soft when he spoke. "White Eagle said he could feel a spirit beside you. He begged the spirit for guidance." He opened his eyes and looked away from her. "He said my eyes would deceive me, but in the end, my heart would speak the truth."

He was silent for several minutes. Nichole watched him struggle to find the right translation, the right words. Finally, he lowered his gaze and studied her face.

Her hair had come undone and spilled down her back. The night breeze teased at the ends and brushed her shoulders. "Tell me," she whispered.

"He said the wind would possess me—consume me. He said I would chase the wind beyond my grave." Merril searched her eyes, as though they might hold the answers.

She shuddered at his words and swallowed. "And... I'm the wind?" Her voice low and even.

"I believe that's what he meant. Yes."

"Merril... something happened to me after the carriage accident. I've changed. I'm not the Nichole you knew anymore."

Merril's eyes opened wide. He spun and paced away from her arms. "No." He stopped, then turned to look at her. In two paces he was upon her. Gripping her shoulders, he stared into her eyes. "If you're not my Nichole, then who the hell are you?" His voice was frightened and desperate.

Terror coursed through her veins. She couldn't answer him because she didn't know. But he believed her. She reached out to him, but he backed away from her touch.

"No. You can't tell me this and then reach for me."

"Merril, I'm sorry. I'm scared, too." She brushed her tears. "When my memory started coming back, and I knew—or I thought—" She stopped her stammered words and her silver-blue eyes met his. "Memories come back in fragments. I remember things that never happened to me... I mean, to Nichole." She sighed and crossed her arms. "But, I remember normal things too. It's all in pieces." She caught her breath and held her hand to her lips to still their quivering. When she found her voice, she raised her eyes. "It wouldn't be fair to you if you didn't know about—whatever this is. I don't know how or why this has happened to me—to us."

She closed her eyes. When they opened, they were directed toward the house. "I'm leaving for Denver in the morning. I can't stay here. I won't marry your brother. He's a monster."

Her gaze shifted to his as she swallowed and took a breath. "Believe me when I tell you that whatever is happening inside my head doesn't change the way I feel about you. Nichole loves—" She stopped and blinked her eyes, brushing the tears away. Then she wrapped her arms around her stomach. "I love you."

She struggled to take a breath and felt his arms go around her. He held her head to his shoulder as she cried. His warmth engulfed her. How could he be so warm when she was so cold? The storm of tears passed, and she found her handkerchief and wiped her face.

"I need to go inside, Merril." She spoke into his chest. "We leave before sunrise."

"We?" He held her at arm's-length and searched her face.

"Amy and Jimmy Leigh are taking me to Denver. I'll be safe there."

"You could leave with me now."

She smiled through her tears and shook her head. "It's already planned. I'll be in Denver tomorrow night."

He tipped his head and ran his hands up and down her arms. "Can I meet you in there? If I leave tonight, I'll be at the house when you and Amy arrive."

Nichole nodded and stepped back into his arms. They folded around her, and she wrapped her arms around his back.

His voice was low when he spoke. "I can't stay here anyway. You know that. They'll charge me with attempted rape and murder."

She closed her eyes nodded against his chest.

They had trapped him, too.

"You certainly did beat the shit out of Kevin." A chuckle escaped her, and Merril laughed. She raised her face to his.

His lips brushed across her cheek and then captured her mouth.

She could taste her tears on his lips.

His hand wound in her hair as he deepened the kiss. When he pulled away, he kissed her eyes and forehead and then held her face in his hands.

Nichole opened her eyes to his smile.

"You had best go in, Nicki. Look for me in Denver."

Nichole nodded, not trusting herself to speak. She stepped away from him and stopped at the corner of the house.

The front porch was empty, and her path to the door was clear. She looked back at Merril and waved her hand, then stepped onto the porch and across to the door.

***

Blackwood Jones

—

Blackwood Jones had left the road and circled the house. Most of the folks at the big shindig were between the house and the barn, leaving the other nice and quiet. He dismounted several yards away and approached on foot.

He heard them talking before he could see where they stood. He crouched low and waited until a movement in the shadow of the tree caught his eye. The couple embraced, and he snickered to himself when they kissed.

The man said, "You had best go in, Nicki. Look for me in Denver."

Jones watched the woman walk toward the house.

Damned if it isn't that blonde-haired bitch.

He waited until she disappeared around the front of the house and then scurried up behind Shilo. He already had his pistol out with a firm grip on the barrel. He brought the butt down on Shilo's head as hard as he could. When the man sank to his knees, he hit him two more times.

Jones flipped the gun around, slipped it back in his holster and smiled. "So they're goin' to Denver." He grabbed Shilo by the boots and pulled him several feet from the house. He chuckled and kicked a tumbleweed over Merril's motionless form. "I'll just have to have a little surprise waitin' for 'em." He kicked Merril twice in the gut and drew his gun from his holster once more. "I should shoot you in the head, but they'd hear it at the party. You're dang near dead, anyway."

He holstered his weapon and captured his horse's reins. "Denver, Denver," he repeated. "Just you wait, you fancy bitch. I'm going to take a peek at what you keep hidden under those satin skirts. Maybe even try a piece." He licked his lips in anticipation.

"Oh, I'll try you out all right. I'll try you out real good ... right before I put a bullet between those pretty blue eyes."

Chapter 36

Nichole Harris

—

Nichole woke to a soft but insistent scratch at her door.

Did I sleep at all?

Her conversation with Merril had replayed in her mind a dozen times as she'd lain in bed and listened to the revelers below.

She turned her eyes to the sound at the door and rolled from her bed to her feet. She slid the chair from beneath the latch and opened the door a crack to peek out.

Amy stood in the hallway dressed to travel with a bonnet and warm coat around her shoulders. She whispered through the opening. "Jim's hitching the wagon. Do you still want to go?"

"Absolutely. I'll be down in a minute." Nichole opened the door a bit more and looked down the hall. "Is anyone else awake?" Her voice was a low murmur.

"No." Amy grinned. "Everyone is asleep. But be as quiet as possible, and hurry. I'll send Jim up for your luggage."

Nichole closed the door and lit the lamp on the dresser. She snatched up the riding habit and underclothes she'd folded on top of the trunk. She dressed in record time, drew her hair back in a ponytail, and tied it with a ribbon. She pulled her flat-brimmed hat onto her head as another scratch sounded at her door.

She peeked first, then opened the door gesturing to the trunk at the foot of her bed.

Jim nodded and moved past her. "Go on down. I'll get the light and the trunk." His voice was a low rumble. "Be sure to bring a wrap. It's a mite brisk this morning."

Nichole tipped her head and opened the wardrobe. She pulled a warm wool cloak out and wrapped it around her. With one more look of understanding between them, she picked up her boots and left the room.

She tiptoed around the banister to the stairs and listened for any movement. A soft snore came from behind Amy and Jason's door. She hurried down the stairs and past the parlor on stocking feet. As soon as she was out the front door, she stopped and allowed herself to breathe.

Moonset had left the western sky studded with tiny stars. To the east, a faint glow outlined the horizon. She stepped into her boots as she scanned the yard for the wagon. Then she saw it, obscured in the darkness beside the house, not far from where she and Merril had spoken last night.

She had no more than stepped from the porch when Jim moved beside her.

He carried her trunk on his shoulder, secured by one long arm. With the other, he guided Nichole to the buckboard. He set her chest on the wagon bed beside two others, and then he helped Nichole up to the seat beside Amy.

Amy's hand found Nichole's and she gave it a reassuring squeeze. Jim stepped in front of the two horses hitched to the wagon. Grasping Sugar's harness, he led them at a slow, even pace toward the road.

Nervous flutters plagued Nichole's stomach as Jim walked the horses down the drive.

They'll catch us.

The creak of the wagon and the chink of the harnesses seemed loud in the morning silence.

Beyond the corral, a few of the overnight guests were breaking camp.

As Jim crossed from The Highlands' drive onto the road, a wagon pulled from the campsite heading west. Jim fell into line behind it, and another team pulled out behind them.

After they crossed the Sandy Creek Bridge, Jim guided the team off the rutted path to a flat place beside the road.

Amy took up the reins as Jim moved to the rear and untied his mount.

"Do you think anyone saw us?" Nichole wondered aloud.

Jim mounted his horse and moved onto the road ahead of the buckboard team.

"We're just one of the guests heading home." Amy shook the reins, and the two-horse team pulled the wagon onto the road behind Jim. "We have a long way to go. Let's hope Jason sleeps for a while. He'll be the first to notice we've gone."

***

Jason Harris

—

Jason moaned and tugged the covers over his head. He eased back into his dream. He and Amy were in Boston. So much in love, he could feel it in his bones. They laughed together and walked hand in hand to her parents' house. They discussed the plans they had for their future. What happened to those dreams?

Still half-asleep, he reached for Amy and found the mattress beside him empty. He pushed the covers away from his face and squinted around the sunlit room. No Amy. Jason sighed and rubbed a hand across his eyes.

He didn't remember seeing her after Kevin's announcement last night, not until he found his way to bed sometime this morning. The fall of light across the room told him the sun was well up. His sweet dream called to him, but he pushed it away. With a grunt of resignation, he sat and swung his feet to the floor.

How have I fallen so low? How do I fix this?

His head shot up, startled by a loud knock.

"Jason? You in there?" Tom spoke through the door.

Jason rubbed his jaw. "Yeah. What do you need, Tom?"

"I'm tryin' to find Jim. Was he doin' somethin' for you this mornin'?"

Jason came slowly to his feet with a groan and opened the door. He studied Tom Baker through bleary eyes and shook his head. "He's probably still asleep."

"I checked his bunk first thing. The buckboard's gone along with two of the tan geldings."

"Maybe he ran an errand for Amy."

"Maybe, but his horse is gone."

Even befuddled with sleep, Jason knew that didn't add up. He rubbed his eyes and peered at Tom. "Is Nichole up?"

"Jeanne said she hasn't come down yet." Tom pulled off his hat and scratched his head. "It don't figure. Where the heck would Jim go with his own horse, two geldings, and a wagon?" Tom replaced his hat and turned toward the stairs. "Sorry to bother you. I thought you might know. We're almost done cleaning up, and everyone that camped overnight has lit out for home."

"Thank you, Tom. If you see Amy, tell her I'd like to speak with her."

"Sure thing, Jase. Sorry to wake ya."

Jason nodded to Tom and turned back to the room. His brow furrowed as he tapped his lips with one finger.

This is very odd.

He pulled on his trousers and then crossed the hall to Nichole's room. He hesitated before knocking. The look in her eyes when Clemens grabbed her rose to haunt his mind. Guilt made him grind his teeth in shame. How had he turned away? He pressed his lips together and knocked.

"Nicki? You awake?" He paused to listen but heard no answer. He pressed his ear to the door. "You disappeared before I could ask you about Kevin's announcement last night. Are you all right?"

He waited, but still no reply. He turned the knob and stepped into her room. The trunk that sat at the end of her bed was gone. Her wardrobe stood open, several drawers in her dressing table were open and empty. He stared at the evidence for only a moment, then spun on his heel and returned to his room.

They wouldn't—Amy wouldn't leave, not like this.

He stopped in the doorway, his gaze darting around his bedroom. Amy stored her trunk in the shed when she first arrived, but he doubted it remained there. He crossed to their wardrobe and opened both doors. Anguish and regret clawed up his throat, and he closed his eyes. Only his clothes hung in the space they shared.

Amy had gone.

On the heels of that thought came another.

Jimmy Leigh.

How often had he heard Jim praise his wife? Jim, who scowled at everyone else, always found a smile for Amy.

Could it be?

Jealous anger blazed through his chest. It made perfect sense. Worst of all, it was his own damned fault. He had told Amy to go.

With a growl, he shrugged into his shirt and grabbed his seldom-used gun belt that hung on a peg near the door. He strapped it on and withdrew his Colt from the dresser drawer. He checked the rounds, slid the Colt into its holster, and pulled on his jacket. This foolishness would end. There was only one place the three of them would go.

Denver.

Jason took the stairs two at a time and grabbed his hat as he went out the front door. He raced across the porch and yard to the stable. "Lloyd!" he hollered across the barn. "I need my horse saddled. Tom? Are you in here?" He stalked past Muffin and her puppies.

Lloyd's head leaned out of the last stall. "I hear ya. Can I finish what I'm doin' first?"

"I'll get it." Tom wiped his hands on a cloth and then opened the stall across from the one he'd been cleaning. He led Jason's brown and white paint to the tack room. "Is this about Jim?" Tom asked as he placed a soft blanket over the gelding's back.

Jason glanced up from buttoning his shirt. "Jim and Amy. Nichole too. They've gone to Denver." Jason unbuttoned his pants and tucked in his shirt.

Lloyd stepped out of the stall and stared at Jason. "You plannin' to ride straight through or stop halfway?"

"I don't know. I know where they're going." Jason hung his head, hands on his hips. When he looked up at Lloyd, he shook his head. "You're right. No use killing myself or Checker. They'll be there tomorrow."

Lloyd bobbed his head in agreement. "Give him a bedroll Tom, in case he decides to stop near the creek. I'll get Cookie to make you a meal for the road."

Jason nodded, and Lloyd walked past him and headed toward the kitchen.

As Tom lifted the saddle onto Checker's back, his gaze met Jason's.

"Did you know they were planning to leave?" Jason asked.

Tom dropped his eyes and adjusted the cinch strap. "I woke you up to find Jim, remember?" He looked over the saddle at Jason. "I didn't know, Jase. I'm sorry."

Lloyd returned with a cloth bag. He tucked it into the saddlebag, then turned to Jason. "What do you want me to tell the men? Jim thought at least a week before the drive, maybe two."

Jason mounted Checker and looked at Lloyd. "Tell them to come back in two weeks. If they have a mind to stay, the bunk is open. I think most will head to town."

"Check the cinch again at the road, Jase. Make sure it's tight."

"Will do, Tom. Thank you, both."

Jason dismounted and tightened the cinch strap at the main road and considered which route they would have gone. Jim would have taken the road due west toward Denver instead of the south road that went past The Shilo Ranch.

Jason decided to head south. He wanted Kevin to know Nicki had taken matters into her own hands and left the ranch. All of Renata's careful planning had gained her nothing. He would have been ecstatic about Nichole slipping out of Kevin's reach if it weren't for Amy and Jim. Jason mounted his horse and pulled the reins to head south.

Ninety minutes later, Jason dismounted in The Shilo yard. The bunkhouse was almost empty now that the roundup was over. He tossed Checker's reins over the corral fence, crossed the wide yard and stepped onto the porch. He knocked and waited.

Katy answered the door, and when she saw Jason, she smiled a welcome. "Hello, Mr. Harris. Renata is still in her room, but if you want to wait, I could fetch her."

"Actually, I'm here to see Kevin." He smiled at the youngster. "Do you know if he's awake?" Katy's momentary surprise didn't escape Jason.

Does everyone know about Renata and me? Does Amy?

"Mister Kevin is in the library," Katy replied and moved back from the door.

Jason stepped past the girl and stopped at the open library door. His gaze swept the familiar room, noting the disarray of papers and books left discarded on the table and chairs. Kevin's gun belt lay across Philip's large oak desk. Jason's attention settled on Kevin at the window, a whiskey glass already in his hand.

"Kevin?" Jason removed his hat and stepped into the room.

"Jason." Kevin turned and stared at Jason. "What brings you here so early? Never mind my question; here, have a drink first," He crossed to the mantel and fumbled with the decanters.

Kevin didn't look well. The bruises from the beating Merril gave him had faded to yellow, but one eye was still swollen. It didn't look as though he'd been to bed yet. He wore the same clothes he had last night.

"Thanks, but no. I can't stay. I wouldn't have stopped at all, but I wanted to be the one to tell you. Amy and Nichole have left The Highlands."

Kevin's head shot up from his glass, and he blinked to clear his vision. "They did what?"

"They're gone, Kevin."

"Gone? Gone where? Is this some trick? Why didn't you stop them?" Kevin set his drink on the desk and advanced on Jason.

Jason refused to step back. "You know why Nichole left, Kevin. God knows you gave her reason enough." Jason looked down at his hat, then back to Kevin. "Amy knows a lot of folks in Denver. Nichole is beyond your reach. It's over." Jason smiled at Kevin's stunned expression.

"And what about you?" Kevin asked. "What are you going to do?"

Jason slid his hat back on his head. "I'm going to collect my wife if I can. I've made enough mistakes already. I'm not about to make this one as well."

He turned to find Renata stood outside the library door. Her hastily donned robe gaped in the front as the sash slipped. The sparkle in her dark eyes no longer had the power to persuade him. He moved past her without a word and walked to the front door.

"Jason! Come back here and explain what happened this instant!" Renata demanded.

Jason paused as his hand touched the door latch, and he turned to look at Renata.

Her fists clenched and unclenched at her sides, working in silent agitation. Her chin was set and angry, but there was just a touch of desperation in her normally smooth voice.

Jason grinned. "Go to hell, Renata." Then he walked out the door.

"Don't you walk away from me, Jason Harris."

Jason slammed the door. He stopped and adjusted his hat, listening to the tirade inside the house. With a satisfied smile on his face, he walked across the dirt yard to Checker, mounted and glanced back at the front door. He half expected Renata to throw open the door and yell at him from the porch, but the door remained closed. He chuckled to himself and felt better than he had in days. With luck, he would see Amy tonight.

He tugged Checker's reins and set a pace on the road to Denver.

***

Kevin Shilo

—

Kevin flinched as the door slammed. The sharp noise reverberated in his skull. He put his hand on the desk to steady himself.

"Stop him, Kevin."

Renata's screech scored his nerves like nails on a chalkboard.

"Stop him yourself, you worthless bitch." Kevin's words were slurred. He stumbled back to the mantel, picking up his glass on the way.

Nichole was gone.

She might have loved him, if not for Renata. "It's over. I'll never have her now. This is your fault. You and your schemes got in the way."

"You're such an idiot." Renata tugged the tie on her satin robe tighter. "All she ever felt for you was pity and disgust. But if you had held up your end of the bargain, she would have been forced to marry you. Now, all our plans are ruined—because of you." She slashed with her hand to emphasize her words and stalked into the library toward Kevin.

Kevin growled and spun to face Renata. "I did everything you asked me to do—more."

"You scared her away, didn't you?" Renata hissed at him. She stepped toward him, pointing her finger. "Not only that, but you didn't go after Merril and finish him as I instructed. She would be here if you had only done what you were told."

Kevin's chest was heavy, and his head pounded. He refilled his glass, drank it down, and choked in his haste. He turned to Renata and wiped the spittle from his mouth. "I did everything." His voice was low and dangerous.

Renata rolled her eyes and crossed to the decanters on the mantel. She took a glass and poured herself a shot. "You are as stupid as your father. Maybe I should have seduced Merril, instead. Now, there's a man with enough ambition and follow-through to get the job done."

Kevin staggered to a standstill, his attention focused on Renata.

I'm what? Stupid like Pa?

He tilted his head and stared hard at the dark-haired woman. "What did you say?" he whispered.

"Now that I think of it, my only real mistake was getting rid of Philip. I was too impatient. Too eager to take what should be mine. He would have married me eventually. I'm sure of it. As I said, he was stupid, pliable. I had only to wait —" Renata turned from the mantel, drink in hand and froze.

Kevin stood beside his father's desk and glared at Renata.

Her only real mistake?

A sob rose in his throat, and he choked it back.

She got rid of Pa?

He brushed at his nose with one hand; in the other, he held his revolver. He thumbed back the hammer and scrubbed at the tears with his shoulder, his gaze never leaving Renata's face.

"You lied to me." His voice wavered, and he cleared his throat. "You never wanted me. You used me, just like you used Pa." A drunken sob escaped him, and the gun lowered.

Renata stepped away from the mantel and edged past the book-lined wall toward the door.

Kevin raised the gun and followed her movements. His lips quivered, and he wiped his arm across his face.

"Put the gun down, Kevin." Renata's voice was soft and wary. "You're drunk, my love. You need some rest. We will talk about all of this later."

"No. I won't listen to you anymore. You're poison." He paused for a moment, his chest heaving in sobs. "Worst of all—the worst thing—you killed my father."

Renata shook her head. "No, no, love. You misunderstood me."

"I heard you say it, just now. He's the only one who loved me, and you killed him." Kevin's voice rose to a screech, and he pulled the trigger. Two more times he cocked the hammer and fired into Renata's body.

That murdering whore.

The first shot took her in the throat and stilled any cry or plea she might have made. The second and third rounds marked her chest. The bark of the Colt left a ringing in his ears that remained long after he stopped firing.

Kevin crossed the library and looked down at her blood-spattered corpse. His breath sawed in and out, and he wiped at his face again, his sleeve soaked with tears and snot. He raised his head at a sound at the library door.

Katy stood silent, her eyes wide. Her trembling hand rose to her mouth as she stared at Renata's body. Her gaze lifted to Kevin.

Kevin stared at Katy for a few moments, then raised the barrel of the gun in her direction.

With a shriek, she ran from the doorway.

Kevin listened as her screams for her mother echoed through the house. Slowly, and with quiet deliberation, he checked the remaining bullets in his gun. Then he sighed in resignation and raised the Colt to his head.

"Forgive me, Pa," he whispered and pulled the trigger.

Chapter 37

Merril Shilo

—

Merril moaned and raised his hand to his head. Pain cleaved his skull behind his ear. The light in his eyes blinded him, and he rolled over. With a grunt, he pushed himself to his hands and knees.

What in the name of all hells had hit him?

He eased to a crouch as the agony reverberated around his skull. He probed his head with his fingers and winced when he pressed the large knot behind his left ear. His fingers came away bloody. He blinked his eyes open and shaded them with his hand while he waited for his vision to clear.

This is The Highlands. Why am I here?

He looked back at the house, and a groan escaped his lips. Horror and adrenaline spiked through him. He closed his eyes and held his head with both hands as it threatened to explode.

It wasn't hard to figure what happened or who hit him from behind and tried to break his skull.

Blackwood Jones.

If he had overheard their plan to meet in Denver—

Merril struggled to his feet and lurched to the tree. He leaned against it and willed the pain and nausea to subside.

What time is it?

He glanced at the sun, but the light pierced his eyes like a dart through his brain, and he turned away. Panic propelled him into motion. He had to find out if they had gone.

He staggered forward and fell to one knee. He rose again and stumbled to the side of the house. Resting his head against the clapboard, he fought to overcome the ache in his skull and the fear in his gut. The wall supported him as he moved toward the porch. He climbed the step and reached the front door, then turned the handle and pushed the door wide open.

"Nicki? Jason?" His voice carried into the house and filled the empty room. He flinched and pressed his hand to his temple.

His knees buckled as hands supported him and guided him to the parlor couch.

"That's it, Mr. Merril, you sit right here. Nichole and Jason aren't at the house just now." Cookie spoke close to him.

He squinted at her as he sat.

Cookie smiled and patted his shoulder. "Jeanne, run and get Amy's medicine kit and the bandages. Mr. Merril's hurt." Cookie's voice carried across the room, and then she ran her hands across his skull.

"Ouch." Merril cringed away as her fingertips pressed the tender spot.

"Who hit you?" Then, in a louder voice, "Lawna, I need warm water and towels. This needs cleaned."

"Cookie, I don't have time for this. Nichole's in danger. Jones knows where they've gone." He tried to pull away, but she had a firm grip on his neck.

"You sit still until I get this cleaned and bandaged. Nichole left early this mornin' with Jim and Amy, or so I hear. Jason went after them a few hours ago." Cookie clucked her tongue as she dabbed blood from Merril's head. "You aren't going to save them right this minute."

Lawna and Jeanne came to Cookie with their hands laden. Lawna set a pan of water near her feet beside the couch, and Jeanne placed the liniment basket on the table.

Deftly, Cookie cleaned the tear in the skin on the back of his head. "The bleeding's stopped, but you have an egg-sized knot behind your ear. Jeanne, hand me the salve. Not that one—Amy's salve, that's it." She dabbed the ointment on the knot and abrasion. "Now, who hit you?" Cookie wiped her hands on a towel and stepped back.

Merril pushed his hair from his face. "I think it was Jones. I'm afraid he overheard Nicki and me make plans last night. How long ago did Jason leave?"

"An hour ago, thereabouts," Cookie replied.

"What time is it now?" Merril looked up at the women. Lawna wrung her hands, and Jeanne chewed on her lip. Cookie shrugged, hands on her wide hips. "Can't be much past ten right now."

"Do you know where they've gone?" Jeanne asked.

Merril's nod was slow and cautious. "Nicki and I were going to meet in Denver. I should already be there. I need to go." He rose to his feet, and the room swam.

Cookie steadied him. "Lawna, step outside and see if you can find Mr. Merril's hat. Jeanne, would you fix a few meals for the road?"

The dizziness passed, and Merril patted Cookie's hand. "I'm better now, Cookie. Thank you. I have to catch Nichole and Amy."

"I know ya do, Mr. Merril. God's speed."

Merril opened the front door just as Lawna stepped onto the porch, dusting off his hat. She offered it to him with a shy smile.

"Thank you. Lawna, is it?" Merril pushed his hair back and slid the hat gingerly over his head.

"Yes, sir."

Merril smiled at the young woman, then stepped off the porch and whistled loudly. Nothing. He waited for a few moments, turned on his heel and headed toward the barn. He would borrow a Highlands' horse from Lloyd if he must.

Tom saw him coming across the yard and yelled back into the barn.

When Merril stepped into the shade of the barn, he saw Lloyd saddling up Midnight with Merril's gear.

"We found him last night. We recognized him right off, but no one could find you. He's fed and watered," Tom explained while Lloyd worked.

"Thank you." He reached for Midnight's nose and patted him with affection and relief.

Lloyd tightened the cinch and looked up at Merril. "What's happened, son?"

Anxiety surged in Merril's chest. "Nicki, Amy, and Jim are headed to Denver. Blackwood Jones knows and has about a seven-hour lead on them. He's going after Nichole."

"Then he's almost there." Tom looked from Merril to his father, alarm on his face.

Merril nodded and looked at both men. "They're riding into an ambush."

"Tom, saddle Ginger and put Rusty in a halter. I'll take care of Sadie." Lloyd began moving with practiced efficiency.

Tom pulled a set of tack together and moved into the third stall.

"What are you doing?" Merril rechecked Midnight's cinch then stepped into his stirrup.

Lloyd led Sadie from her stall and stopped to adjust the halter he had fit over her head. "They're too far ahead of you. You'll run that big horse of yours to death and have nothin' to show for it. Tom's goin' with you, and you'll both lead a spare mount."

Merril settled onto Midnight's saddle. Lloyd grinned and handed Merril the long lead rope for Sadie.

Tom mounted Ginger and tied Rusty's lead to his saddle horn. He reined Ginger alongside Midnight at the barn entrance.

Lloyd took hold of Midnight's and Ginger's halters, getting both riders' full attention. "You're not gonna catch 'em going fast, though I know you'll want to. You'll injure your horses—kill 'em, most like—and not make it to town. This is a long race, not a sprint like these horses are used to. Vary a trot and lope for no more than forty minutes, then walk them for ten, then stop. Rest the horses, water them, saddle the fresh horse, give yourselves a rest, then go again. You should catch Jason in about four or five hours, maybe sooner. When you do, put his saddle on the freshest horse and let Tom take any that are winded or have gone lame. Your animals are gonna be hurtin' by then."

Lloyd looked up at his son. "Take the spent horses on to Denver. It'll be closer than trying to come back. Let 'em rest for at least three days before you even think about bringin' 'em home."

Tom nodded in understanding.

Across the yard, Cookie called out, moving as fast as her large frame could carry her. She had two burlap bags, one in each hand. As she ran up to the men, she handed one to Merril and one to Tom. "There's enough for each of ya, not that you'll be stoppin' to eat." Cookie patted Tom's leg and stepped back. "Take care of yourselves, now."

"Thank you, Cookie," Merril replied gravely. Both men secured their food bag in their saddlebag.

As Merril guided Midnight out of the barn's shadow, he saw Timothy and Lawna watching from the kitchen step. Jeanne stood on the front porch and waved as the men rode past.

Merril turned right at the end of the drive toward Denver, and Tom followed his lead.

***

Blackwood Jones

—

It was midmorning when Jones arrived on the outskirts of Denver. He'd spent a long night on the road, stopping only for a short nap after the moon set.

He passed several wagons moving along Fifteenth Street. Some hauled construction materials, while others transported goods to the market. No one gave Jones a second glance. There were plenty of cowboys in town.

He bypassed three stables because he wanted to find one closer to his destination. He turned northwest at the diagonal street, Park Avenue.

Wranglers had talked in the bunkhouse about the ride between the Denver house and the ranch all the time. With Mrs. Harris in town and Jason at the ranch, letters and banknotes were run twice a month between the two homes. Jones knew right where he was headed, even though he'd never made the run himself.

The small livery stable at the edge of the neighborhood was just what he wanted. He turned his tired animal over to a young boy, along with a few pennies, took his bedroll and saddlebag over his shoulder, and paused to remember the directions. The wranglers had said it was a red brick, two-story just a couple of blocks east of Park, on Pence, easily recognized by the large 'H' old Quincy used to decorate the front door.

Jones smiled as he walked along Pence Street. It felt good to stretch his cramped legs. The residential area still had houses going up. Most of the lots remained empty.

Two blocks down, he spotted it. A smug grin stretched his face as he gazed across the street at the 'H' on the door. A chuckle escaped his tobacco stained lips, and he spat a long string of tobacco on the road.

The curtains were drawn, and windows closed. The house looked empty. He crossed the street and moved along the side of the building and into the small back yard. A carriage house sat to the right of the main building at the back of the lot. He passed it, stepped onto the back door landing and tested the door. Locked. The door to the carriage house proved to be locked as well. He took a step back and gazed up at the second floor. A small balcony jutted from a back bedroom. An easy jump from the roof of the carriage house.

Jones pulled himself to the roof and tossed his bags onto the balcony. He jumped to the edge and stepped over the rail, giggling as tobacco juice ran down his chin. He couldn't stop smiling.

He tried the balcony door, then removed his scarf, wrapped it around his fist and hit the window beside the door hard enough to break the pane. The tinkling sound of broken glass was loud in his ears. He stood still and listened. Not even a dog barked. He chuckled as he removed several long shards, then reached in and unbolted the latch. He was in. Now, all he had to do was have a small snack from his bag, a nap on the bed, and wait for the ladies. He tossed his bedroll and pack in the corner and flopped down on the bed.

He had thought about that blonde-haired bitch all the way from The Highlands. She had looked so fancy in the moonlight wearing that expensive dress. He would have taken her right there if it hadn't been for that Shilo boy. He hadn't been able to hear too much of their conversation, but that was no matter. He'd heard enough to know she would meet him in Denver today.

He reached down and rubbed his crotch. He was hard just thinking about the pretty little Harris girl. He turned and spat a long stream of tobacco against the wall and chuckled as the brown stain ran down to the floor. A few more hours and he'd have her right where he wanted her. Then, he'd tell that uppity little bitch just what he thought of her. He loosened his belt and rubbed himself. He would show her what he thought of her all right, and then he'd fuck her every which way he could think of.

***

Merril Shilo

—

Merril and Tom kept a steady pace toward Denver. They rotated saddles and packs to the extra horses at each rest period.

It was good Tom was with him, Merril decided. His impatience thrust them forward, and Tom's good sense and care for their mounts kept them at an even pace.

They talked as they rode. Tom told Merril what he knew of Blackwood, what type of gun the man carried and how well he rode. Jones had kept to himself around the bunkhouse. The wranglers disliked the man's arrogant and spiteful ways and tended to avoid him.

Merril's anxiety and fear kept him in the saddle. Amy's ointment helped the pain in his head but made him weary to the bone. He talked to stay awake more than anything else. He told Tom about their run-in with Jones at the pond and their rescue by the Cheyenne. He explained why Jim, Amy, and Nichole had left without warning for Denver. Merril told Tom all he had learned about his brother's and Renata's attempt to force Nichole to wed Kevin.

"Jones is a mean old cuss," Tom agreed. "But for the life of me, I don't see how Jason let Kevin and Renata get away with forcing that announcement at the party. Nichole has *always* been your girl—at least, as far as I knew."

Merril caught Tom's sympathetic glance. "It came as a shock to me as well."

They topped a rise, and the land ahead sloped down into a long shallow valley. A half-mile away, a man walked his horse along the side of the road.

"There's Jason," Merril commented.

"Yup," Tom replied.

Tom sounded so much like his father, Merril smiled. They picked up the pace to catch Nichole's cousin.

Jason turned when they drew near and waited for them to approach. "What's this?" he called as they reined in and dismounted beside him.

Tom walked to Jason's gelding and took the reins. He ignored Merril and Jason as he looked Checker over.

Merril stepped toward Jason, too many contradictory feelings and emotions in his mind. He didn't know what to do first—demand to know why he allowed Nichole to be bullied, punch him in the face, or tell him his wife was in mortal danger. He stopped walking and stared down into Jason's face.

"Jones overheard Nicki and I talk last night about meeting in Denver today," Merril said, his voice low and controlled.

"You knew they were leaving?" Jason asked, clearly surprised.

Merril's grin ticked up, and he clenched his teeth. He nodded once while he held Jason's gaze. "I was headed to Denver last night, but Jones got the drop on me and pistol-whipped the shit out of my head. I was out until this morning. You'd already left when I came around."

Jason looked at Merril and Tom, each leading an extra horse. His brow furrowed, and he looked back at Merril. "I'm sorry you were injured, but why are you both here now?"

"I believe Jones left for Denver last night." Merril rested his hands on his belt.

Jason's gaze rested on Tom as he moved Jason's saddle to one of the extra horses. "Well, then... he could—he might already be in town!" Blue eyes widened in horrified understanding, and his voice rose in alarm. "You're trying to catch up with Amy and Nichole."

"You know, Jason, you could have prevented all this. Just how the hell does a man as smart as you muck things up as bad as you have?" Merril shook his head in disgust.

Outrage flashed in Jason's eyes, then his fair skin flushed, and he looked away. "Renata," he muttered under his breath, only loud enough for Merril to hear.

"Yeah, well, I warned you about her." Merril watched Tom work with the horses. "Renata set up the fight between Kevin and me, and then cried rape."

"I assumed that," Jason replied. "Nicki was desperate to find you when she heard."

Tom finished tacking Sadie with Jason's saddle and bent to unbuckle Merril's saddle from Ginger.

"Let me do that, Tom." Merril lifted the leather seat from Ginger.

"You're still eight miles out, at least," Tom said to Merril as he placed the blanket on Midnight's back. Merril set it on the blanket, and Tom reached for the cinch straps from beneath.

"They could already be there," Merril commented, adjusting the equipment while Midnight stretched his neck to bite at grass near the road.

"Probably not," Tom replied. "Don't panic yet. Keep the pace."

With no water nearby for the horses, Tom pulled a large tin bowl from his pack and an extra canteen. He put the pan on the ground and filled it to the rim, catching the interest of all five horses. He let the three horses they had been riding drink first, then refilled the bowl and allowed Sadie and Midnight to drink their fill. Soon, the horses were grazing alongside the road, and the three men stood silent, looking west.

"It's farther than it looks," Jason commented. A low haze lay across the valley below the mountains.

"You should be able to make it to the house from here if you don't push your mounts too hard." Tom glanced from the valley to the horses. "They're about spent." He studied Jason and Merril then nodded toward the animals. "I'll stay with Checker, Rusty, and Ginger. After they've rested, I'll walk 'em the rest of the way into town."

"Let's go, then." Merril caught Midnight's reins and checked the saddle, his rifle, and his gun. After he mounted, he looked over at Jason, already astride Sadie. Their eyes met with the complete understanding of what was at stake.

"Keep them to a trot. Any faster than that and they'll fall out, or come up lame," Tom advised.

Merril reached down to Tom, and the men shook hands. "Thank you. Wish us luck. I hope to see you at the house this evening."

Merril glanced at Jason, then shook his reins and headed down into the valley.

Chapter 38

Nichole Harris

—

After several hours, Jim informed Nichole and Amy that they hadn't been followed. They stopped to rest the horses for thirty minutes and then continued.

During their second break, Amy pointed out the halfway campsite. She gestured to a stand of trees about a hundred feet from the road. "At the end of that trail, there's a small creek and fire pit. June, Tom, and I camped there on our way to The Highlands last week."

Jim unhitched the horses from the buckboard and walked them to the water while Amy and Nichole strolled the other way to stretch their legs.

As soon as they separated from Jim, Nichole whispered to Amy, "I spoke to Merril last night."

Amy smiled. "I never saw him. I hoped he would come."

"He was angry about the wedding announcement."

Amy chuckled and shook her head. "Did you tell him about Clemens?"

"Yes." Nichole paused to choose her next words. "We talked about White Eagle and the things he said about me. Merril knows I've been different since the accident. I told him that I remember things that don't belong to me—to Nichole."

Amy stopped and stared at her. "He knows you aren't *you* anymore?"

Nichole blinked and caught her breath in astonishment. She'd only begun to wrap her mind around the possibility that something inexplicable had happened, yet Amy seemed willing to accept the miraculous. "Doesn't that frighten you?" Nichole whispered.

"Heavens, no! I like you more now than I did before." She paused and raised a brow. "Do you know if—should I call her 'old Nichole'—if she died? Is that what my vision foretold?"

"No." Nichole shook her head. "She's not gone."

It helps to talk with Amy.

Amy gaped at Nichole. "What do you mean?"

Jim had returned to the wagon with the horses, and the women turned around and headed back.

"I'm still me, in one sense. Half of the memories that come back are familiar. I still feel like me," Nichole answered softly. "It's the other memories that confuse me. They're mine too, but they don't belong here, or maybe, they don't belong to *now*."

Amy arched one brow at Nichole. "Fascinating."

Nichole's serious face broke into a huge smile as she stared back at Amy.

"What?" Amy grinned at Nichole in confusion.

Nichole shook her head and chuckled. "It's nothing. I'm just glad you're not freaked out."

"Freaked out?"

Nichole laughed again. "Yeah, you know, hysterical and terrified."

Amy made a funny noise and waved her hand. "I guess not much freaks me out, then."

When they reached the buckboard, the horses were hitched and ready. Jimmy helped both women up to the high seat.

"I hate this seat," Nichole commented as Jim mounted his mare. Both he and Amy laughed.

"No, seriously. It should be padded and have an awning over the top to keep the sun off our necks."

Jim chuckled as he rode ahead.

Nichole turned to Amy who also had a strange smile on her face. "What's so amusing?"

"You just described the carriage you asked Jason to order for you. You and Jason discussed at length whether you needed one, and how well it would hold up on these roads." Amy hesitated, then added, "It's the carriage that overturned when you were injured."

They reached the outskirts of Denver late in the afternoon. As they passed the first few buildings, Nichole felt relieved. The long ride was almost over, and Merril would be waiting for her.

The street was powder-dry, and a dust cloud hung in the air along the roadway, kicked up by horse and wagon traffic on the main thoroughfare. Nichole gazed spellbound at the storefronts as shoppers, soldiers, cowboys, and fancy women moved along the street.

Jim rode slightly ahead of the wagon. At a diagonal cross street, he turned right, and Amy followed him.

"We're almost there," Amy commented as she turned the team right again.

Without the busy street and shops, it seemed to Nichole as though they were heading out of town. Then they passed several houses, and she realized they were in a new residential area.

"We're home, gals," Jimmy called back. He rode up the street, then stopped and dismounted in front of a narrow two-story red brick house.

Amy pulled the reins and brought the team to a stop before the residence.

Nichole stared at the richly carved 'H' on the front door.
So this is home. I don't remember it.

"Here we are." Amy dropped the reins and stretched her tired back with a sigh.

Jim dusted his pants with his hat and then slid it onto its resting place. "Why don't you ladies go on inside? I'll take the team around back and take care of the horses. I'll bring our things in when I'm done."

"That sounds marvelous, Jim," Amy replied with a quick smile. "I don't know about you Nicki, but I need a bath."

"Merril said he would be here." Nichole reminded them as Jim helped Amy down from the seat, then came around to help her.

"The house is locked up." Amy opened a pouch she had tied to her skirt and removed a key. "He couldn't get in. He's probably in town and will be along soon."

Jim led the team and his mare around the side of the house.

Nichole climbed the steps to the covered front porch. Alone at the door, she turned around to find Amy.

Amy remained at the edge of the street looking up at the house.

"Is something wrong?" Nichole asked as Amy continued to search the windows.

Nichole returned to Amy and looked up at the house. The windows were closed, and the curtains were drawn. She glanced at Amy who still gazed up, key in hand.

"What's the problem?" Nichole asked again.

"Nothing." Amy shook her head. "I don't know." Amy continued to the front door, inserted the key in the lock, and opened the door. She looked back at Nichole who followed her onto the porch.

"I saw damage to the window upstairs, but when I looked again, everything was fine."

"A premonition?"

"It could mean anything." Amy shrugged. "Or nothing. Come in. I'll show you the house."

Nichole followed Amy's example and removed her hat, hanging it and her wrap on decorative wooden pegs near the door, and looked around.

"The receiving area." Amy gestured to the front parlor with one hand, as she closed the door and turned the bolt. A double-cushioned love seat faced two matching chairs across a small table. If the curtains had been open, the windows would look onto the porch.

They walked through a small dining room to the back of the house and into the kitchen. Amy pushed back the curtains, and they could see Jim busy with the horses in the carriage house.

"The privy is out the back steps to the left. We can bathe at the foot of the stairs, near the fireplace over there." She pointed to a small area near the stairs. "There's a curtain for privacy. The bedrooms are upstairs."

Nichole nodded and started up the narrow stairs. With the curtains drawn, the upper floor was shadowed.

Amy followed her, and at the top, directed Nichole to a room facing the street.

The tidy bedroom was empty of personal effects. A large wardrobe stood to one side, and a quilted blanket was spread neatly across the bed.

Amy crossed to the windows and opened the curtains. She checked the latch, then looked at the sill on both sides.

"Is that the window you saw?" Nichole asked. Amy nodded and turned back to Nichole—then froze.

"Welcome home, ladies," a menacing voice taunted from behind them. "I been waitin' for you all day."

Nichole spun around and took a step back.

Blackwood Jones stood in the doorway, with a revolver pointed at her. Bareheaded, his thin, greasy hair was pulled across his forehead and secured behind his ear. He was in stocking feet with his belt and pants undone.

"You." He indicated Amy with his gun. "I got no quarrel with you."

"Then let her go," Nichole begged. She reached back and clasped Amy's hand.

Amy's grip was strong, but she was shaking.

"Can't do that. She'd go for help, and what I have in mind may take a while." Jones grinned at Nichole and spat into the hall. "I don't want to be interrupted." He ran his tongue over his yellow-black teeth and smacked his lips.

He looked around the room, then reached over and opened the wardrobe door. The end of the gun moved from Nichole to Amy.

Jones lifted his chin at Amy. "Get in there." He waved his gun in the direction of the open cabinet.

Amy released Nichole's hand and stepped around the bed, closer to Jones. She bent her head and squeezed into the closet, and then cried out as Jones slammed the door shut.

Nichole winced at the sound. Her mouth had gone dry, and her heart pounded in terror.

"A snug fit," Jones commented with a chilling laugh.

With the gun pointed at Nichole, he picked up a candleholder from the nightstand and shoved it through the wardrobe handles locking Amy inside.

"Now, you." He advanced on Nichole, gun first, then reached out with his other hand and grabbed a handful of her hair just above her ear. "I've been thinkin' about this all day." He holstered his gun, punched Nichole in the stomach and slung her down hard on the bed.

***

Merril Shilo

—

The horses trudged forward with their heads down. Their breath labored. Pressing them to greater speed proved useless—they had nothing left to give.

Merril had tried to keep them at a slow trot, but Jason kept riding ahead. He had to remind Jason to slow down. Not that he wanted to go slower; he understood Jason's terror. Shadows were long, and he needed to find Nichole.

Precaution didn't matter. Just before they reached the small livery near the house, Sadie stopped walking altogether. Jason dismounted and coaxed her forward, but she wouldn't move. Head down, she had bloody froth at her mouth and was blowing hard.

"Leave her," Merril said. "We can send someone back from the livery."

Jason tossed down Sadie's reins, grabbed his rifle, and ran up the street.

Merril urged Midnight past Jason and dismounted at the stable. Midnight hung his head blowing hard as well. Merril patted his neck and yelled for assistance.

A boy of about twelve came out at a run. When he saw Midnight's condition, his eyes grew large.

"There is another one down the road that needs care."

The boy nodded his head and watched as Jason ran past, turning down Pence Street.

"We'll be at the Harris house. You know the place?" Merril's skin crawled. He needed to run.

The boy nodded again. Merril handed him Midnight's reins just as the horse dropped to his front knees.

"Damn," Merril muttered. His heart broke for Midnight. When he looked up, he noticed a Shilo-branded pony in the corral and his heart filled with dread. He pulled his rifle from its sheath and ran after Jason.

"He's here!" Merril yelled to Jason as he passed him with his long stride.

The house looked empty. Merril leaped the front steps, tried the door and found it locked. He turned and motioned to Jason, who had just made it to the yard.

"Go around back. This is locked."

Jason nodded and ran along the side of the house. Merril hopped the porch rail and together, they raced into the back yard. As he rounded the corner, Merril spotted Jim near the carriage house with Amy's trunk in his arms. Both Merril and Jason came to a stop and struggled to catch their breath.

"Where's Amy?" Jason panted, hands on his knees.

"Jones is here," Merril gasped at the same time.

At Merril's words, Jim raised his eyes to the balcony. The big man let out a growl of pure rage and tossed the trunk aside. In two strides, he crossed the yard and put his shoulder to the latched kitchen door. It opened with a crash. Without pause, he turned and ran up the stairs with Merril and Jason at his heels.

***

Blackwood Jones

—

Blackwood Jones punched Nichole hard again and waited for her to whimper. He'd worked her over pretty good. Her nose was bloody, and her lips torn and bleeding. One eye had swollen closed. He could hear Amy crying softly in the wardrobe. It was so good. Now that the fancy little bitch was put in her place, it was time for the main event.

He reached down and tore her blouse open, then ripped her chemise down the middle. He laughed out loud when her breasts were exposed.

Nice.

He squeezed them hard with both hands, but the bitch didn't make a sound. That was all right. He was almost done.

He freed his erection from his trousers and pushed her skirt up, spreading her knees wide with his own.

The loud crash at the back door startled him. He paused, crouched over Nichole, as he fumbled for his gun. Just as he drew it from his holster and pointed it at the door, Jimmy Leigh was on him, screaming like a banshee.

Jim wrapped an arm around Jones's chest and lifted him clear of Nichole. His forward motion and mass propelled them both across the room, against the far wall, and out the window with a crash.

Jones pulled the trigger as they fell.

***

Amy Harris

—

Crouched inside the wardrobe, Amy heard a bang downstairs. It shook the house. Then the thumping of boots on the stairs.

Jim's coming.

An instant later, she heard Jim scream—a bloodcurdling battle cry that filled her heart with something inexplicable. The house shook again. Into the sudden silence, she heard the sound of falling glass.

"Help me! Jim, are you there?" She pounded on the inside of the cabinet. Powerless and blind, terror consumed her, and she succumbed to panic. Yet, part of her mind stood aside, calm, almost observant—a part she couldn't reach. Blood drummed in her ears like a kettledrum, and she gasped for air as terror threatened to suffocate her.

It felt as though she'd been trapped in the darkness, listening to Nichole cry out and Jones's snickering, for an eternity.

"Let me out!" she rasped as she pounded on the door again. She stilled when she heard a scrape on the wall outside her prison, then light and fresh air rushed in as the doors opened wide.

Jason gripped her arms and pulled her from the cramped interior.

Crushed to the safety of Jason's chest, she sobbed and held tight to his shoulders. Her back ached, and her legs buckled, as though they couldn't support her weight any longer. Something inside her remained disconnected. Watchful.

Her head came up over Jason's shoulder, and her eyes grew wide. "Oh, no!" The window and a good portion of the wall were gone.

"Nichole? Oh, sweet Jesus," Merril's cry filled the room. He turned from the gaping hole in the wall and fell to his knees beside the bed. He pushed the blood-soaked hair from her face and ran his hand down her neck. "Nicki, I'm so sorry. Please don't go—stay with me." His voice was choked and broken. "Amy—she's not breathing!"

Merril's cry galvanized Amy. She tried to push Jason away, but his arms locked around her. "Jason, let me go."

"I need to know you're all right."

The terror in Jason's voice reached her, and she looked up at her husband's face. She placed her palm on the side of his cheek. "Yes. I'm uninjured, but you need to let me go. I have to help Nichole." She shoved at him again, and he released her. "Go help Jim. Merril and I will take care of Nichole. Hurry!" Amy pointed toward the door.

Jason took a step back, then turned and ran from the room.

Merril wrapped the quilt around Nichole. He sat on the bed and pulled her into his lap. He whispered into her ear as he searched for a pulse. His face crumbled, and he shook his head at Amy. He hugged her to his chest as grief overwhelmed him. "No, no, *no*!"

"I need you to lay her down. Merril, listen to me." Amy gripped his arm. "Unwrap the blanket and lay Nichole on her back."

Merril looked up at Amy, confusion and grief etched on his face.

"Do it now. There isn't much time for this to work. I don't even know if I can, but I have to try. It may already be too late."

"For what to work, Amy?" He laid Nichole on the bed and ran both hands over his face.

Amy stepped in front of him and opened the quilt. She turned Nichole's head to the side.

Nichole's eyes were partly open and dull. Blood oozed from her open lips. "Try to get the blood out of her mouth."

Merril pulled the handkerchief from his neck and wiped Nichole's mouth clear of blood.

Amy climbed on top of the bed and straddled Nichole's hips. She placed one hand between her breasts and one on her abdomen. Her hands trembled as she pushed her sight into Nichole.

A golden aura shimmered around her hands and bled down onto Nichole's skin. Amy could see inside Nichole. Lungs filled with blood. A broken rib's jagged edge pierced her lung. The liver bruised—the spleen torn—her heart still.

Anguish filled Amy's chest. She could see the damage with her *Earth-Sight*, but she couldn't mend the bone or spark her heart. She couldn't fill Nichole's lungs with air. She knew she couldn't. She'd tried to heal before and failed.

The part of her she had sensed, the calm watchful presence in the wardrobe—moved. It twisted around Amy, inside her, then reached through Amy's connection to Nichole and began to mend the damage. The Entity straightened the rib, removed it from Nichole's lung, and knitted the shattered bone. The liver healed, and the tear in the spleen mended.

The presence nudged Amy, and somehow, she understood. She widened her vision. Nichole's bruises were touched, her loose teeth reset. Lastly, a fiery spark shocked Nichole's heart, and air pushed the remaining blood up and out through her mouth.

Amy watched her heart falter, then begin to beat on its own.

Nichole struggled to take a breath.

Without breaking the connection to the other presence, Amy opened her inner vision and found a translucent mirror. The face reflected was her own, but she knew it wasn't her. The Entity mimicked her face and gazed back at her. The moment seemed suspended in time as she stared into eyes identical to her own.

Slowly, the Entity pulled away. It whispered into Amy's mind.

I will find you.

Then, it was gone.

Chapter 39

Courtney Veau

—

Present-day – Denver, Colorado

Courtney blinked, and the attic came into focus. Cobwebs hung like wraiths in the beam of her flashlight. The old photo frame lay in her lap. How long had she sat in the dust remembering her short time as Nichole? She looked down at the sepia-toned photograph, and her fingertips caressed the curved glass above Merril's face. "I'm sorry, my love."

She leaned her head against the wall and closed her eyes. He called to her from across the years. What was the pulling sensation inside her chest whenever she heard his voice?

His words—so close—she could almost feel his lips against her ear. *Come back, my love.*

She let her senses follow him, and then her eyes snapped open, and she gasped for breath.

The filthy old attic still surrounded her, but for an instant, she could have reached out and touched him. Her hand trembled as she lifted it to the light, expecting to find blood on her fingertips, but there was none. Only tears.

His voice had grown distant again, calling to her from far away. A hard shiver shot down her spine. Granny Curtis would have said someone stepped on her grave.

Tears blurred her vision as she looked down at the photograph.

I don't want to be here without you.

She closed her eyes and threw her senses wide. What if she let the pull of Merril's voice take her? Could she follow him back?

Hadn't White Eagle said she was the wind? What were his words?

"...a day will come when the wind will choose a direction. A time will come when the door must close."

Was this the day? Was now the time to choose?

Courtney took a deep trembling breath and looked toward the attic doorway Dessa had left open. If this worked, how would Dessa feel when she found her? Courtney had no doubt she would die when she let the voice take her. She didn't know if she would wake in Merril's arms, or simply follow him into death.

This would be a blind leap of faith.

She closed her eyes and clutched the oval frame to her chest. She opened herself to Merril's voice as it came near her once more. He was on the stairway—in the attic—right beside her.

Her breath rushed out, and she reached for the sound of his voice.

His lips were beside her ear. His breath soft on her face. "Nicki, please. Come back."

"I'm coming, Merril," she said softly. "I'm coming."

***

Amy Harris

—

June 12, 1875

Amy gasped at the Entity's sudden departure and moved from the bed. Nichole coughed the blood from her lungs and struggled to breathe.

Merril rolled her onto her side and rubbed her back. "It worked." Tears streaked his dirty face, and his sudden laugh became a sob.

Amy stumbled around the bed and knelt beside Merril. The sense of duality had vanished from her mind but left her shaken. She ran her hand over Nichole's face and choked back tears of relief.

Oh, blessed Lord and Lady, whatever that was, I thank you.

Merril looked from Nichole's face to Amy. "I've known the healing power of your salve. It works like a miracle, but this—I've never seen anything like it." His voice dropped to a whisper. "Are you a healer, Amy?"

"No, I'm not." Amy couldn't hide the tremor in her voice. "I've never done—or experienced something like this before."

"You could've fooled me. Look at her face." He pulled back Nichole's hair and held it away from her cheeks.

Nichole's eyes remained closed. Tears poured from them as she coughed and battled to breathe. Her skin, beneath the blood and tears, continued to heal. The bruises cleared, and the cuts closed. The swelling around her eye diminished, and her appearance returned to normal.

Amy rose from Merril's side. "I'll get some water and towels." She took the pitcher from the dresser and left the room to the sound of Nichole's stirring—coming back from the dead. She stopped just outside the door and held the pitcher close to her chest to stop its shaking.

Nichole was alive, but not because of her; or maybe not *just* because of her. Something had joined with her, entwined its magic with hers. More terrifying yet was the promise that echoed in her mind.

I will find you.

Jason's voice carried to her from downstairs as he spoke with Jim.

Concern for Jim and her errand to tend to Nichole forced her to put aside her own worries and speculations. With a trembling hand, she wiped the tears from her face. She needed to go downstairs, but not yet—not until she knew her legs would hold. She took a deep breath and watched the magical glow fade from her arms.

What have I done?

***

Nichole Harris

—

Nichole blinked and brought her hand to her face. "Merril?" She wheezed, and then coughed again.

"I'm here, my love. You'll be all right." Merril's voice choked off, and his lips quivered. He pressed them into a hard line.

Nichole nodded and covered her face with her hands. Uncontrollable emotion welled up inside her, and she sobbed.

Merril wrapped the quilt around her, lifted her into his arms, and sat on the bed with her on his lap. He rocked and whispered to her as she cried. "I've got you, sweetheart. I won't let you go. I love you."

Nichole sniffed and rubbed the bedcover beneath her nose. She closed her eyes and rested her head against Merril's chest. He smelled of dust, and horse, and man. The scent anchored her and made closing her eyes bearable. As long as she could feel his arms around her, and smell the dust on his shirt, she knew he was real and no longer a ghost.

Her breath hitched, and his arms tightened.

"Do you feel better now?" Merril's voice rumbled through his chest under her ear.

"Yeah. I think so. My lungs hurt—and I feel nauseous."

He dropped his chin to the top of her head, and his hand ran up and down her back.

"I could hear you, you know," she murmured, and a tear escaped from under her lashes and slid down her cheek. "You were looking for me." Her breath caught, and she paused to still the quiver in her voice. "You searched every night. I even saw you once, but you couldn't see me. I almost left the house after that." Those memories were too close—too raw. Emotion crawled up her throat and choked off her voice.

"What house, Nic?" Merril held her away from his chest.

She opened her eyes and saw he studied her face with a furrowed brow. His brown hair had pulled free from its binding and hung tangled to his shoulders. His deep-set eyes were dark with worry and fatigue.

"This house." Her chin trembled as she struggled to explain. "White Eagle said you would chase the wind, remember?" Her voice dropped to a whisper.

"And I was the wind." She pressed her lips to still their trembling but didn't drop her gaze.

Concern filled his eyes. "Do you know where you are, Nicki?"

She almost laughed. A hoarse sound escaped her throat, and when her eyes closed, the unshed tears rained down her face. "I do." She nodded and opened red-rimmed eyes. "I do indeed know where I am."

She tried to offer him a smile and took a deep breath into her burning lungs. "Do you... do you remember the talk we had behind the house the night of The Highlands barbecue?"

"You mean last night?" Merril grinned and pushed a curl behind her ear.

"That was last night?" Her voice rose, and nausea rolled in her stomach. *How could that be?*

She wasn't missing time; in fact, she had too much of it.

"We talked beside the tree near your balcony. You left the ranch this morning with Amy and Jim. We planned to meet in Denver." He shook his head and dropped his eyes. "What happened to you—it's my fault."

"How? Why didn't you come?" Nichole tipped her head to see his face.

When he lifted his gaze, guilt and regret filled his green eyes. "Jones must have overheard us talking. He bushwhacked me after you went inside. I didn't come to until this morning. By then, you'd already gone."

"So, how is this your fault?" She shook her head and looked out the broken wall. The sun threw long shadows across the dirt road.

How many times had she—had Courtney Veau—stared out that window at sunset?

"At least you got here in time," she whispered.

His hand on her back stopped moving.

"What is it?" She pushed back from his chest to see his face.

He swallowed, glanced into her eyes, then looked away. Grief distorted his face. "I—" His reply choked off as he turned his head and clenched his jaw. When he spoke, his voice was low. "We didn't make it in time. Jones had—you were—"

"I was what?" She freed her arm from the coverlet and pushed the hair from his face. Her arm and hand were covered with blood.

"You were... dead, Nic." His voice broke. "You were already gone."

Nichole stared as he struggled to compose himself, but her focus had turned inward.

Of course. I was dead.

She had to have died to return to Courtney's time—even for a moment. She blinked at the realization that she retained both sets of memories—the future and the present. "Who revived me?"

"Revived?" Merril looked up. "Amy did. She touched you and... I don't know how she did it." He shrugged and shook his head. "You began to choke and breathe again. She says she's not a healer, but I swear to you Nicki, she brought you back."

Nichole freed her other hand and captured his face. Their gazes locked—ice-blue and emerald. She drew his mouth to hers, tasting his tears as they mingled with her own. Their kiss deepened, completing her soul's journey—to have her heart beat next to his.

He pulled back to look deep into her eyes. "That's the second time I lost you. Never again."

"I won't leave your side." She tipped her head and kissed him softly. "Next time you say you're going somewhere, I'll damn well go with you. And whatever happens, we'll be together."

Soft kisses feathered across her face, and then he pulled her close to his chest again. "You'd better. You're a part of me, Nic. I never want to lose you."

"I felt that way the first time I saw you. You rode up to the house with Kevin and your dad, remember? I was quite taken with you."

"You remember that?" He set her away from him again and searched her face. "Your memory's returned?"

Nichole nodded. "All of it."

And more.

"Whatever magic Amy used must have healed my head injury, too. I remember everything."

Both lives.

Her desire to tell Merril about Courtney filled her mind with possible words, but the tale stuck in her throat. They had begun this conversation the night of the barbecue. Last night. She didn't have answers then, and although her memories were back, she needed time to sort things out.

She smiled up at Merril. "I'll tell you about it another time. Just hold me, Merril."

Nothing matters but this. I'm home.

He pulled her close to his chest, his touch saying everything he didn't speak aloud.

Their future was uncertain; but Nichole silently vowed, they would never be separated again.

A Sneak Peek at Prophecy

The Soul of the Witch Saga continues in Book 4:
Prophecy

Chapter 1

Dr. Frank Phelps

—

Present day – Fort Worth, Texas

Dr. Frank Phelps rushed down the hall and squeezed between the elevator doors just before they closed. He took a quick breath, reset the computer bag on his shoulder, and then pressed the button for the third floor.

The medical conference in Geneva had been a treasure trove of both practical psychiatry and theoretical psychology. He'd been able to obtain a series of audio lectures on cutting-edge psych research. A now familiar Swiss accented voice spoke through his earbuds and explained the latest hypothesis on counter-intuitive diagnoses.

He caught sight of his disheveled image in the reflective elevator door.

I should have stopped by the house.

He ran a hand through his thinning brown hair and straightened his jacket and glasses. Thankfully, he had no appointments—just a quick check-in with

Marcia, and he would have the rest of the day and weekend to himself. *Ding*. He adjusted his collar as the elevator doors slid open.

When he entered his office, his receptionist, Marcia Brice, rose to her feet and hurried around her desk. Her wide, blue-eyed gaze and pale face stopped his progress through the reception area.

He pulled out the earbuds and his pulse quickened. "What's wrong?"

"You've not seen the news?" Her eyebrows rose toward her hairline.

He shook his head and flinched when the phone rang.

Marcia ignored it and after two rings the tone discontinued. "The service has picked up our calls for the last five days, on advice from the attorney."

"Whose attorney? What's happened?" Dr. Phelps set his shoulder bag on a chair, never taking his gaze from Marcia.

"One of our patients, Courtney Veau, was found inside an abandoned property in Denver. She's dead, Frank."

"What?"

This doesn't make sense.

"I saw her but two weeks ago." His mouth went dry and his pulse quickened when he recalled the photo of a house and the map of Denver she had placed on his desk.

"I tried to reach you."

"I was at a conference. I switched off my cell."

"I left messages at your hotel." Her voice rose as the phone rang again. They both ignored it.

"I never checked—" Dr. Phelps ran his hand over his face. "When? When did this happen?"

Marcia picked up the remote and turned on the DVD player. "Courtney's... body was found on the twenty-third. Her funeral took place yesterday, here, in Fort Worth."

Dr. Phelps directed his attention to the television. The flat-screen showed a distance shot of the residence, the house cordoned off by police tape. A small crowd gathered to watch the officer's work. The house appeared a perfect match to the photo Courtney had slapped on his desk.

Marcia handed him the remote. "Greta said I should record this news report, and have you watch it when you returned to the office. She wants to speak with you before you take calls from reporters or the Denver detective."

"Greta?" He echoed—heart still racing. "Detectives?"

"Greta James, Courtney's attorney. Well—*former* attorney. Just watch." Marcia pointed toward the flat-screen.

"This was the scene last week when the body of Russell Veau's daughter, Courtney, was found in an abandoned house near downtown Denver. Our viewers may remember Russell Veau from his 90s hit TV show, The Psychic Connection.

"On an anonymous tip, police were sent to this address on Pence Street in Denver, where the young heiress was found and pronounced dead at the scene."

The screen changed to a familiar blonde-haired woman in the newsroom. *"That was Kent Davis, our reporter on the scene last week at the house where the body of Courtney Veau was discovered. The Denver police have ruled out homicide and are waiting for toxicology results to confirm if this was a possible suicide or overdose.*

"As our viewers will remember, Courtney Veau, a Fort Worth resident, sustained serious injuries earlier this month in an automobile accident. She was admitted to the hospital for observation, then released three days later."

Dr. Phelps sank into one of the waiting room chairs and increased the volume. "Her injuries weren't serious," he muttered at the television.

"The staff physician at JPS, Dr. Milton Chambers, released Courtney for follow-up care to a Dr. Frank Phelps. Dr. Phelps, a psychiatrist and psychologist, has been unavailable for comment. Police have confirmed that prescription medications were found on the scene, but they will not confirm if a suicide note has been discovered."

"Who's on Courtney's HIPAA?" Frank whispered as Marcia slid into the seat beside him.

"Greta James. Her attorney."

"Did she ask for my notes on Courtney's visit?" He turned to Marcia and decreased the volume on the set.

"You know she did. It's the first thing she wanted." Marcia's cell phone rang, and she pulled it from her pocket. She held up a finger to Dr. Phelps. "Hello? Yes. Yes, he is." She looked at her boss and handed him her cell. "Greta James, for you."

"I think I should speak to our own attorney first." Dr. Phelps stared at Marcia's cell.

"Then just listen to her," Marcia suggested. "You've done nothing wrong, and she gave me advice when I couldn't reach you."

With reluctance, Dr. Phelps took the phone and held it for a moment to his ear before he spoke. "Hello?"

"Dr. Phelps?" a soft professional voice responded.

"Yes. Ms. James, is it? How may I help you?"

"I hoped we might meet. I have information—not released to the public—which may interest you regarding Courtney Veau's death. You have two voicemails from her I would like to hear."

He heard the familiar elevator chime in the hallway and through the phone. His eyes turned to the office door. "I'm unaware of any messages, Ms. James. If you'd like to make an appointment to meet, I'll hand you back to Marcia. She maintains my schedule." He rose from the chair just as the office door opened.

Greta James smiled at Dr. Phelps, closed her phone and dropped it into her briefcase. "No need to bother Marcia, unless she would be willing to make a pot of coffee."

Greta stepped across the waiting room and held out her hand to Dr. Phelps.

He returned the phone to Marcia and shook the attorney's hand. "Ms. James."

"Please, call me Greta." Her smile was filled with concern, and a touch of grief.

She was tall. Almost as tall as his own six-foot height. He glanced at her shoes and confirmed she wore a high stylish heel. Her calves were toned. Her modest length skirt flared around her knees but tightened along her slim hips. By the time his gaze made it past the curve of her silk blouse and crescent moon necklace, to her amused hazel eyes and full-lipped smile, he was convinced there was some sort of mistake. Women like this didn't walk through his door and ask to be called by their first name.

Greta tipped her head toward his private office. "Shall we?" She released his hand, smiled at Marcia, and strode into the next room. Her shoulder strap slid down her arm as her leather case landed in the guest chair. "Oh, and Marcia? Please lock the front door." Her gaze switched to Dr. Phelps. "I apologize for giving orders in your office, but Detective Hernandez is in town to speak with you. You should expect a visit from him today." She took a seat in the other guest chair, crossed her legs, and then turned her head to meet Frank's eyes. "This shouldn't take too long, but I don't want to be interrupted."

Frank tore his gaze away from Greta and looked toward Marcia. "Courtney's file?"

"On your desk." Marcia changed the time on the 'We'll be back at' sign on the door to noon, then locked the door and stepped to the coffee maker.

Frank took a moment to gather his senses.

What the hell have I come home to?

The unexpected and upsetting events left a hollow feeling in the pit of his stomach. His young patient was dead—one who had been vibrant and full of life.

Is her death my fault?

He lifted his black framed glasses with the back of his hand and rubbed his tired eyes, then gripped his case and walked into his office.

Courtney Veau's file sat in the middle of his desk. He took his seat and flipped open the file. He didn't need to read his notes; he could remember his conversation with Courtney word for word.

"Let's start with the messages she left you," Greta suggested, her voice soft.

Dr. Phelps nodded but didn't reach for his cell phone. Instead, he focused on the woman across the desk. She was dressed to distract him, and her smooth cultured voice had an almost hypnotic quality to it. Soothing. Manipulative. He used hypnosis and distraction enough to know when he was being coerced. Ms. Greta James certainly had game, but she appeared far too young to be Courtney Veau's trust attorney. Despite how lovely she looked, she didn't add up.

"I think not, Ms. James." He raised his hand to forestall her protest. "I'm sorry—Greta. I've not heard those messages myself. I'm sure you understand my need to be cautious. Malpractice lawsuits are rampant, and I must vet everything I hand over to my client's—*former* client's attorney. Please understand, I've only just learned of Courtney's death."

Greta nodded and ran the heel of her hand across her cheek and her nails along her temple, dislodging a few auburn strands of hair. As though a mask fell away, her fatigue became apparent. "I understand, and I do apologize. I've simply been on my feet since Detective Hernandez contacted me a week ago. Why don't I go first, then?

"My family has worked closely with the Veau family for years. I became Russell Veau's attorney when my father took on other clients. Even before any direct contact with the Veaus, I grew up with their—peculiarities—through my father's practice."

She paused as though considering her words. "When Courtney's parents were killed in the plane crash, I became the estate and trust manager. Courtney has always been more to me than a mere client." She reached over, pulled a tissue from her bag, and then dabbed her eyes and nose.

"I'm sure this is difficult for you—"

"As I said, I'm just tired." The tissue disappeared into her fist, and liquid gray eyes assessed him. "Dr. Phelps—"

"Call me Frank."

"Thank you, Frank. Let me assure you; Courtney's death is not your fault. There's nothing you could have done to prevent her from making this decision."

Frank's breath caught for a moment. "You believe it may have been suicide."

Greta shook her head. "No, not precisely." Her voice remained slow, considerate. "Courtney comes from a long line of powerful mediums—spiritualists, if you will. Their power is inherent. In the normal course of events, she would have learned these skills from her father, but she never had that chance."

They paused while Marcia brought them coffee. When she left the office, she closed the door behind her.

Greta set her Styrofoam cup on Frank's desk and cleared her throat. "Let me tell you what I know, and what I gleaned from several sources. Correct me if am mistaken."

Elbows on his desk, Frank laced his fingers and rested his chin on his thumbs. "Go ahead."

Greta sat forward. "Courtney Veau barely survived a serious car accident. Her heart stopped twice. Both the EMT's and the ER staff feared she had sustained a traumatic brain injury, but the MRI scans came back clean. She spent the next three days in the hospital under observation, but was released with only a deeply bruised leg, facial abrasions, and a black eye."

Frank nodded and shifted in his chair. "The rounding doctor was Dr. Chambers."

"Yes, I've spoken with him." Greta smiled and nodded at Frank's interruption.

"Dr. Chambers referred Courtney to me due to emotional instability. He felt the imbalance could have been caused by her near-death experience. I've done several research papers on the subject. He thought I might be able to help her."

Greta shook her head and raised her eyebrows. "But it wasn't a typical near-death experience, was it? Courtney claimed to have returned to a past life. She even brought you proof in the form of a photograph and map to a house in Denver."

"Yes." Frank pressed his lips and looked away. "She didn't reveal her plan to travel there."

They were both silent for a moment, and then Greta spoke. "The detective told me they've preliminarily dismissed drug overdose as the cause of death—pending the toxicology report. There were no marks on the body and the prescriptions in her possession were practically untouched. I know they've had the MRI's reviewed by their own experts. Nothing was missed. COD is likely to remain a mystery."

"Unless there is something on my phone that could tell us what happened."

Their gazes locked. The fatigue and grief he recognized in her eyes made him reach for his phone. "All right. This goes against my better judgment, but I'm curious as well." He turned the device on. As soon as the screen lit up, he touched the voicemail icon, turned the speaker on, and hit play. There were ten messages. The first two were from men. He paused and passed them. On the third recording, they heard Courtney's voice.

"Uh—Hi, Dr. Phelps? This is Courtney Veau. Don't be upset, but I wanted to let you know I'm in Denver." Her voice went up a pitch and her words tumbled out with excitement. *"I found the house—the one in the picture I showed to you—and they had a room for rent—so I took it. I can't believe I'm really here. The landlady said the rent was month-to-month when she gave me the key. I'll call you when I get back to town. Buh-bye."*

Frank's gaze lifted from the phone to Greta. "They said on the news the house was abandoned."

"It is. I've read the police reports. They don't know how she got in and out. The doors were locked and so corroded they had to bust them down to gain entrance. They did find a single silver key in her purse, but it didn't fit any of the locks. A landlady, she says. That's interesting."

Frank skipped three more calls, and then heard Courtney's voice again.

"Hi, Dr. Phelps. It's me again." Her voice was slow and strained this time—nasally, as though she had been weeping. *"I'm hearing voices, well... one voice. He whispers to me—I mean to Nichole. I have my father's journal, and I've tried to make Merril hear me, but it hasn't worked. I know he loved me in my other life. I know the time I spent there was real. But I don't know what to do now. I think I might come home. Call me when you get this."*

Frank covered his mouth with his hand and shook his head. Courtney's words pierced him.

Could I have stopped her death with a phone call?

His chest ached, and his eyes burned. "She doesn't sound good."

Greta didn't appear to notice his distress. She tipped her head to try to read his phone. "No, she doesn't. What is the date on the message?"

He looked at the screen. "April twenty-first." The glass on the phone went dark and he slid it into his bag. "So, what happened between the twenty-first and the twenty-third?"

Greta ran her fingers across her brow and sat back in the chair. "She found the photo."

Frank's head came up. "What photo?"

"The official police report states they found Courtney in the attic, an old photo clutched to her chest. The report goes on to describe the photo, but here—" She reached into her bag and withdrew an antique framed oval photograph. She laid it on the desk in front of him and pointed to a woman, seated between two standing men. "This is Nichole Harris. The photo appears to have been taken in the early 1870s." She tapped the raised glass above the tall gentleman on Nichole's left. "I suspect this handsome young man is Merril."

"How did you obtain this?" He glanced from the photo to Greta.

A shadow of a smile moved across Greta's face. "There's no official crime scene. Nothing held as evidence. The building, and all the items in the attic, including this photo, belong to The Hawthorn Group—an investment company. I reached out to THG and offered to repair the doors that were damaged when the officers entered the house in search of my client. In return, I asked to purchase this photograph—an out-of-court settlement. They agreed."

"Why would you want it?" His gaze returned to the photo. The blonde woman's eyes seemed to draw him in. He took in every inch of the photograph.

"I don't. It's not for me."

The tone of her voice drew his attention back to her face. Her eyes smiled first, and then her lips. "I read another report, filed by an officer who never entered the house. This officer maintained crowd control and checked ID badges of those who required access to the house during the site investigation. According to his report, an elderly woman approached him. She informed him, in no uncertain terms, that the photograph 'in the poor girlie's hands', should be given to her doctor for the long table under his clock."

Frank's gaze shot to his credenza beneath his office clock and then back to Greta. "How is this possible?"

Greta shrugged. "By the time Detective Hernandez read the report, the elderly woman had vanished. I'm surprised the officer even mentioned her comment. The old woman must have made quite an impression on the young man."

Greta closed her bag and stood. "Thank you for your time, Frank, and for sharing Courtney's phone calls with me."

"You're welcome." Frank came to his feet. "You seem relieved. Do you have a better understanding of what happened to Courtney?"

"Actually, I do." She gave him a genuine smile. "You remember, I told you her spiritual powers were inherent. Although she never trained with her power, she really only needed two things—desire and belief. We know she had the desire." Greta tapped the oval glass above the photo. "When she found the photo, it suspended her disbelief and she knew she could find her way back to him."

"Then, you're saying that—" Frank blinked and shook his head. "You believe Courtney returned to her previous life?"

Greta shrugged, picked up the long strap of her bag and hung it on her shoulder. "I have no reason to believe otherwise."

"But, that's not possible." He rounded his desk and stared into Greta's gray eyes.

She smiled. "Suspend your disbelief, Frank. You didn't cause this, and you couldn't have averted the outcome." Greta picked up the photograph and placed it in Frank's hands. "Courtney's gone back to her life as Nichole. She returned to Merril, and she wanted you to have this."

Chapter 2

Amy Harris

—

June 12, 1875 – Denver, Colorado

Amy Harris stood in the hallway outside the bedroom door, an empty ceramic water pitcher clutched to her chest. When her knees threatened to buckle, she locked them tight and leaned her back against the wall.

Calm yourself.

Her eyes fluttered closed, and she urged her heart to regain a slow even pace. She pushed a ragged breath through clenched teeth and pressed lips. Her inhale hitched as she struggled to fill her lungs.

You will not cry. The worst is over.

Her body trembled, and her heart rate accelerated, despite her attempt to quiet her mind. The terror that had overwhelmed her in the dark confines of the locked wardrobe clawed at her throat.

With a gasp, she opened her eyes and searched the empty hallway. Daylight shone through the broken bedroom wall and illuminated the corridor with an unfamiliar glow.

Everything has changed.

From the bedroom behind her, Nichole coughed the last blood from her lungs, while Merril repeatedly assured Nichole, and himself, she would be all right. The opening in the exterior wall channeled the worried shouts of neighbors, who had been drawn to the sound of a single gunshot, followed by the crash of the porch collapse.

Jim must be hurt. I need to move.

The tall Highlands foreman, Jimmy Leigh, had gone through the window, taking the madman Blackwood Jones with him. But Jim's heroic attempt to save Nichole had come too late. The thought of Nichole's battered, and bloody body filled Amy's mind along with memory of Merril's anguished cry.

Amy would have fallen to her knees in defeat as Jason pulled her from the wardrobe, were it not for the Entity.

The Entity's composed presence had calmed her mind and given Amy the strength to push her husband away. She'd directed Jason to go outside and aid Jim as she turned to Nichole's broken body. The moment she had placed her hands on Nichole's lifeless chest and pushed her *earth-vision* into Nichole, Amy felt the Entity move across her consciousness and interlace with her own limited magic. No longer a simple spectator, the Entity not only saw through Amy's eyes, but it also healed through her hands.

Amy relaxed her grip on the urn enough to brush the auburn hair from her face. She paused and held the trembling hand before her eyes. With a thought, she pushed her vision past her skin to see bone and tendons—the absolute extent of her ability. She had neither the *fire-skill* to knit bone, nor the *air-skill* to fill Nichole's collapsed lung. She had only *Earth* and *Water*.

The Entity had observed the damage inside Nichole through Amy's vision, then extended its reach and used the delicate touch of fire to knit her splintered rib and mend her lung. In the end, it had been the Entity who pushed air into Nichole's chest and sparked the beat of her heart.

Whoever... or whatever, had invaded Amy's mind, had healed Nichole and then departed with a whispered promise. *"I will find you."*

Another tremor moved down her spine, and she gripped the empty urn with both hands.

Find your center—calm yourself. Jim needs you. Nichole needs you. Your husband—

Amy's thoughts ground to a halt. This entire unspeakable episode could be laid at his feet. Her anger at Jason steadied her.

Two more quick breaths, a prayer to the Goddess for strength, and she pushed herself away from the wall. Her emotional stability returned as she navigated the steep staircase with the urn cradled in her arm. At the base of the kitchen stairs, she paused when Jason helped Jim through the broken back door.

"Is Nichole all right?" Jim grimaced as he limped forward, his bloody side toward Amy, with his opposite arm thrown across Jason's shoulders for support. He faltered and took another quick step into the kitchen.

"She'll recover—with rest." Amy's gaze cataloged the big man's injuries with growing concern. A scraped chin and bloody elbow were minor. And although he favored his right leg, it was the blood on his left side and down his leg that concerned her the most. "She's in better shape than you. Jason, sit him at the table. Jim, you'll need to remove your shirt."

Albert Fielding, their closest neighbor, stood in the broken doorway. His clothes were covered with blood from assisting Jim into the house.

"Hello, Mr. Fielding. Thank you for your help." Her calm voice held no trace of her pent-up fury. She handed him the ceramic urn, retrieved the bucket from under the kitchen counter, and held it up for him to take. "Would you be so kind as to bring me water from the pump at the well? It flows much faster than the pump in the kitchen."

Mr. Fielding took the bucket in his other hand and disappeared out the back door with a nod.

She turned her gaze from the retreating neighbor, flicked a brief glance at her husband, and focused on Jim's muscular frame. "What happened to Jones?"

Jim held his bloody shirt above his head as he twisted to view the gunshot wound along his side. Although the flow of blood had slowed, his denim trousers were soaked red from his belt to his boot. "He's dead. The fall broke his neck."

"I can't say I'm sorry about that." Amy's hand touched the skin above the wound as her *earth-sight* penetrated. The injury had already begun to mend. "This will require stitches." A quick appraisal of his other injuries told her his knee had been wrenched but would also heal at a remarkable pace. She raised her gaze from the wound to Jim's eyes.

His dark stare held hers for a moment before he turned his head and nodded. "Do what you have to."

Jason's blue eyes, so similar to Nichole's, turned from the deep slice along Jim's ribs to Amy. "Shouldn't we take him to the hospital?" Blond curls clung to the perspiration on his forehead, his face still red from the race to the house.

Anger hardened Amy's heart. "No. That won't be necessary." She stood and stepped to a tall linen closet tucked beneath the stairs. "I can manage a few stitches." She brought Jim a folded linen cloth. "Hold this to the wound until I return." The back door squeaked on its broken hinge. "Thank you, Mr. Fielding." She took the urn from the neighbor's hand and pointed toward the floor. "Please, set the bucket next to Jim's chair." She held the urn to her chest, withdrew additional linen towels from the closet, and then turned to mount the stairs. "I'll be right back."

"Here, let me help," Jason offered, a footstep behind her

Amy stopped and faced her husband. "No. Thank you. I can manage." She tipped her head toward the back door. "You should wait out front for the coroner and police chief. I imagine they'll be along shortly."

"But Nichole—"

"Is in good hands." Amy turned from Jason's injured gaze and looked up the steps. "Besides, I doubt Nichole would care to see you just now." Her clipped tone brooked no argument. Thankful the urn was only half-full, she pressed the linens under her arm, grasped her skirt with her hand, and ascended the steps.

Merril and Nichole's soft voices caught her ear as she passed the first room. She paused and looked in on the couple.

Merril sat at the head of the bed, his back rested against the headboard. He held Nichole in his lap, the bedcover wrapped around her to keep her warm. His long dark hair, loose and dusty from the race to her side, curtained both their heads as he whispered to her.

They both looked up as she entered the room.

"I have water and towels for you. I'll put these in the room down the hall. This room needs to be—repaired." Her gaze flicked toward the hole in the wall, then settled on Nichole.

Nichole's mouth moved without sound, and her crystal blue eyes filled with tears. She reached out her hand and whispered, "Amy."

Amy set the urn and towels on the dresser and took Nichole's hand. "My dear, what's the matter?" Amy sank to her knees beside Nichole and wrapped her arms around her. "Shh, now. You're safe."

Nichole's blonde curls nodded against Amy's shoulder. "I know," she rasped, her voice thick with emotion. "I just missed you so much."

"You missed me?" Amy exchanged a confused glance with Merril.

Nichole pulled back and wiped a tear from her cheek. "I have to explain so many things."

Amy smiled and placed a hand on each side of Nichole's face. "We'll have time to talk soon, my dear. For now, you need to move to a different room and clean up." Amy stood and stepped back. "Blackwood Jones is dead."

She waved her hand toward the missing wall. "Jones and Jim went out the window and took the wall out as well. The porch broke their fall."

"What?" Nichole cleared her throat and looked from the hole in the wall back to Amy. "Is Jim all right?"

"He took a jolt from the fall. He's injured, but nothing is broken," Amy assured Nichole. The worst harm is from the bullet wound."

"Jim's been shot?" Merril asked, shock and concern evident in his tone.

"Yes. Luckily, the wound is only a deep graze, no penetration. It could have been much worse." Amy retrieved the water and towels. "I'm going to put this down the hall. Merril, if you could help Nichole change rooms, and then fetch her travel case, I would be most appreciative."

The Soul of the Witch Saga continues in Book 4:
Prophecy

Also by

Soul of the Witch Saga

Prodigy – Book 1

Pyromancer – Book 2

Passage – Book 3

Prophecy – Book 4

Paradox – Book 5

Patriarch – Book 6

—

J.L.'s Timeless Quest

Aubrielle's Call

The Corsair's Tempest

Hawthorn and Mistletoe

—

The Hunter Chronicles

Hunter's Gamble

Hunter and Lily Graham

The Kid in Black

Penelope's Heart

All of these stories take place within the same shared universe.

About the Author

C. (Connie) Marie Bowen writes paranormal romance and historical fantasy set within a richly layered, persistent universe. Her award-winning novel *Passage* launched the *Soul of the Witch* series, introducing a world where magic, loyalty, and sacrifice intertwine.

Bowen's stories span multiple series, with characters crossing paths and timelines within the shared universe of the Soul of the Witch Saga. Figures such as Hunter from *The Hunter Chronicles* and J.L. from *The Timeless Quest* play meaningful roles within this interconnected world.

Born in Denver, Colorado, Bowen grew up with a love of ghost stories and storytelling. She now lives in the greater Chicagoland area with her husband and two rescue pets, Abigail and Rousseaux.

Visit https://www.cmariebowen.com to explore her connected series and learn more.

www.ingramcontent.com/pod-product-compliance
Lightning Source LLC
Chambersburg PA
CBHW072129250626

47159CB00007B/2627